ADVENTURE TIME™

BITTER SWEETS

ROSS RICHIE CEO & Founder • MARK SMYLIE Founder of Archaia • MATT GAGNON Editor-in-Chief • FILIP SABLIK President of Publishing & Marketing • STEPHEN CHRISTY President of Development
LANCE KREITER VP of Licensing & Merchandising • PHIL BARBARO VP of Finance • BRYCE CARLSON Managing Editor • MEL CAYLO Marketing Manager • SCOTT NEWMAN Production Design Manager
IRENE BRADISH Operations Manager • CHRISTINE DINH Brand Communications Manager • DAFNA PLEBAN Editor • SHANNON WATTERS Editor • ERIC HARBURN Editor • REBECCA TAYLOR Editor
IAN BRILL Editor • CHRIS ROSA Assistant Editor • ALEX GALER Assistant Editor • WHITNEY LEOPARD Assistant Editor • JASMINE AMIRI Assistant Editor • CAMERON CHITTOCK Assistant Editor
KELSEY DIETERICH Production Designer • JILLIAN CRAB Production Designer • DEVIN FUNCHES E-Commerce & Inventory Coordinator • ANDY LIEGL Event Coordinator • BRIANNA HART Administrative Coordinator
AARON FERRARA Operations Assistant • JOSÉ MEZA Sales Assistant • MICHELLE ANKLEY Sales Assistant • ELIZABETH LOUGHRIDGE Accounting Assistant • STEPHANIE HOCUTT PR Assistant

Created by Pendleton Ward

Written by **Kate Leth**
Illustrated by **Zachary Sterling**
with Chrystin Garland

Inks by **Jenna Ayoub**
& Brittney Williams

Colors by **Whitney Cogar**
with Fred Stresing

Letters by **Aubrey Aiese**

"Forest Princess Gets a Pet"
Written and Illustrated by **Meredith McClaren**

Cover by **Stephanie Gonzaga**

Designer **Kara Leopard**
Assistant Editor **Whitney Leopard**
Editor **Shannon Watters**

With Special Thanks to Marisa Marionakis, Rick Blanco, Jeff Parker, Laurie Halal-Ono, Nicole Rivera,
Conrad Montgomery, Meghan Bradley, Curtis Lelash and the wonderful folks at Cartoon Network.

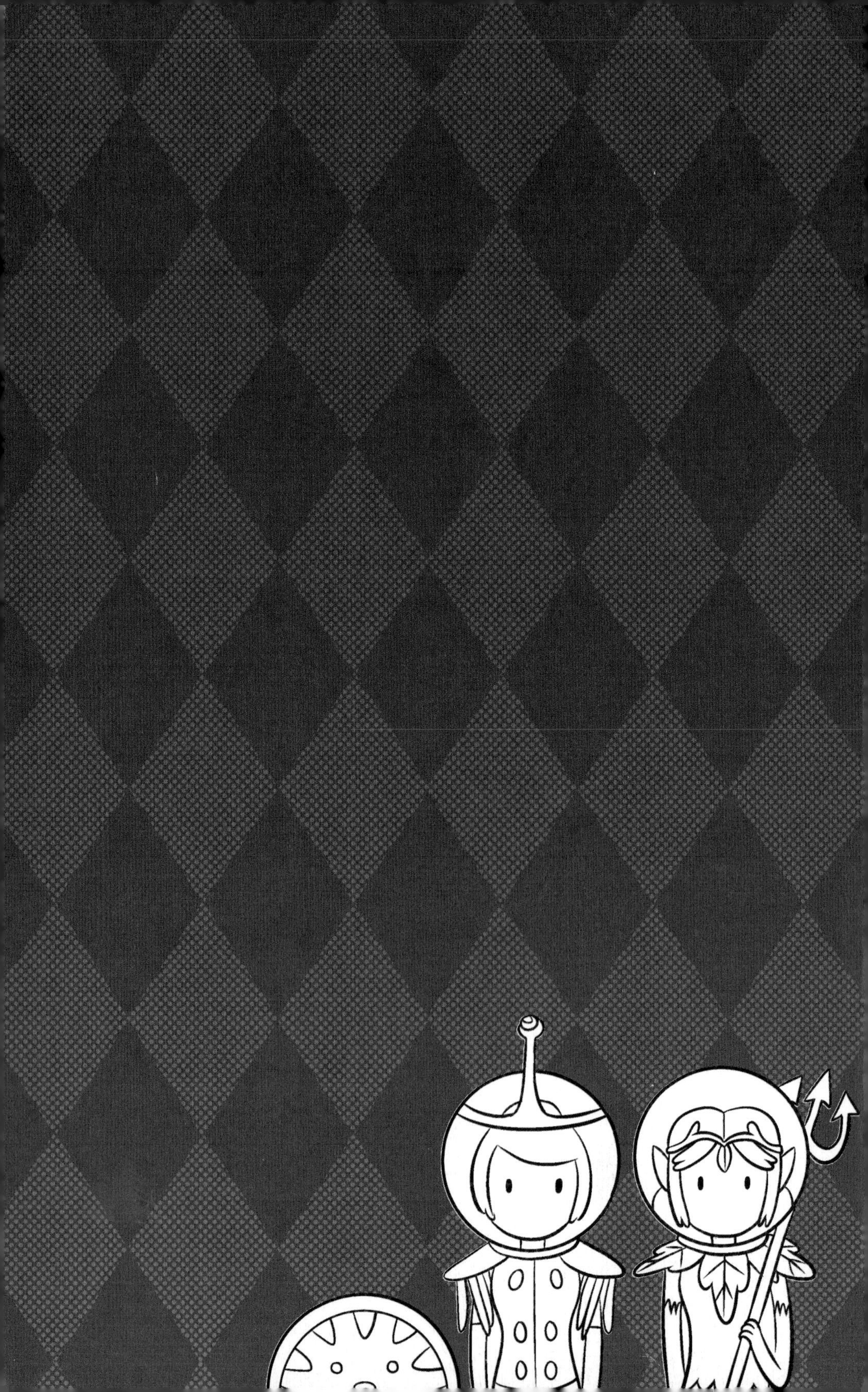

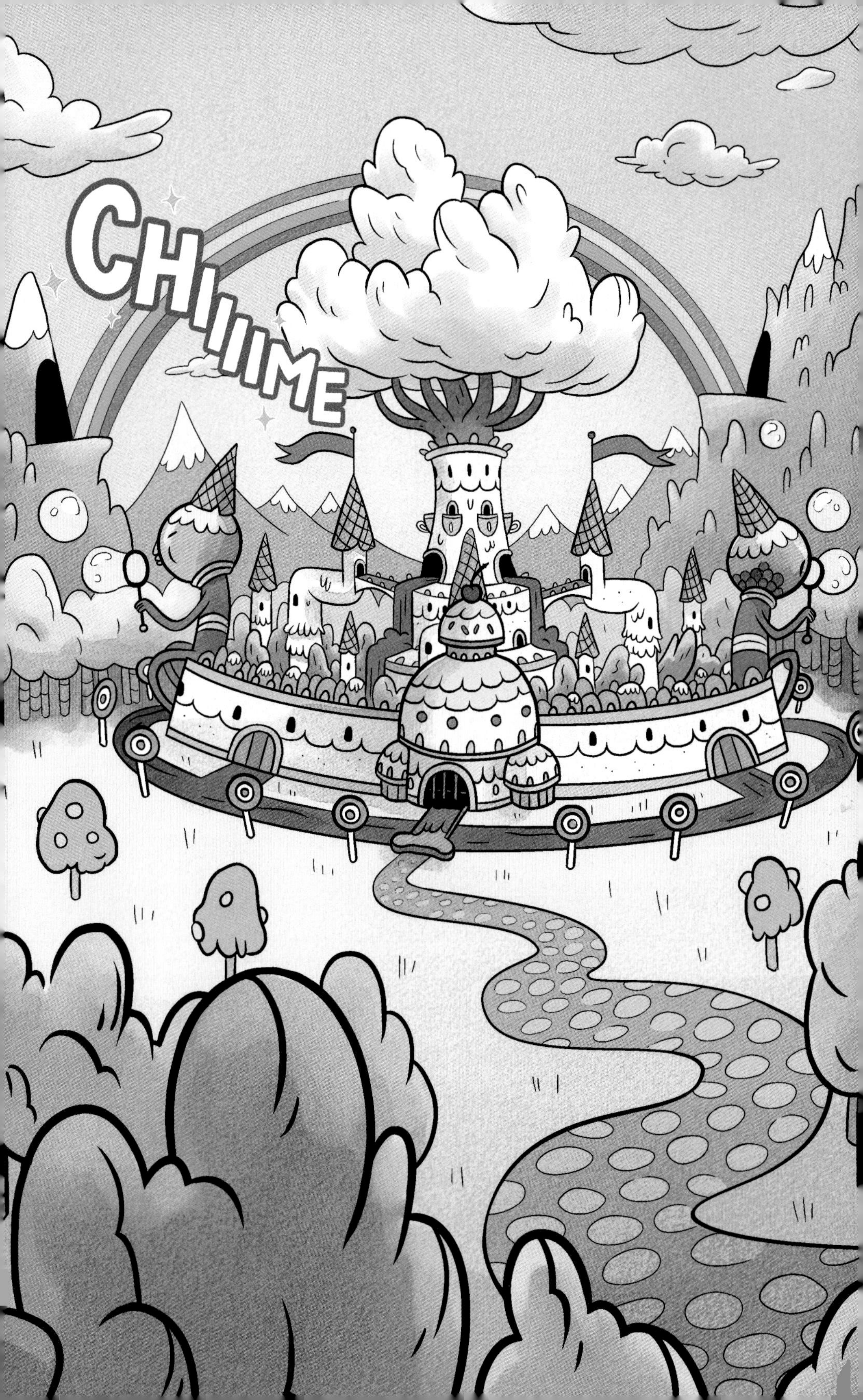
CHIIIIME

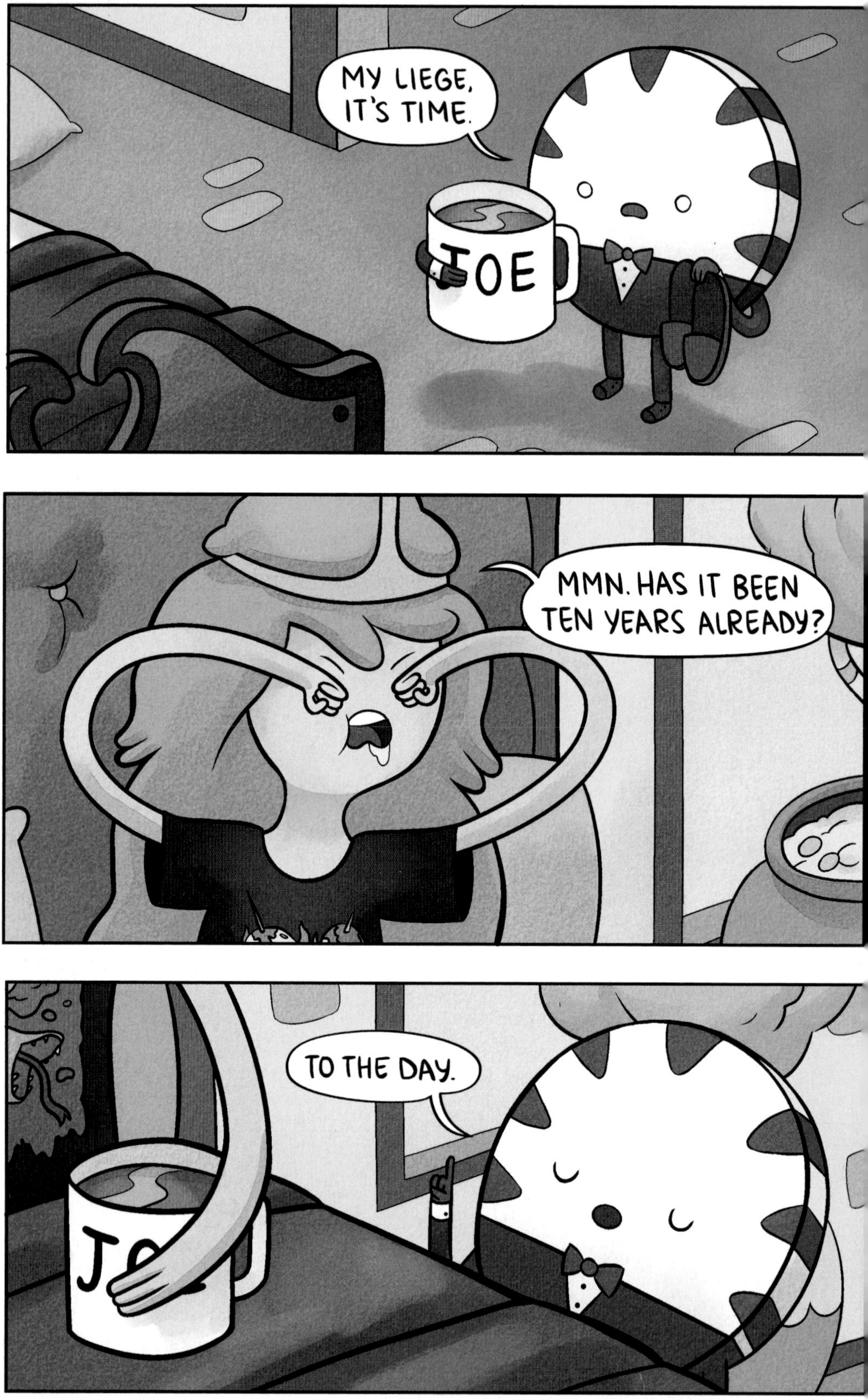
MY LIEGE, IT'S TIME.
JOE
MMN. HAS IT BEEN TEN YEARS ALREADY?
TO THE DAY.

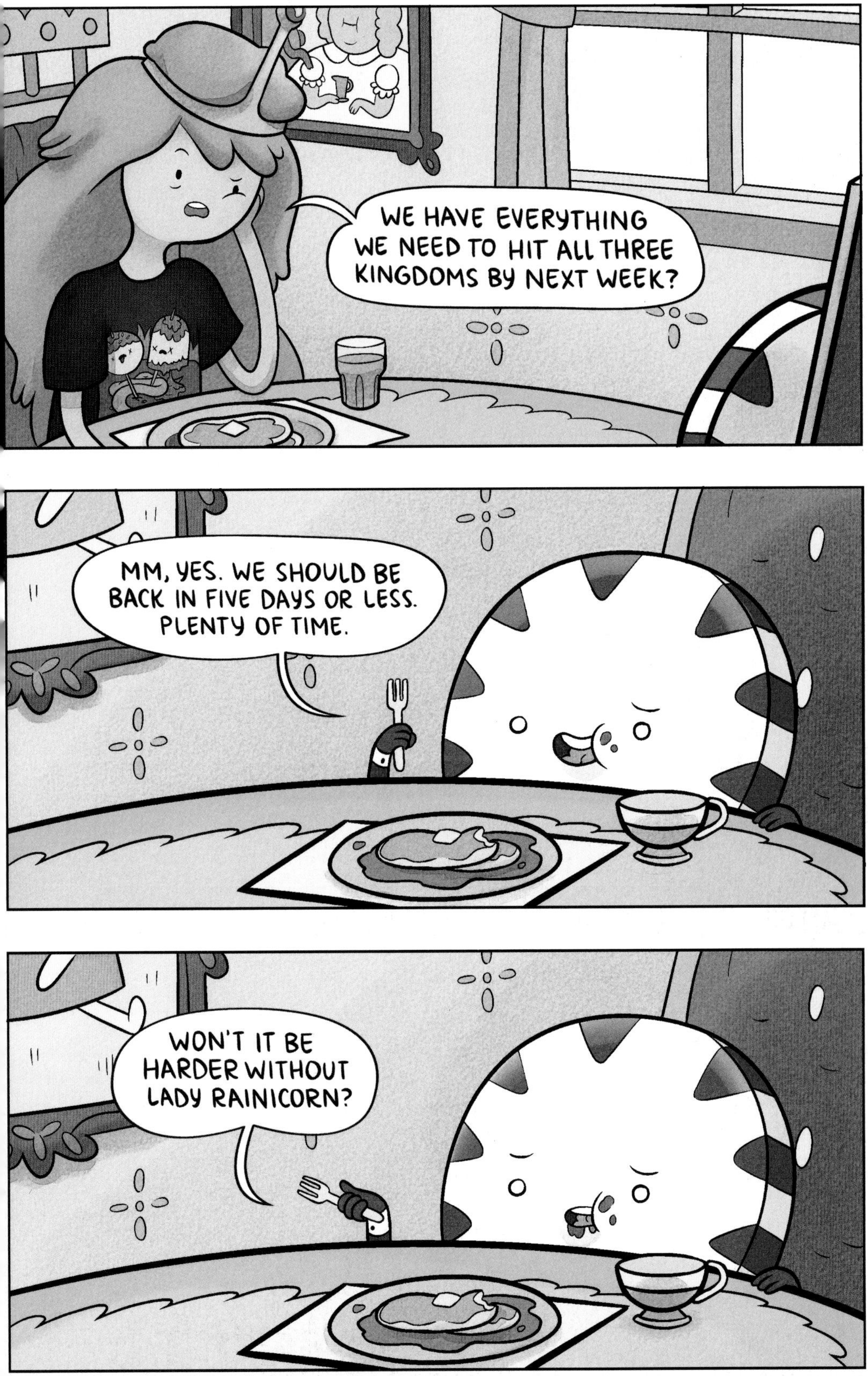
WE HAVE EVERYTHING WE NEED TO HIT ALL THREE KINGDOMS BY NEXT WEEK?
MM, YES. WE SHOULD BE BACK IN FIVE DAYS OR LESS. PLENTY OF TIME.
WON'T IT BE HARDER WITHOUT LADY RAINICORN?

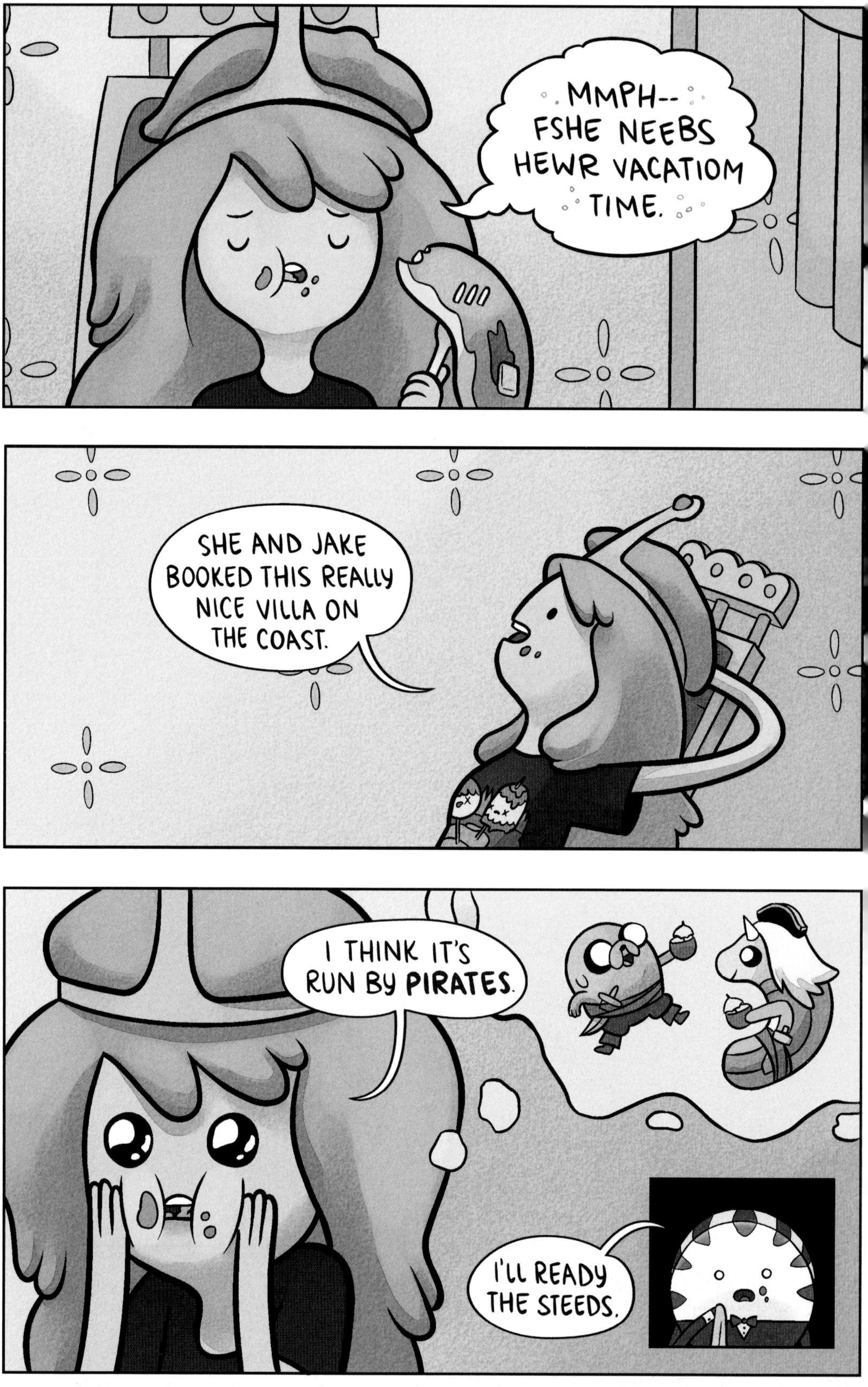
MMPH-- FSHE NEEBS HEWR VACATIOM TIME.
SHE AND JAKE BOOKED THIS REALLY NICE VILLA ON THE COAST.
I THINK IT'S RUN BY PIRATES.
I'LL READY THE STEEDS.

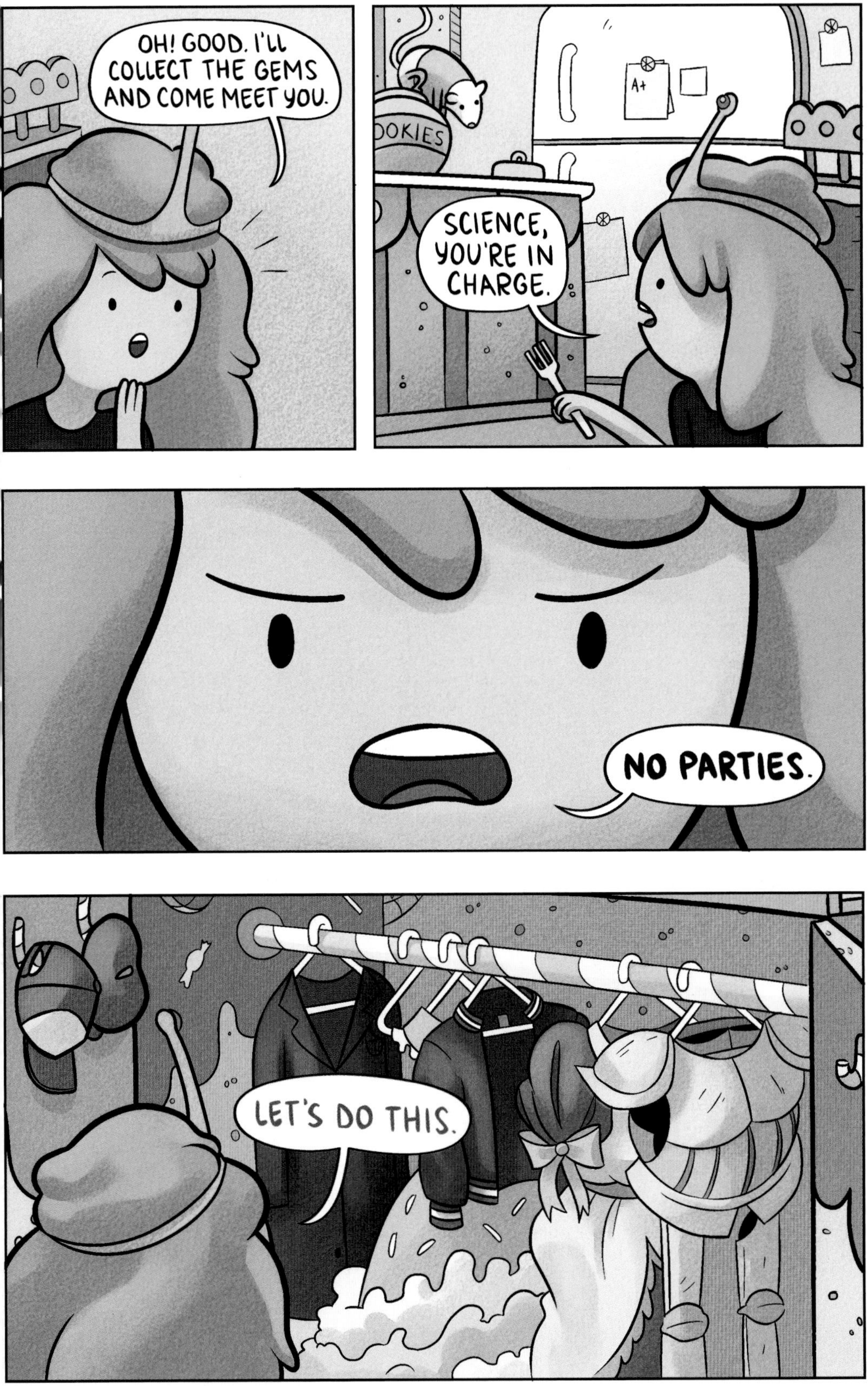
OH! GOOD. I'LL COLLECT THE GEMS AND COME MEET YOU.
OOKIES
A+
SCIENCE, YOU'RE IN CHARGE.
NO PARTIES.
LET'S DO THIS.

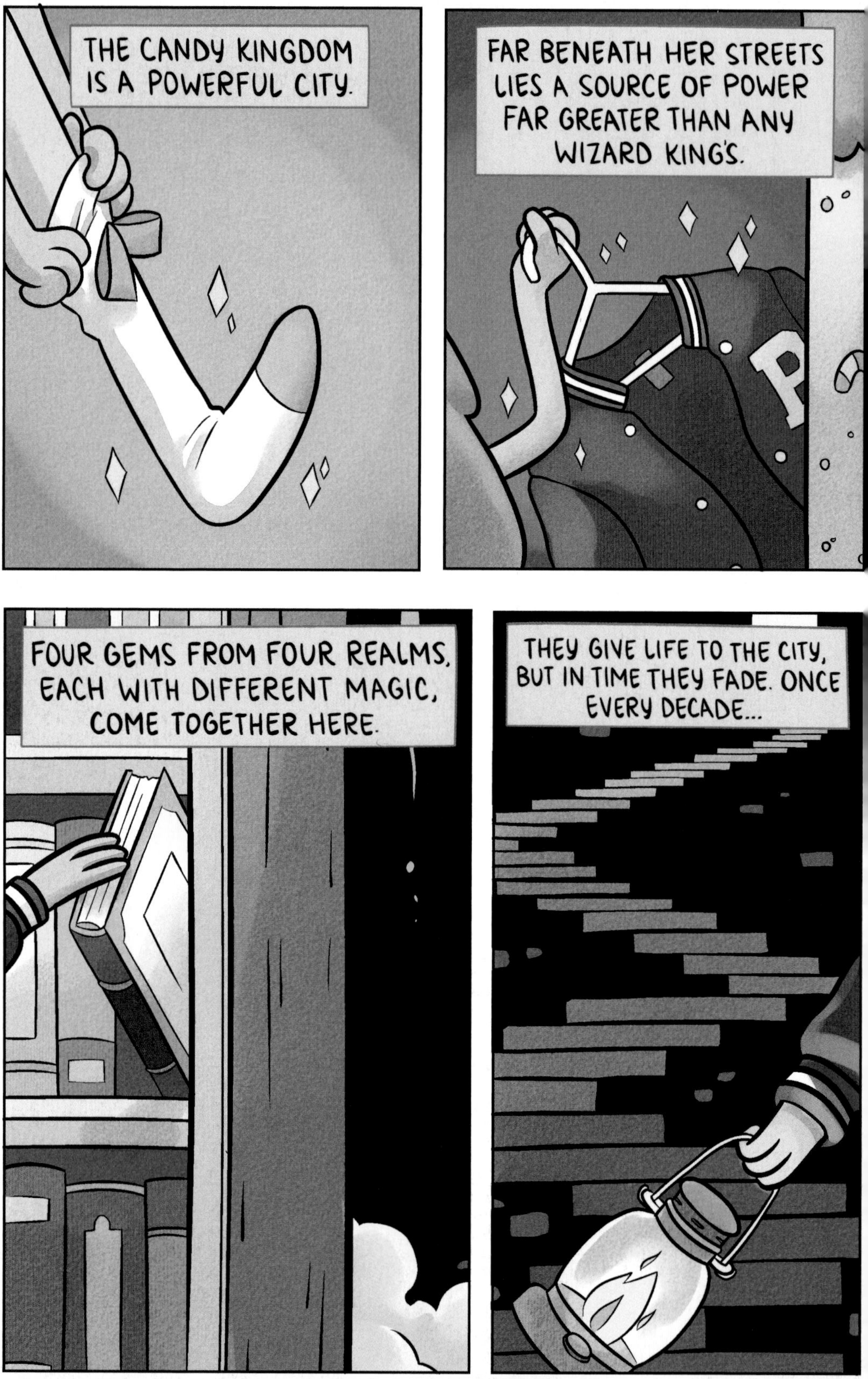
THE CANDY KINGDOM IS A POWERFUL CITY.
FAR BENEATH HER STREETS LIES A SOURCE OF POWER FAR GREATER THAN ANY WIZARD KING'S.
FOUR GEMS FROM FOUR REALMS, EACH WITH DIFFERENT MAGIC, COME TOGETHER HERE.
THEY GIVE LIFE TO THE CITY, BUT IN TIME THEY FADE. ONCE EVERY DECADE...

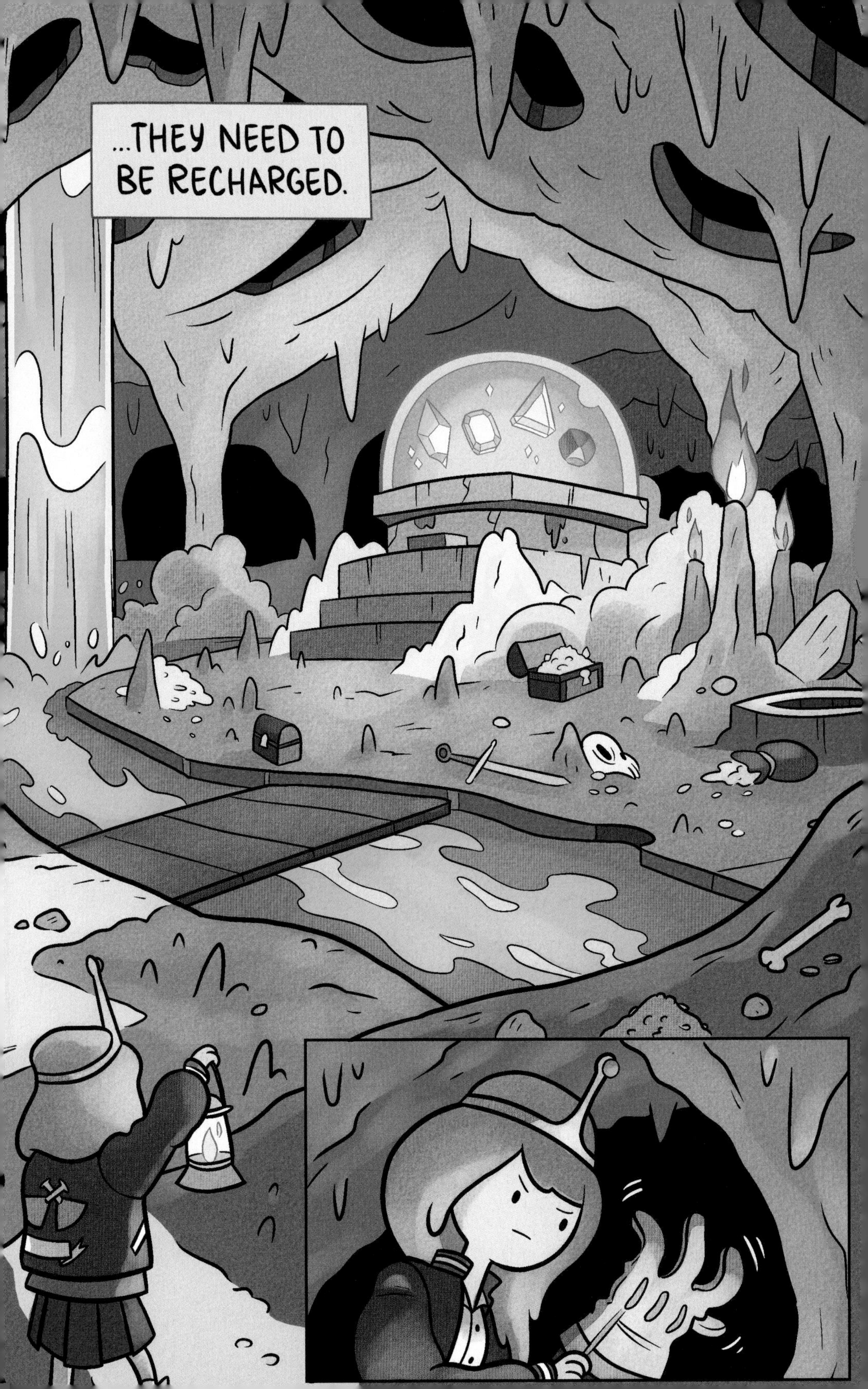
...THEY NEED TO BE RECHARGED.

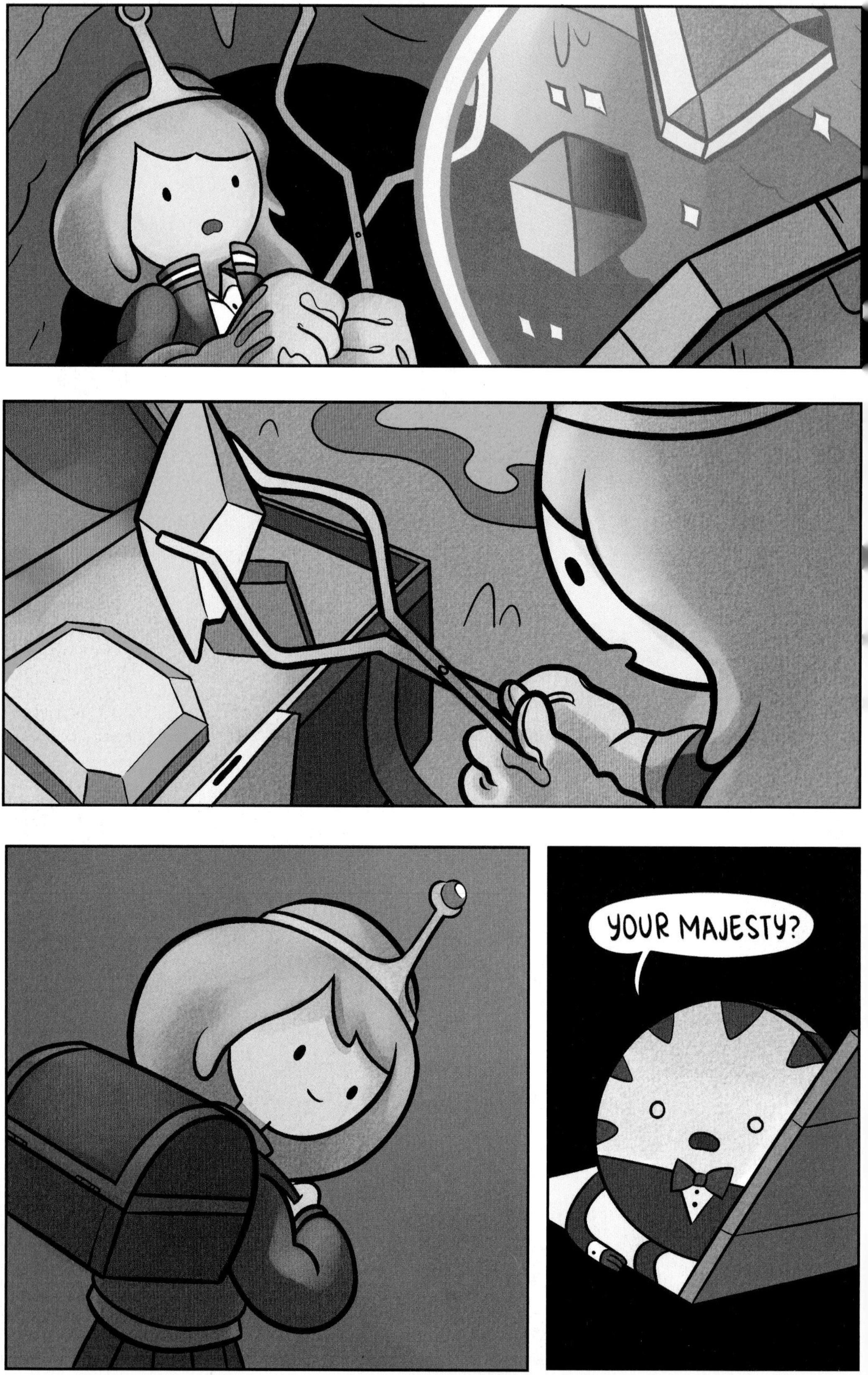
YOUR MAJESTY?

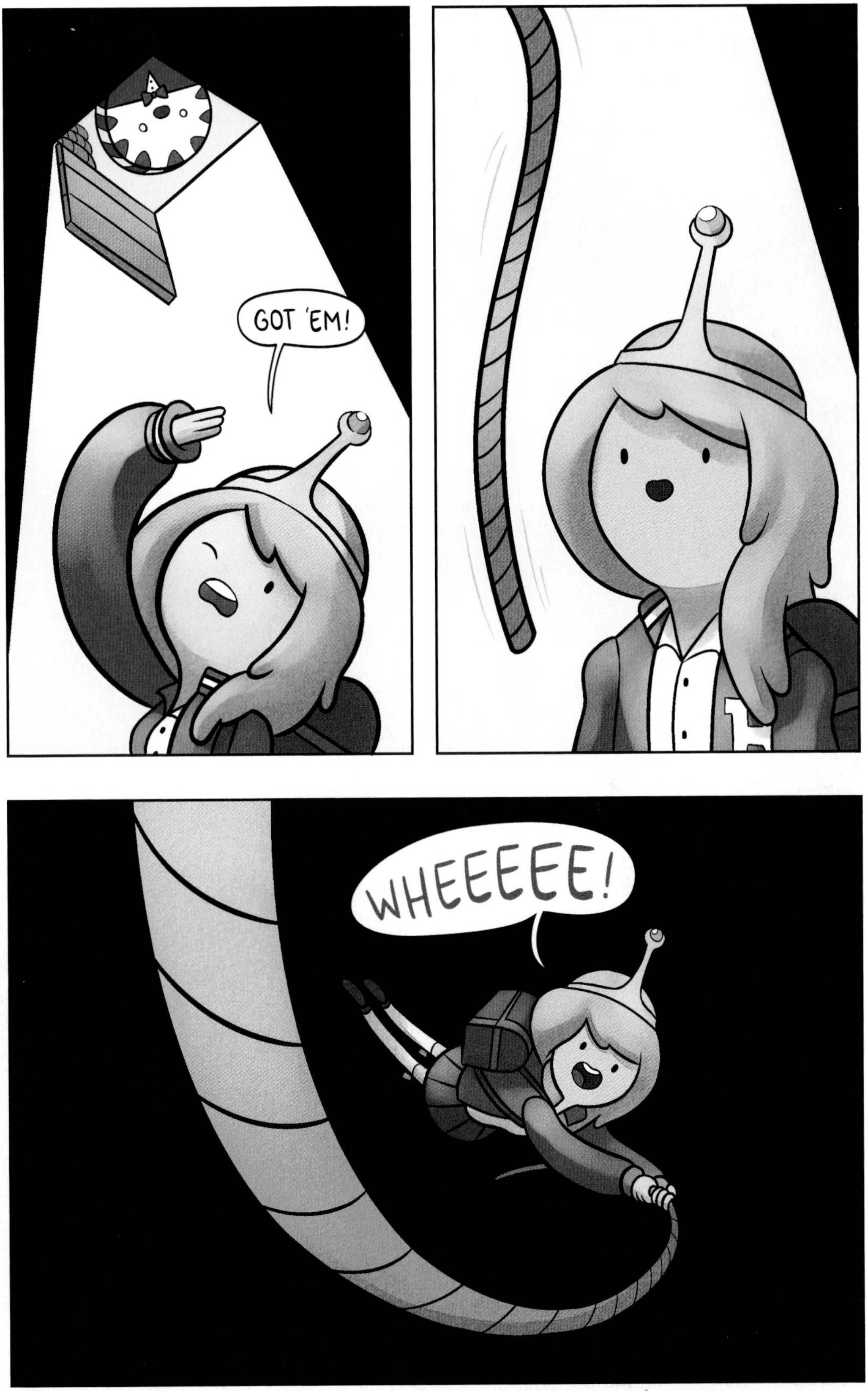
GOT 'EM!
WHEEEEEE!

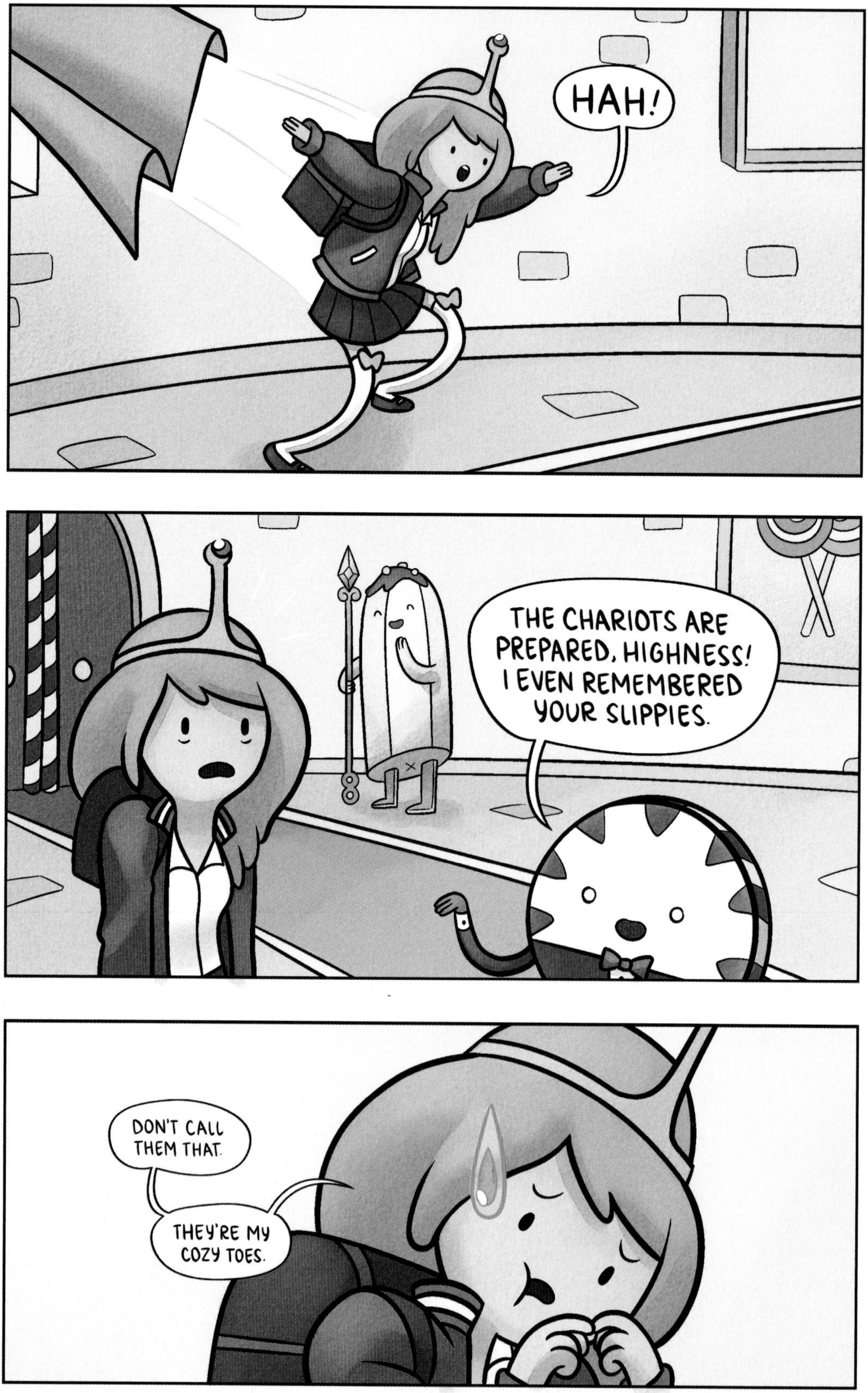
HAH!
THE CHARIOTS ARE PREPARED, HIGHNESS! I EVEN REMEMBERED YOUR SLIPPIES.
DON'T CALL THEM THAT.
THEY'RE MY COZY TOES.

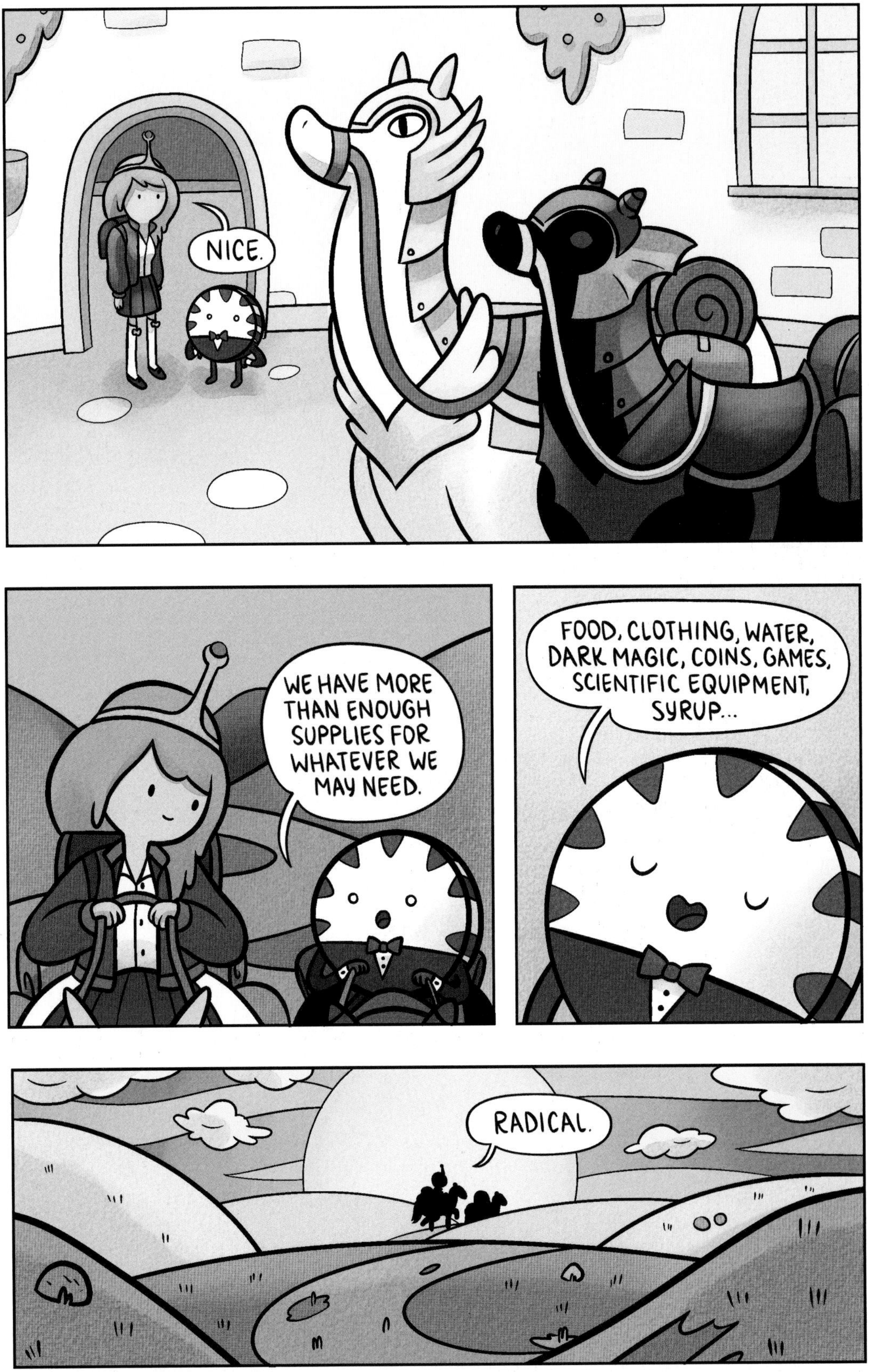
NICE.
WE HAVE MORE THAN ENOUGH SUPPLIES FOR WHATEVER WE MAY NEED.
FOOD, CLOTHING, WATER, DARK MAGIC, COINS, GAMES, SCIENTIFIC EQUIPMENT, SYRUP...
RADICAL.

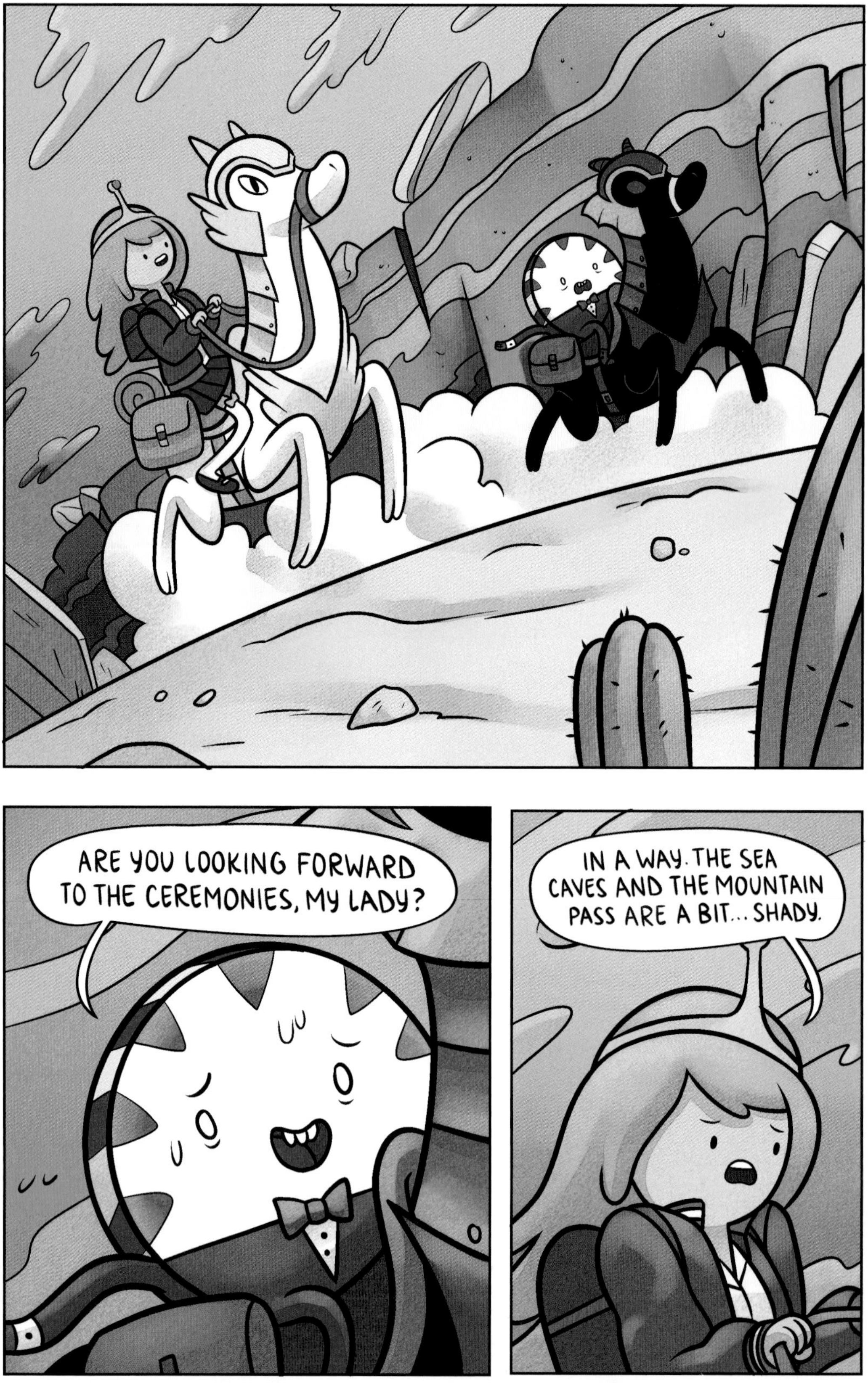
ARE YOU LOOKING FORWARD TO THE CEREMONIES, MY LADY?
IN A WAY. THE SEA CAVES AND THE MOUNTAIN PASS ARE A BIT... SHADY.

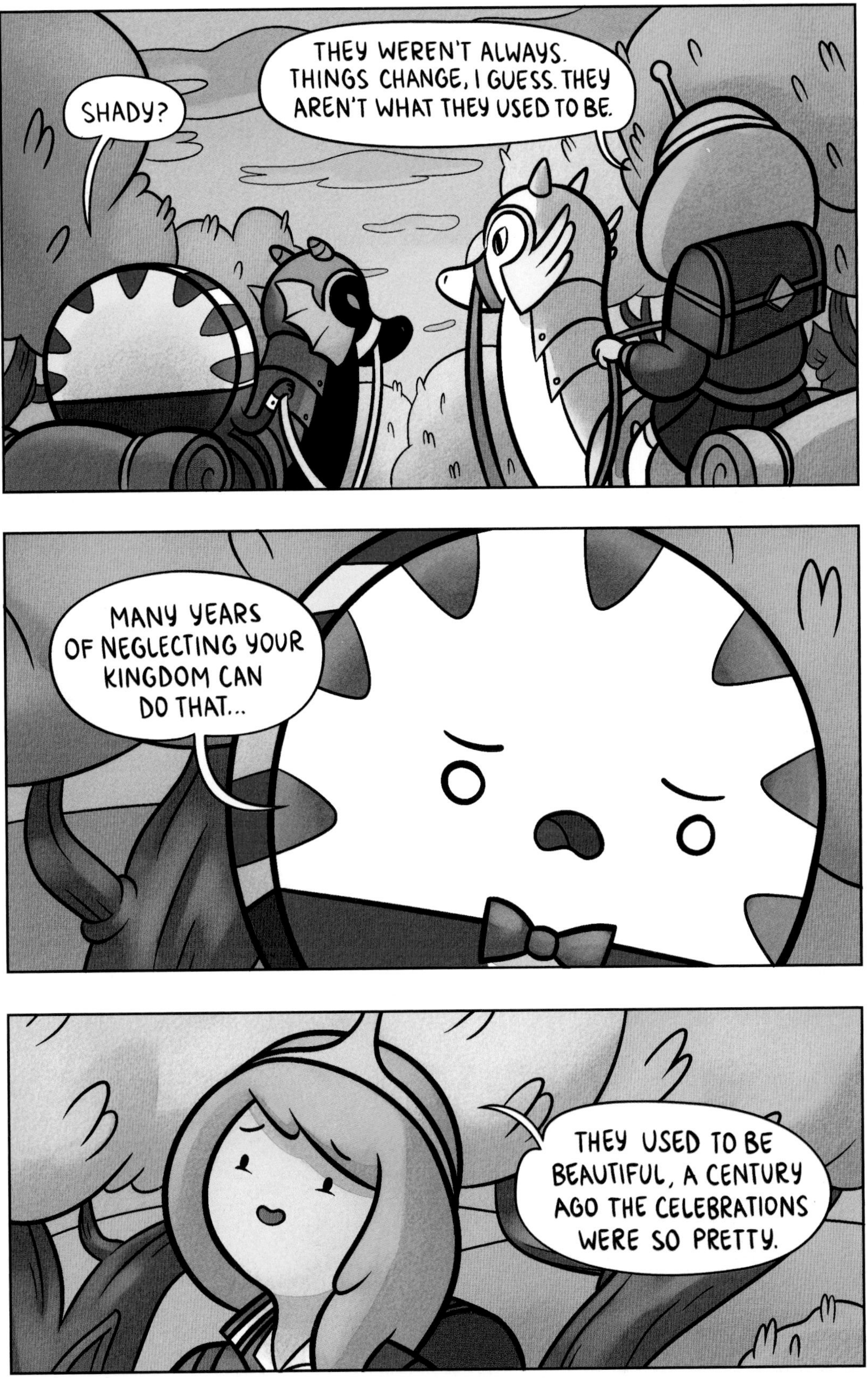
SHADY?
THEY WEREN'T ALWAYS. THINGS CHANGE, I GUESS. THEY AREN'T WHAT THEY USED TO BE.
MANY YEARS OF NEGLECTING YOUR KINGDOM CAN DO THAT...
THEY USED TO BE BEAUTIFUL, A CENTURY AGO THE CELEBRATIONS WERE SO PRETTY.

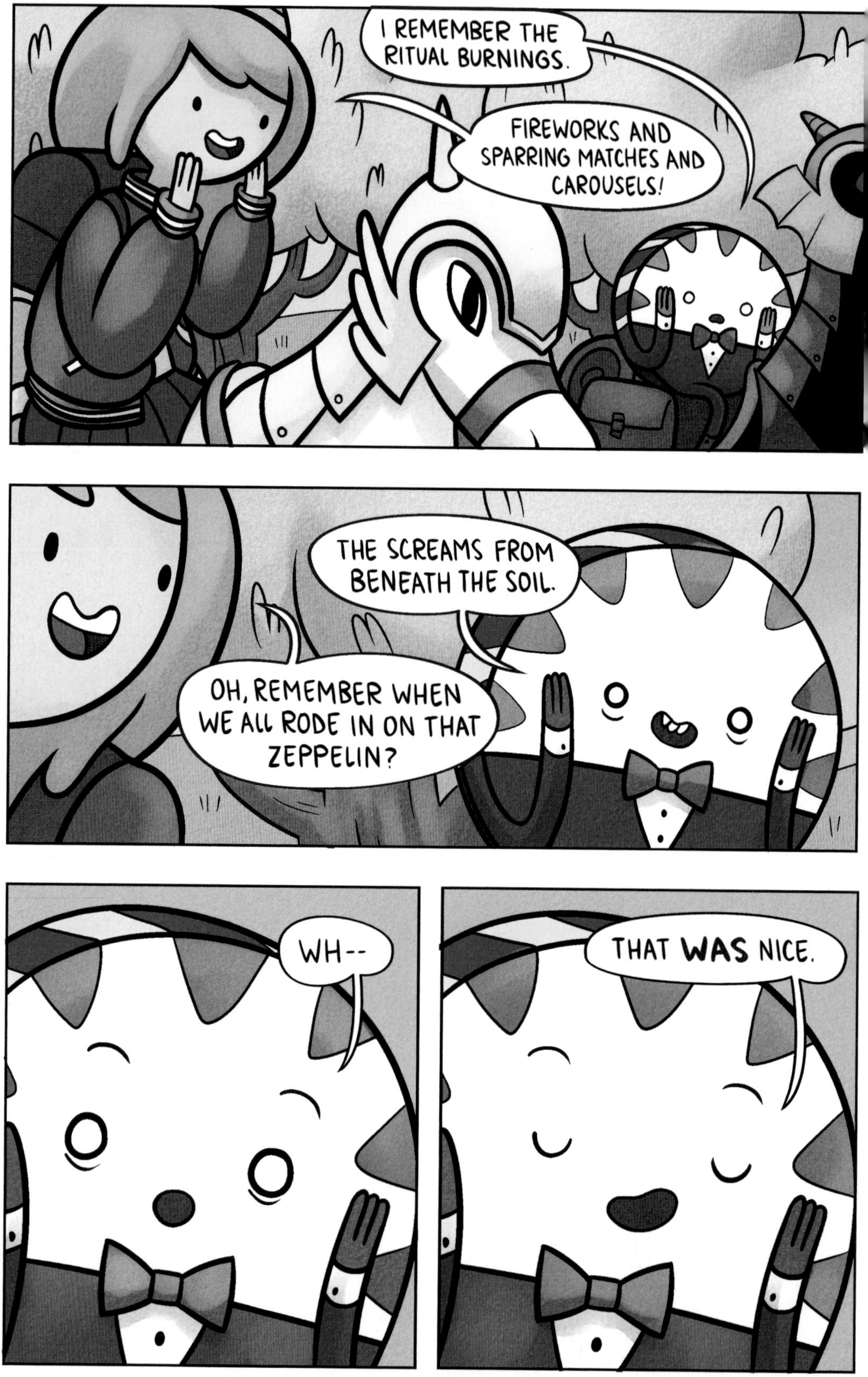
I REMEMBER THE RITUAL BURNINGS.
FIREWORKS AND SPARRING MATCHES AND CAROUSELS!
THE SCREAMS FROM BENEATH THE SOIL.
OH, REMEMBER WHEN WE ALL RODE IN ON THAT ZEPPELIN?
WH--
THAT **WAS** NICE.

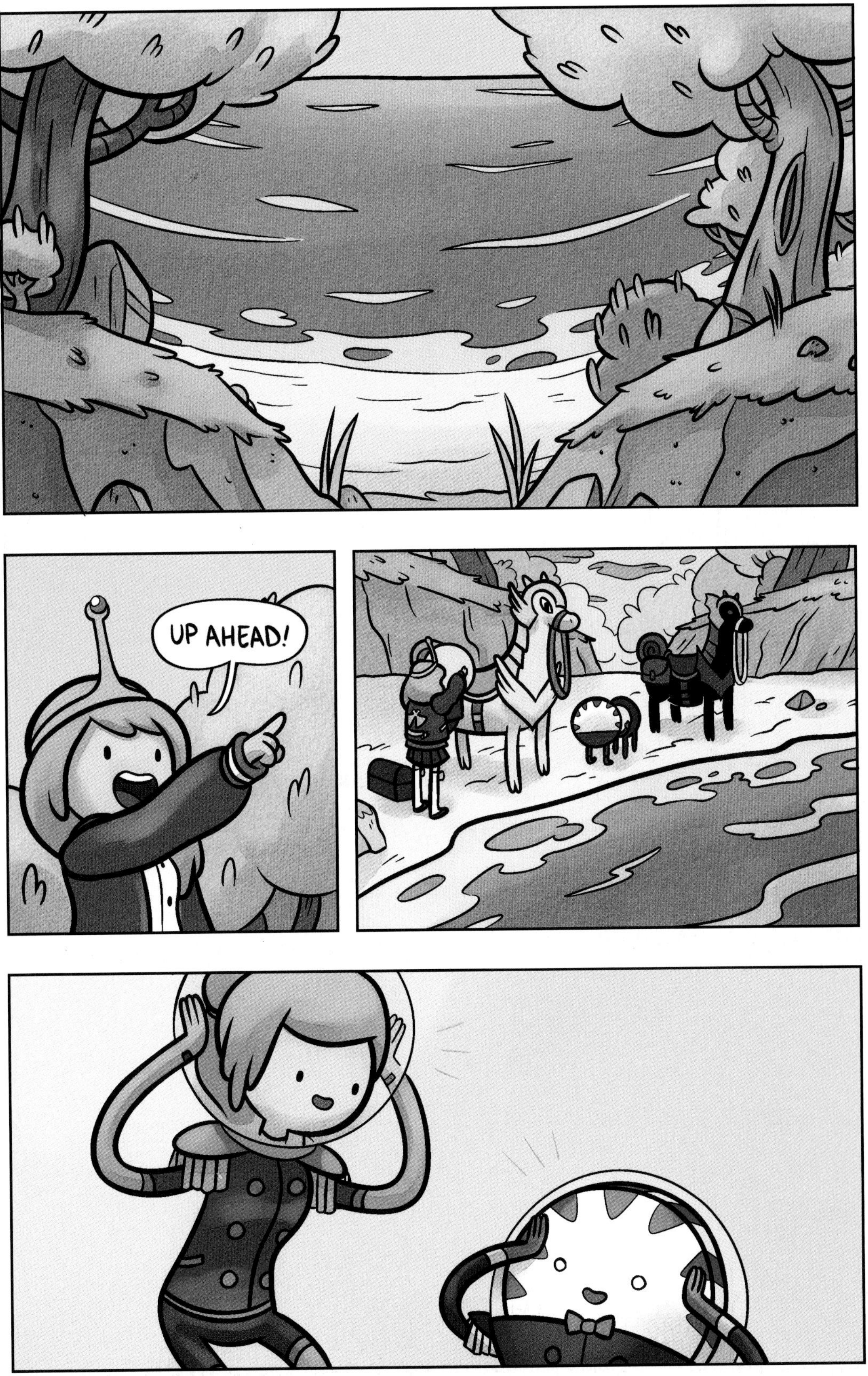
UP AHEAD!

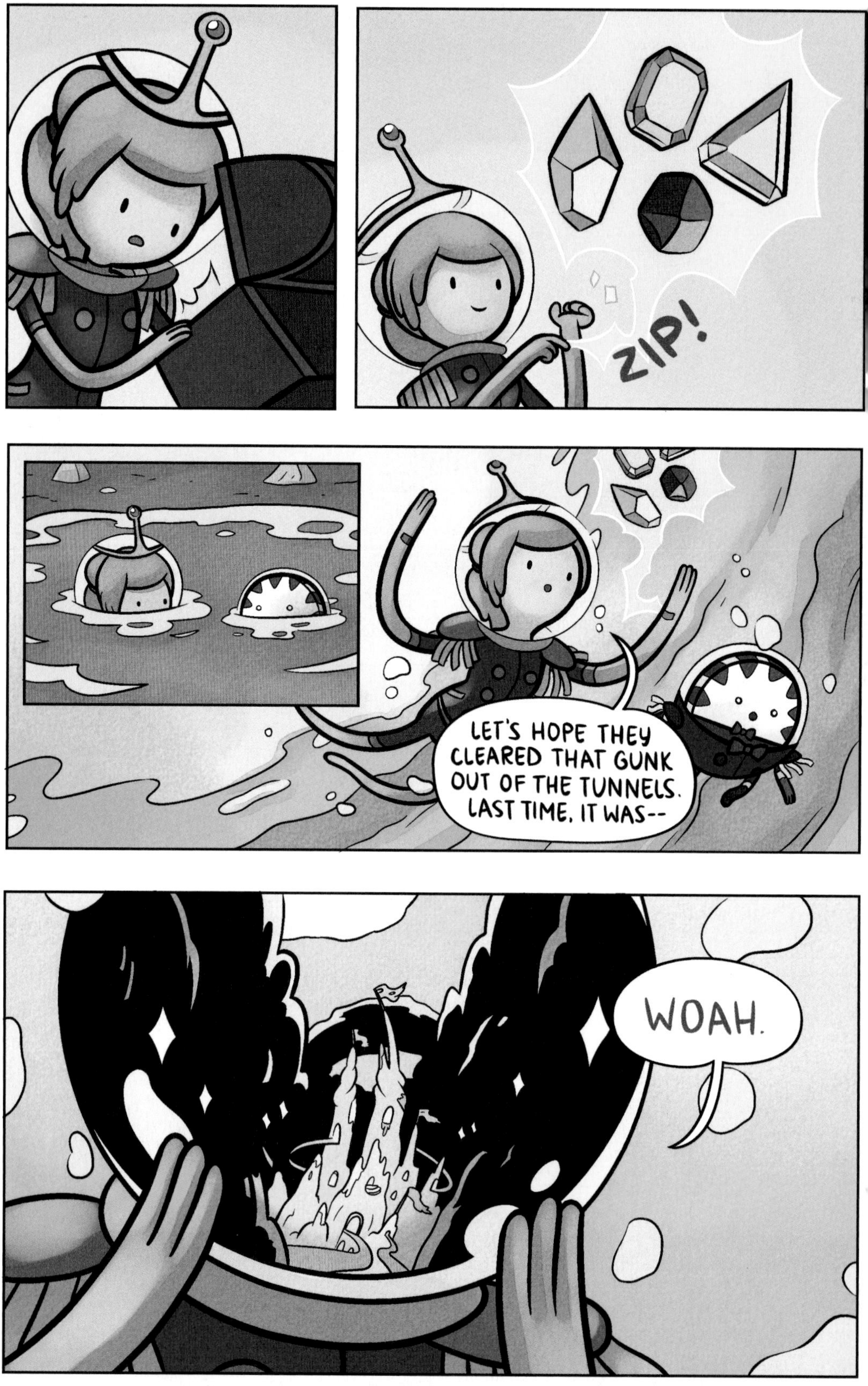
ZIP!
LET'S HOPE THEY CLEARED THAT GUNK OUT OF THE TUNNELS. LAST TIME, IT WAS--
WOAH.

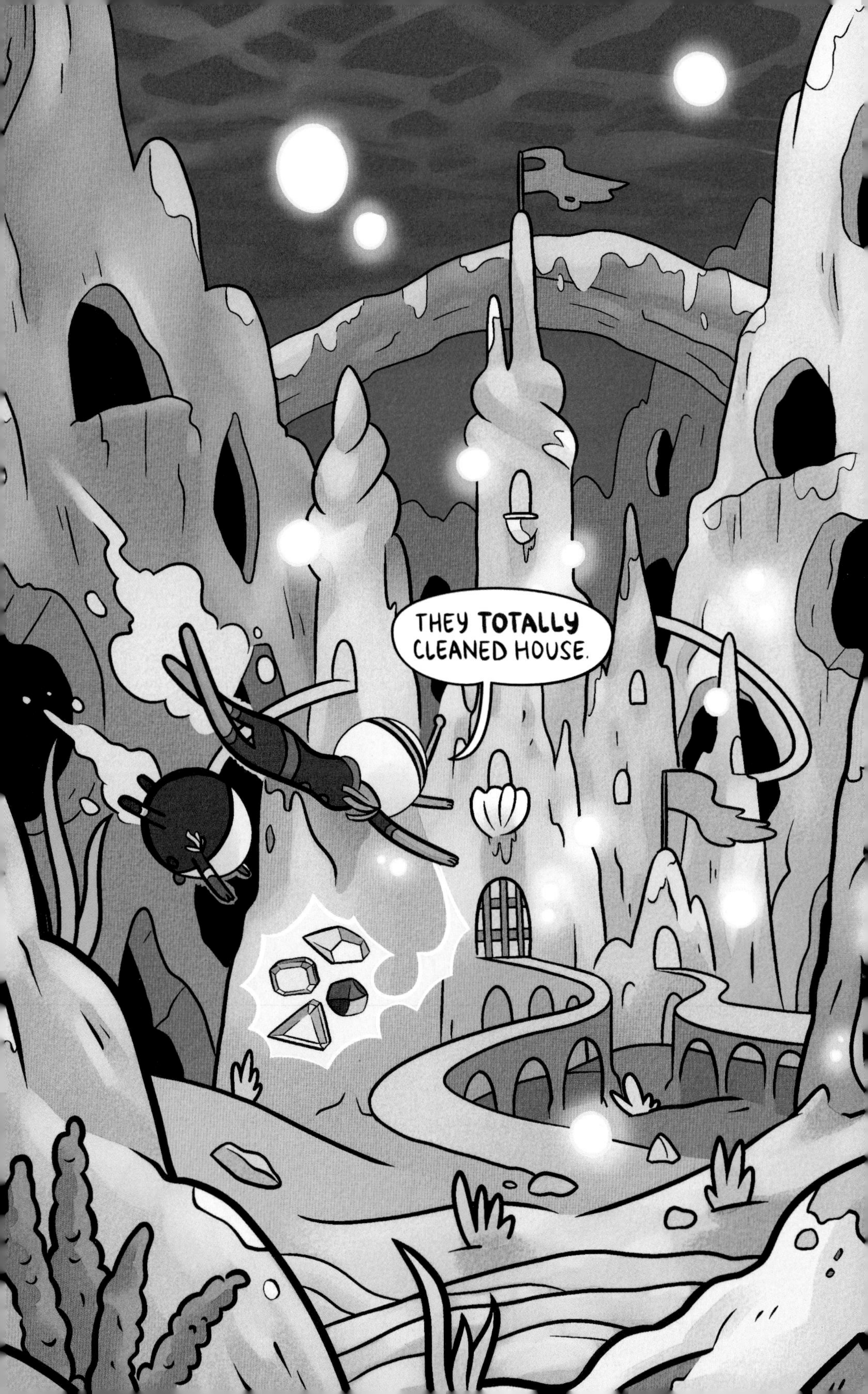
THEY **TOTALLY** CLEANED HOUSE.

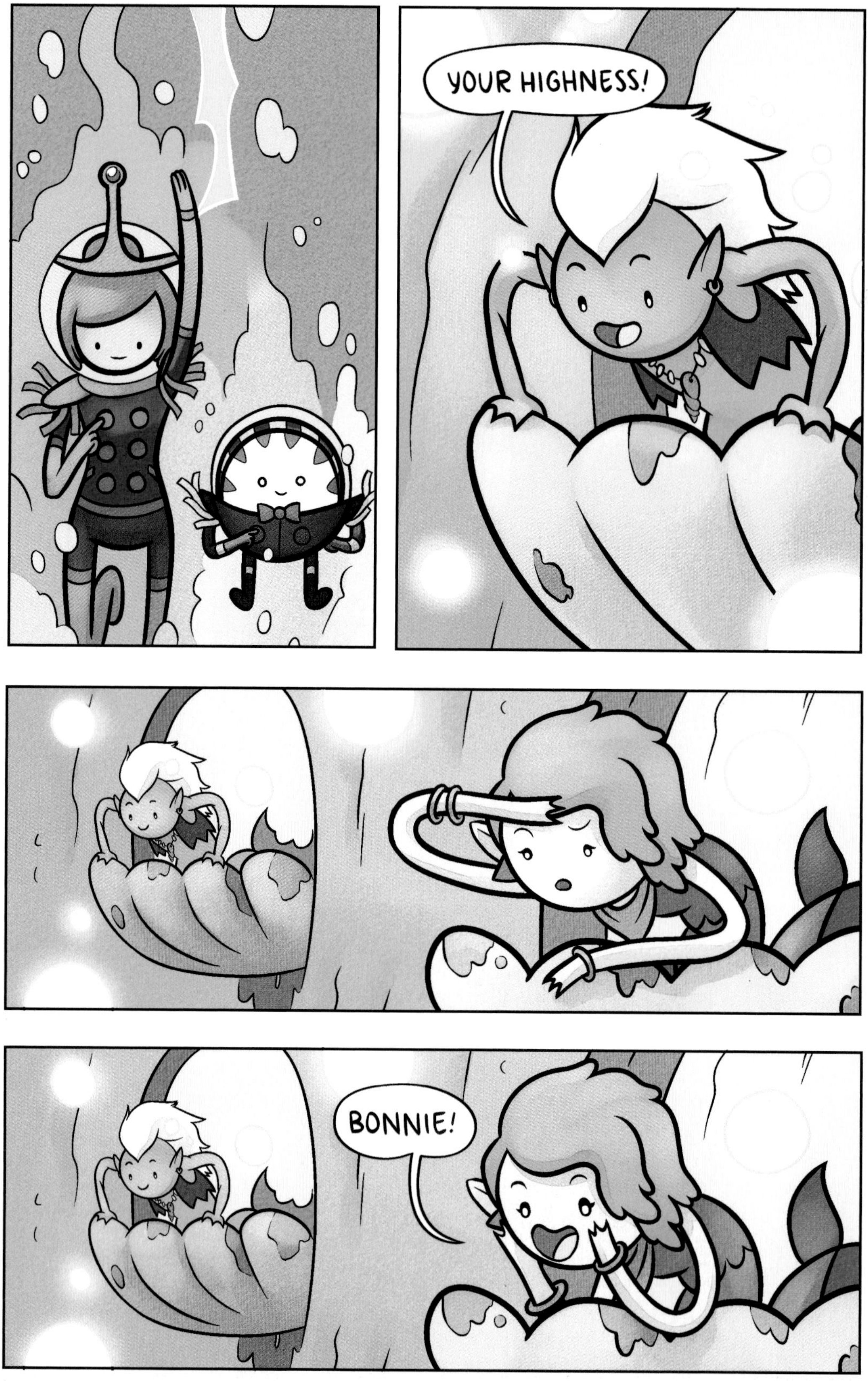
YOUR HIGHNESS!
BONNIE!

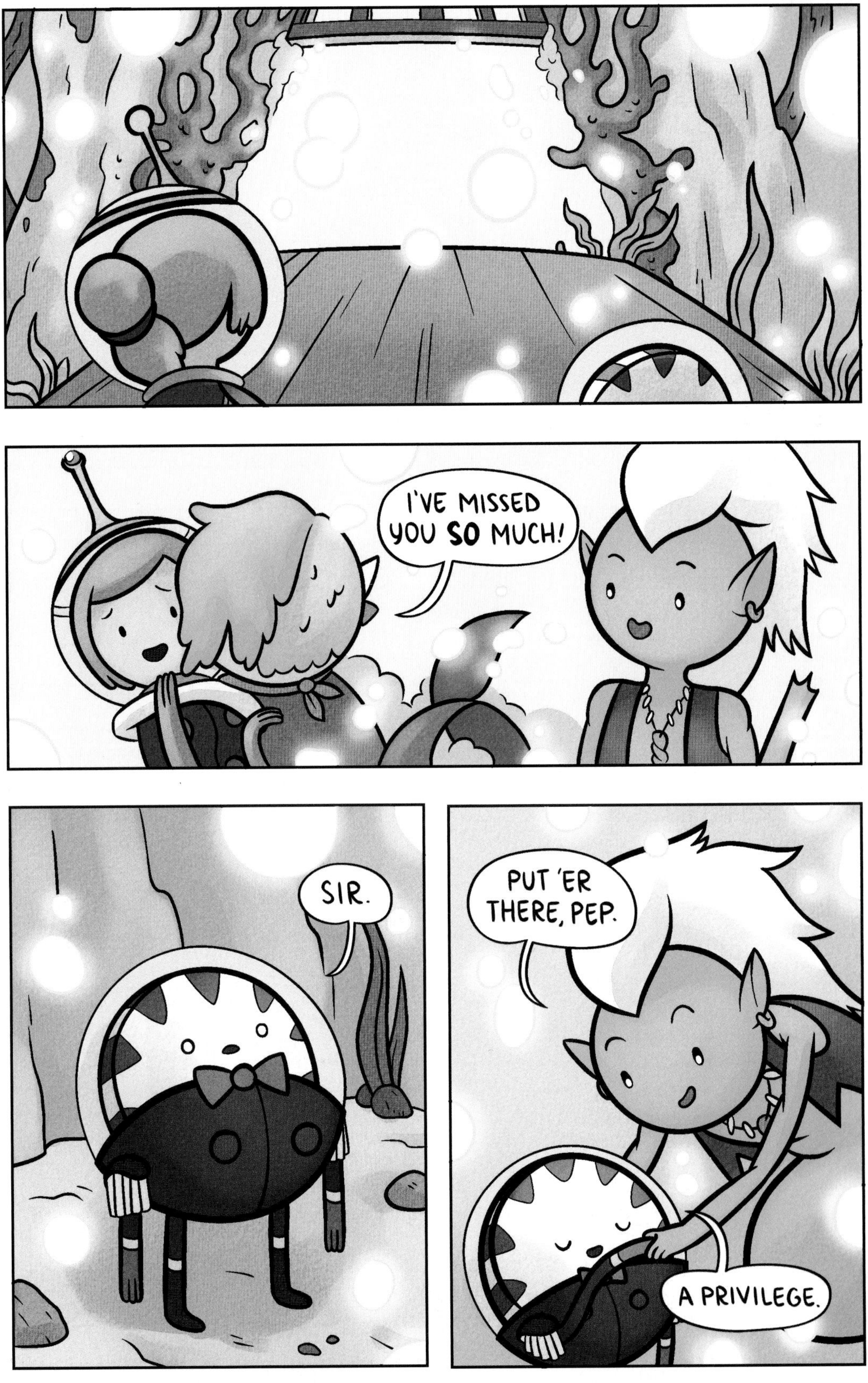
I'VE MISSED YOU SO MUCH!
SIR.
PUT 'ER THERE, PEP.
A PRIVILEGE.

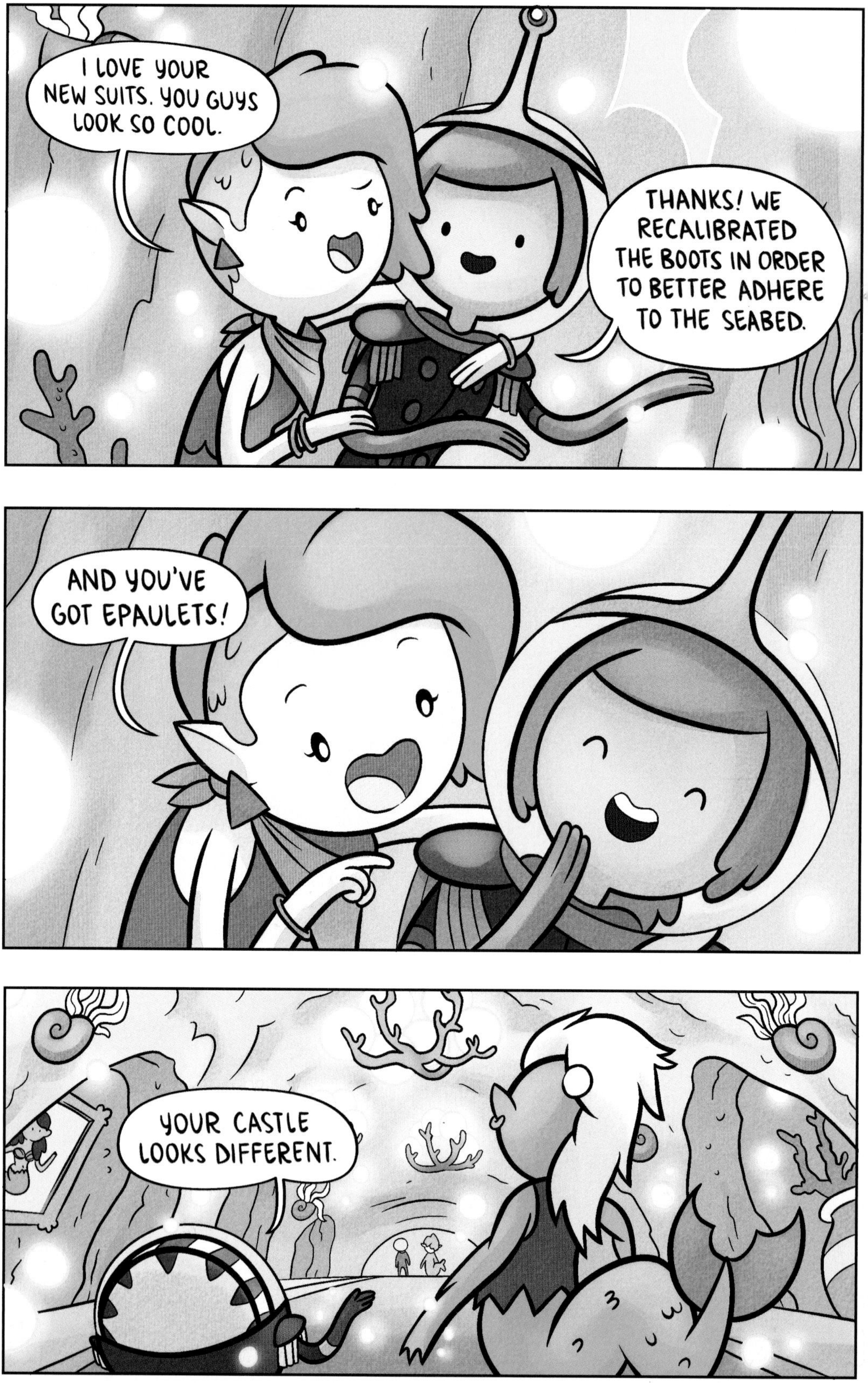
I LOVE YOUR NEW SUITS. YOU GUYS LOOK SO COOL.
THANKS! WE RECALIBRATED THE BOOTS IN ORDER TO BETTER ADHERE TO THE SEABED.
AND YOU'VE GOT EPAULETS!
YOUR CASTLE LOOKS DIFFERENT.

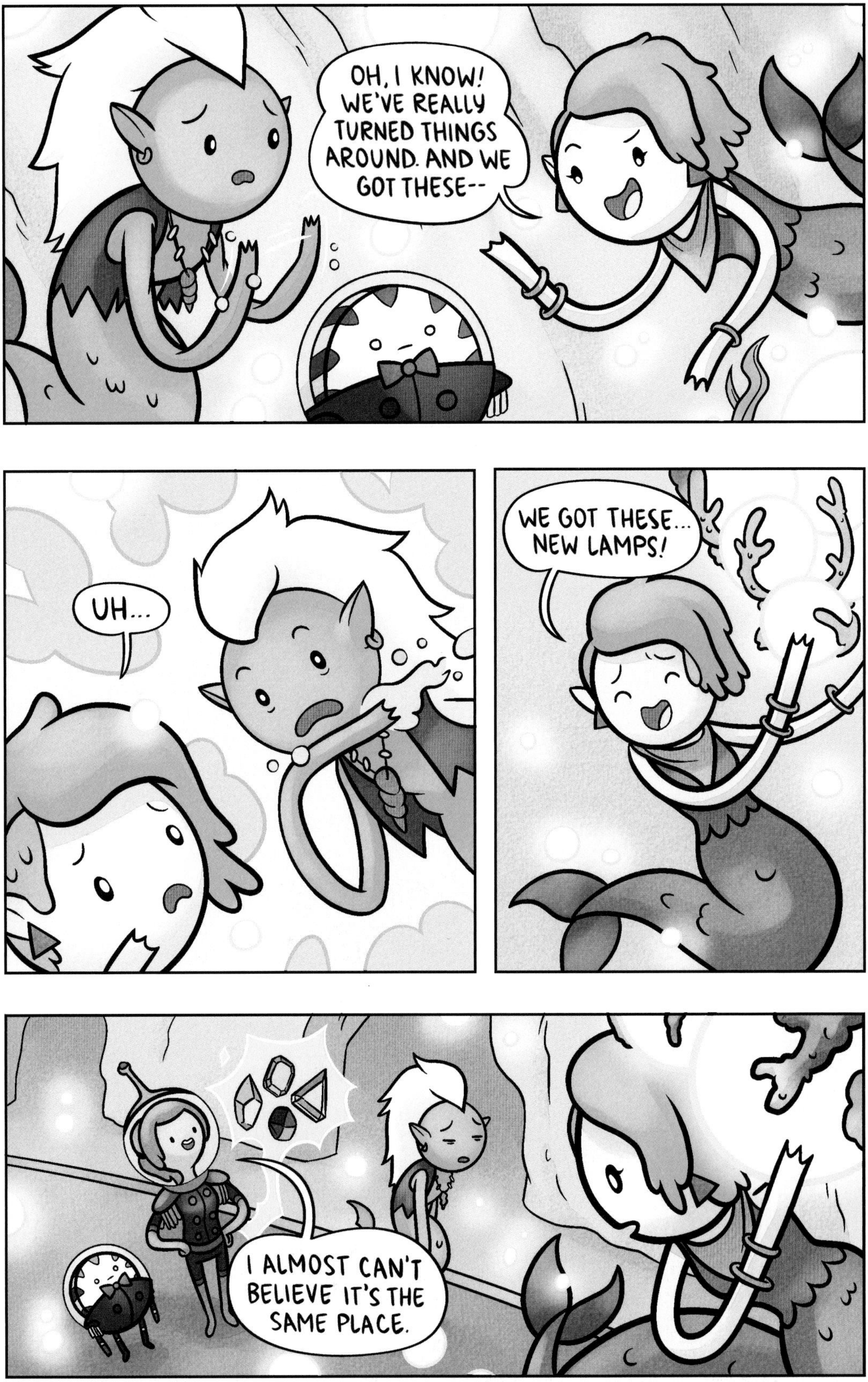
OH, I KNOW! WE'VE REALLY TURNED THINGS AROUND. AND WE GOT THESE--
UH...
WE GOT THESE... NEW LAMPS!
I ALMOST CAN'T BELIEVE IT'S THE SAME PLACE.

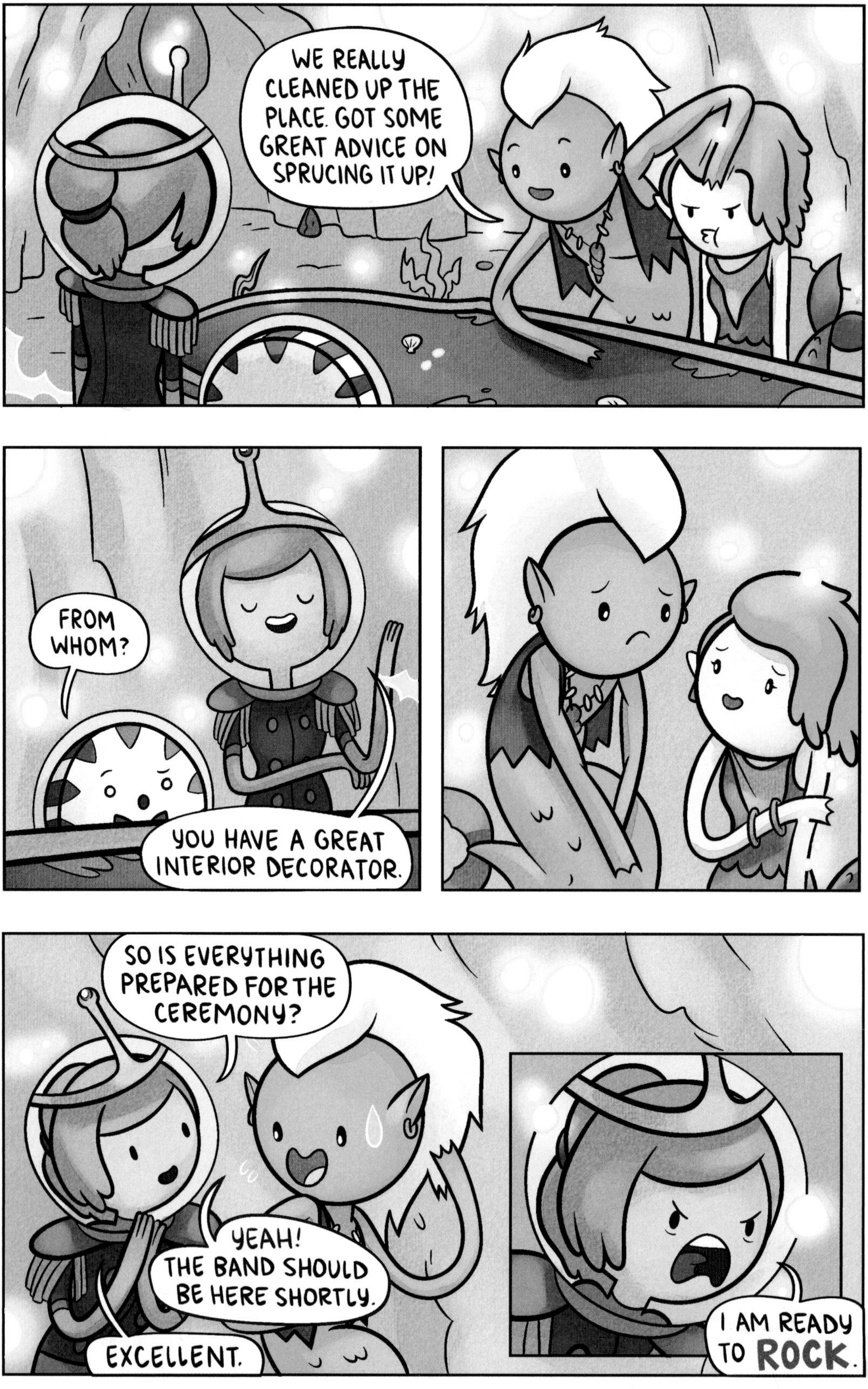
WE REALLY CLEANED UP THE PLACE. GOT SOME GREAT ADVICE ON SPRUCING IT UP!
FROM WHOM?
YOU HAVE A GREAT INTERIOR DECORATOR.
SO IS EVERYTHING PREPARED FOR THE CEREMONY?
YEAH! THE BAND SHOULD BE HERE SHORTLY.
EXCELLENT.
I AM READY TO ROCK.

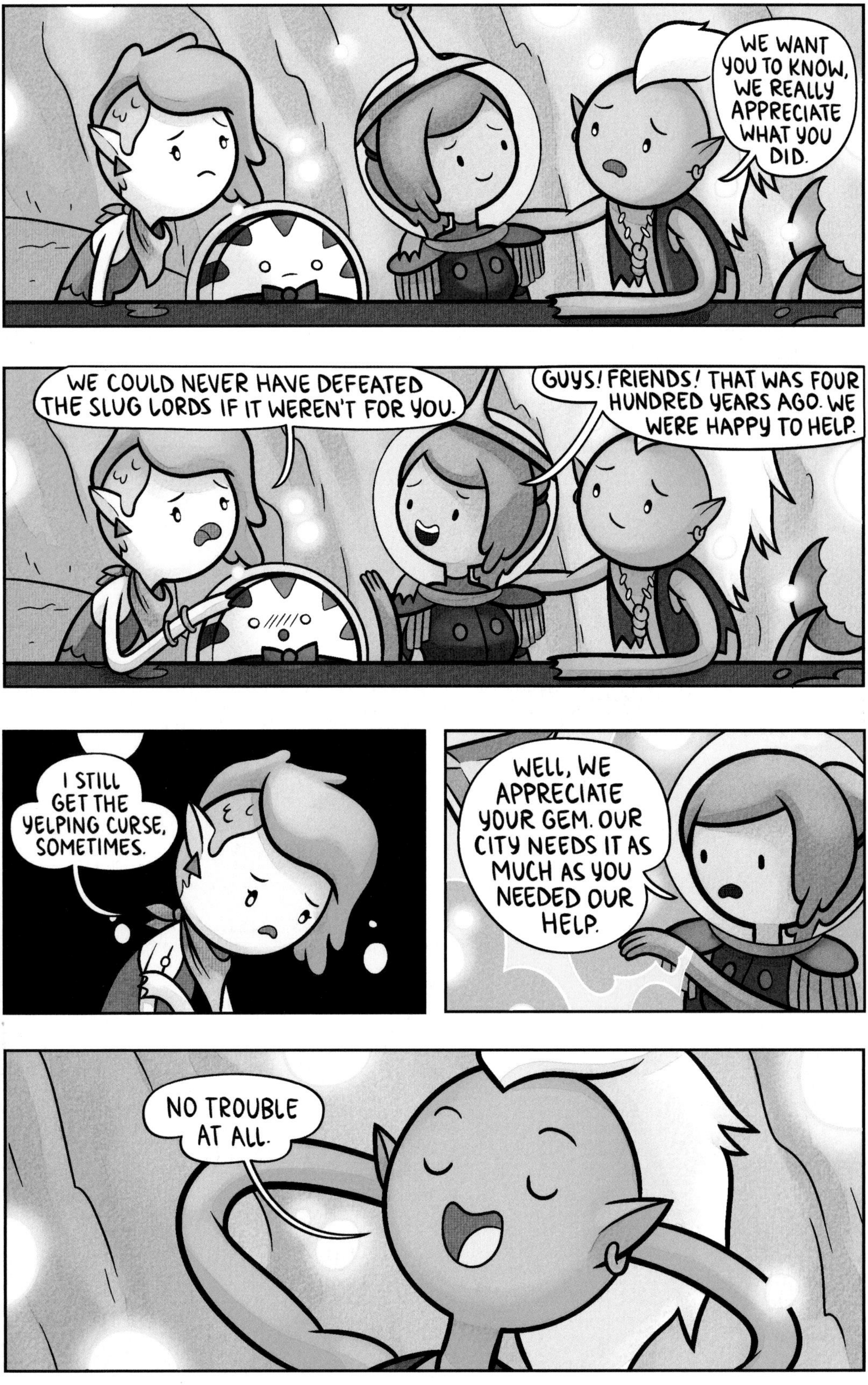
WE WANT YOU TO KNOW, WE REALLY APPRECIATE WHAT YOU DID.
WE COULD NEVER HAVE DEFEATED THE SLUG LORDS IF IT WEREN'T FOR YOU.
GUYS! FRIENDS! THAT WAS FOUR HUNDRED YEARS AGO. WE WERE HAPPY TO HELP.
I STILL GET THE YELPING CURSE, SOMETIMES.
WELL, WE APPRECIATE YOUR GEM. OUR CITY NEEDS IT AS MUCH AS YOU NEEDED OUR HELP.
NO TROUBLE AT ALL.

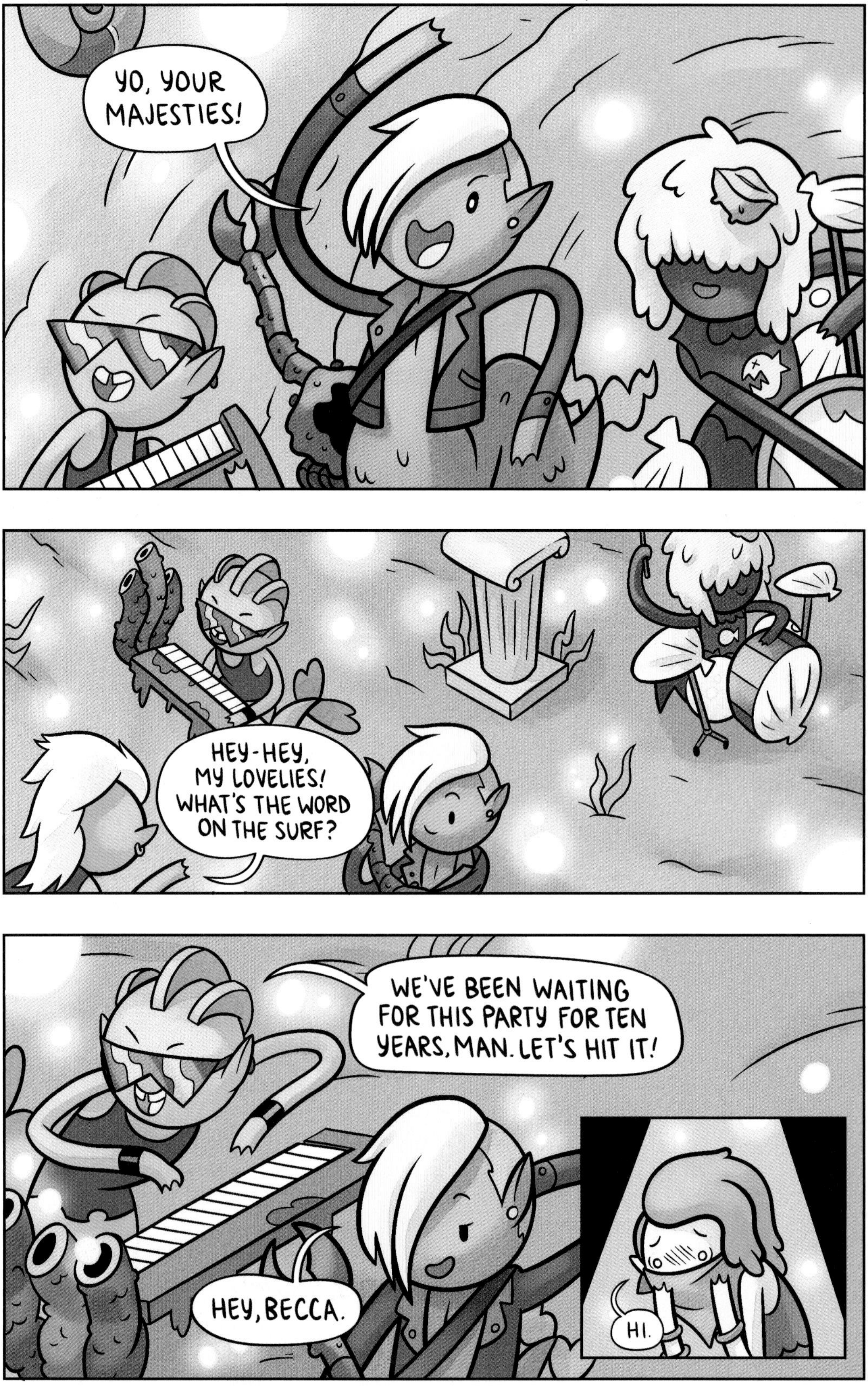
YO, YOUR MAJESTIES!
HEY-HEY, MY LOVELIES! WHAT'S THE WORD ON THE SURF?
WE'VE BEEN WAITING FOR THIS PARTY FOR TEN YEARS, MAN. LET'S HIT IT!
HEY, BECCA.
HI.

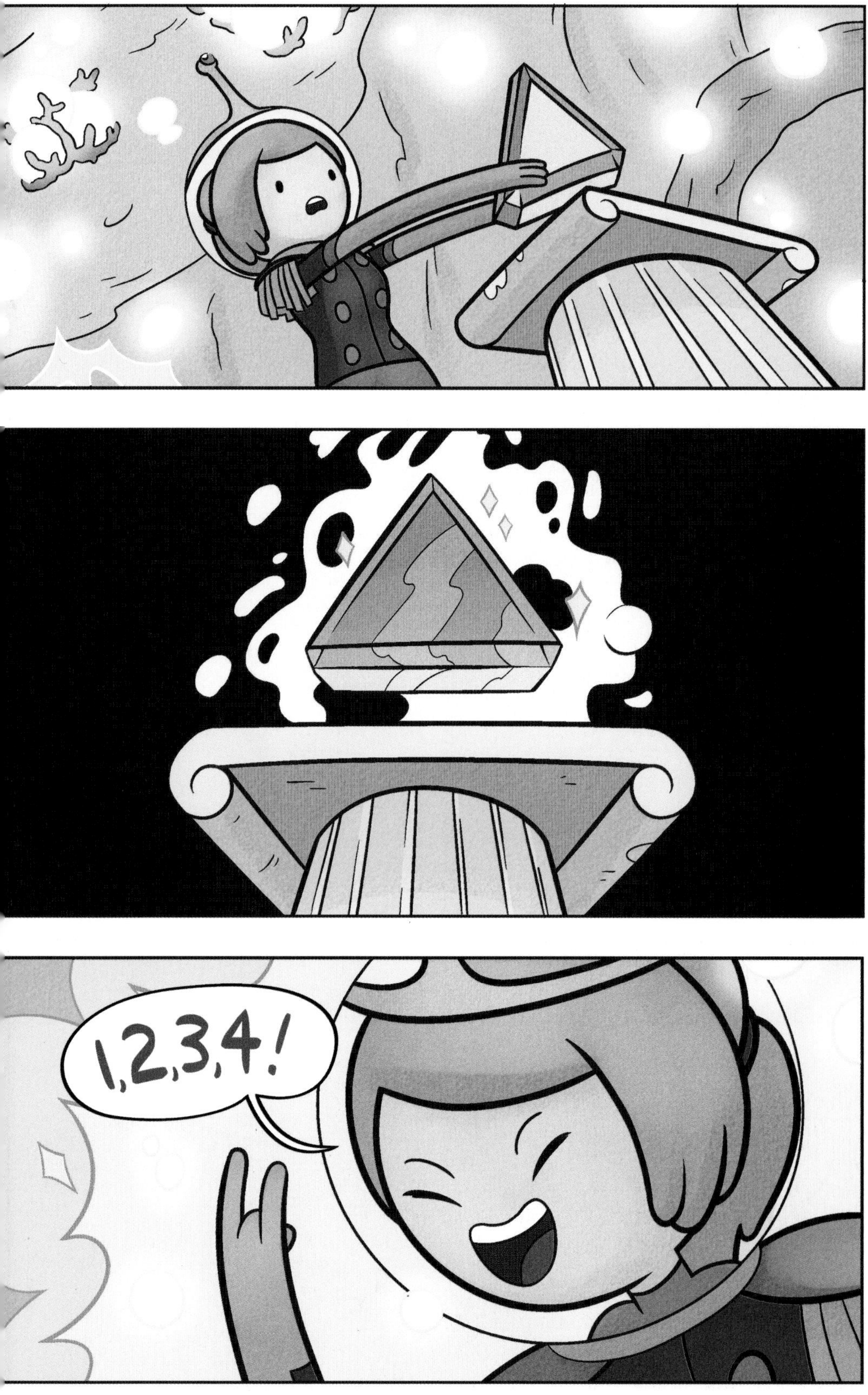
1,2,3,4!

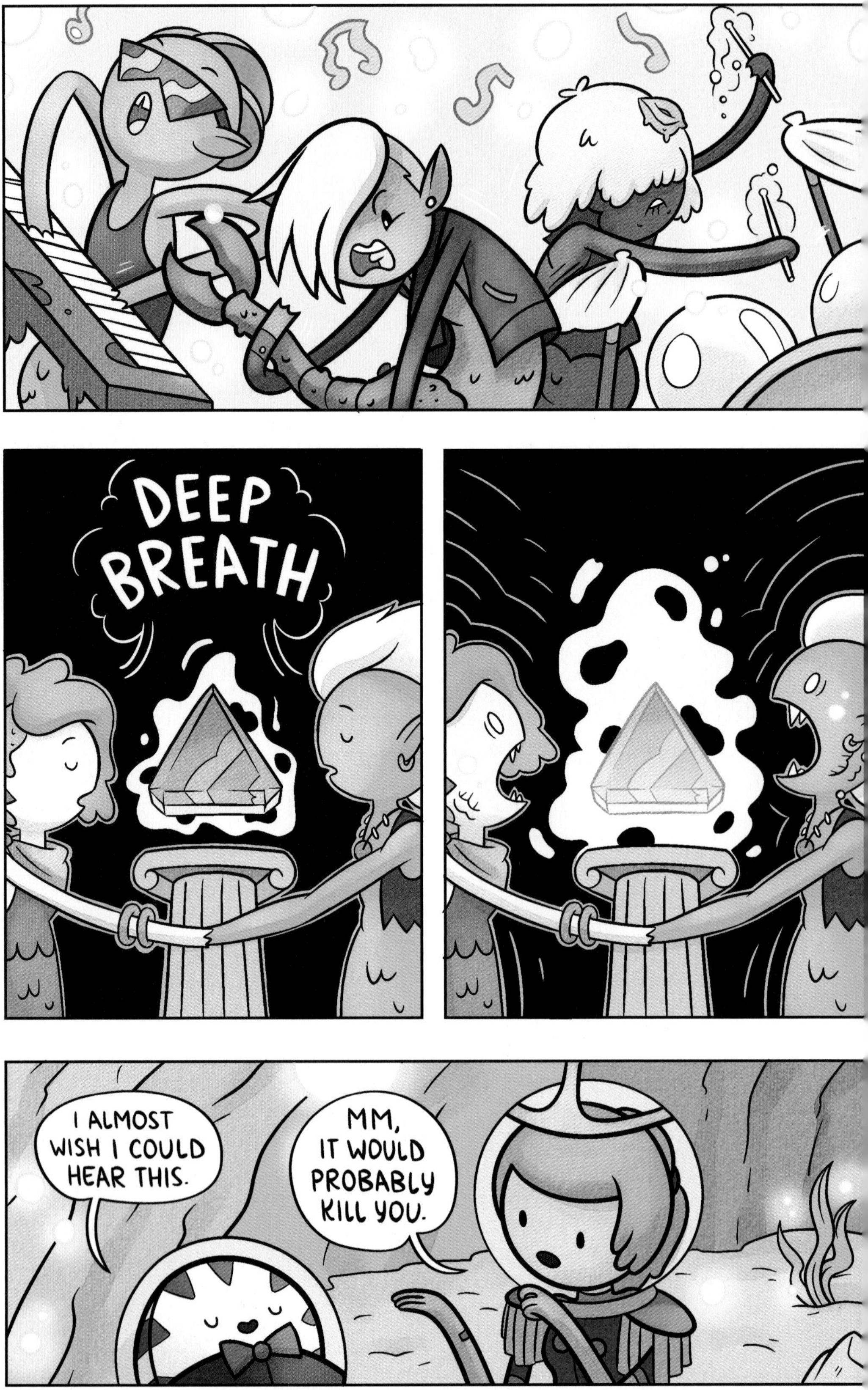
DEEP BREATH
I ALMOST WISH I COULD HEAR THIS.
MM, IT WOULD PROBABLY KILL YOU.

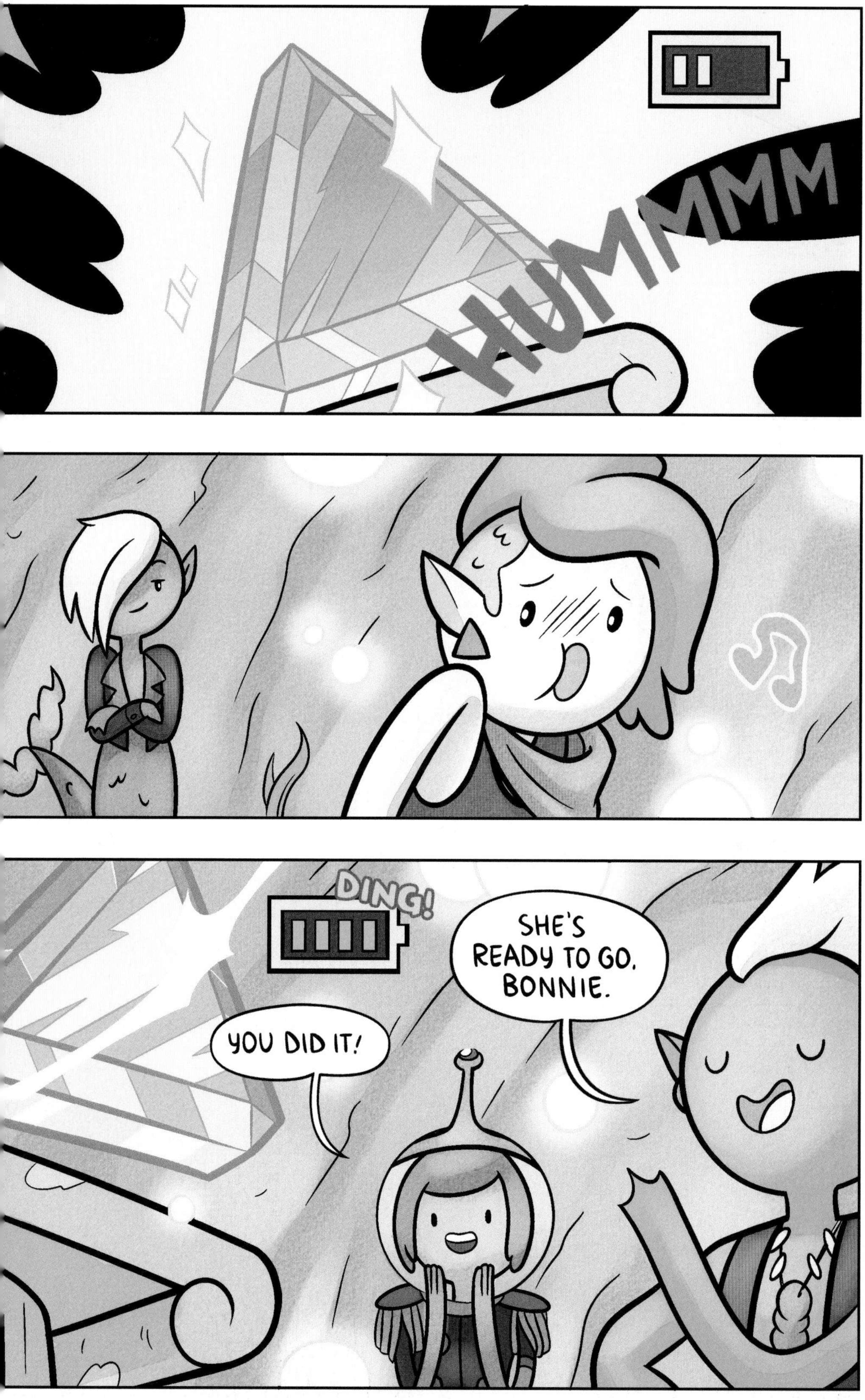
HUMMMM
DING!
SHE'S READY TO GO, BONNIE.
YOU DID IT!

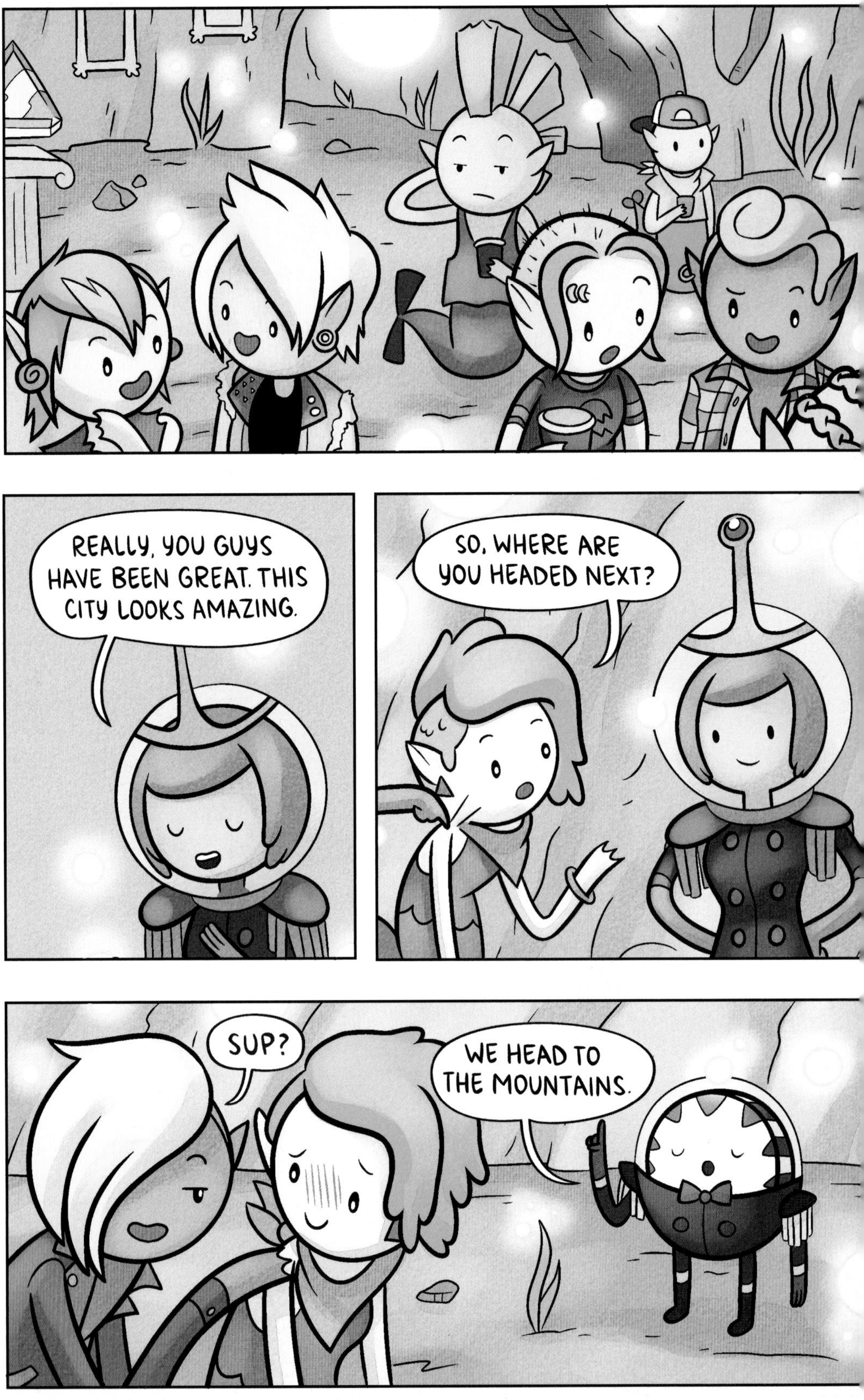
REALLY, YOU GUYS HAVE BEEN GREAT. THIS CITY LOOKS AMAZING.
SO, WHERE ARE YOU HEADED NEXT?
SUP?
WE HEAD TO THE MOUNTAINS.

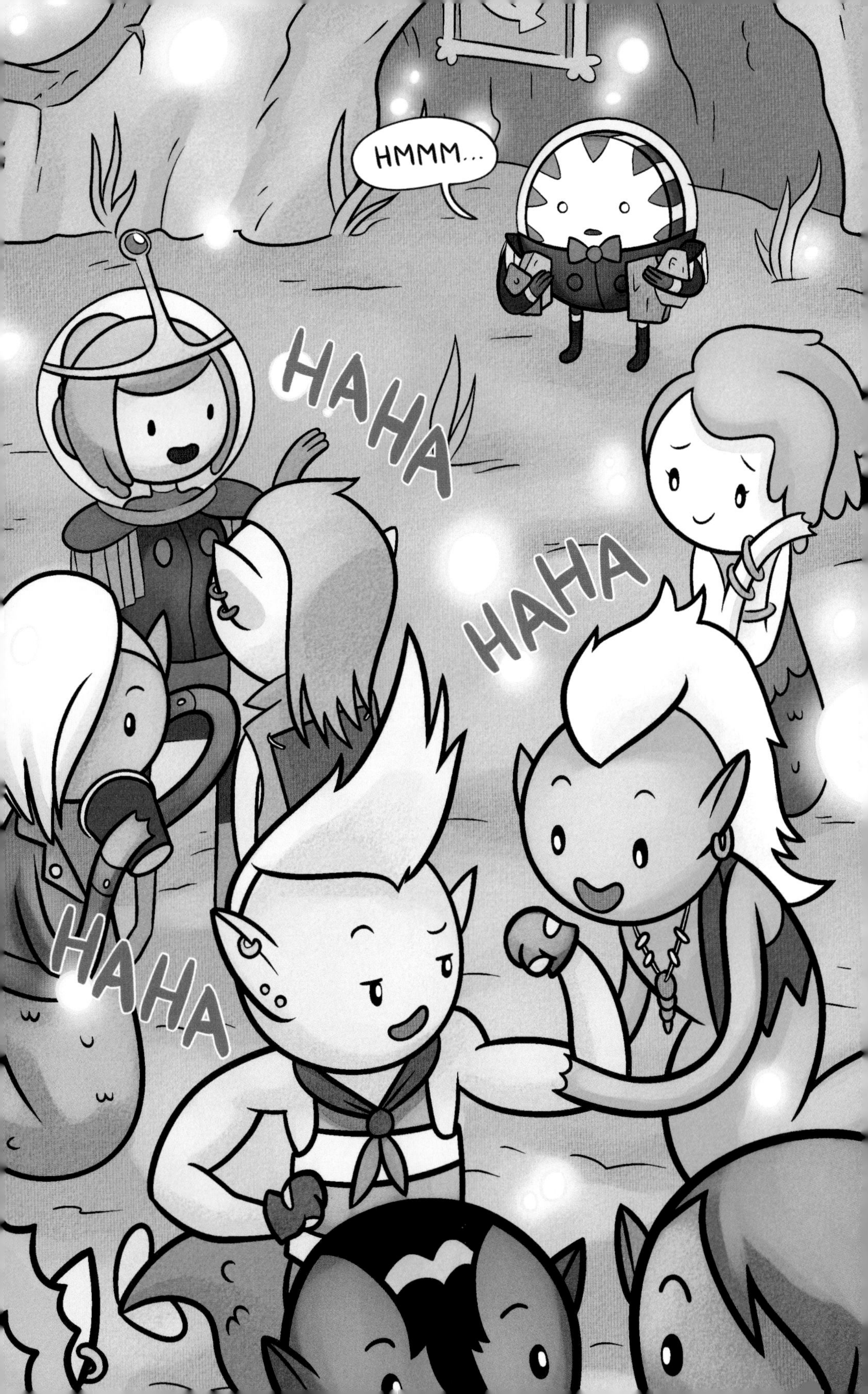
HMMM...
HAHA
HAHA
HAHA

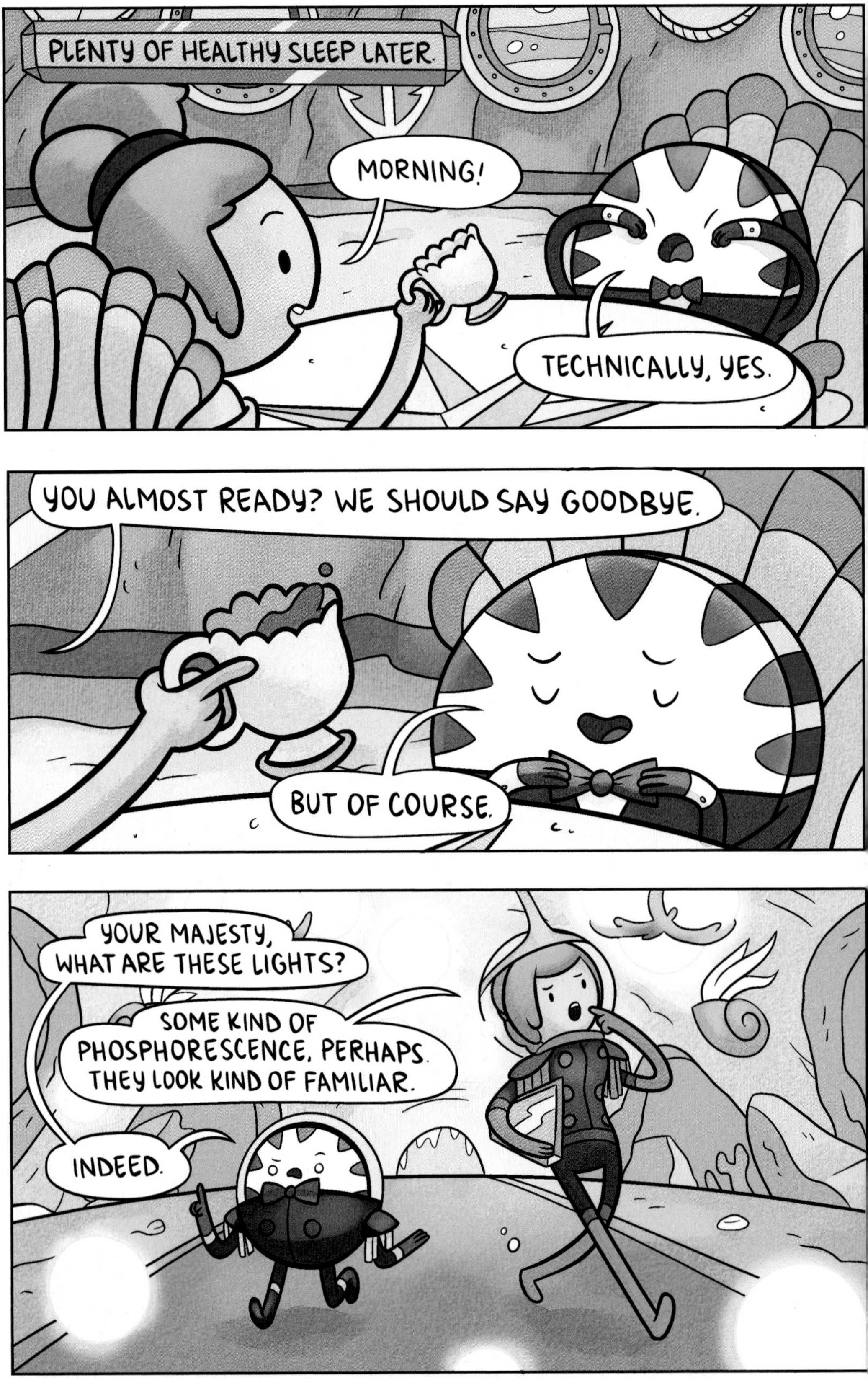
PLENTY OF HEALTHY SLEEP LATER.
MORNING!
TECHNICALLY, YES.
YOU ALMOST READY? WE SHOULD SAY GOODBYE.
BUT OF COURSE.
YOUR MAJESTY, WHAT ARE THESE LIGHTS?
SOME KIND OF PHOSPHORESCENCE, PERHAPS. THEY LOOK KIND OF FAMILIAR.
INDEED.

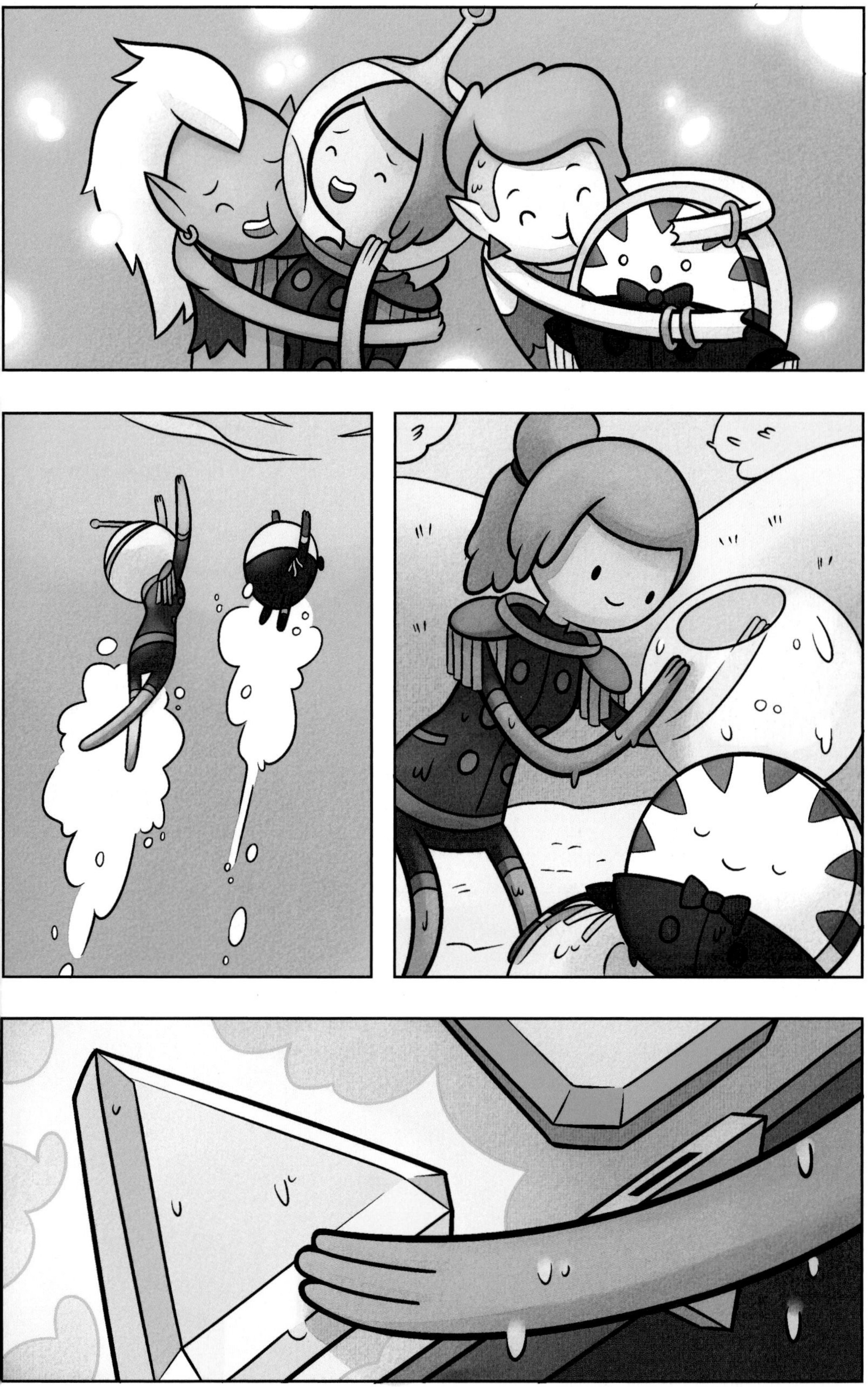

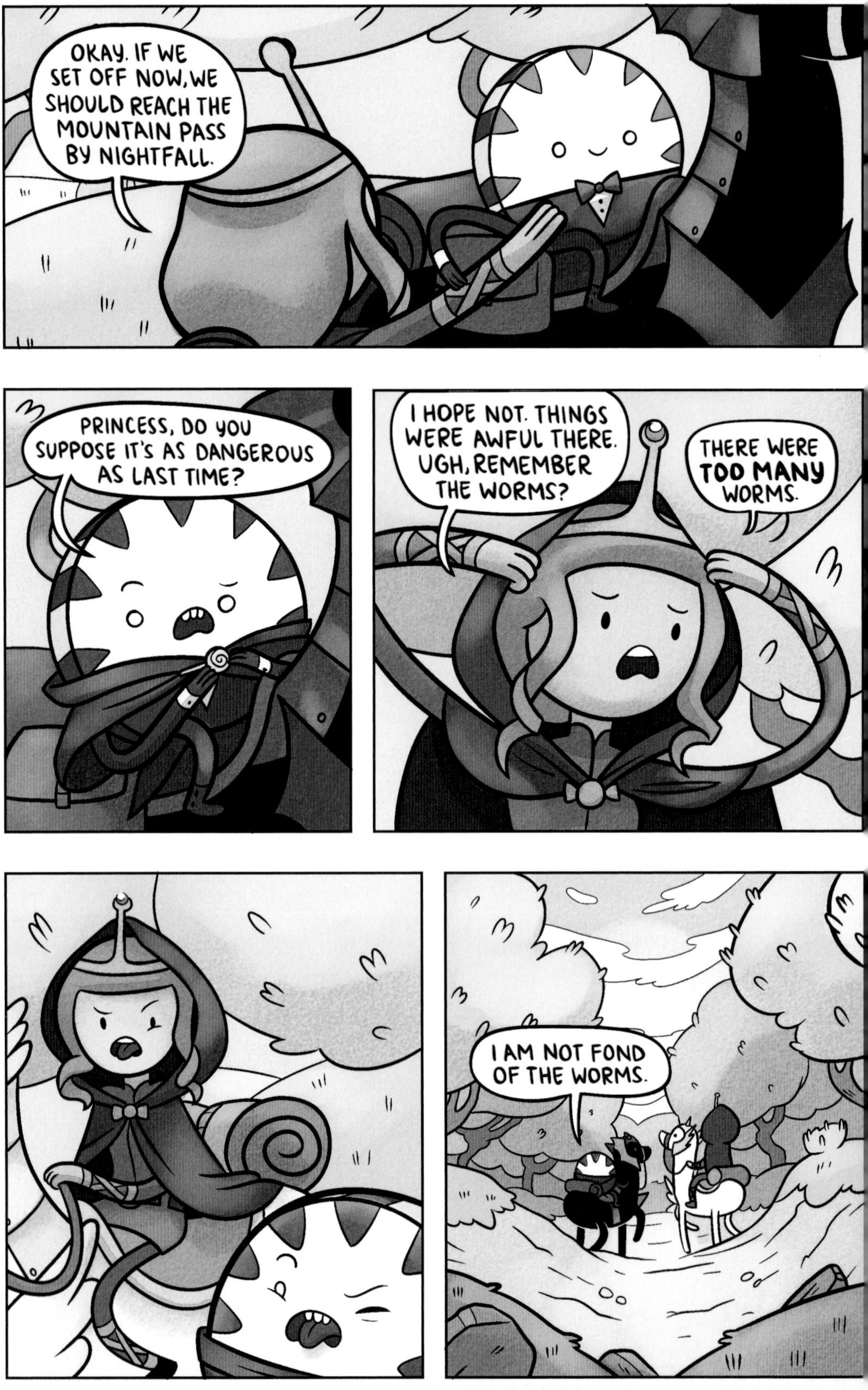
OKAY. IF WE SET OFF NOW, WE SHOULD REACH THE MOUNTAIN PASS BY NIGHTFALL.
PRINCESS, DO YOU SUPPOSE IT'S AS DANGEROUS AS LAST TIME?
I HOPE NOT. THINGS WERE AWFUL THERE. UGH, REMEMBER THE WORMS?
THERE WERE **TOO MANY** WORMS.
I AM NOT FOND OF THE WORMS.

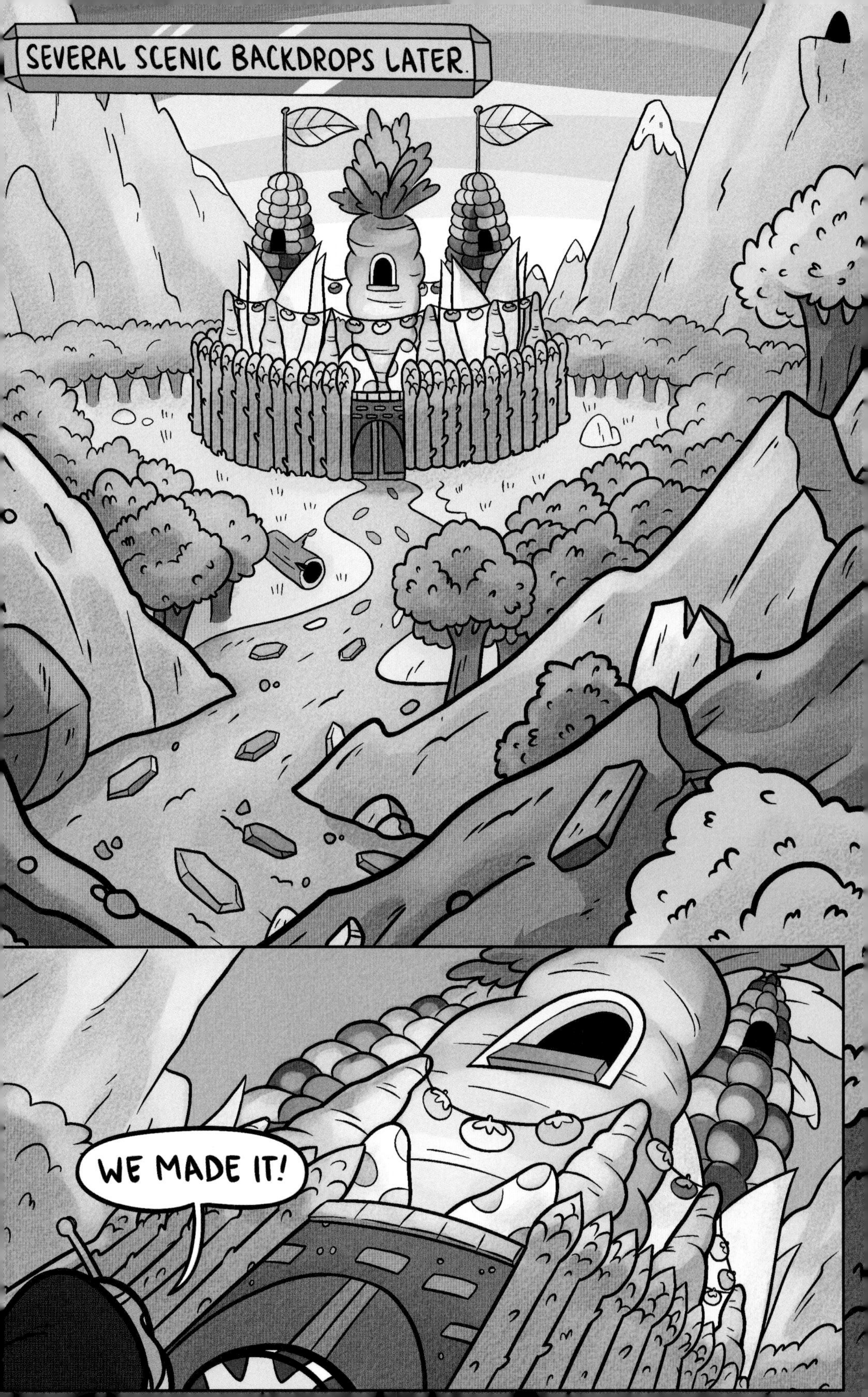
SEVERAL SCENIC BACKDROPS LATER.
WE MADE IT!

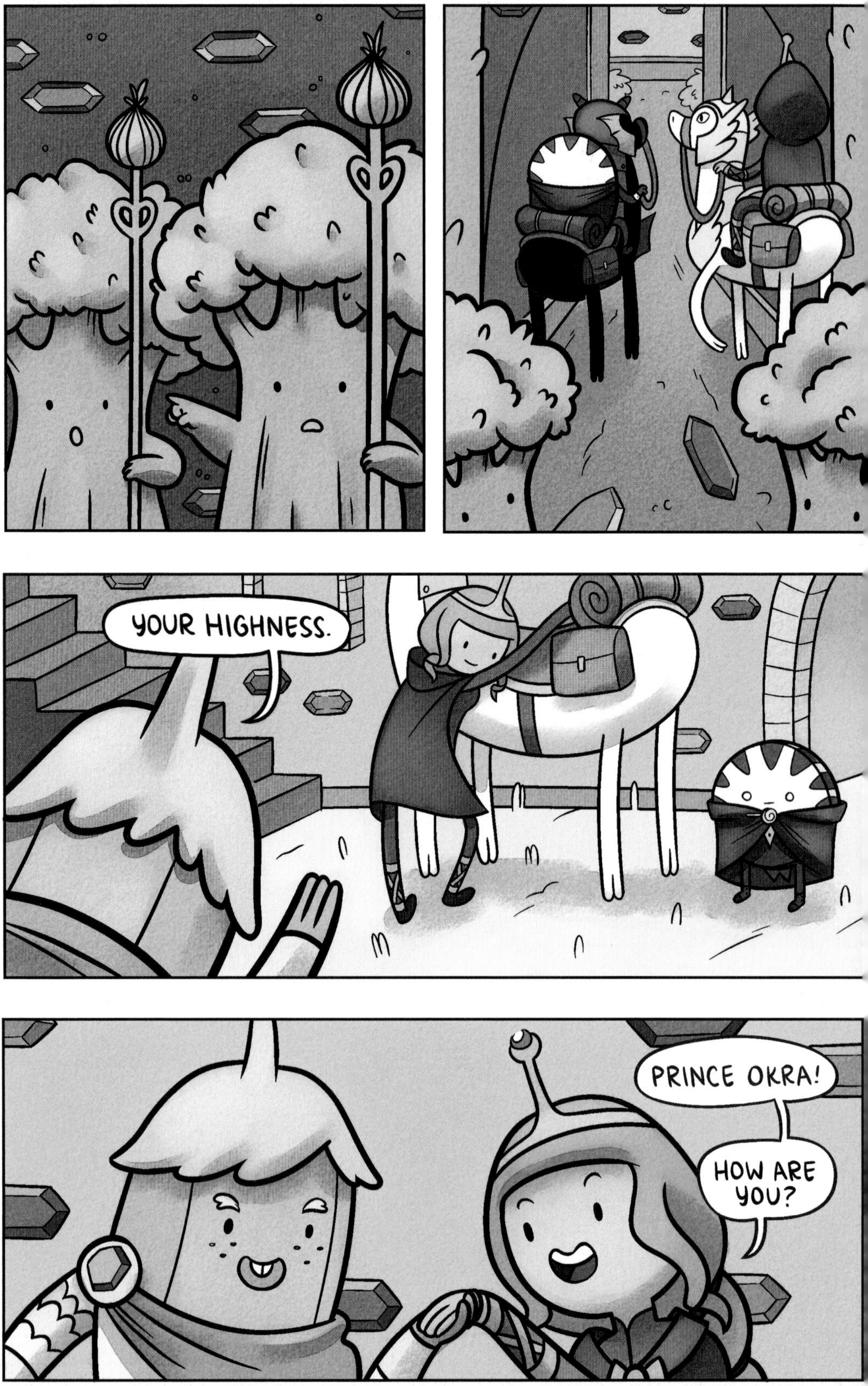
YOUR HIGHNESS.
PRINCE OKRA!
HOW ARE YOU?

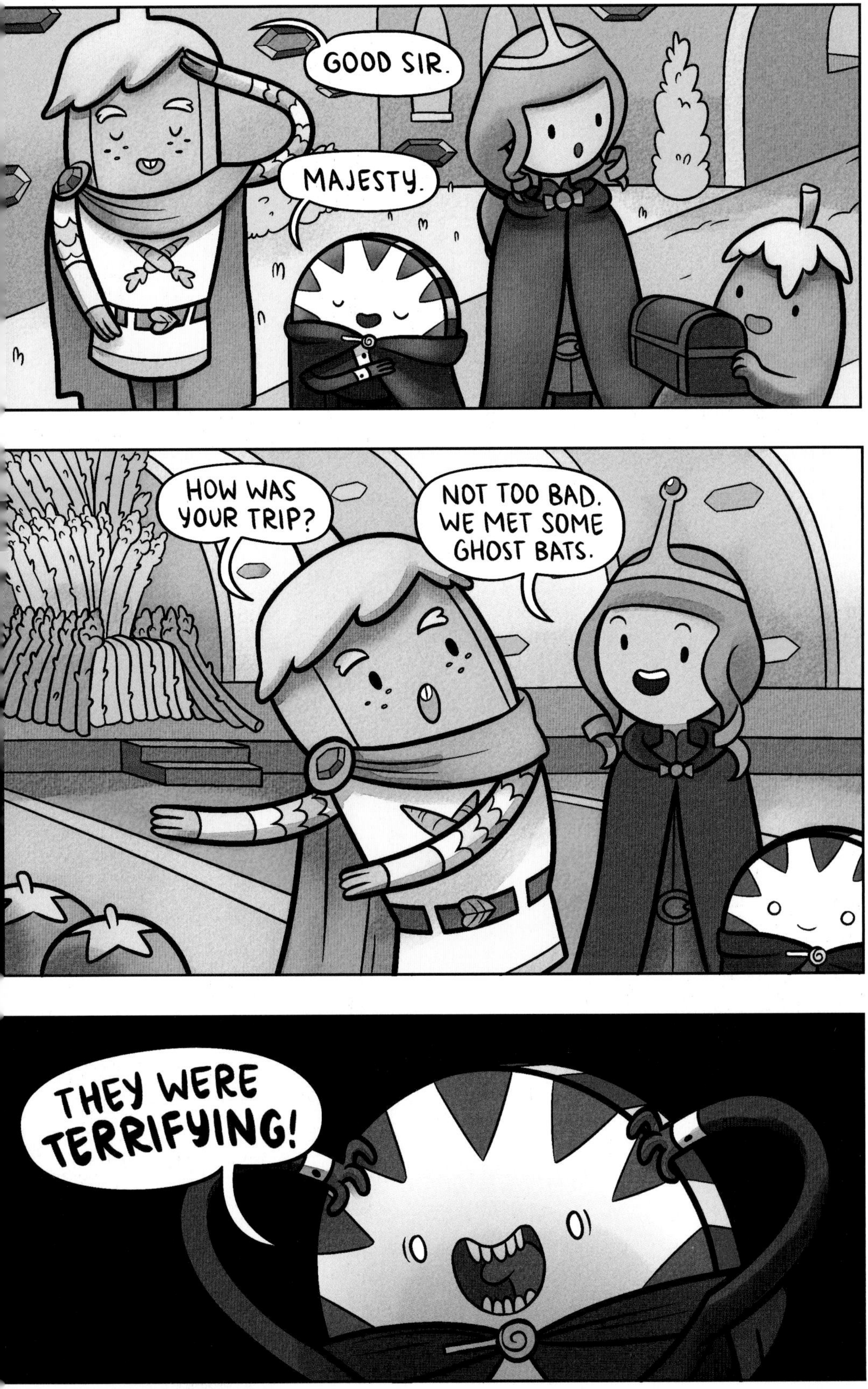
GOOD SIR.
MAJESTY.
HOW WAS YOUR TRIP?
NOT TOO BAD. WE MET SOME GHOST BATS.
THEY WERE TERRIFYING!

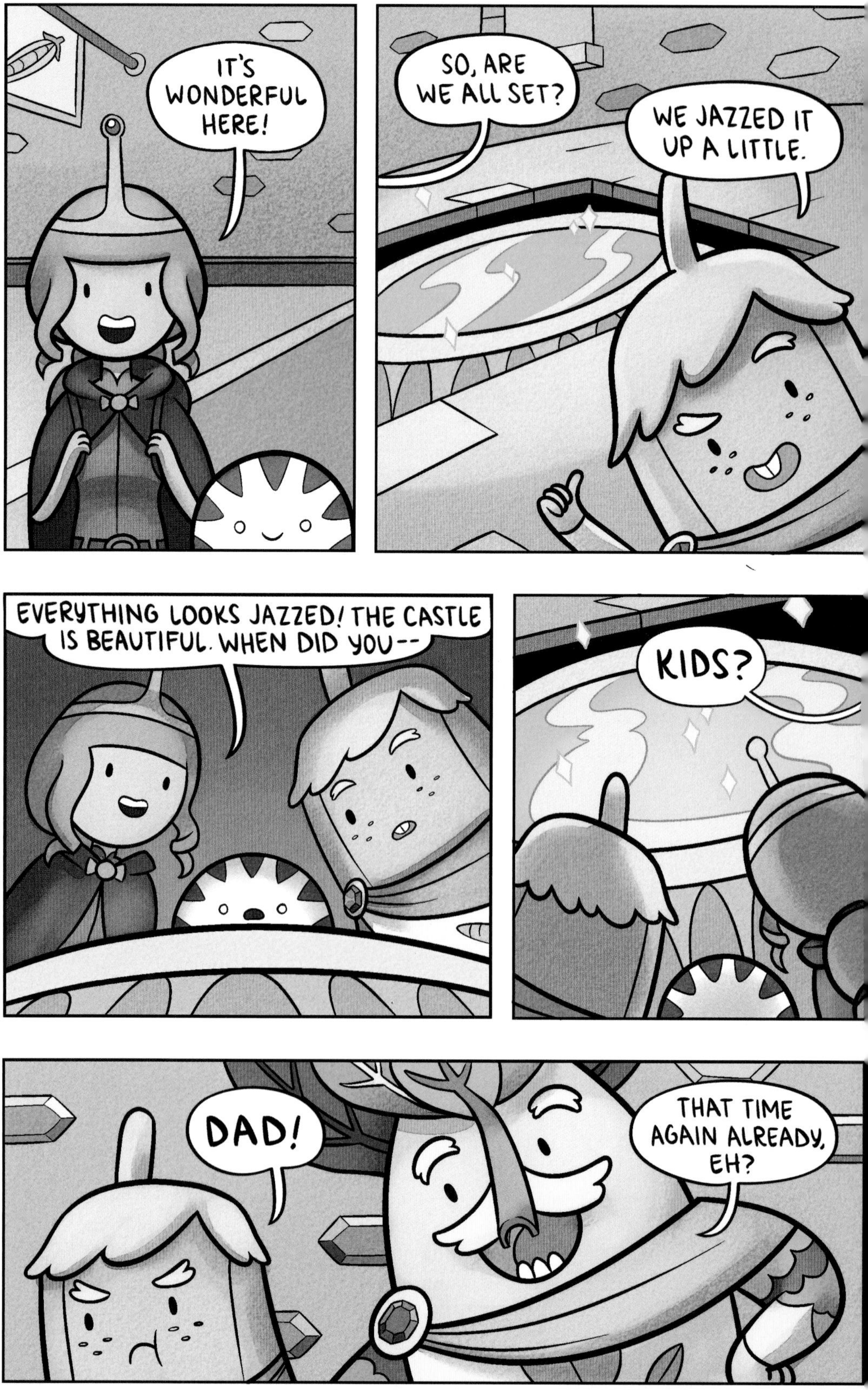
IT'S WONDERFUL HERE!
SO, ARE WE ALL SET?
WE JAZZED IT UP A LITTLE.
EVERYTHING LOOKS JAZZED! THE CASTLE IS BEAUTIFUL. WHEN DID YOU--
KIDS?
DAD!
THAT TIME AGAIN ALREADY, EH?

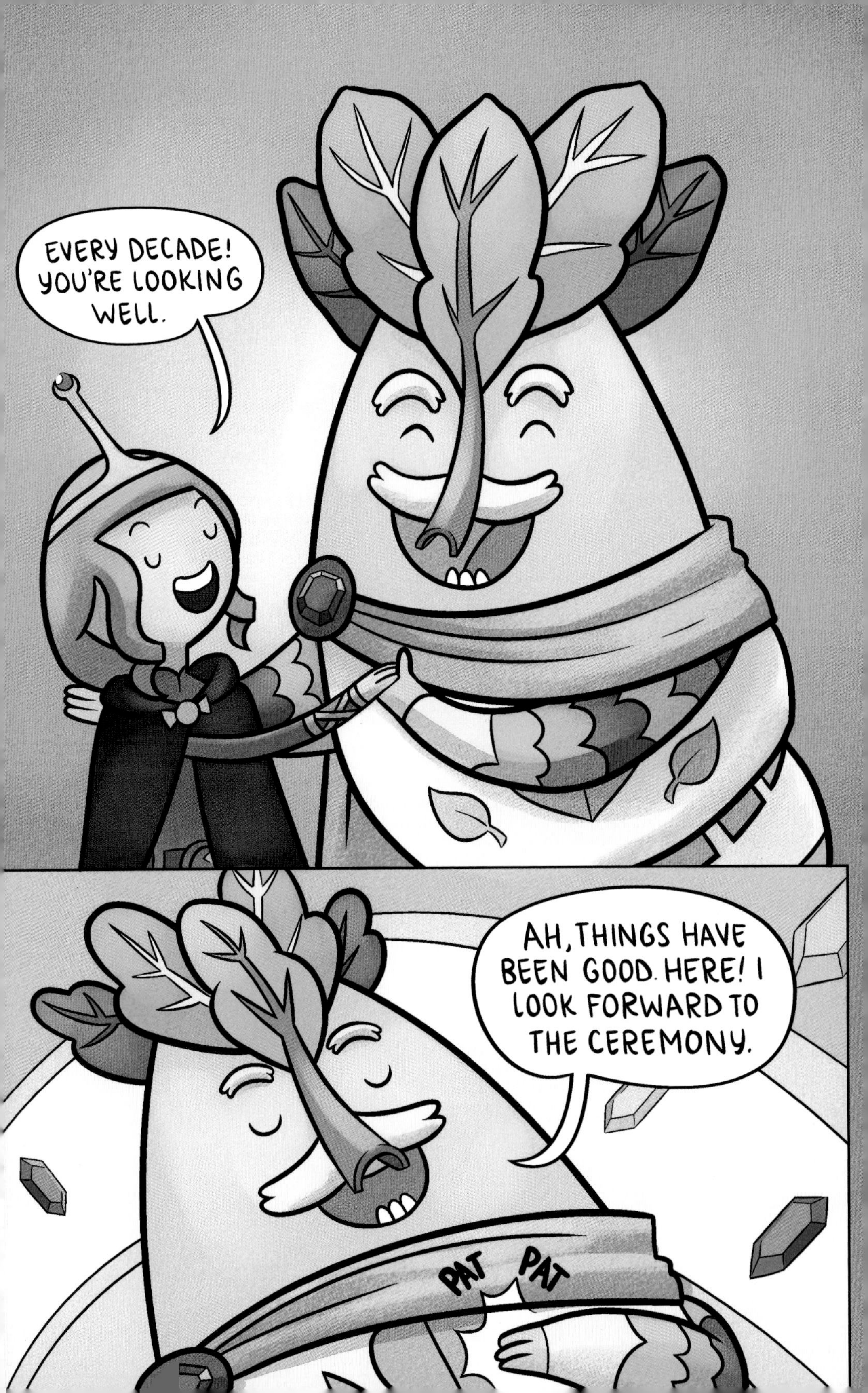
EVERY DECADE! YOU'RE LOOKING WELL.
AH, THINGS HAVE BEEN GOOD. HERE! I LOOK FORWARD TO THE CEREMONY.
PAT PAT

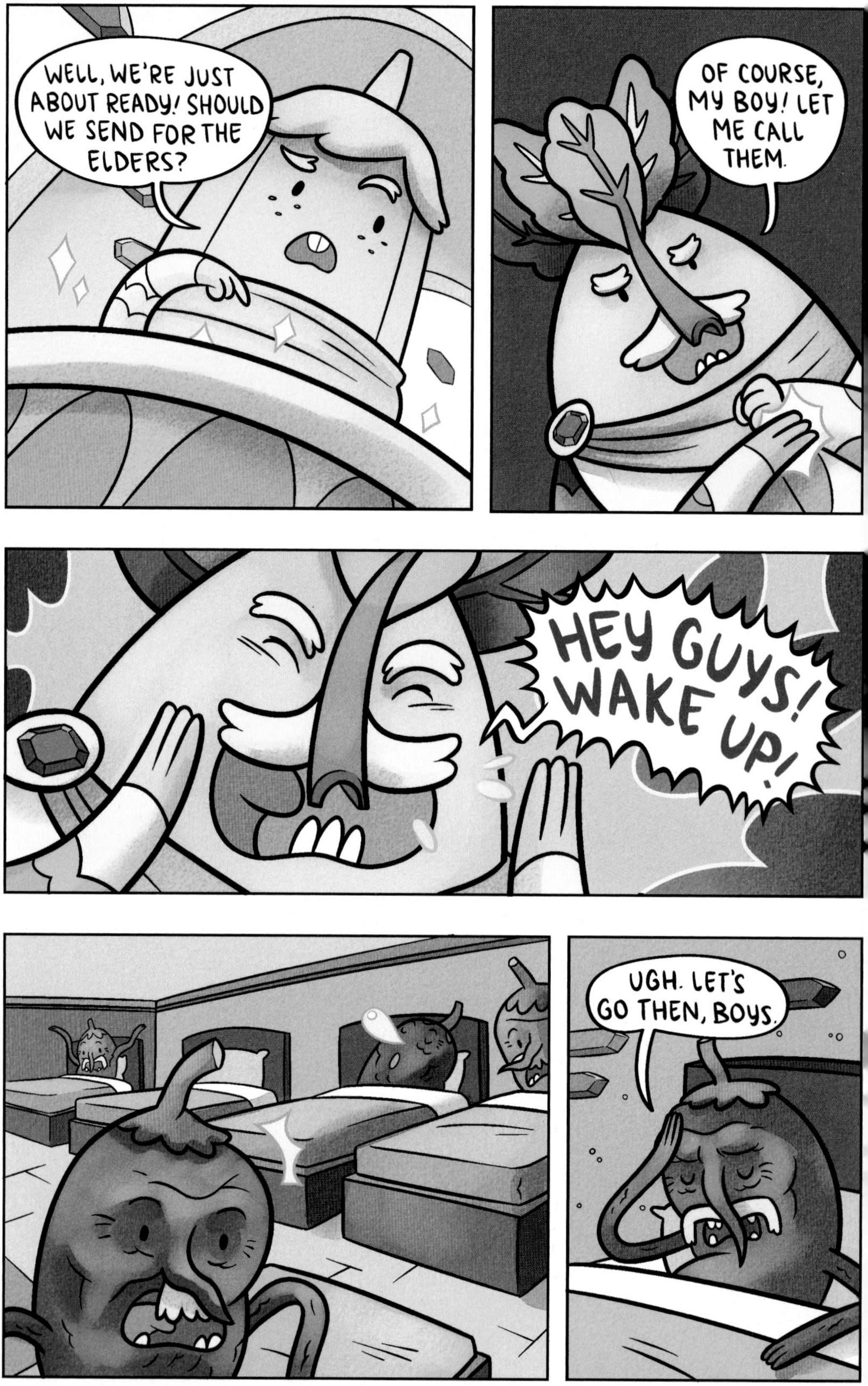
WELL, WE'RE JUST ABOUT READY! SHOULD WE SEND FOR THE ELDERS?
OF COURSE, MY BOY! LET ME CALL THEM.
HEY GUYS! WAKE UP!
UGH. LET'S GO THEN, BOYS.

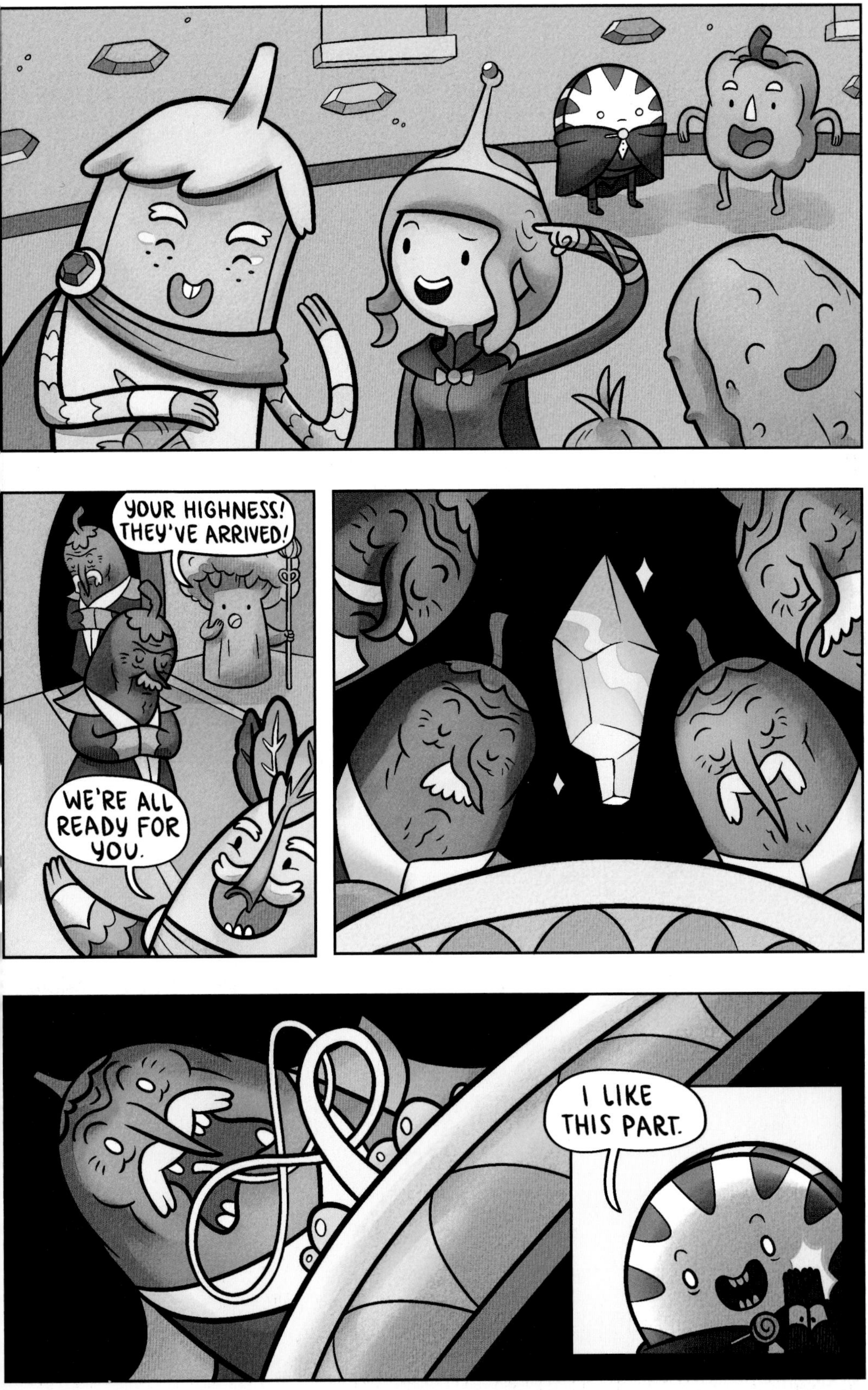
YOUR HIGHNESS! THEY'VE ARRIVED!
WE'RE ALL READY FOR YOU.
I LIKE THIS PART.

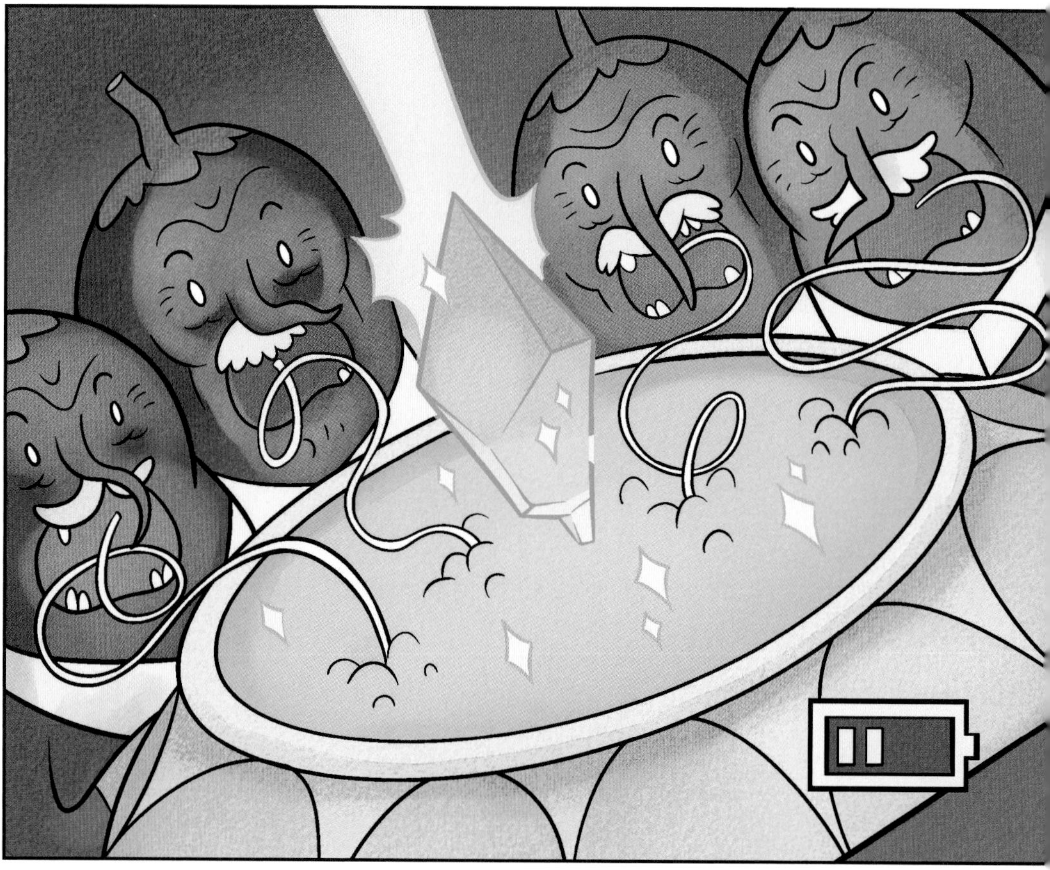

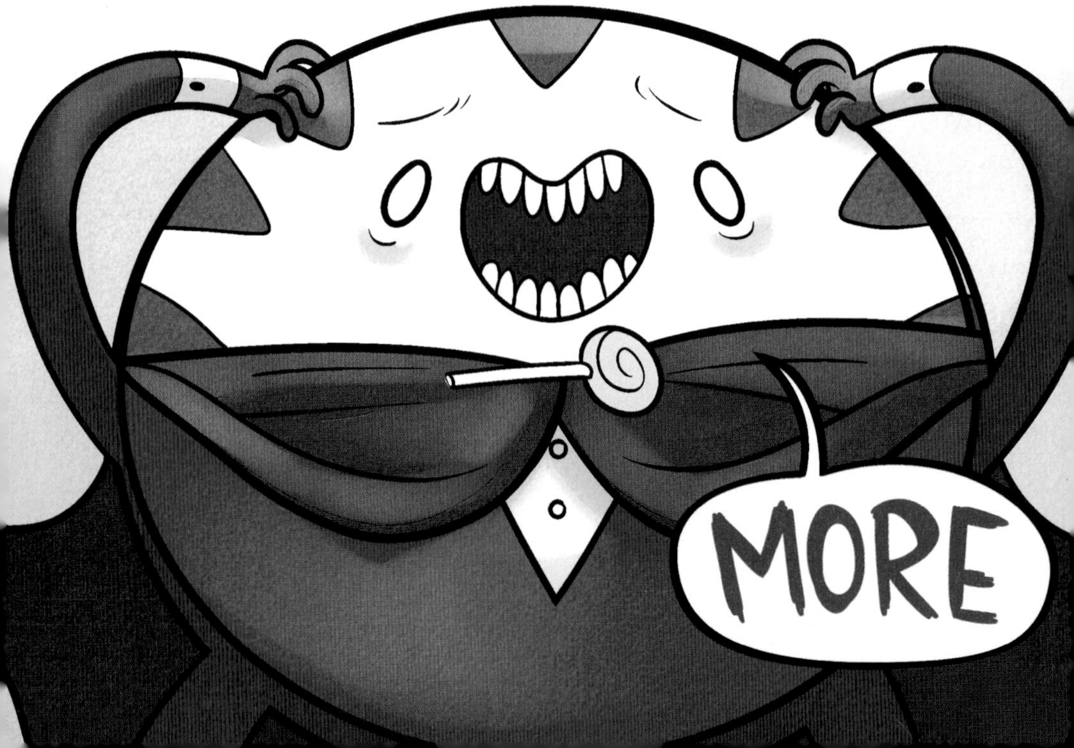
MORE

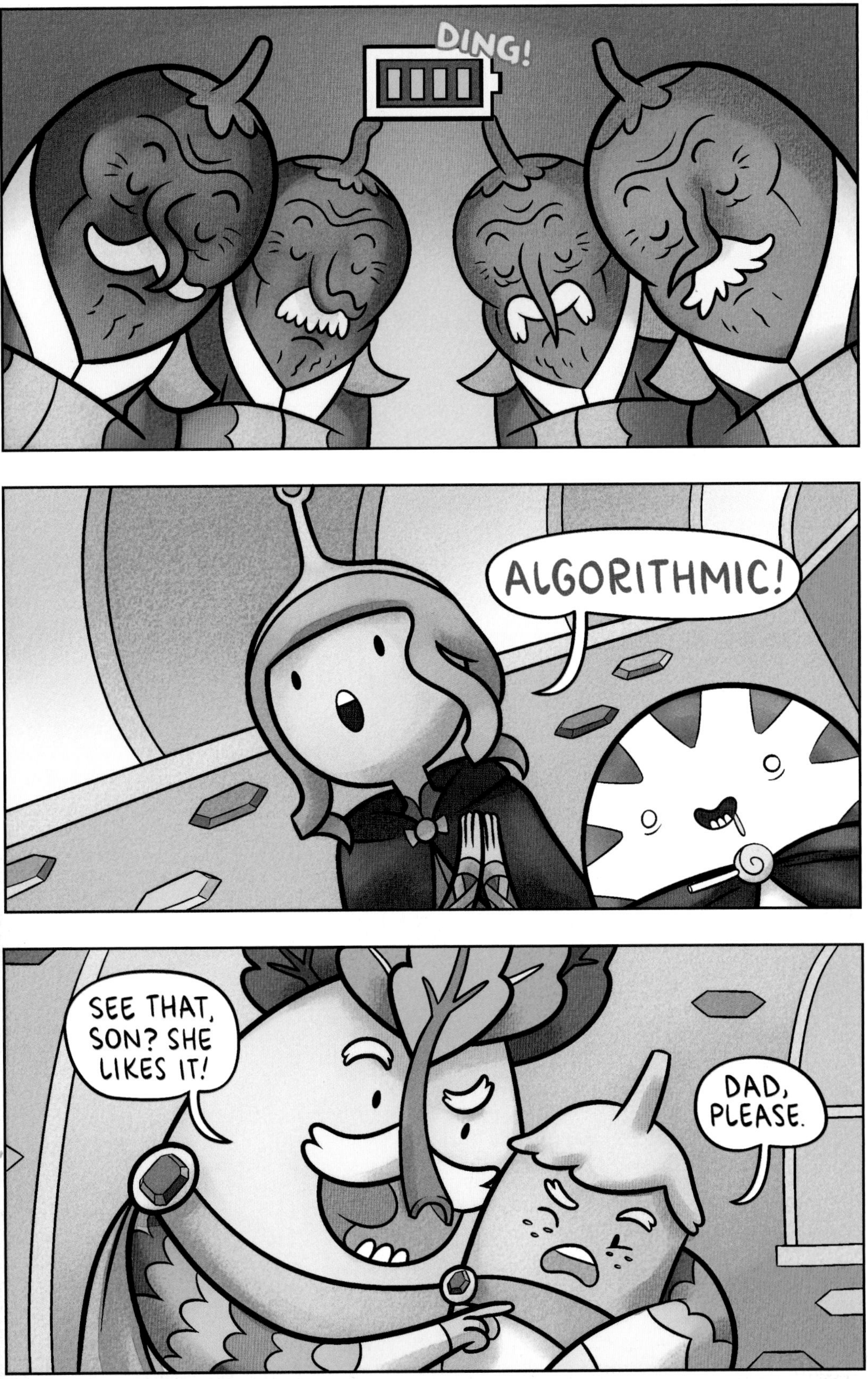
DING!
ALGORITHMIC!
SEE THAT, SON? SHE LIKES IT!
DAD, PLEASE.

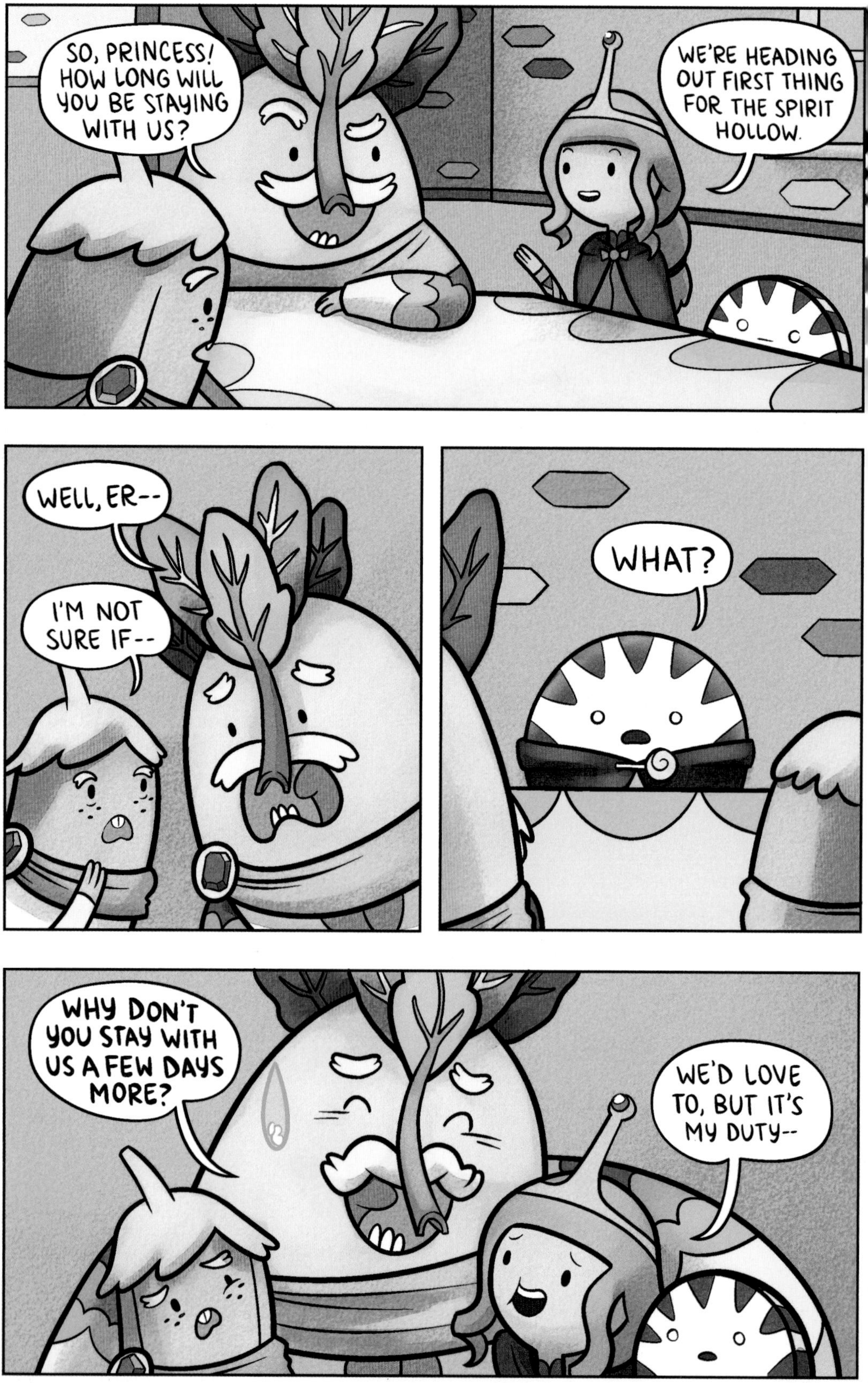
SO, PRINCESS! HOW LONG WILL YOU BE STAYING WITH US?
WE'RE HEADING OUT FIRST THING FOR THE SPIRIT HOLLOW.
WELL, ER--
I'M NOT SURE IF--
WHAT?
WHY DON'T YOU STAY WITH US A FEW DAYS MORE?
WE'D LOVE TO, BUT IT'S MY DUTY--

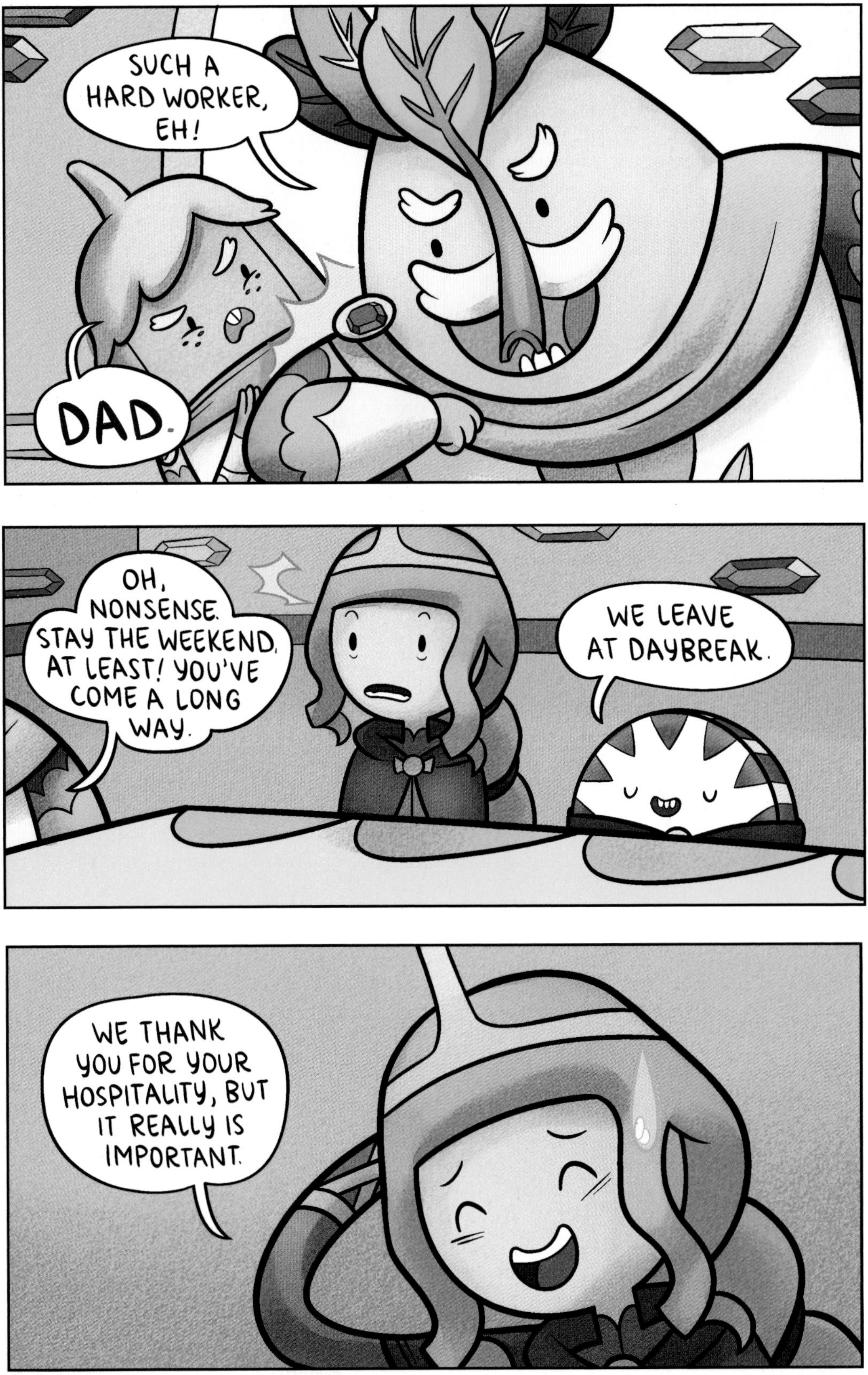

SUCH A HARD WORKER, EH!
DAD.
OH, NONSENSE. STAY THE WEEKEND, AT LEAST! YOU'VE COME A LONG WAY.
WE LEAVE AT DAYBREAK.
WE THANK YOU FOR YOUR HOSPITALITY, BUT IT REALLY IS IMPORTANT.

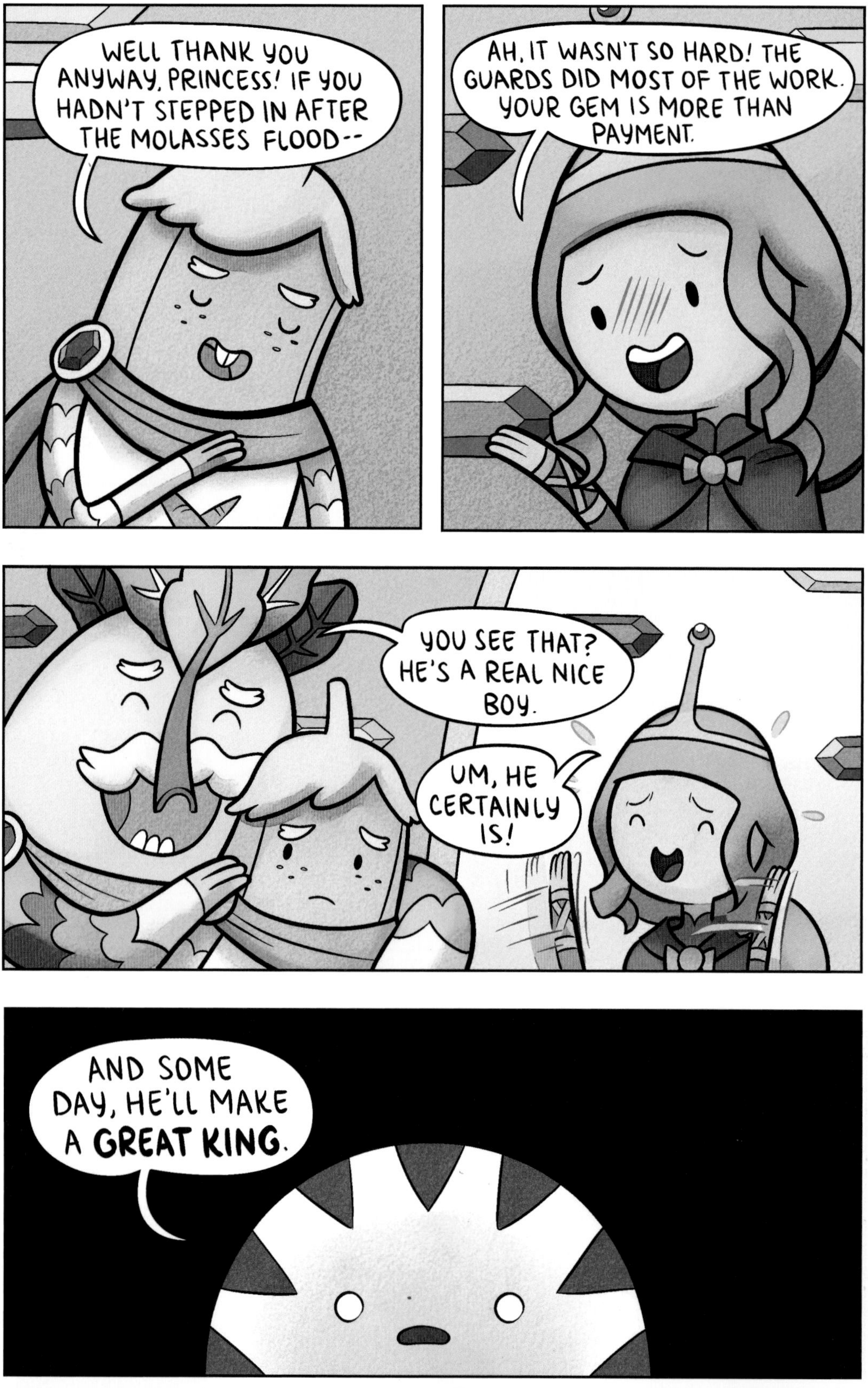
WELL THANK YOU ANYWAY, PRINCESS! IF YOU HADN'T STEPPED IN AFTER THE MOLASSES FLOOD--
AH, IT WASN'T SO HARD! THE GUARDS DID MOST OF THE WORK. YOUR GEM IS MORE THAN PAYMENT.
YOU SEE THAT? HE'S A REAL NICE BOY.
UM, HE CERTAINLY IS!
AND SOME DAY, HE'LL MAKE A **GREAT KING**.

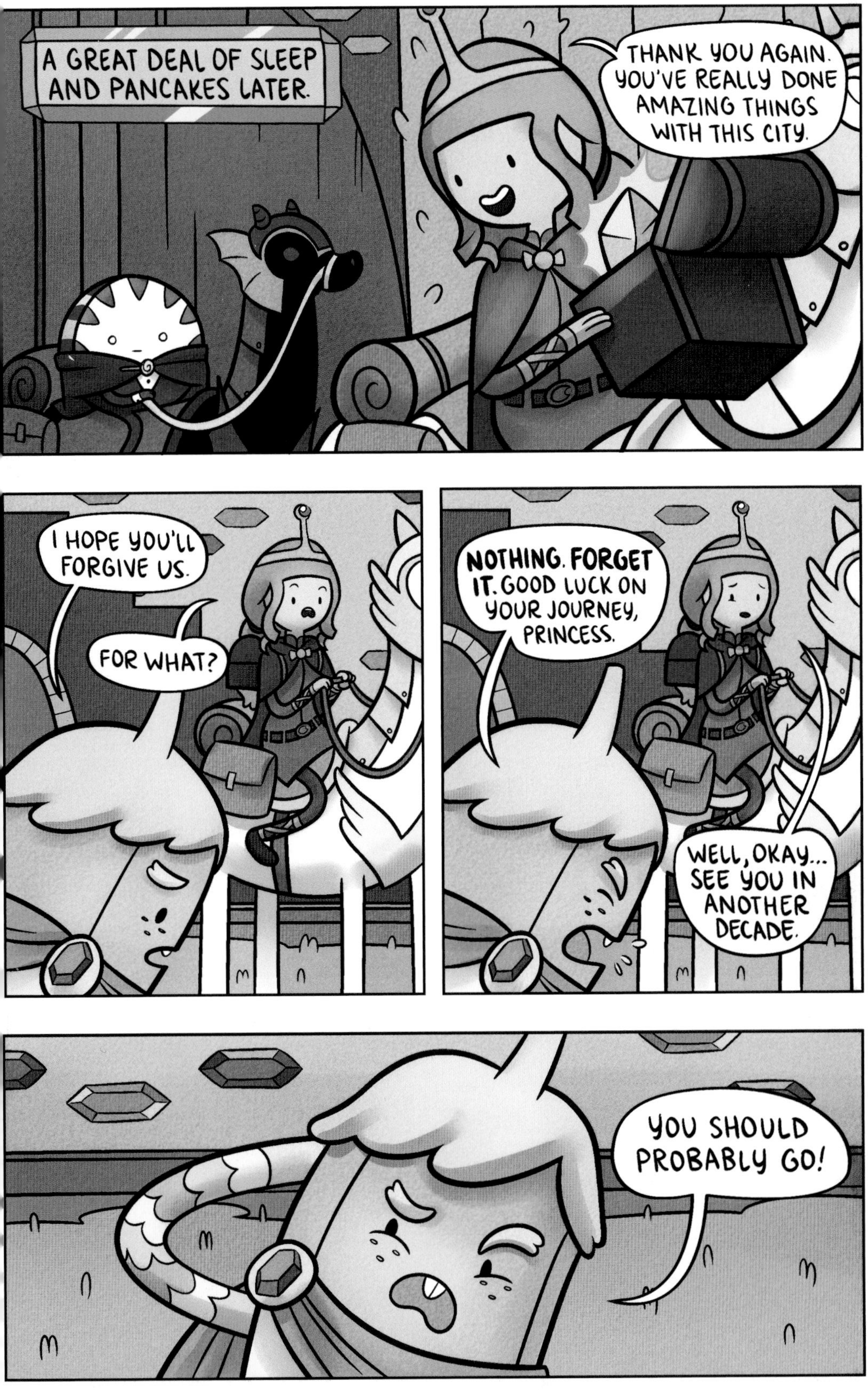
A GREAT DEAL OF SLEEP AND PANCAKES LATER.
THANK YOU AGAIN. YOU'VE REALLY DONE AMAZING THINGS WITH THIS CITY.
I HOPE YOU'LL FORGIVE US.
FOR WHAT?
NOTHING. FORGET IT. GOOD LUCK ON YOUR JOURNEY, PRINCESS.
WELL, OKAY... SEE YOU IN ANOTHER DECADE.
YOU SHOULD PROBABLY GO!

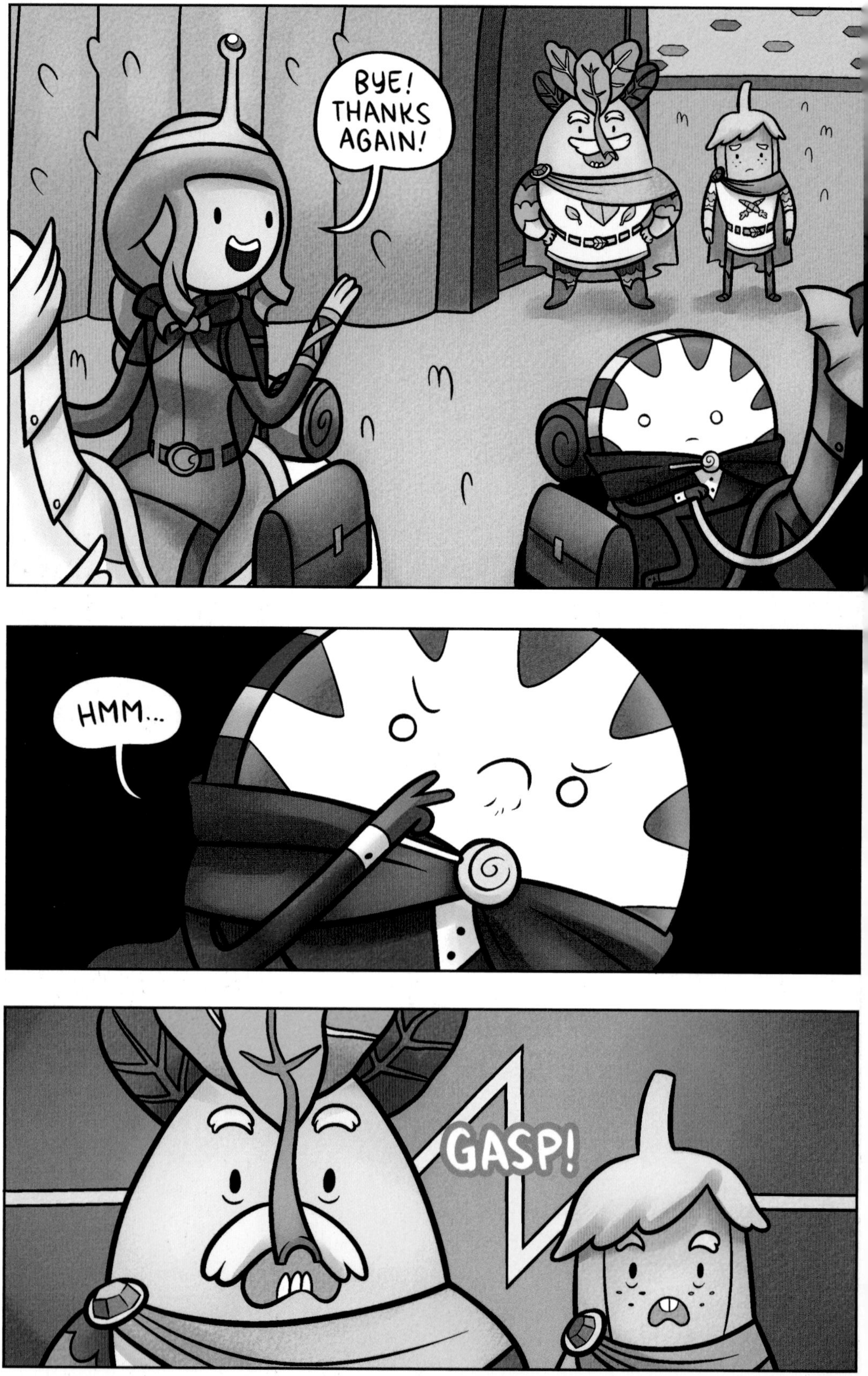
BYE! THANKS AGAIN!
HMM...
GASP!

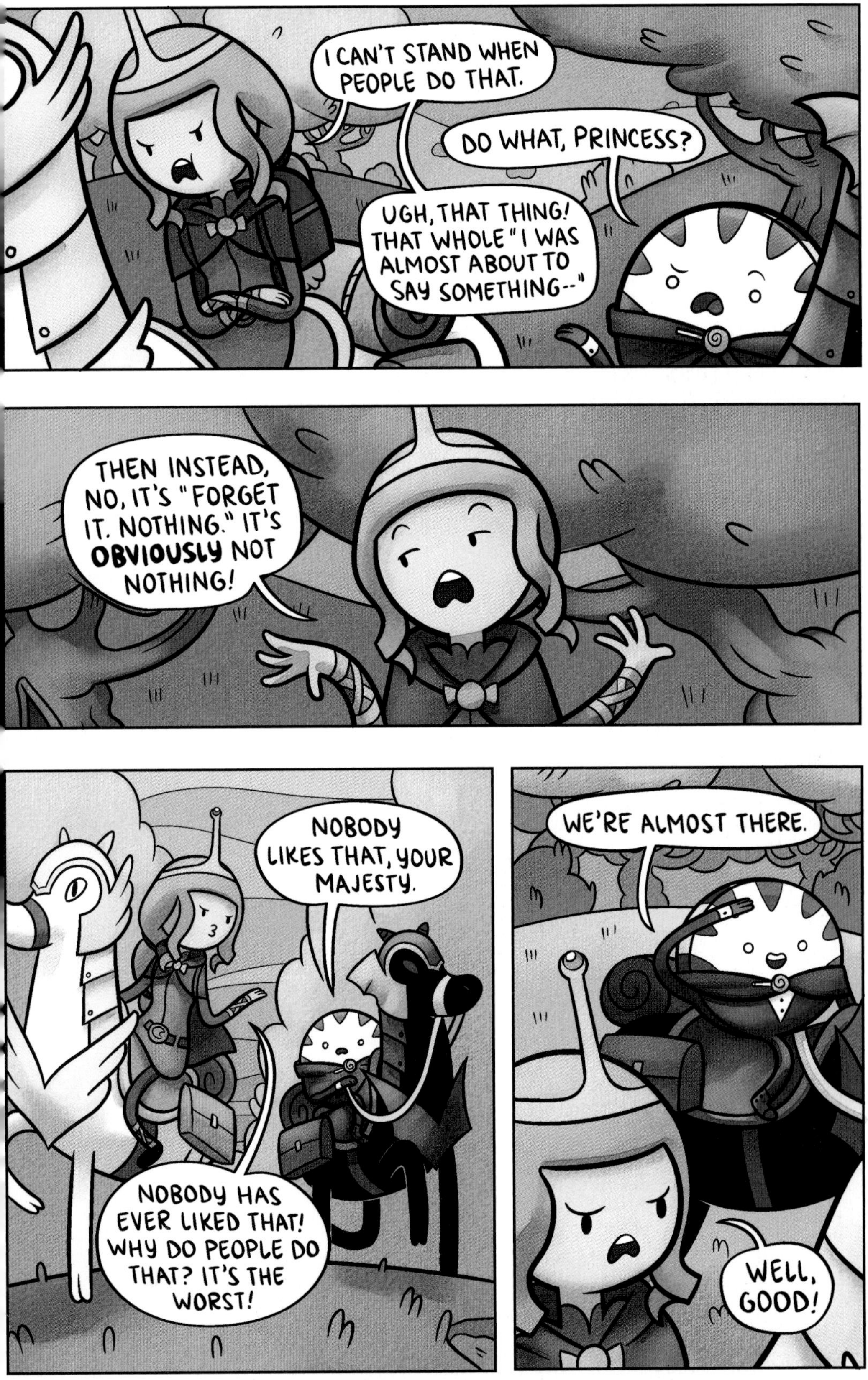
I CAN'T STAND WHEN PEOPLE DO THAT.
DO WHAT, PRINCESS?
UGH, THAT THING! THAT WHOLE "I WAS ALMOST ABOUT TO SAY SOMETHING--"
THEN INSTEAD, NO, IT'S "FORGET IT. NOTHING." IT'S **OBVIOUSLY** NOT NOTHING!
NOBODY LIKES THAT, YOUR MAJESTY.
NOBODY HAS EVER LIKED THAT! WHY DO PEOPLE DO THAT? IT'S THE WORST!
WE'RE ALMOST THERE.
WELL, GOOD!

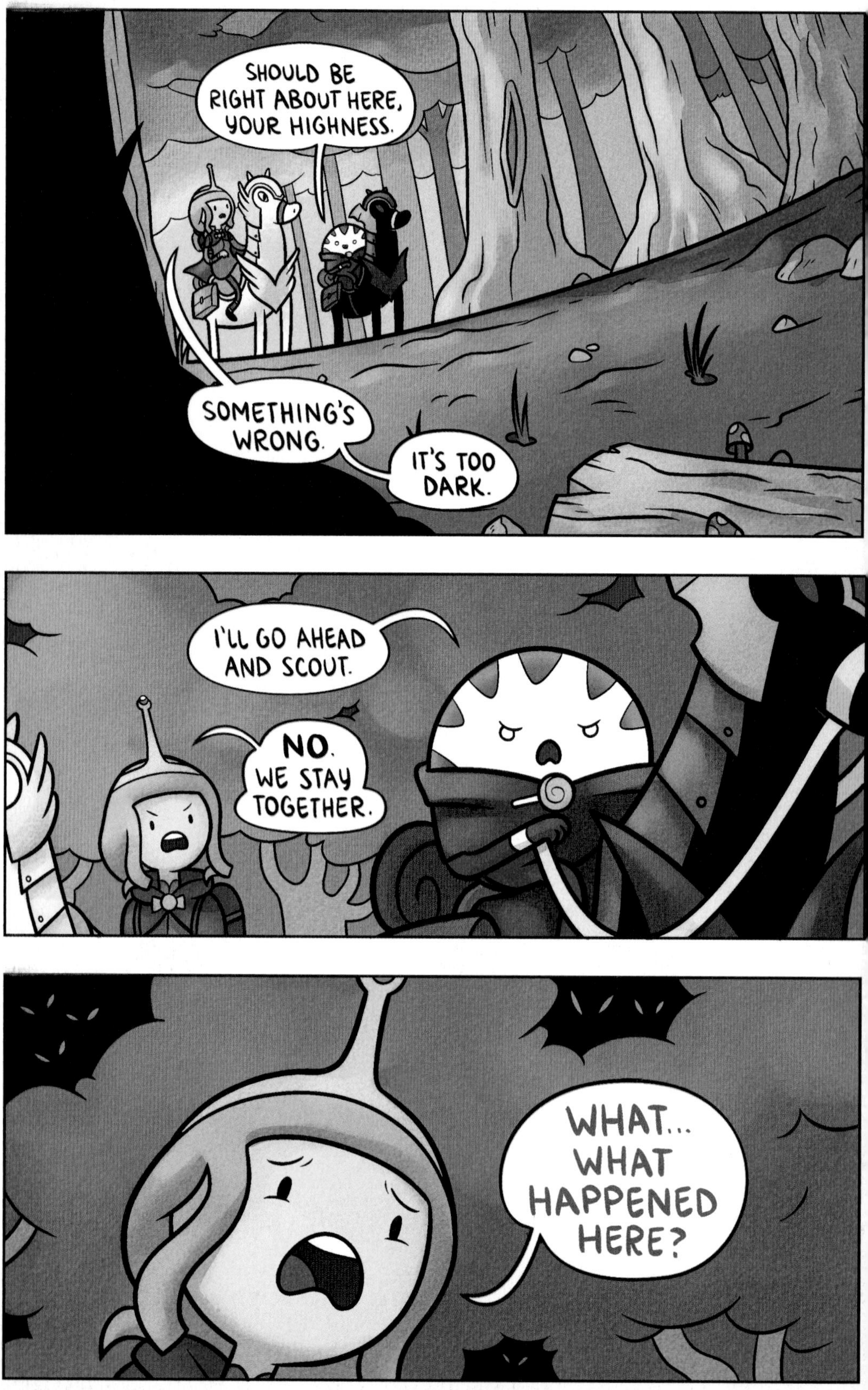
SHOULD BE RIGHT ABOUT HERE, YOUR HIGHNESS.
SOMETHING'S WRONG.
IT'S TOO DARK.
I'LL GO AHEAD AND SCOUT.
NO. WE STAY TOGETHER.
WHAT... WHAT HAPPENED HERE?

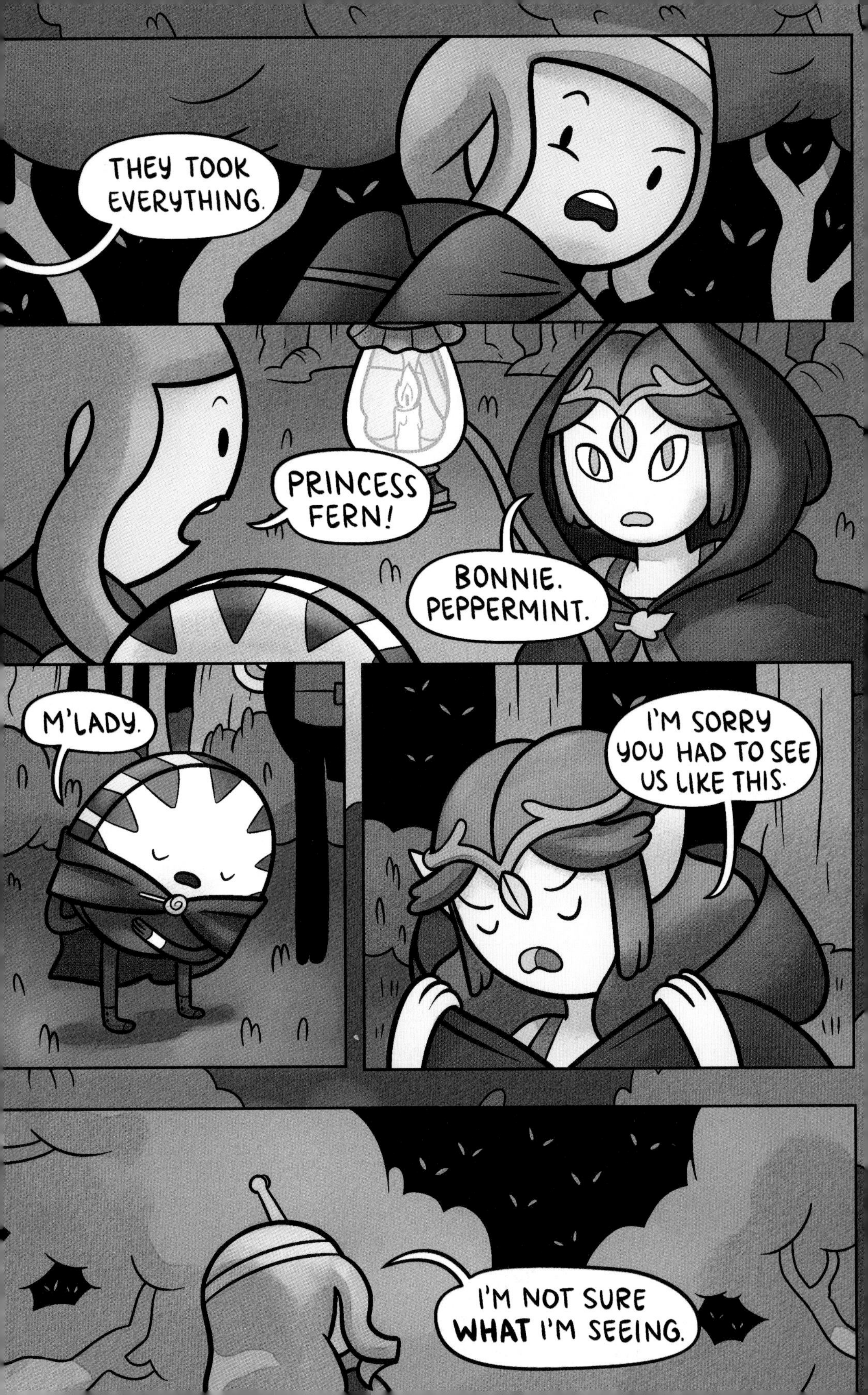
THEY TOOK EVERYTHING.
PRINCESS FERN!
BONNIE. PEPPERMINT.
M'LADY.
I'M SORRY YOU HAD TO SEE US LIKE THIS.
I'M NOT SURE **WHAT** I'M SEEING.

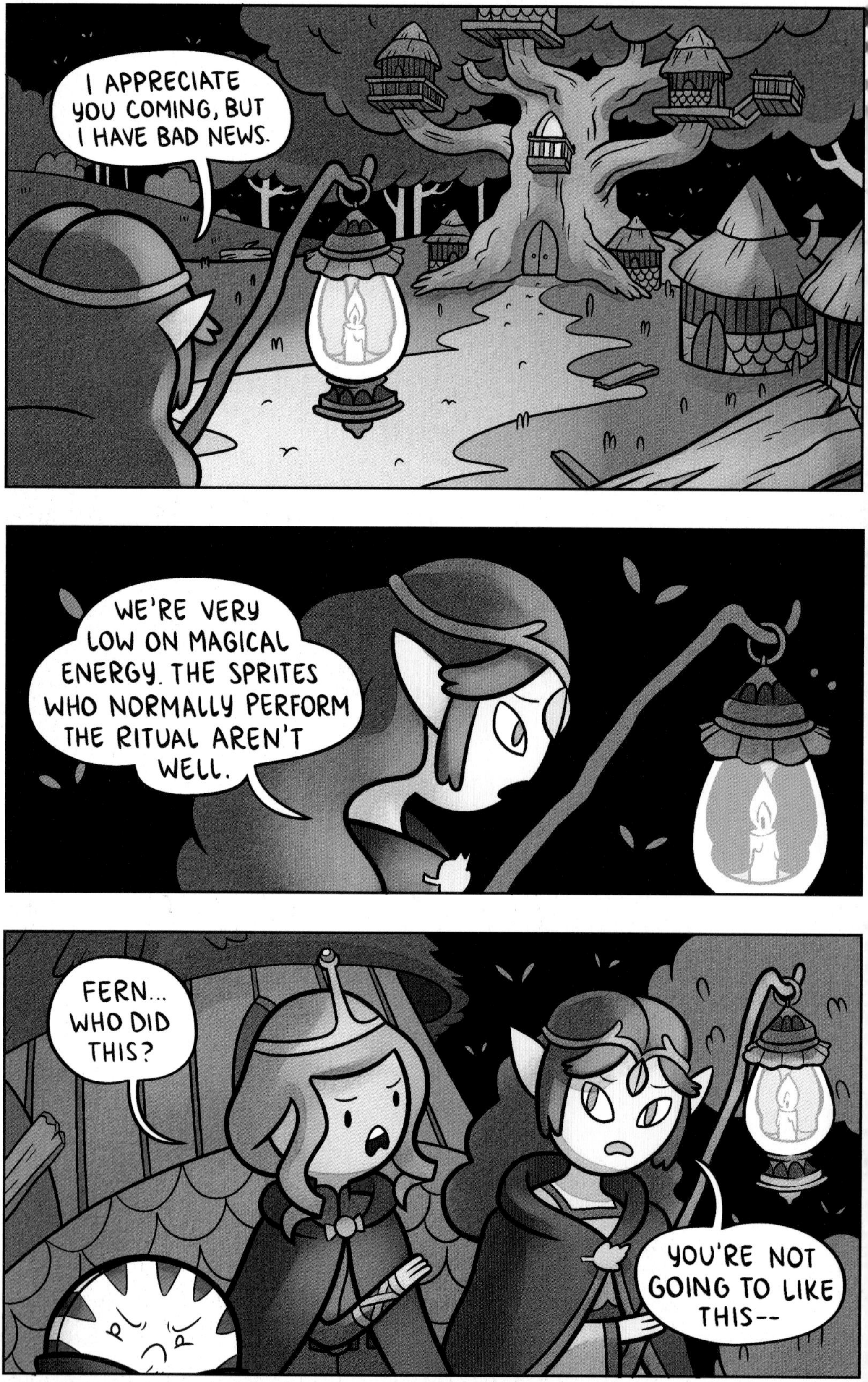
I APPRECIATE YOU COMING, BUT I HAVE BAD NEWS.
WE'RE VERY LOW ON MAGICAL ENERGY. THE SPRITES WHO NORMALLY PERFORM THE RITUAL AREN'T WELL.
FERN... WHO DID THIS?
YOU'RE NOT GOING TO LIKE THIS--

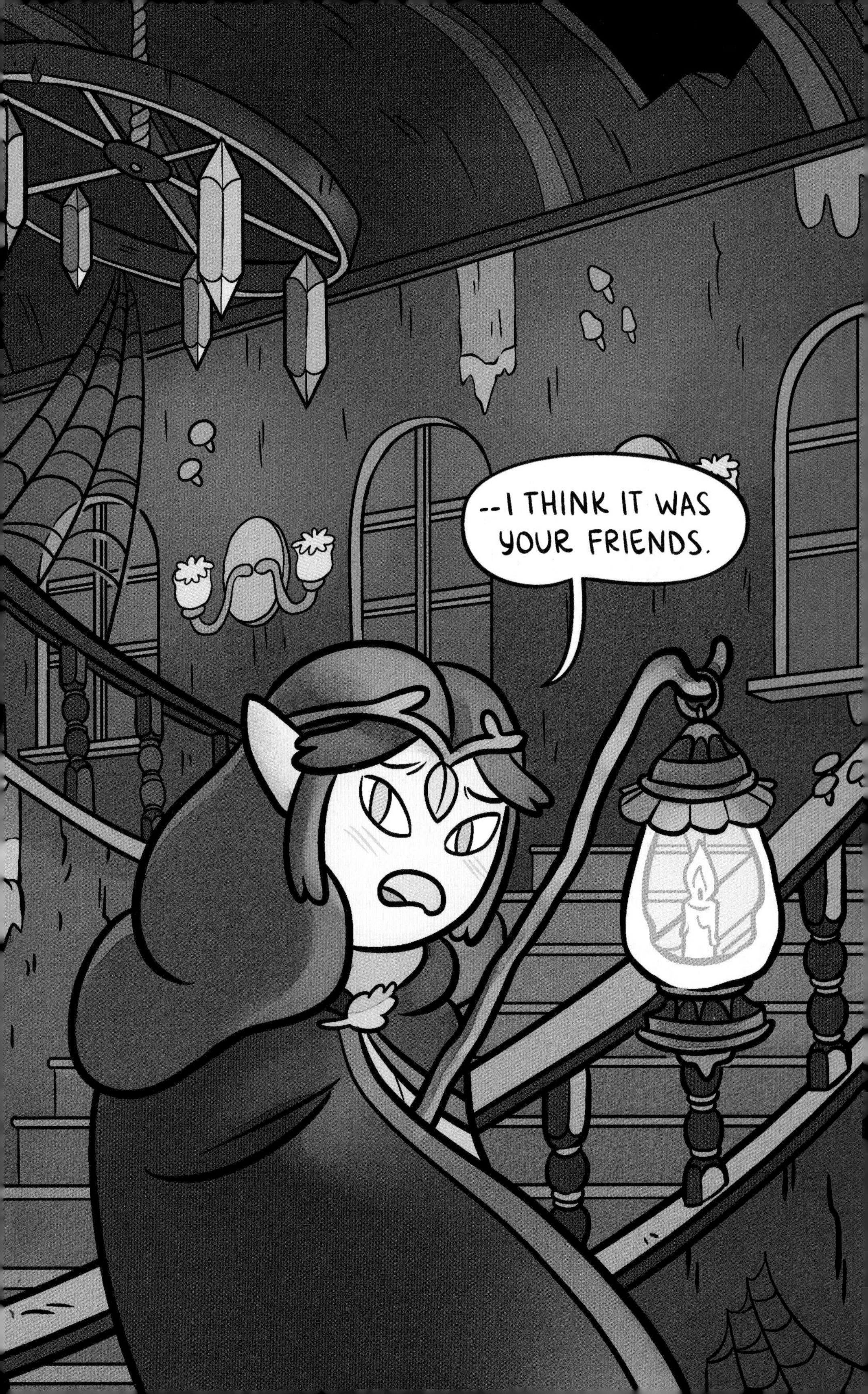
--I THINK IT WAS YOUR FRIENDS.

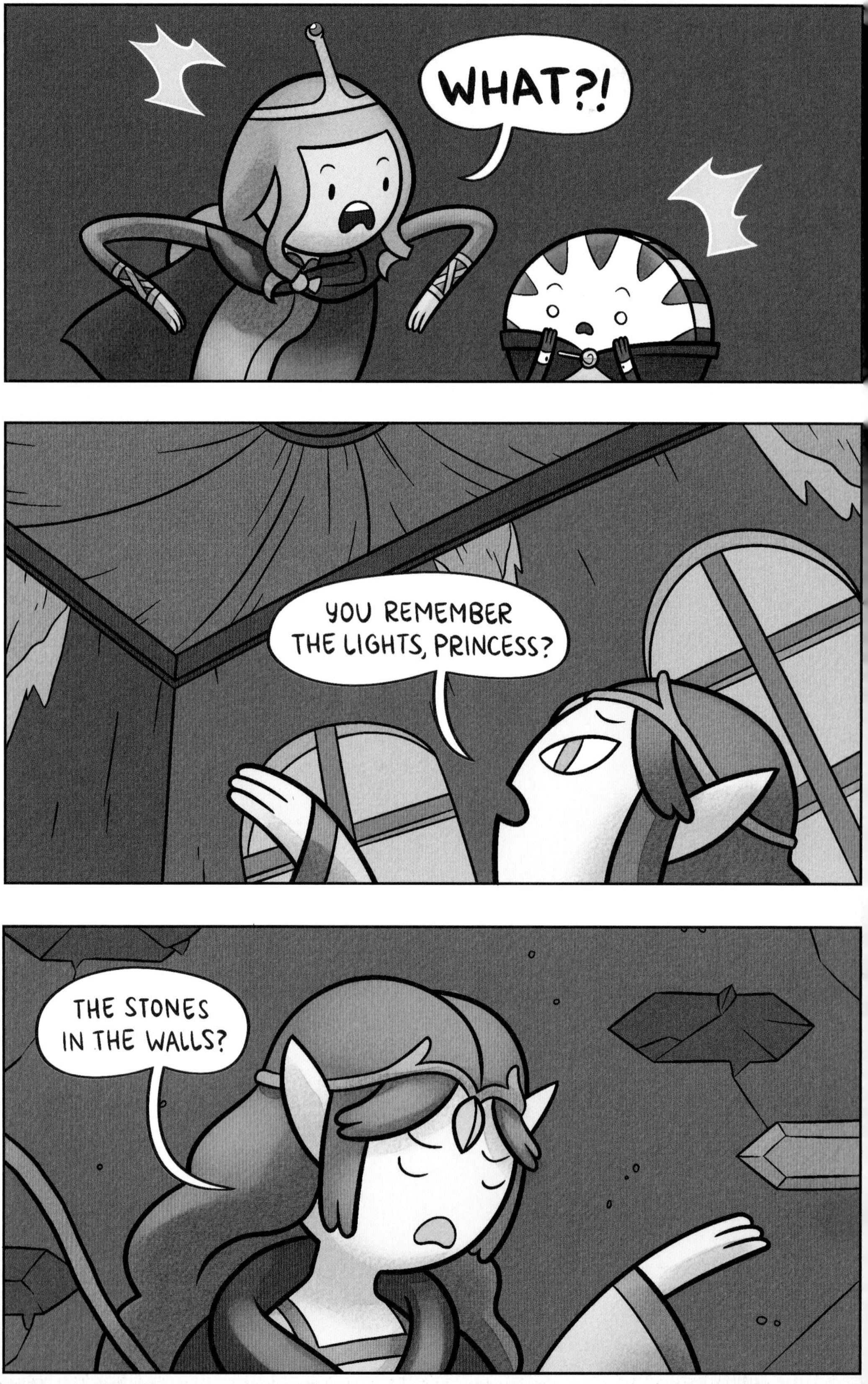
WHAT?!
YOU REMEMBER THE LIGHTS, PRINCESS?
THE STONES IN THE WALLS?

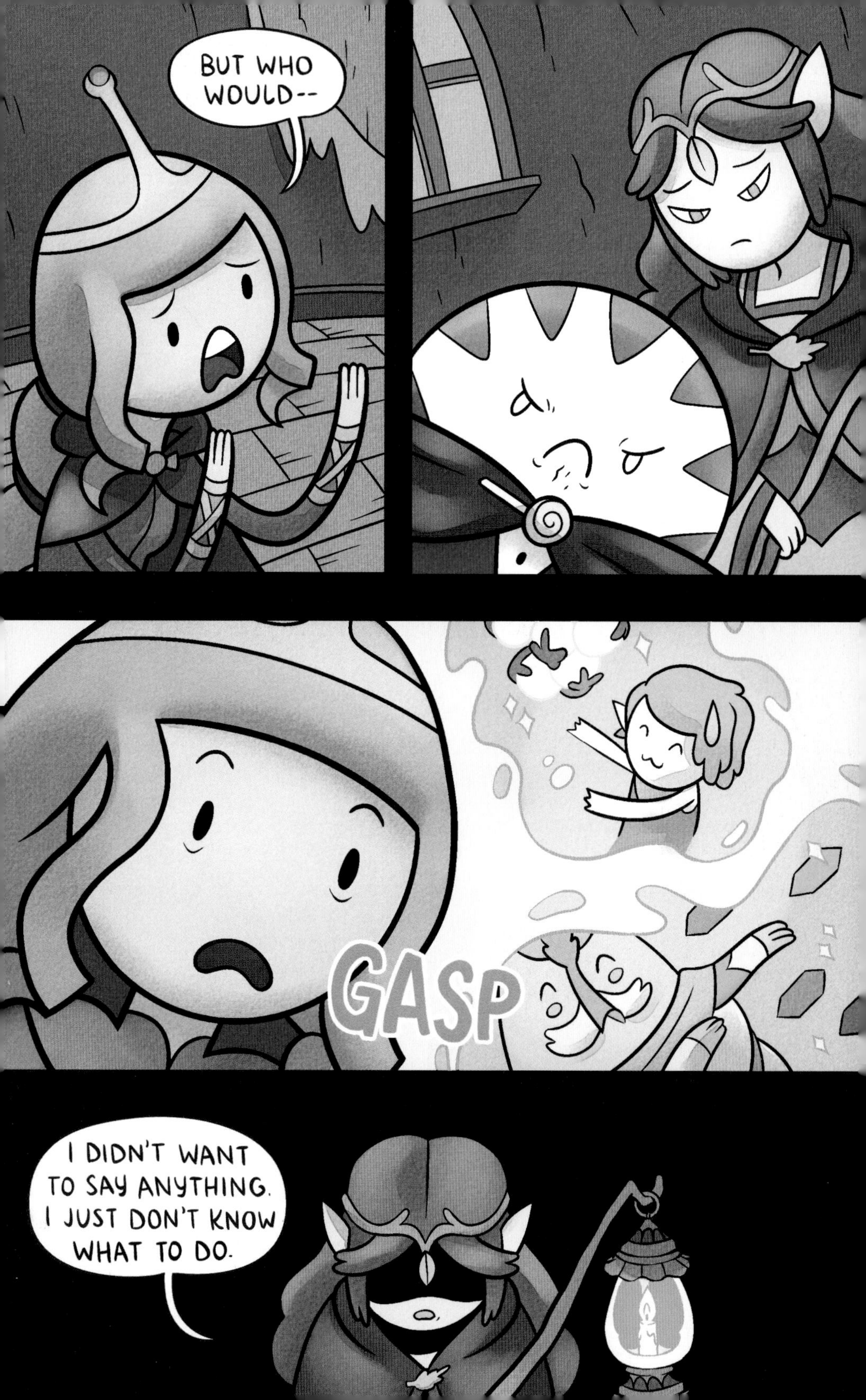
BUT WHO WOULD--
GASP
I DIDN'T WANT TO SAY ANYTHING. I JUST DON'T KNOW WHAT TO DO.

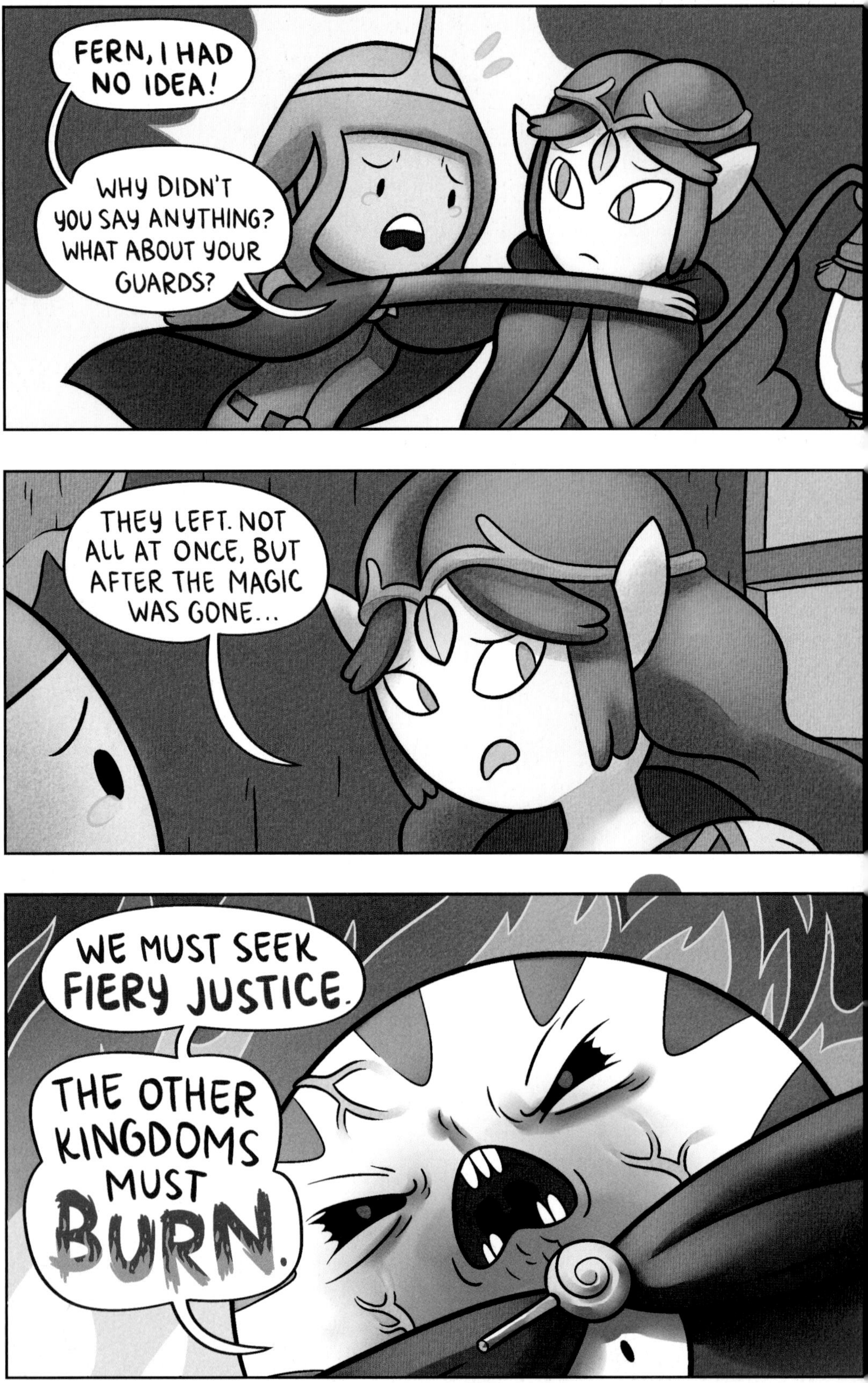
FERN, I HAD NO IDEA!
WHY DIDN'T YOU SAY ANYTHING? WHAT ABOUT YOUR GUARDS?
THEY LEFT. NOT ALL AT ONCE, BUT AFTER THE MAGIC WAS GONE...
WE MUST SEEK FIERY JUSTICE.
THE OTHER KINGDOMS MUST BURN.

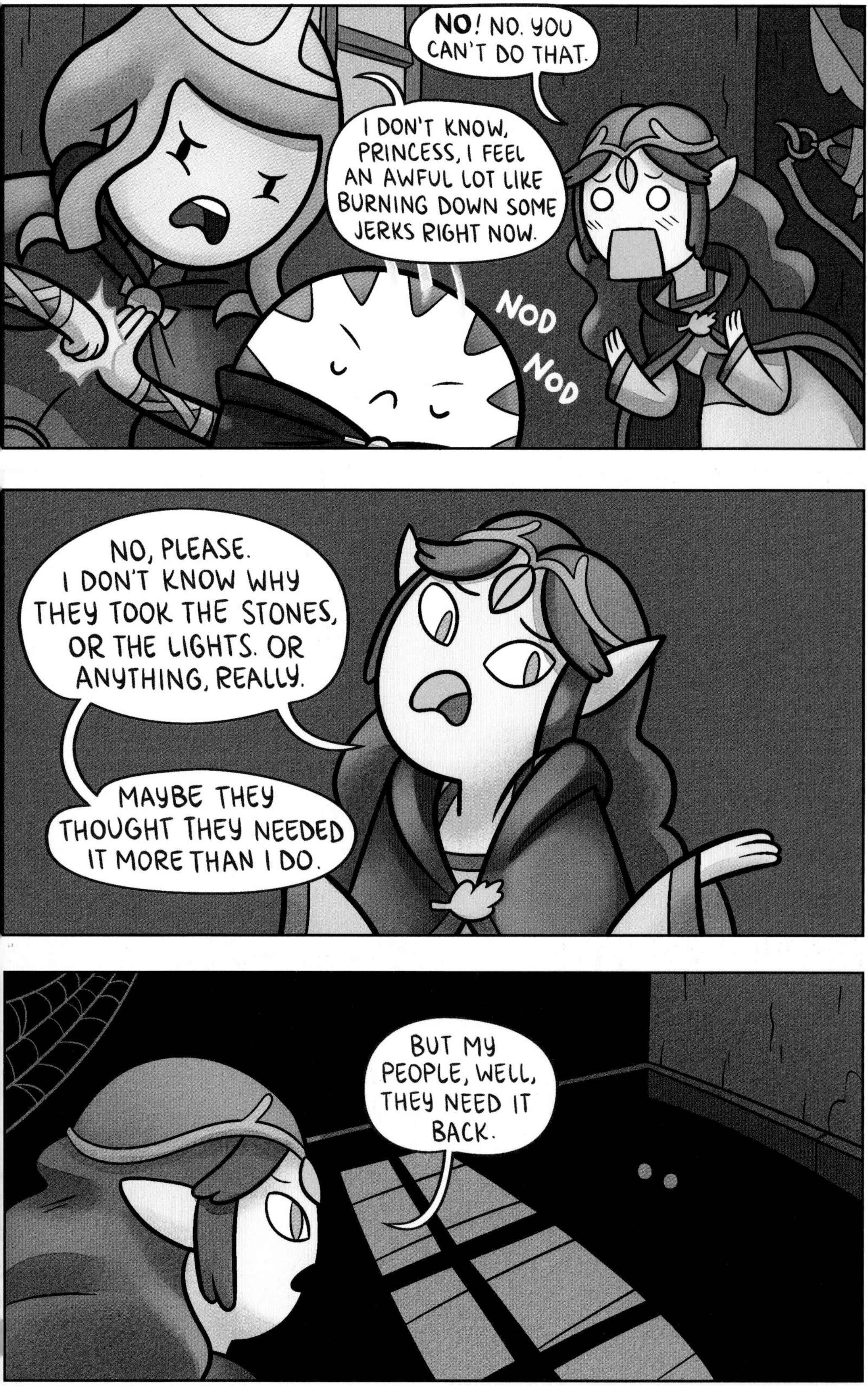
NO! NO. YOU CAN'T DO THAT.
I DON'T KNOW, PRINCESS, I FEEL AN AWFUL LOT LIKE BURNING DOWN SOME JERKS RIGHT NOW.
NOD NOD
NO, PLEASE. I DON'T KNOW WHY THEY TOOK THE STONES, OR THE LIGHTS. OR ANYTHING, REALLY.
MAYBE THEY THOUGHT THEY NEEDED IT MORE THAN I DO.
BUT MY PEOPLE, WELL, THEY NEED IT BACK.

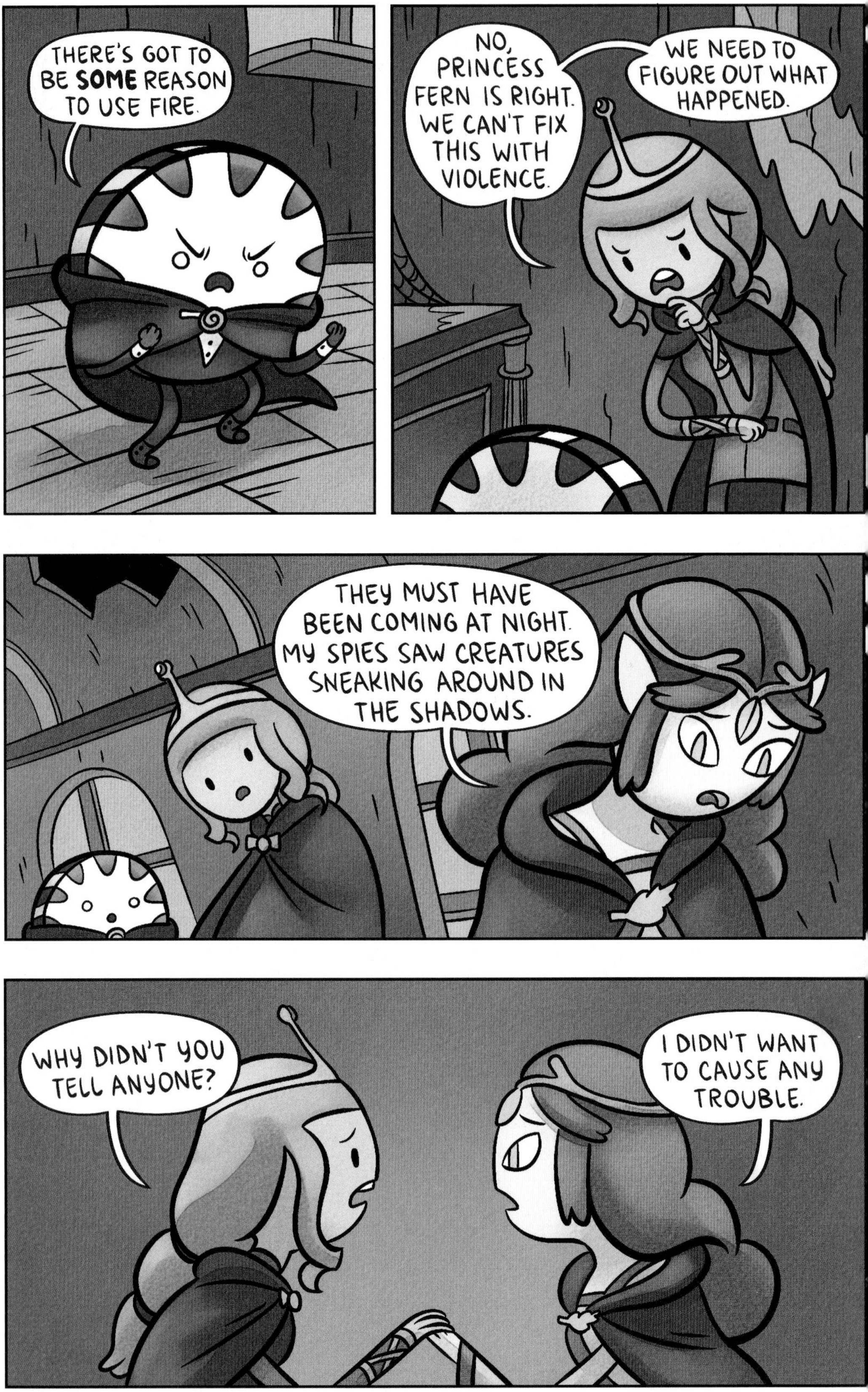
THERE'S GOT TO BE **SOME** REASON TO USE FIRE.
NO, PRINCESS FERN IS RIGHT. WE CAN'T FIX THIS WITH VIOLENCE.
WE NEED TO FIGURE OUT WHAT HAPPENED.
THEY MUST HAVE BEEN COMING AT NIGHT. MY SPIES SAW CREATURES SNEAKING AROUND IN THE SHADOWS.
WHY DIDN'T YOU TELL ANYONE?
I DIDN'T WANT TO CAUSE ANY TROUBLE.

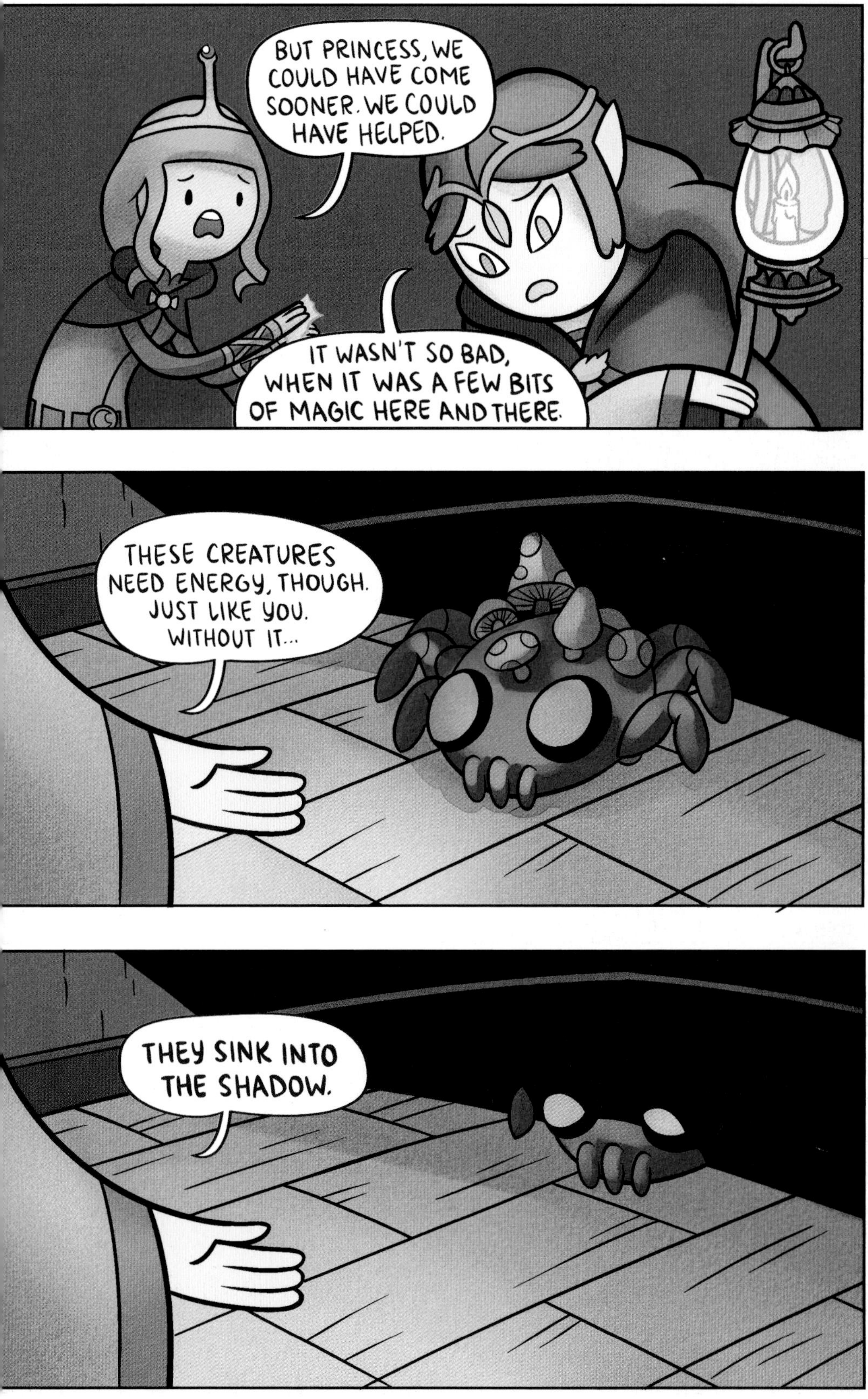
BUT PRINCESS, WE COULD HAVE COME SOONER. WE COULD HAVE HELPED.
IT WASN'T SO BAD, WHEN IT WAS A FEW BITS OF MAGIC HERE AND THERE.
THESE CREATURES NEED ENERGY, THOUGH. JUST LIKE YOU. WITHOUT IT...
THEY SINK INTO THE SHADOW.

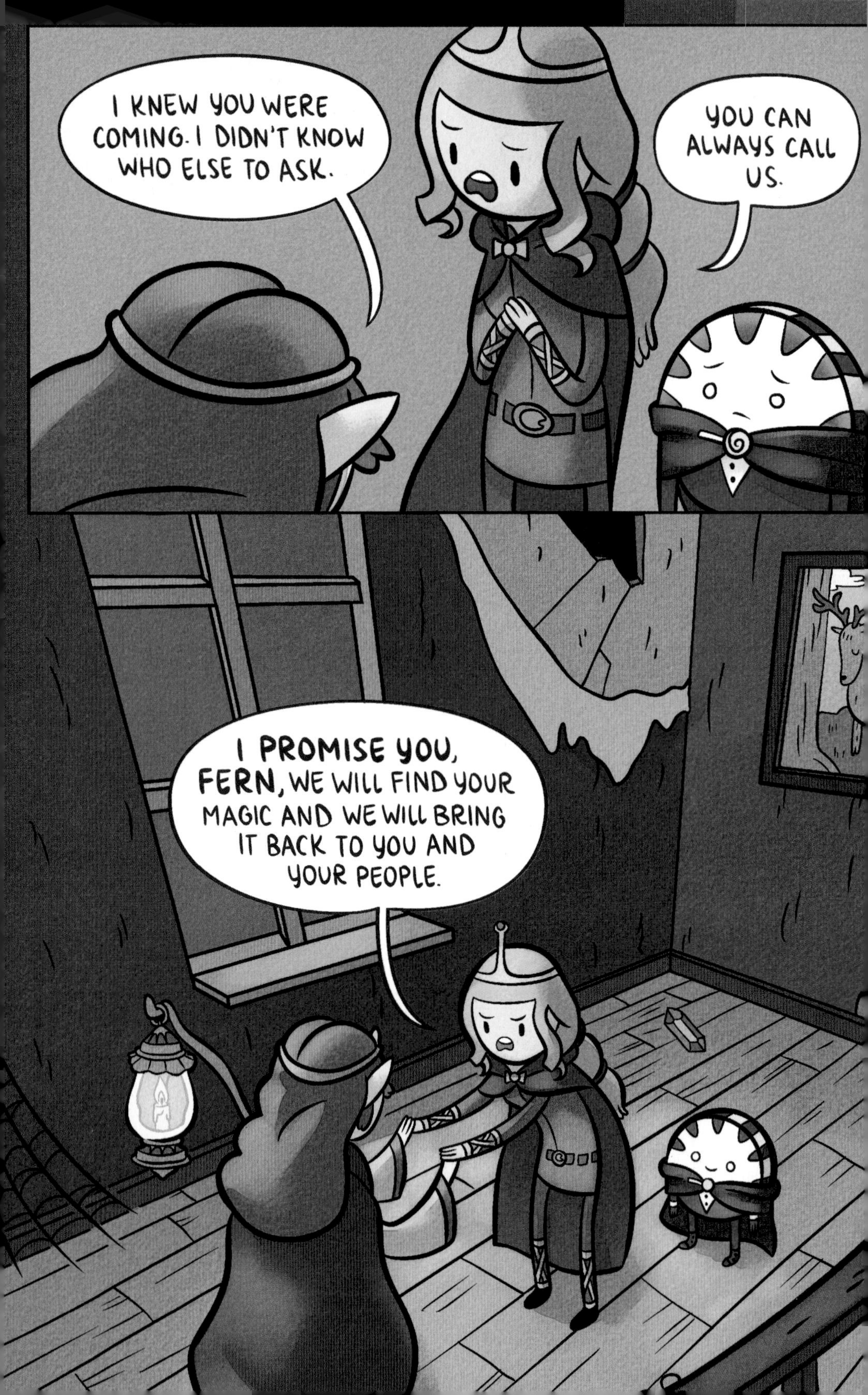
I KNEW YOU WERE COMING. I DIDN'T KNOW WHO ELSE TO ASK.
YOU CAN ALWAYS CALL US.
I PROMISE YOU, **FERN,** WE WILL FIND YOUR MAGIC AND WE WILL BRING IT BACK TO YOU AND YOUR PEOPLE.

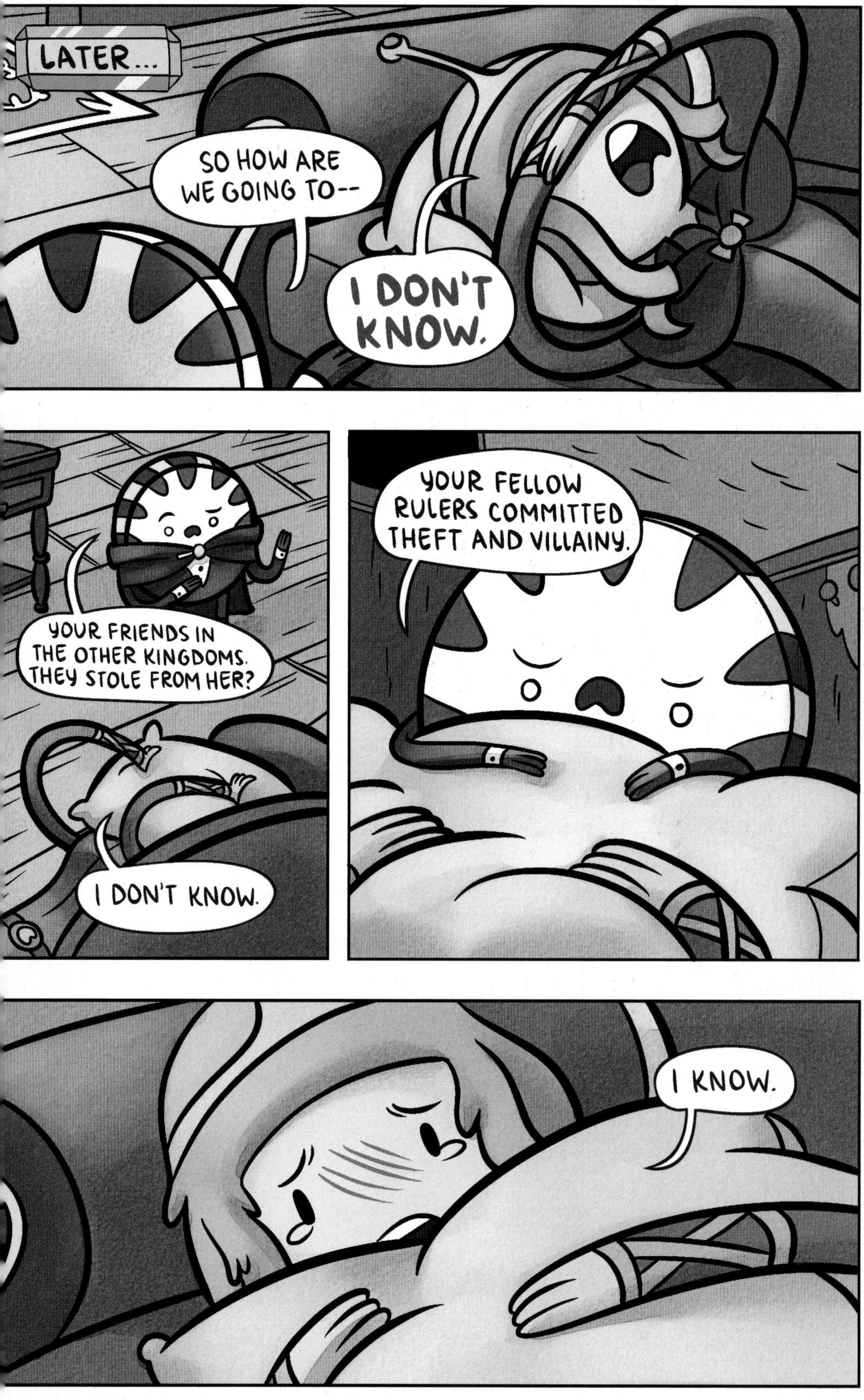
LATER...
SO HOW ARE WE GOING TO--
I DON'T KNOW.
YOUR FRIENDS IN THE OTHER KINGDOMS. THEY STOLE FROM HER?
I DON'T KNOW.
YOUR FELLOW RULERS COMMITTED THEFT AND VILLAINY.
I KNOW.

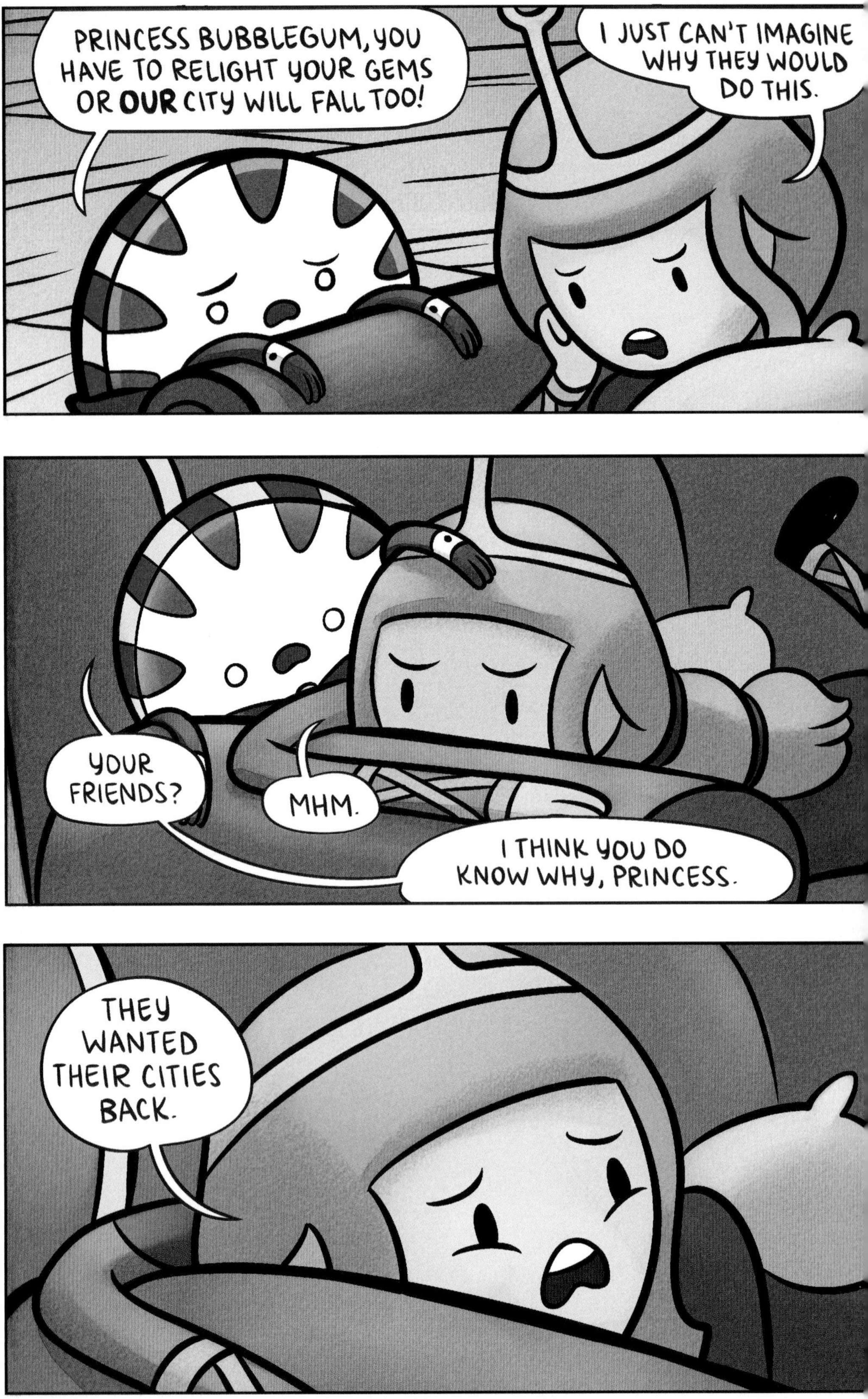
PRINCESS BUBBLEGUM, YOU HAVE TO RELIGHT YOUR GEMS OR OUR CITY WILL FALL TOO!
I JUST CAN'T IMAGINE WHY THEY WOULD DO THIS.
YOUR FRIENDS?
MHM.
I THINK YOU DO KNOW WHY, PRINCESS.
THEY WANTED THEIR CITIES BACK.

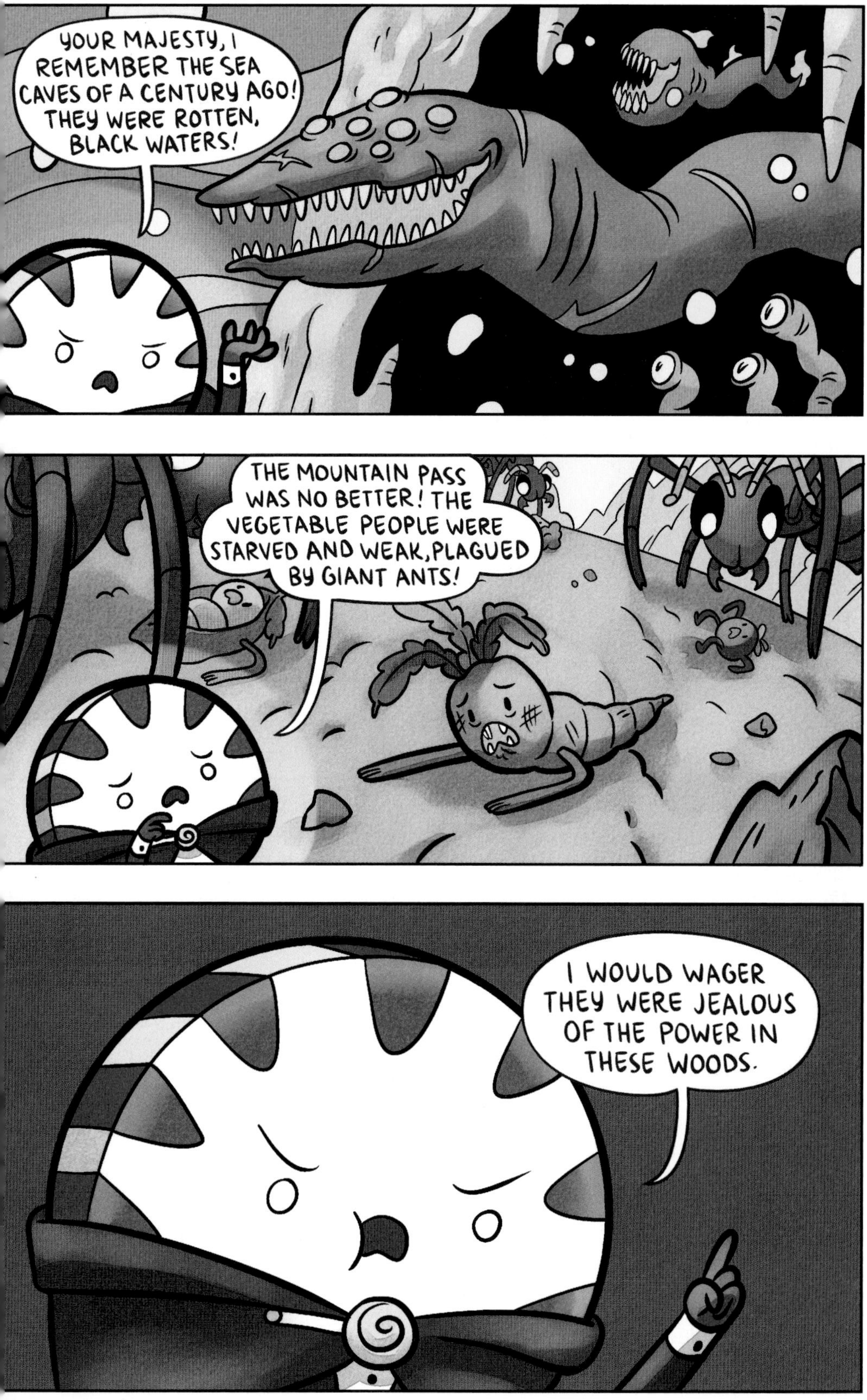
YOUR MAJESTY, I REMEMBER THE SEA CAVES OF A CENTURY AGO! THEY WERE ROTTEN, BLACK WATERS!
THE MOUNTAIN PASS WAS NO BETTER! THE VEGETABLE PEOPLE WERE STARVED AND WEAK, PLAGUED BY GIANT ANTS!
I WOULD WAGER THEY WERE JEALOUS OF THE POWER IN THESE WOODS.

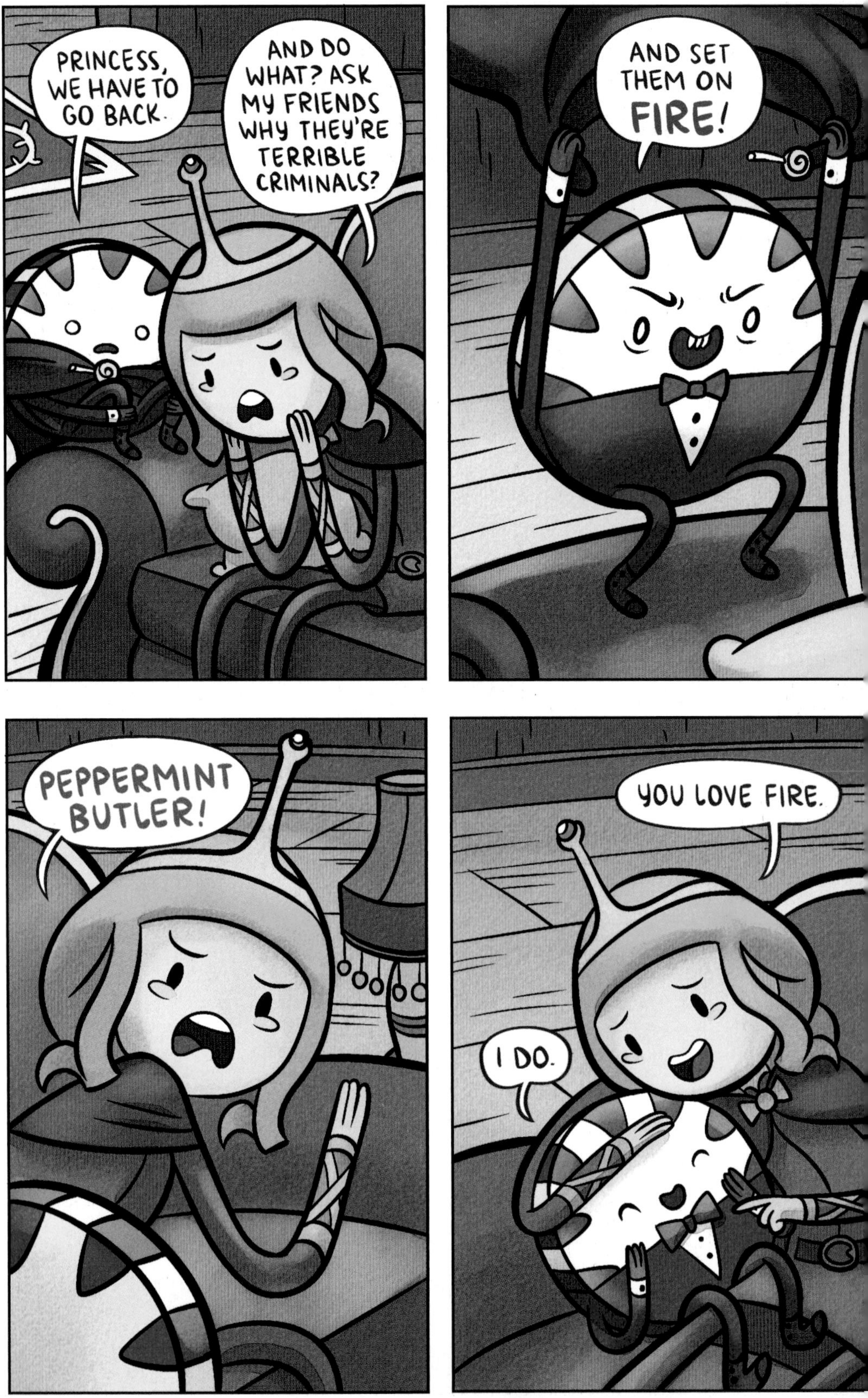
PRINCESS, WE HAVE TO GO BACK.
AND DO WHAT? ASK MY FRIENDS WHY THEY'RE TERRIBLE CRIMINALS?
AND SET THEM ON FIRE!
PEPPERMINT BUTLER!
YOU LOVE FIRE.
I DO.

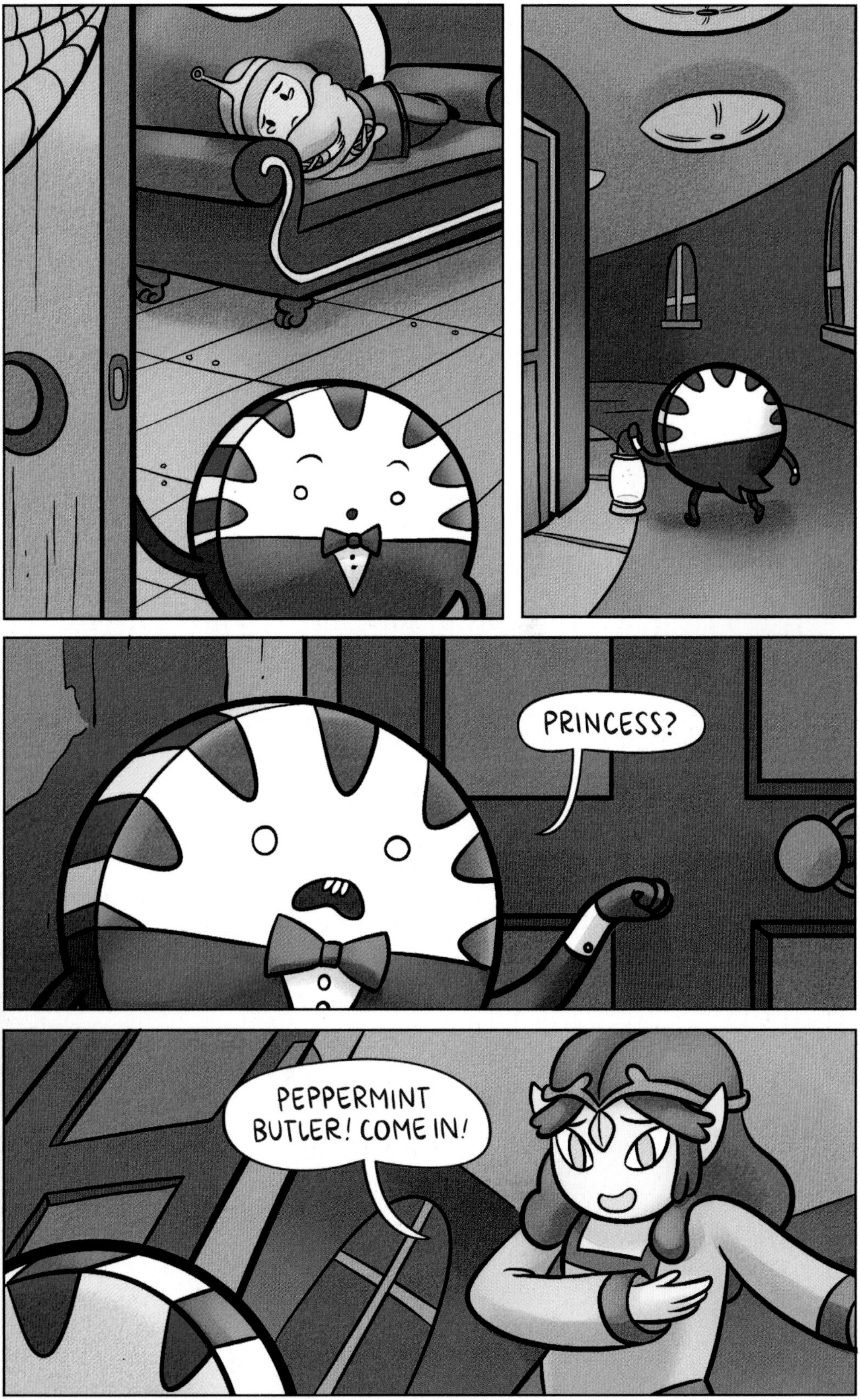
PRINCESS?
PEPPERMINT BUTLER! COME IN!

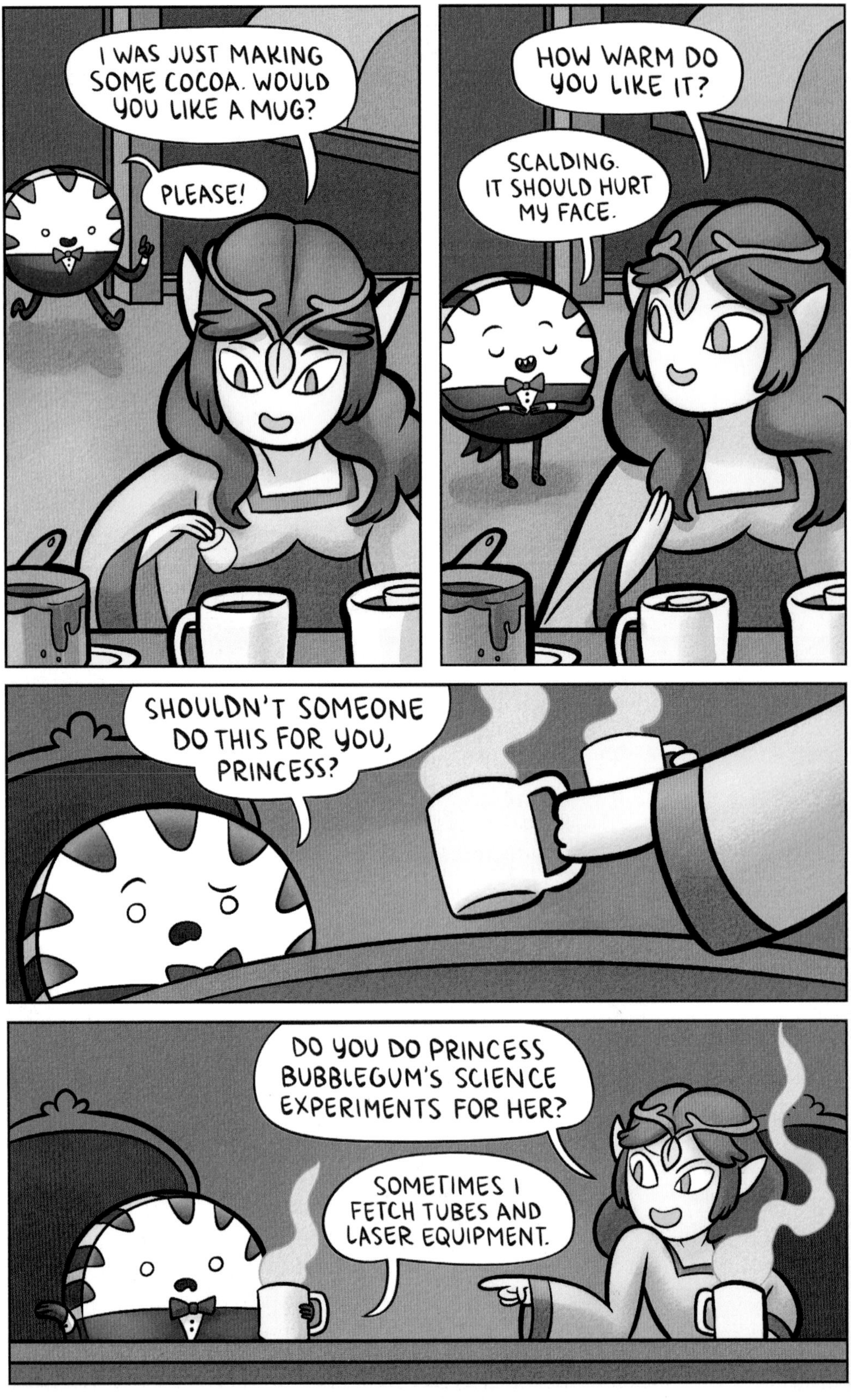
I WAS JUST MAKING SOME COCOA. WOULD YOU LIKE A MUG?
PLEASE!
HOW WARM DO YOU LIKE IT?
SCALDING. IT SHOULD HURT MY FACE.
SHOULDN'T SOMEONE DO THIS FOR YOU, PRINCESS?
DO YOU DO PRINCESS BUBBLEGUM'S SCIENCE EXPERIMENTS FOR HER?
SOMETIMES I FETCH TUBES AND LASER EQUIPMENT.

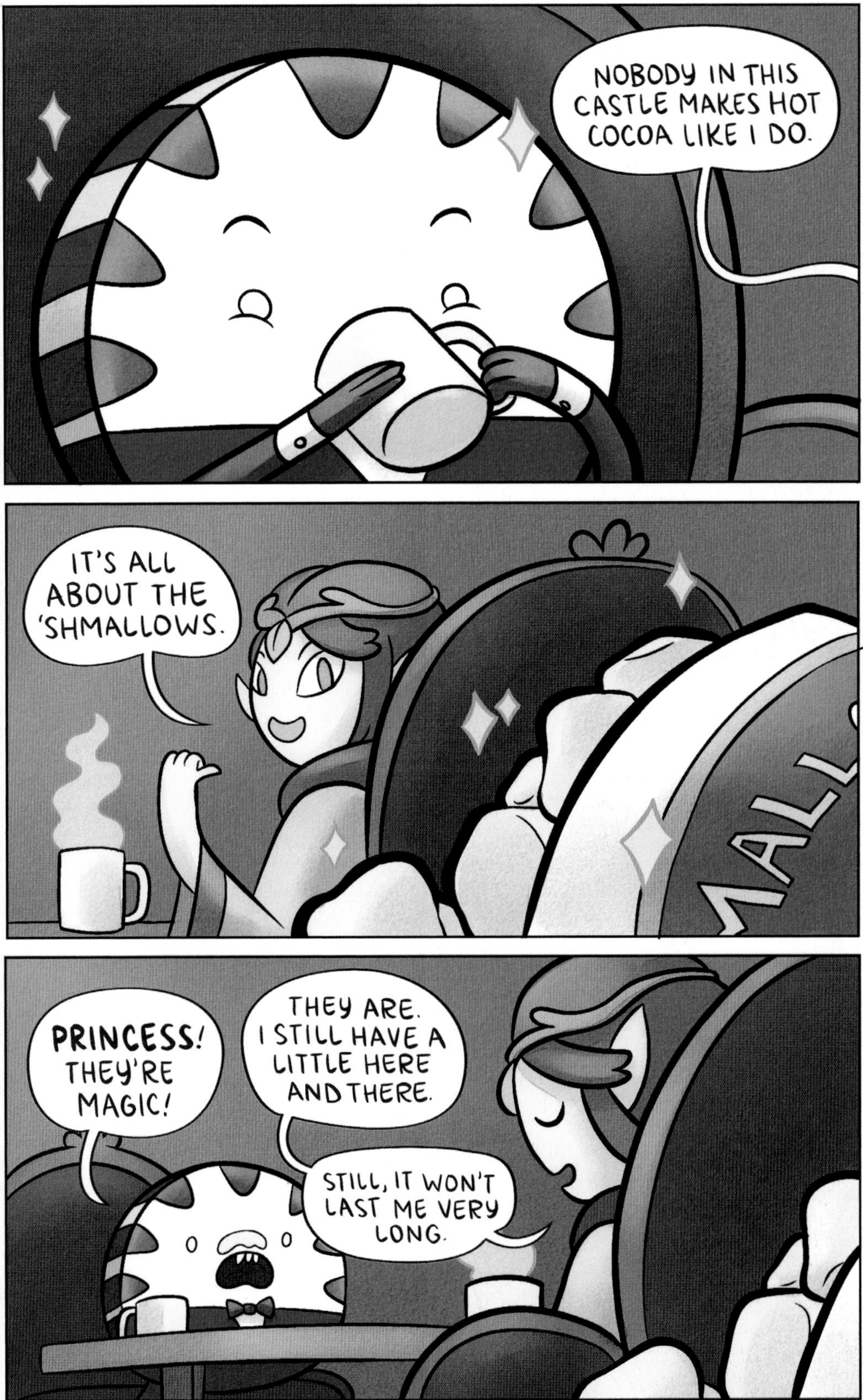
NOBODY IN THIS CASTLE MAKES HOT COCOA LIKE I DO.
IT'S ALL ABOUT THE 'SHMALLOWS.
MALL
PRINCESS! THEY'RE MAGIC!
THEY ARE. I STILL HAVE A LITTLE HERE AND THERE.
STILL, IT WON'T LAST ME VERY LONG.

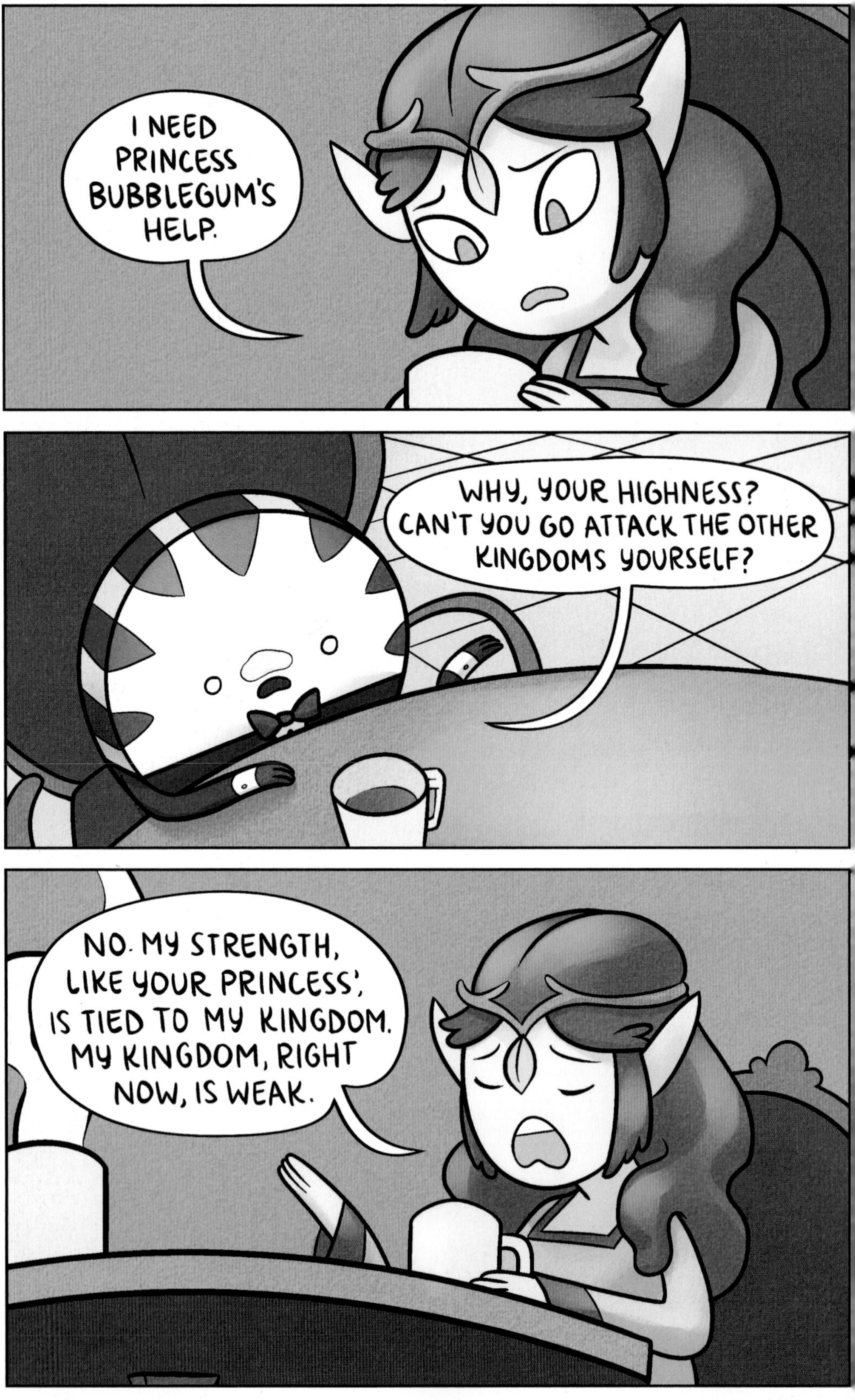
I NEED PRINCESS BUBBLEGUM'S HELP.
WHY, YOUR HIGHNESS? CAN'T YOU GO ATTACK THE OTHER KINGDOMS YOURSELF?
NO. MY STRENGTH, LIKE YOUR PRINCESS', IS TIED TO MY KINGDOM. MY KINGDOM, RIGHT NOW, IS WEAK.

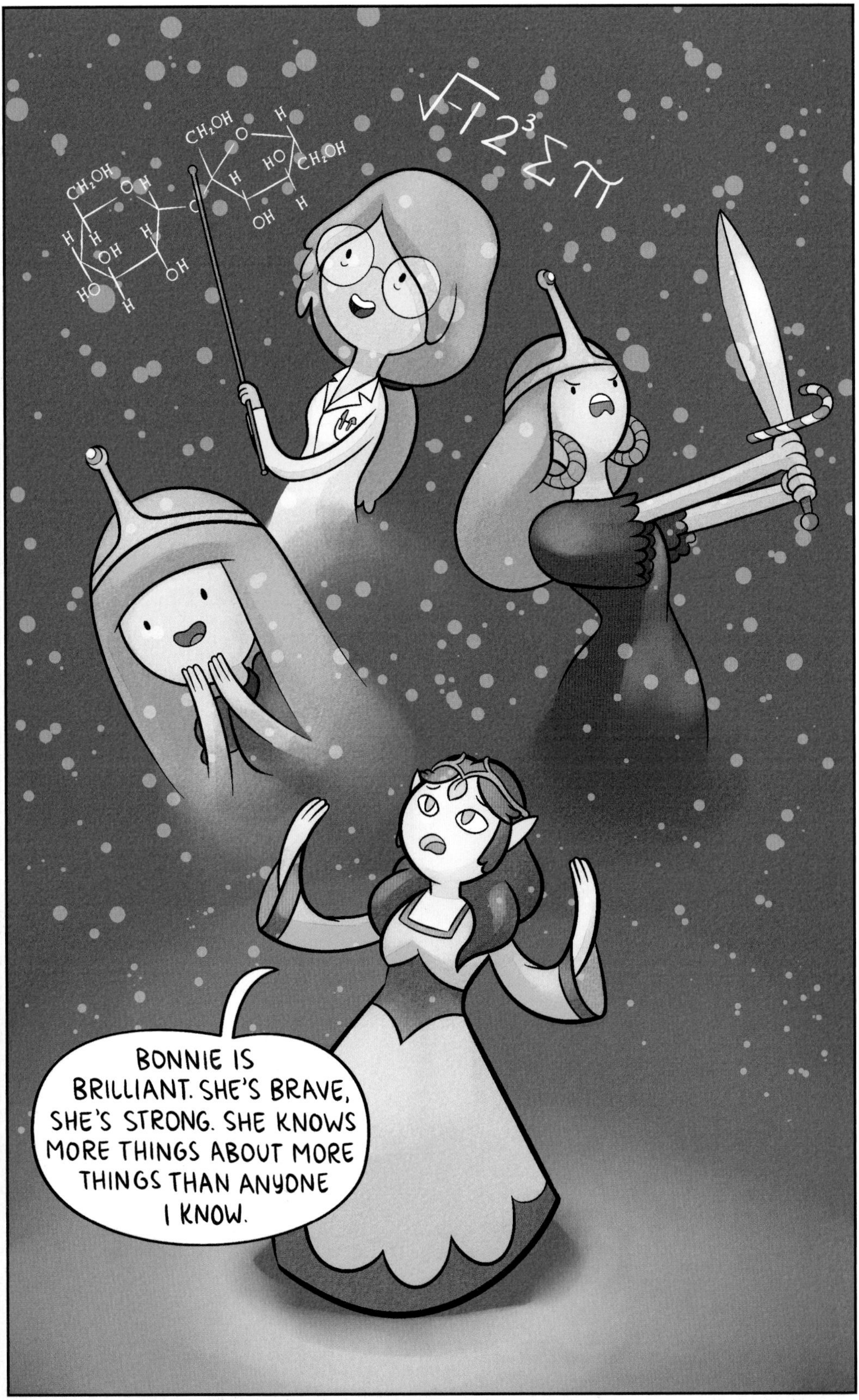
BONNIE IS BRILLIANT. SHE'S BRAVE, SHE'S STRONG. SHE KNOWS MORE THINGS ABOUT MORE THINGS THAN ANYONE I KNOW.

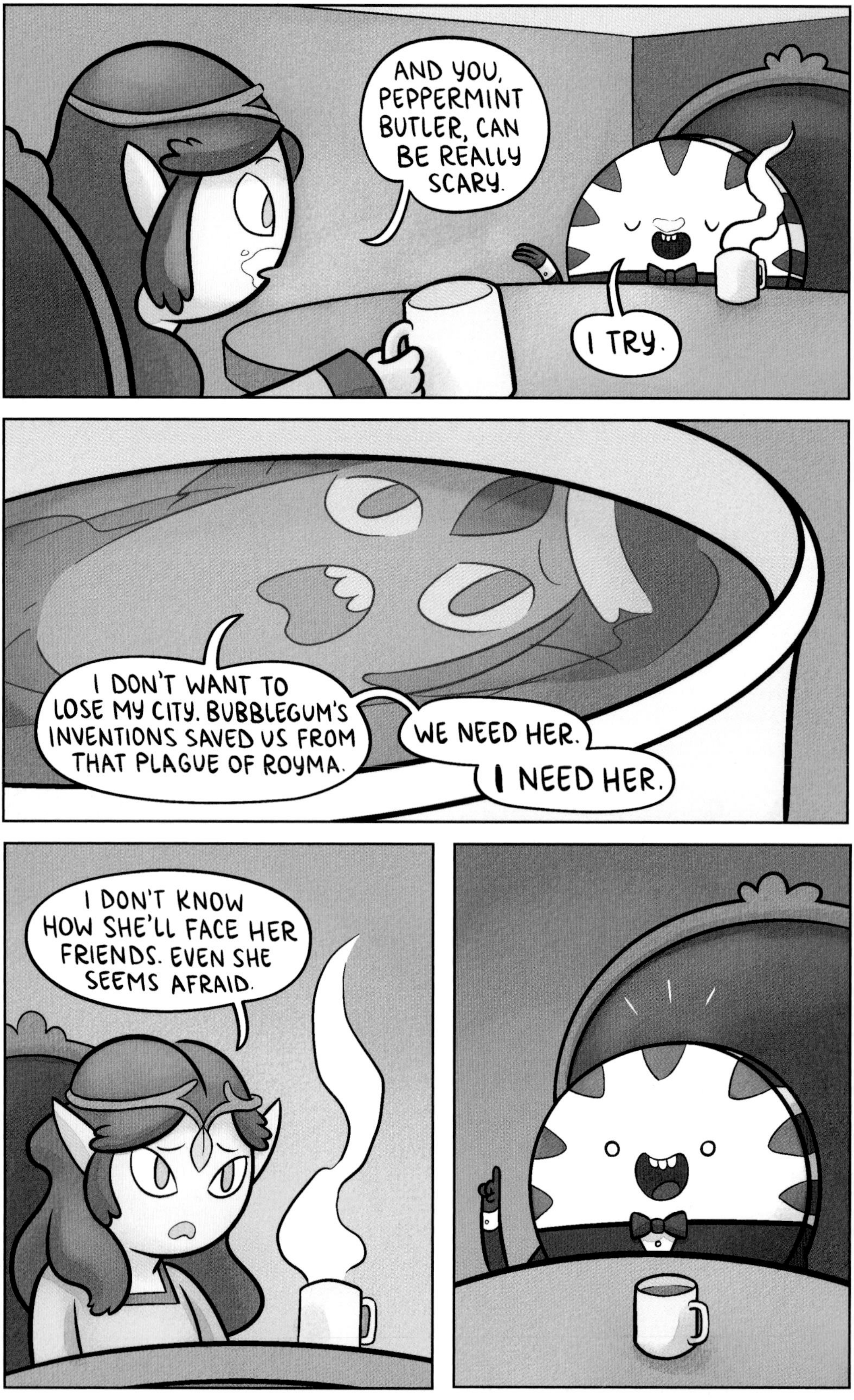
AND YOU, PEPPERMINT BUTLER, CAN BE REALLY SCARY.
I TRY.
I DON'T WANT TO LOSE MY CITY. BUBBLEGUM'S INVENTIONS SAVED US FROM THAT PLAGUE OF ROYMA.
WE NEED HER.
I NEED HER.
I DON'T KNOW HOW SHE'LL FACE HER FRIENDS. EVEN SHE SEEMS AFRAID.

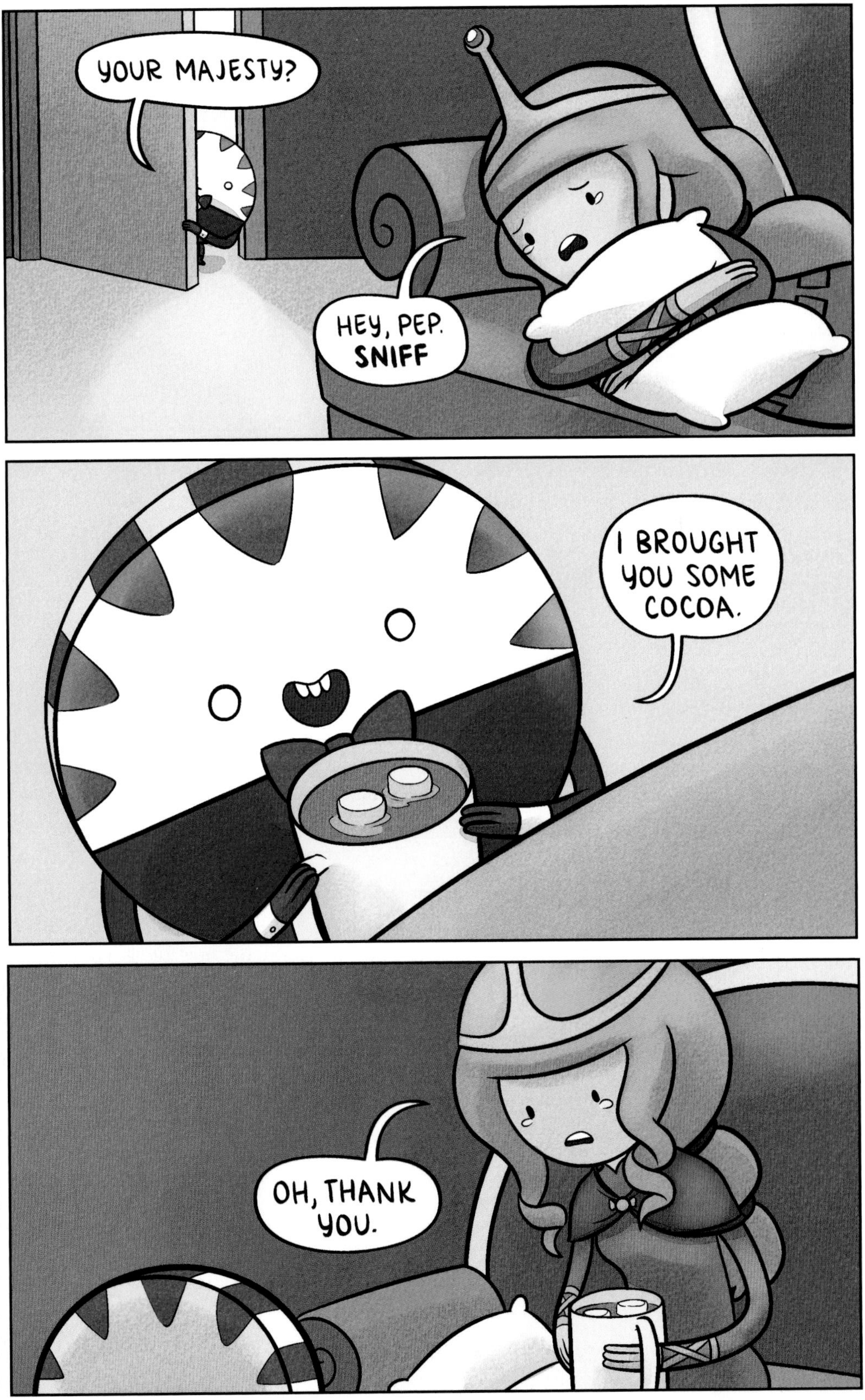
YOUR MAJESTY?
HEY, PEP. SNIFF
I BROUGHT YOU SOME COCOA.
OH, THANK YOU.

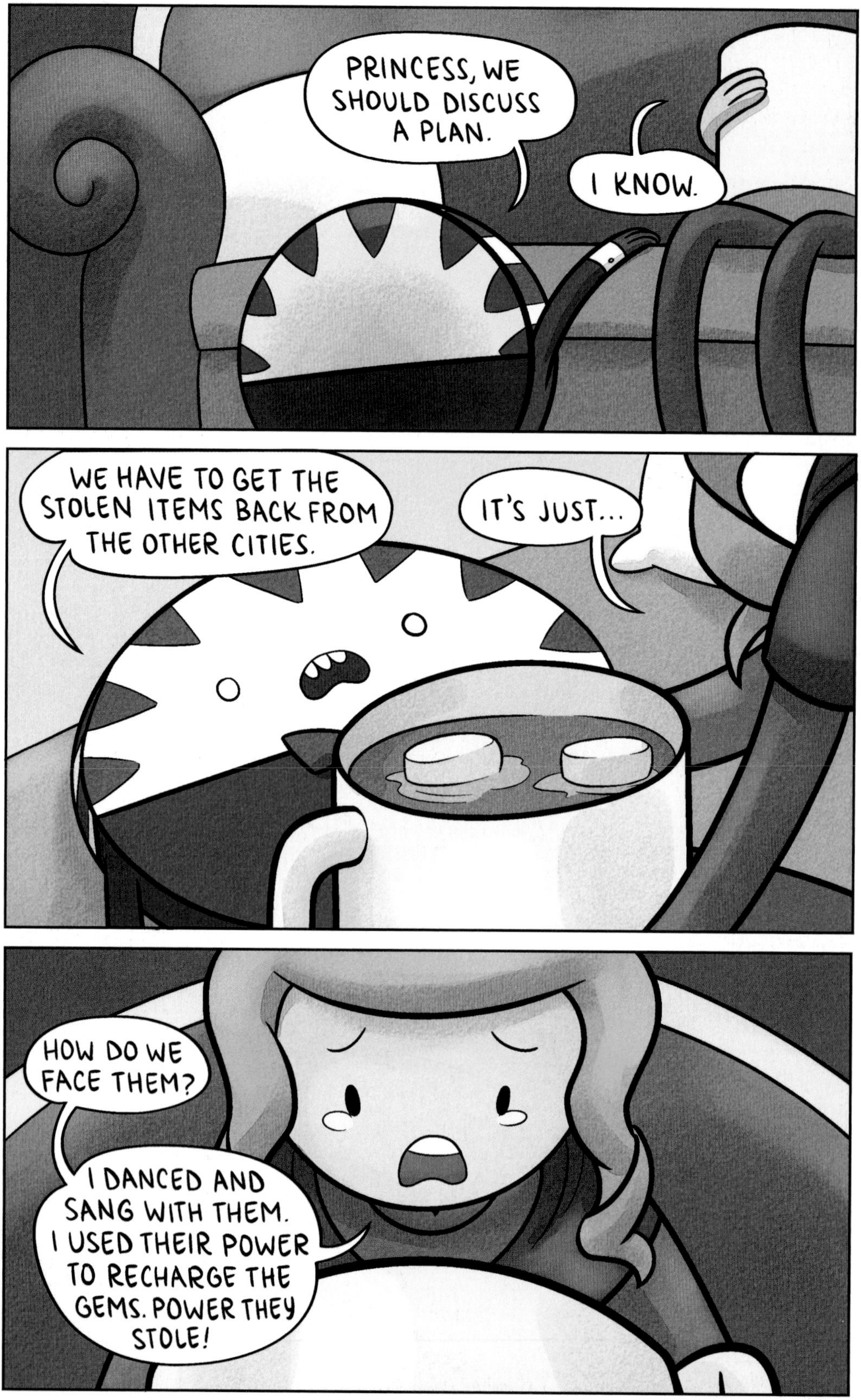
PRINCESS, WE SHOULD DISCUSS A PLAN.
I KNOW.
WE HAVE TO GET THE STOLEN ITEMS BACK FROM THE OTHER CITIES.
IT'S JUST...
HOW DO WE FACE THEM?
I DANCED AND SANG WITH THEM. I USED THEIR POWER TO RECHARGE THE GEMS. POWER THEY STOLE!

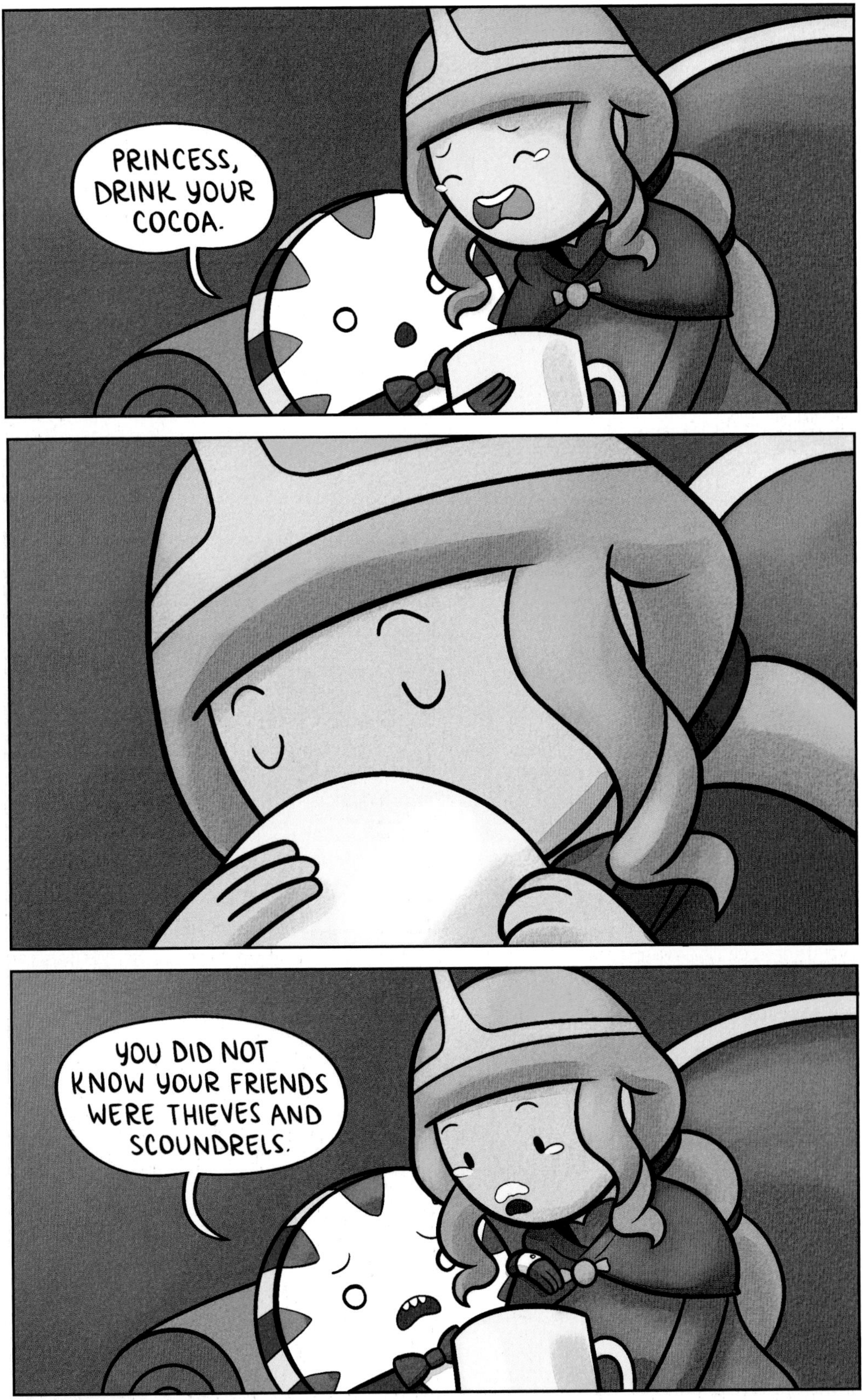
PRINCESS, DRINK YOUR COCOA.
YOU DID NOT KNOW YOUR FRIENDS WERE THIEVES AND SCOUNDRELS.

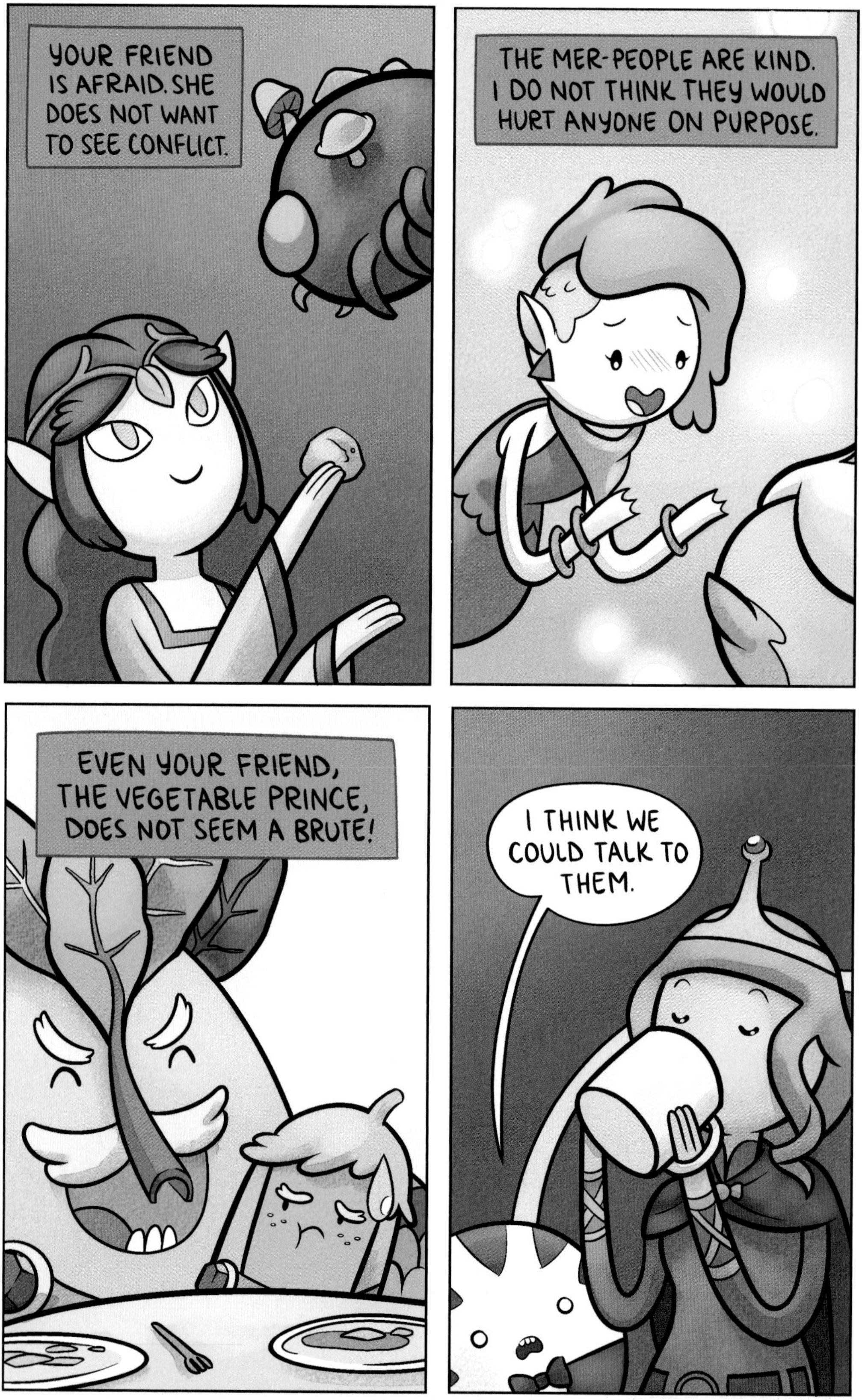
YOUR FRIEND IS AFRAID. SHE DOES NOT WANT TO SEE CONFLICT.
THE MER-PEOPLE ARE KIND. I DO NOT THINK THEY WOULD HURT ANYONE ON PURPOSE.
EVEN YOUR FRIEND, THE VEGETABLE PRINCE, DOES NOT SEEM A BRUTE!
I THINK WE COULD TALK TO THEM.

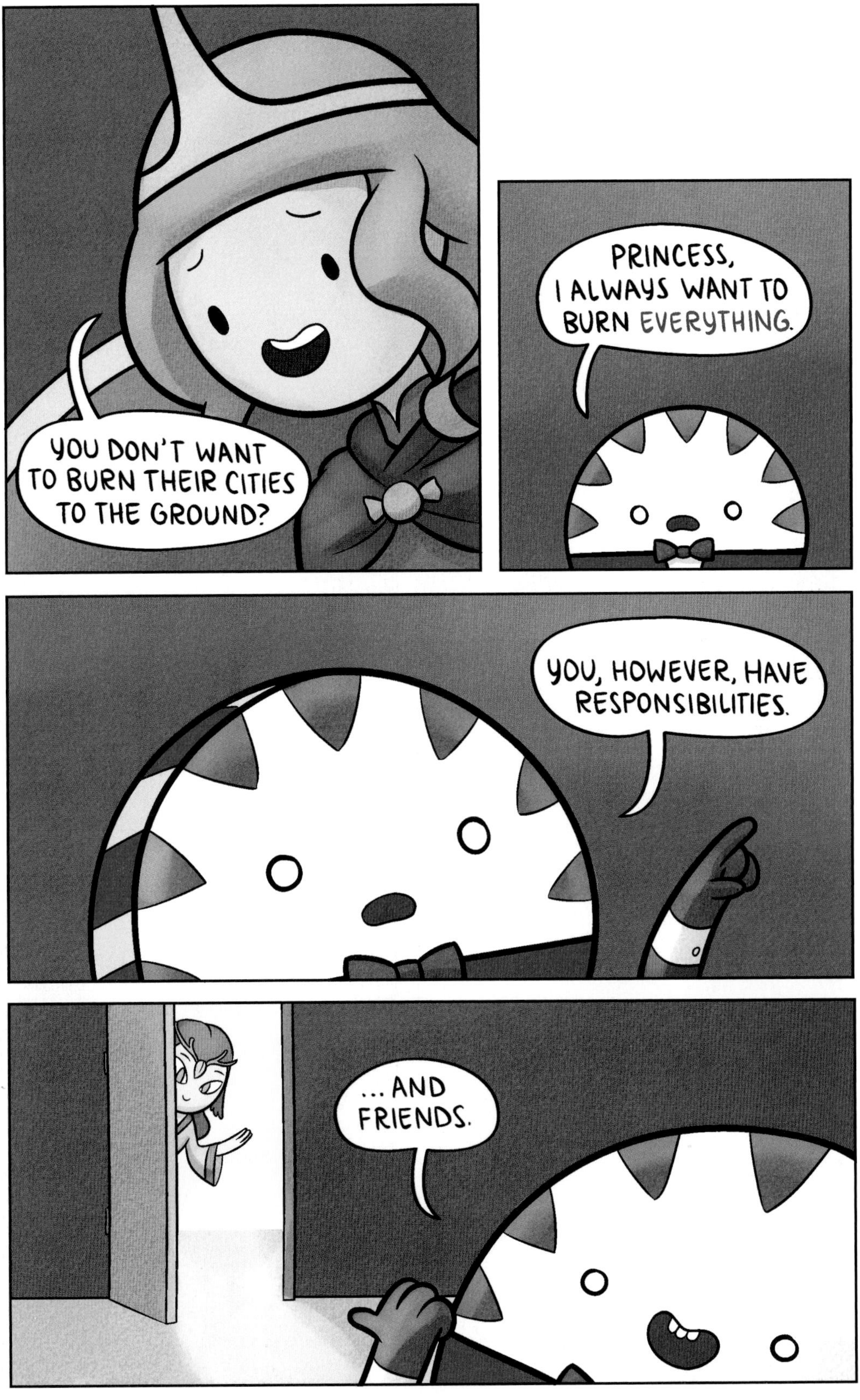
YOU DON'T WANT TO BURN THEIR CITIES TO THE GROUND?
PRINCESS, I ALWAYS WANT TO BURN EVERYTHING.
YOU, HOWEVER, HAVE RESPONSIBILITIES.
...AND FRIENDS.

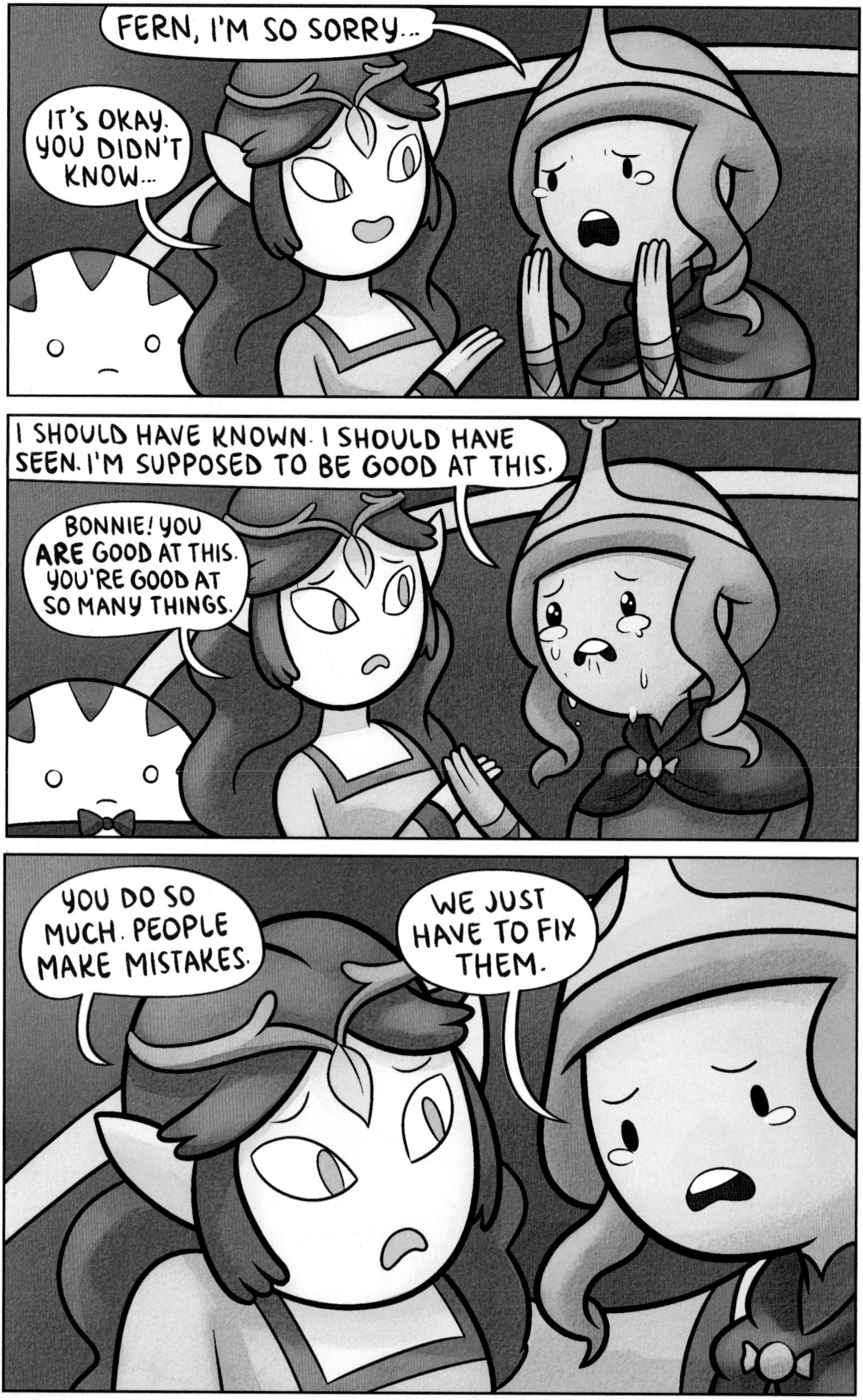
FERN, I'M SO SORRY...
IT'S OKAY. YOU DIDN'T KNOW...
I SHOULD HAVE KNOWN. I SHOULD HAVE SEEN. I'M SUPPOSED TO BE GOOD AT THIS.
BONNIE! YOU **ARE** GOOD AT THIS. YOU'RE GOOD AT SO MANY THINGS.
YOU DO SO MUCH. PEOPLE MAKE MISTAKES.
WE JUST HAVE TO FIX THEM.

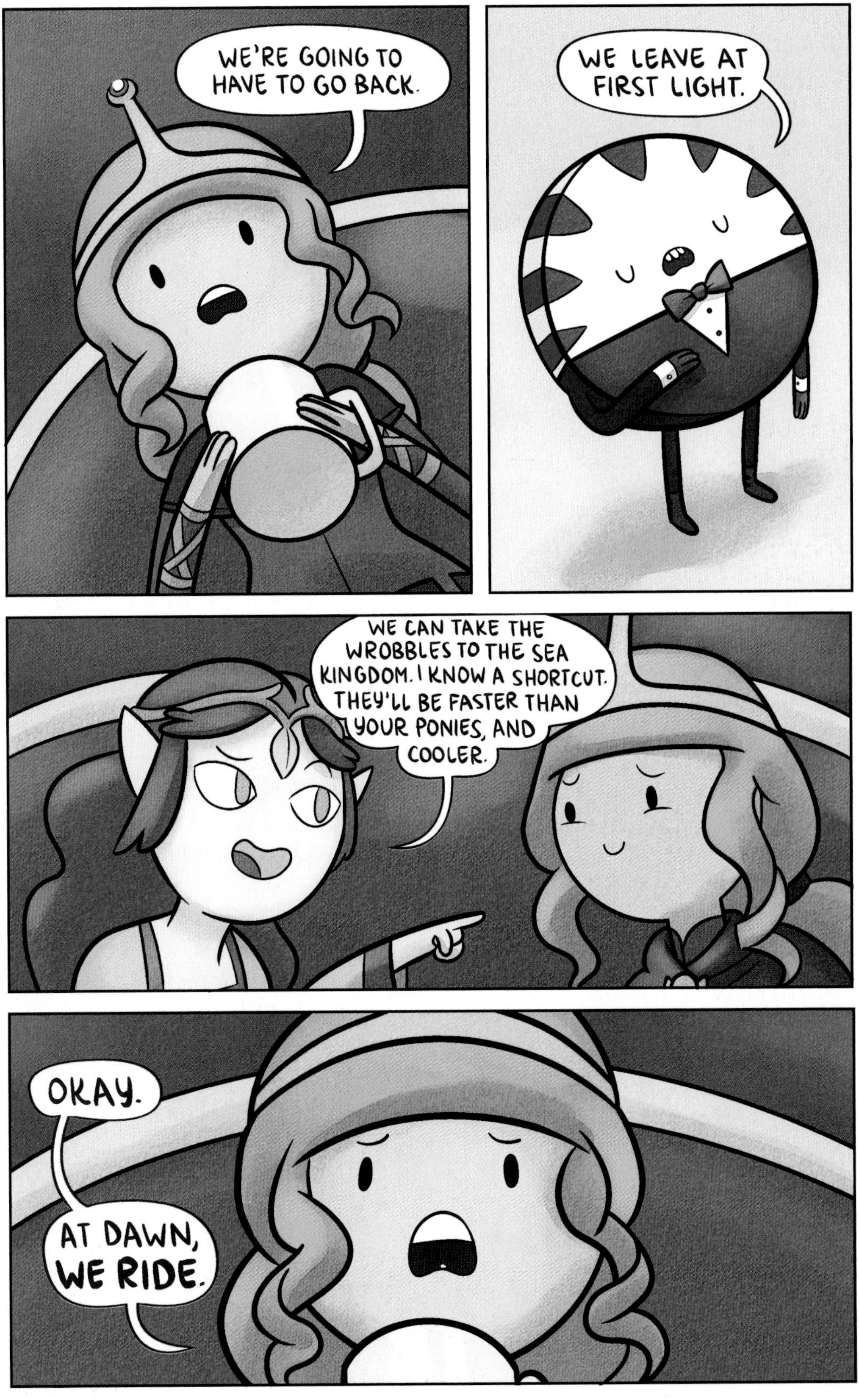
WE'RE GOING TO HAVE TO GO BACK.
WE LEAVE AT FIRST LIGHT.
WE CAN TAKE THE WROBBLES TO THE SEA KINGDOM. I KNOW A SHORTCUT. THEY'LL BE FASTER THAN YOUR PONIES, AND COOLER.
OKAY.
AT DAWN, WE RIDE.

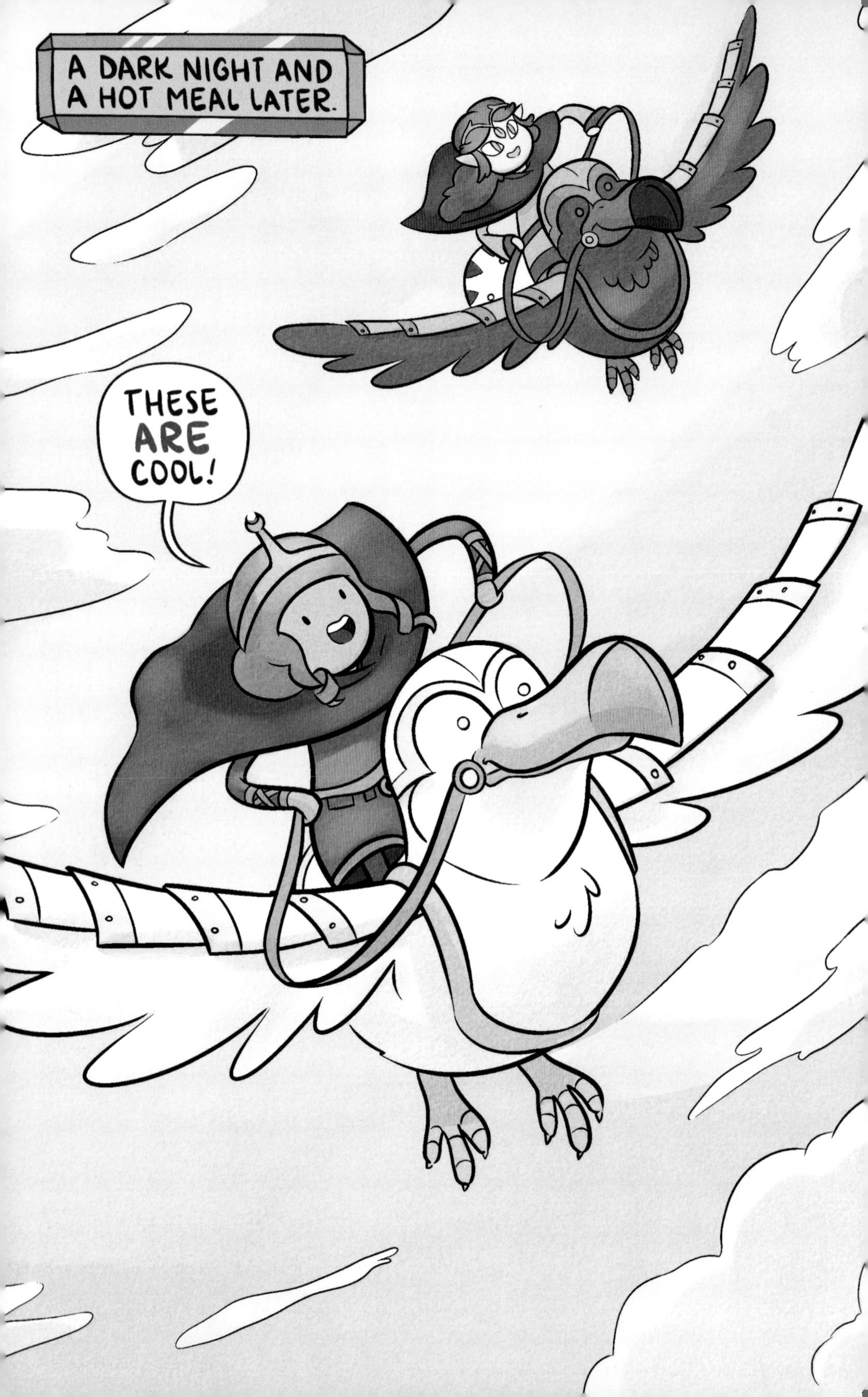
A DARK NIGHT AND A HOT MEAL LATER.
THESE ARE COOL!

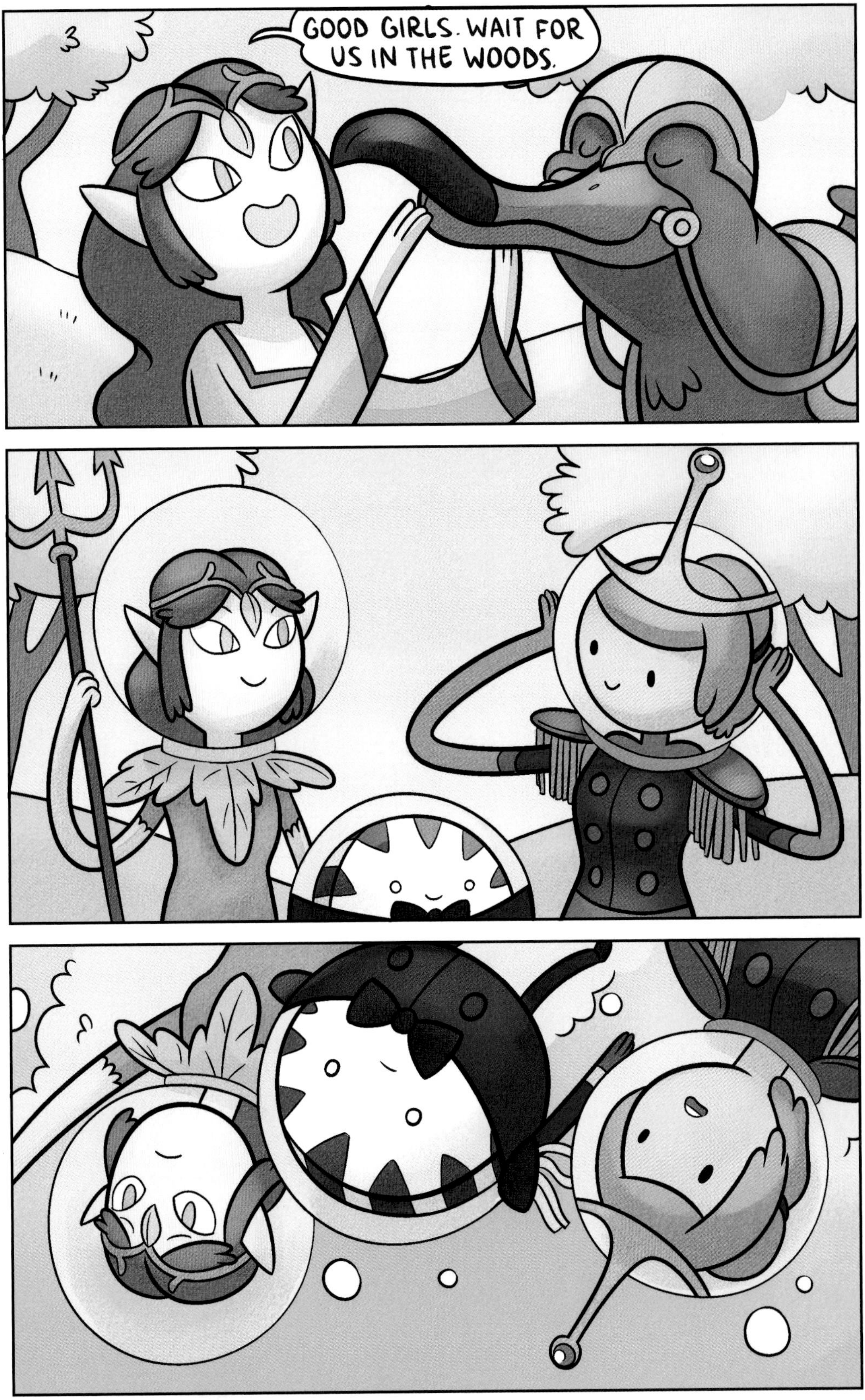
GOOD GIRLS. WAIT FOR US IN THE WOODS.

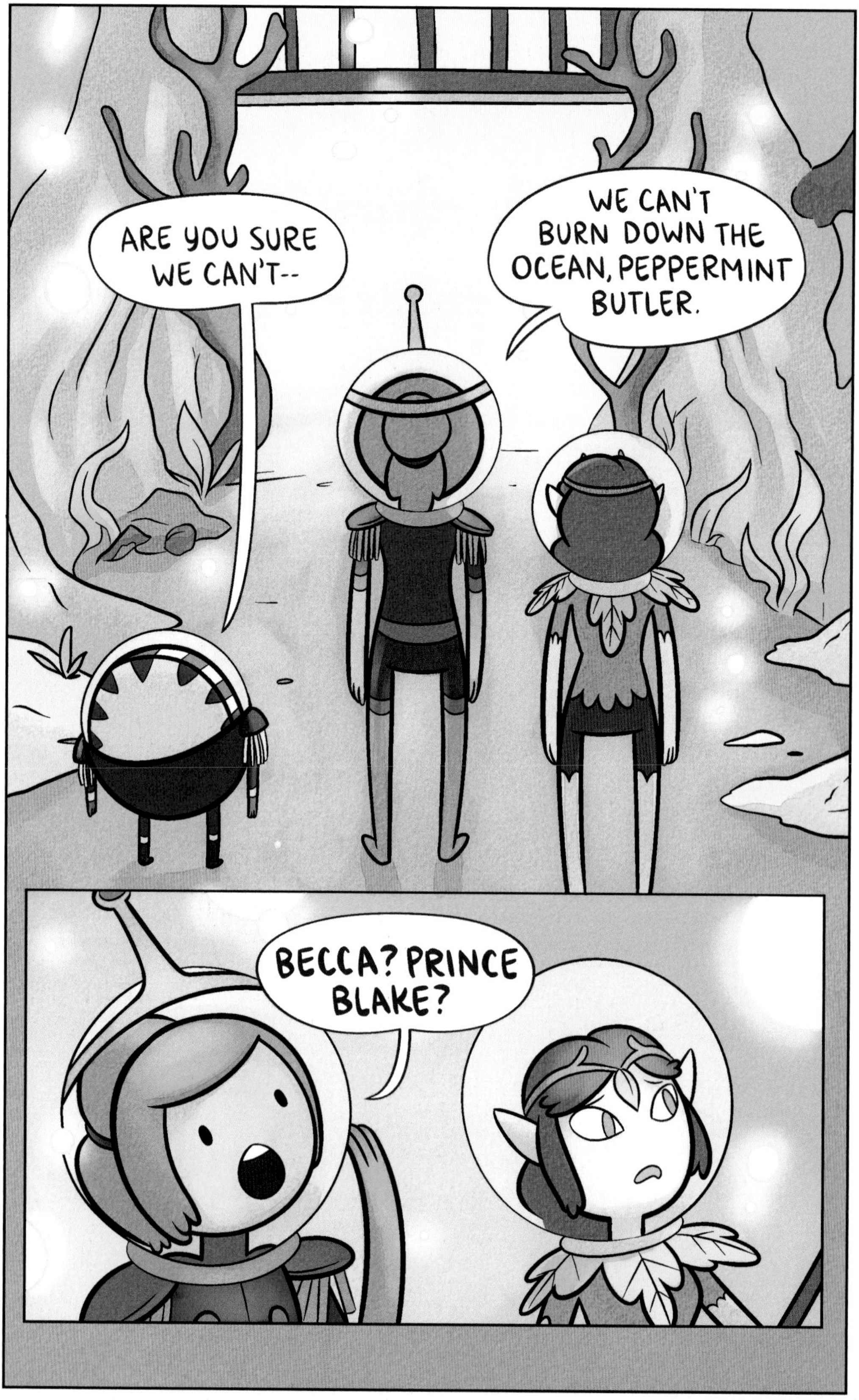
ARE YOU SURE WE CAN'T--
WE CAN'T BURN DOWN THE OCEAN, PEPPERMINT BUTLER.
BECCA? PRINCE BLAKE?

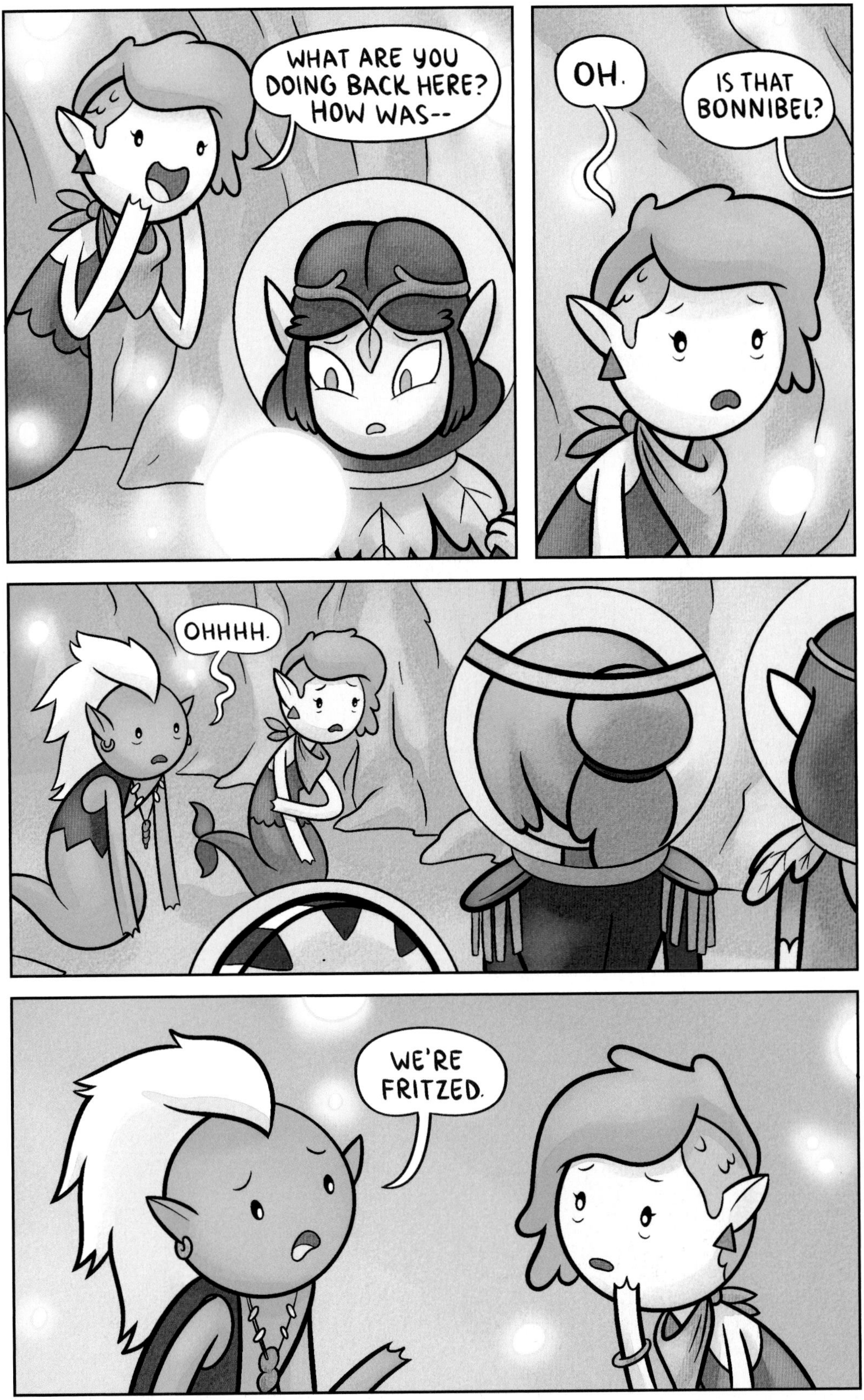
WHAT ARE YOU DOING BACK HERE? HOW WAS--
OH.
IS THAT BONNIBEL?
OHHHH.
WE'RE FRITZED.

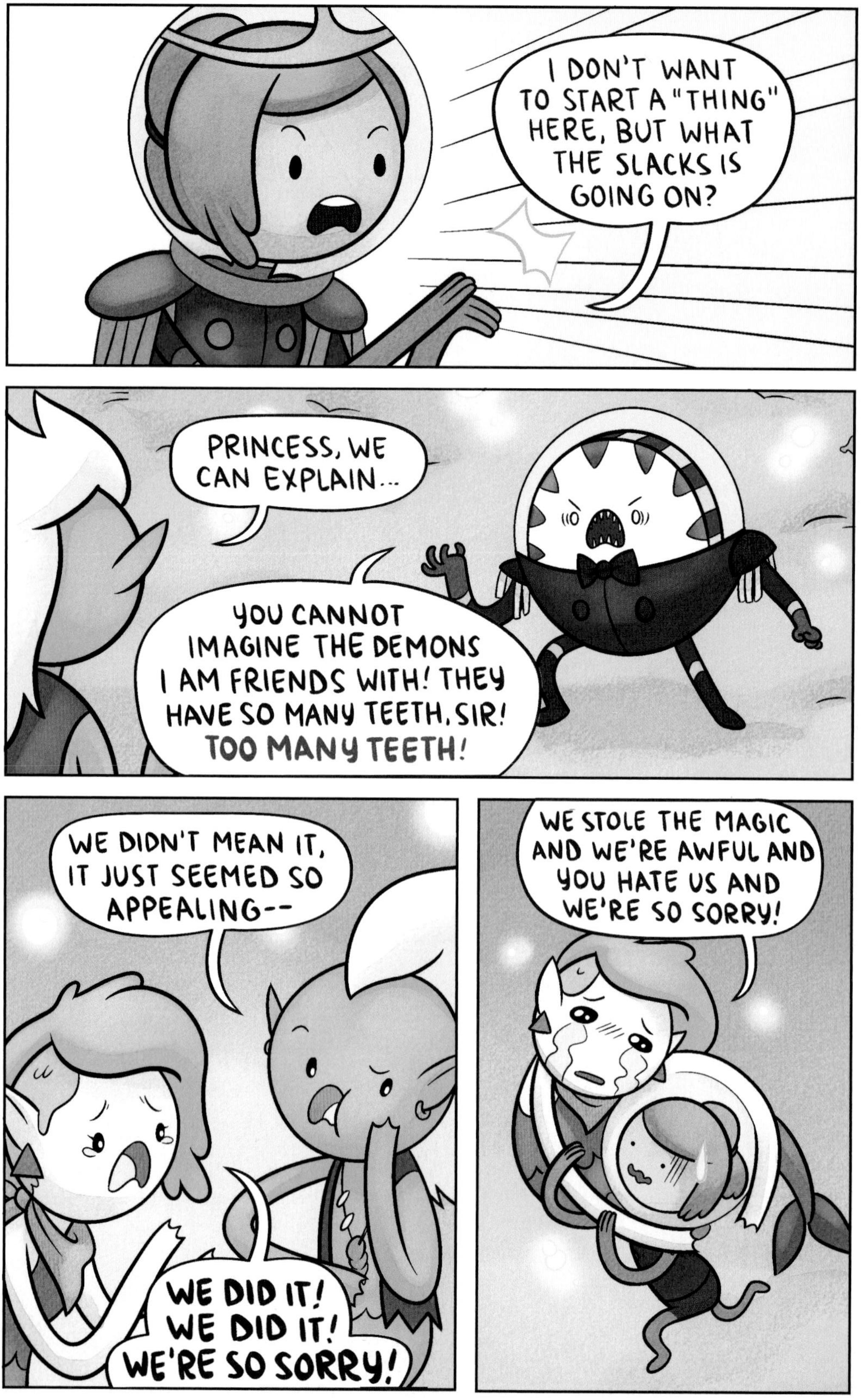
I DON'T WANT TO START A "THING" HERE, BUT WHAT THE SLACKS IS GOING ON?
PRINCESS, WE CAN EXPLAIN...
YOU CANNOT IMAGINE THE DEMONS I AM FRIENDS WITH! THEY HAVE SO MANY TEETH, SIR! TOO MANY TEETH!
WE DIDN'T MEAN IT, IT JUST SEEMED SO APPEALING--
WE DID IT! WE DID IT! WE'RE SO SORRY!
WE STOLE THE MAGIC AND WE'RE AWFUL AND YOU HATE US AND WE'RE SO SORRY!

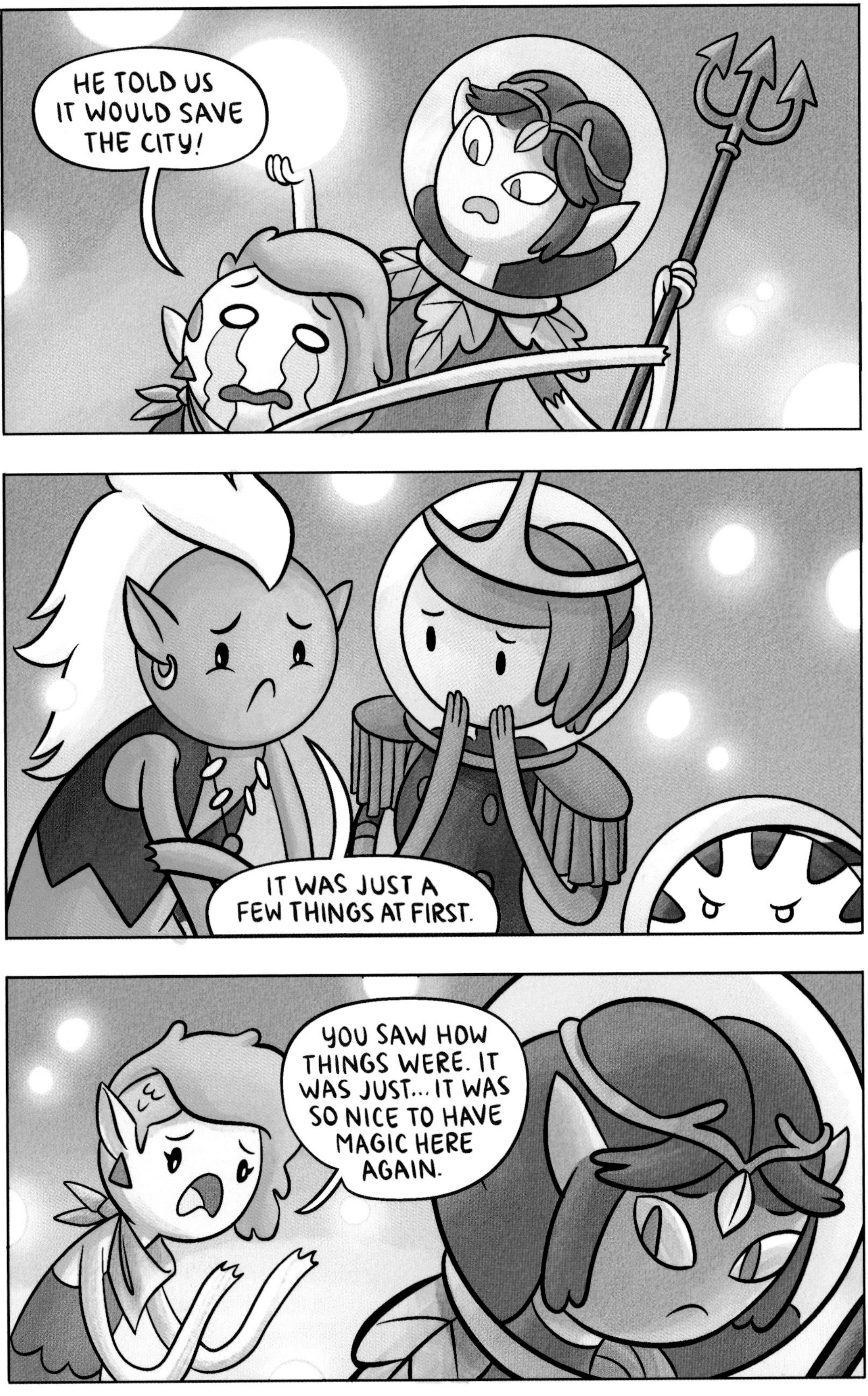
HE TOLD US IT WOULD SAVE THE CITY!
IT WAS JUST A FEW THINGS AT FIRST.
YOU SAW HOW THINGS WERE. IT WAS JUST... IT WAS SO NICE TO HAVE MAGIC HERE AGAIN.

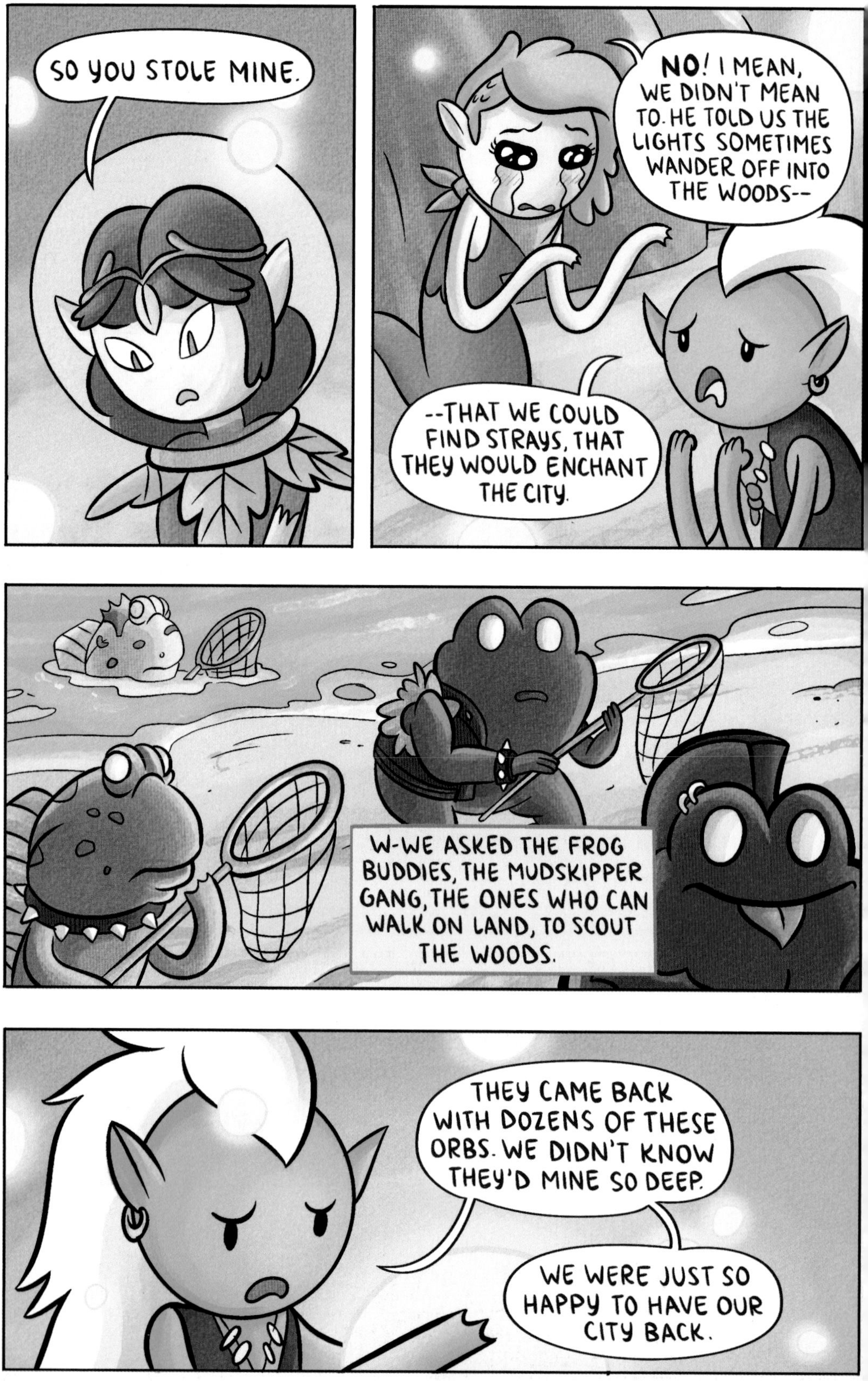
SO YOU STOLE MINE.
NO! I MEAN, WE DIDN'T MEAN TO. HE TOLD US THE LIGHTS SOMETIMES WANDER OFF INTO THE WOODS--
--THAT WE COULD FIND STRAYS, THAT THEY WOULD ENCHANT THE CITY.
W-WE ASKED THE FROG BUDDIES, THE MUDSKIPPER GANG, THE ONES WHO CAN WALK ON LAND, TO SCOUT THE WOODS.
THEY CAME BACK WITH DOZENS OF THESE ORBS. WE DIDN'T KNOW THEY'D MINE SO DEEP.
WE WERE JUST SO HAPPY TO HAVE OUR CITY BACK.

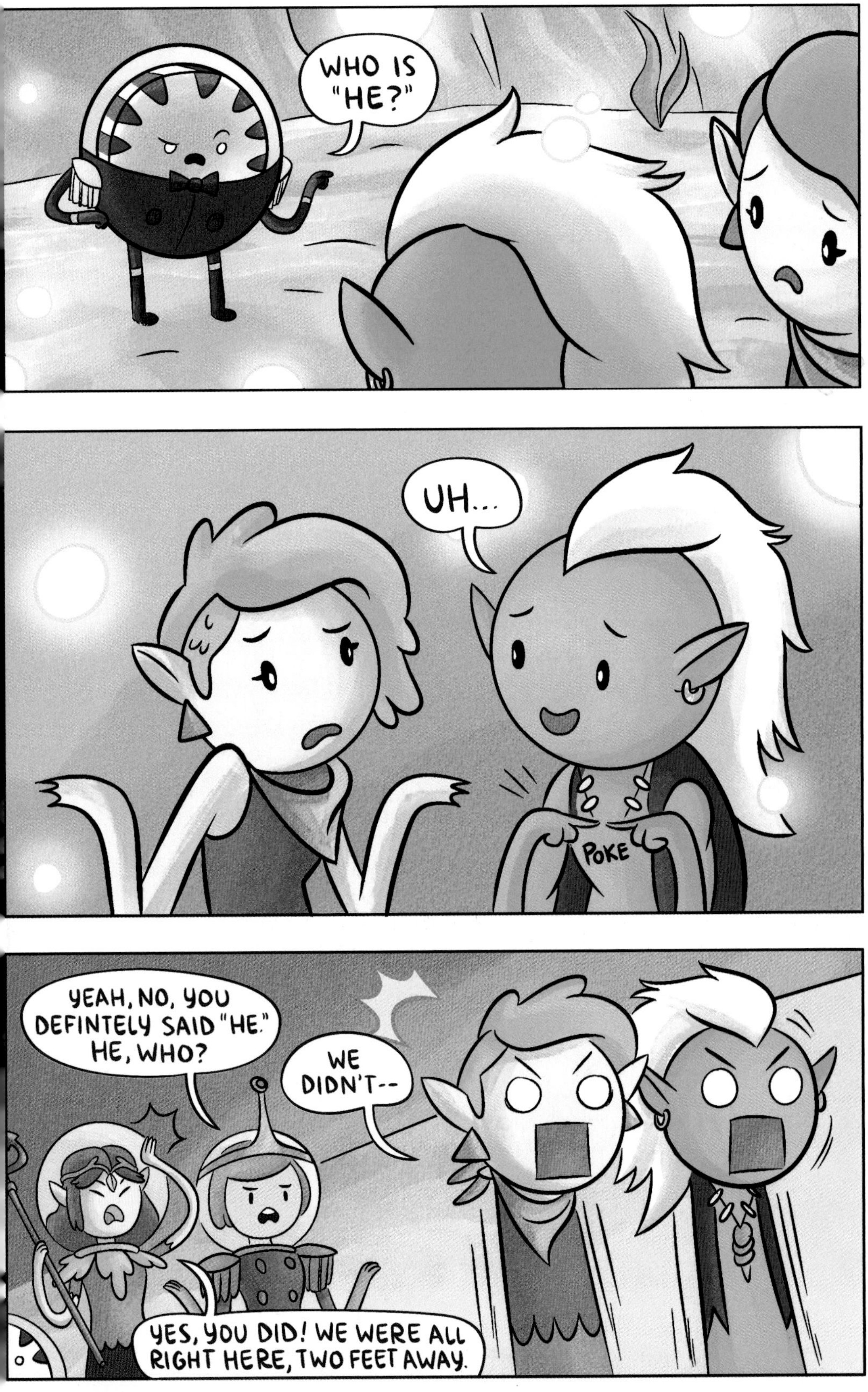
WHO IS "HE?"
UH...
POKE
YEAH, NO, YOU DEFINTELY SAID "HE." HE, WHO?
WE DIDN'T--
YES, YOU DID! WE WERE ALL RIGHT HERE, TWO FEET AWAY.

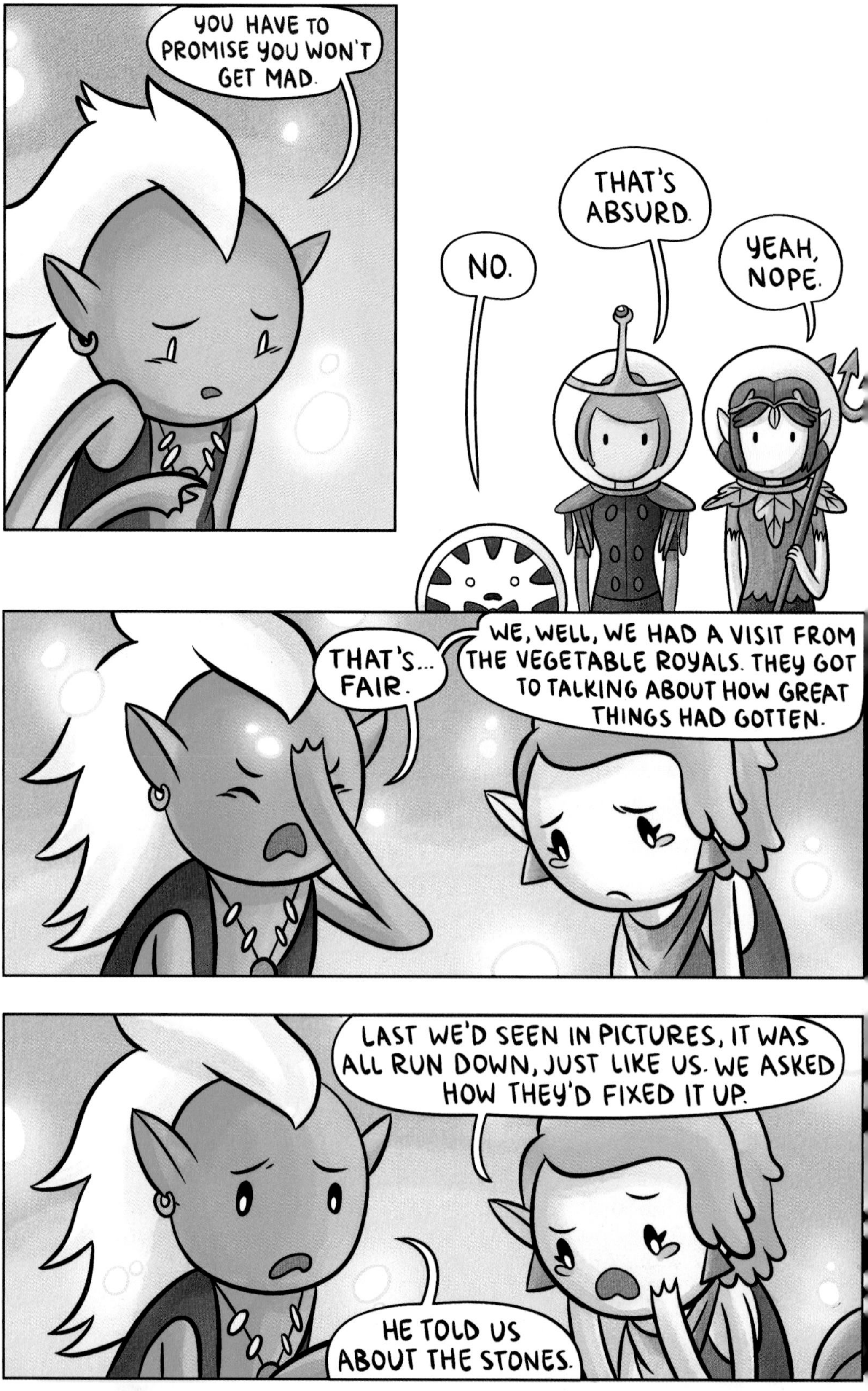
YOU HAVE TO PROMISE YOU WON'T GET MAD.
NO.
THAT'S ABSURD.
YEAH, NOPE.
THAT'S... FAIR.
WE, WELL, WE HAD A VISIT FROM THE VEGETABLE ROYALS. THEY GOT TO TALKING ABOUT HOW GREAT THINGS HAD GOTTEN.
LAST WE'D SEEN IN PICTURES, IT WAS ALL RUN DOWN, JUST LIKE US. WE ASKED HOW THEY'D FIXED IT UP.
HE TOLD US ABOUT THE STONES.

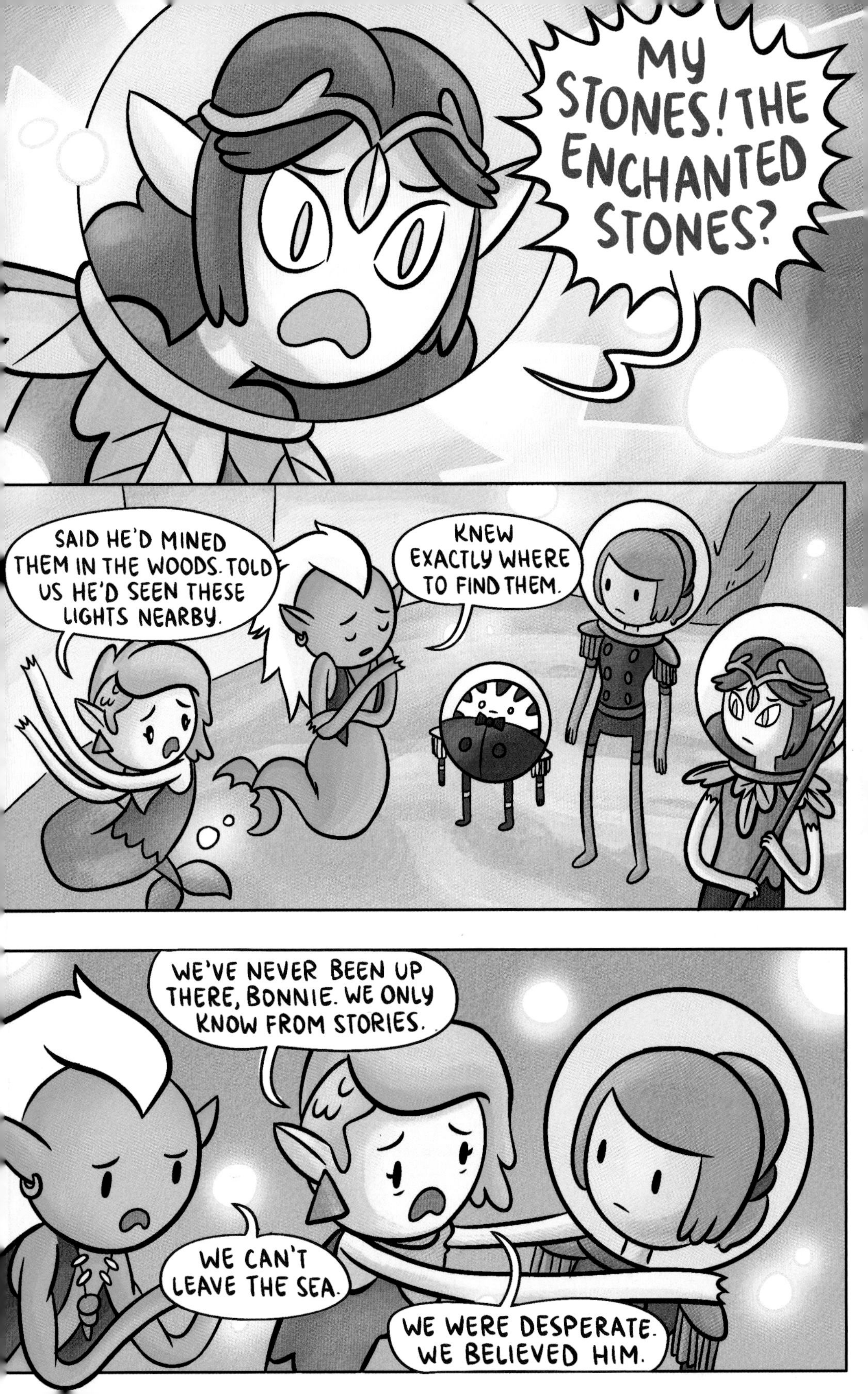

MY STONES! THE ENCHANTED STONES?
SAID HE'D MINED THEM IN THE WOODS. TOLD US HE'D SEEN THESE LIGHTS NEARBY.
KNEW EXACTLY WHERE TO FIND THEM.
WE'VE NEVER BEEN UP THERE, BONNIE. WE ONLY KNOW FROM STORIES.
WE CAN'T LEAVE THE SEA.
WE WERE DESPERATE. WE BELIEVED HIM.

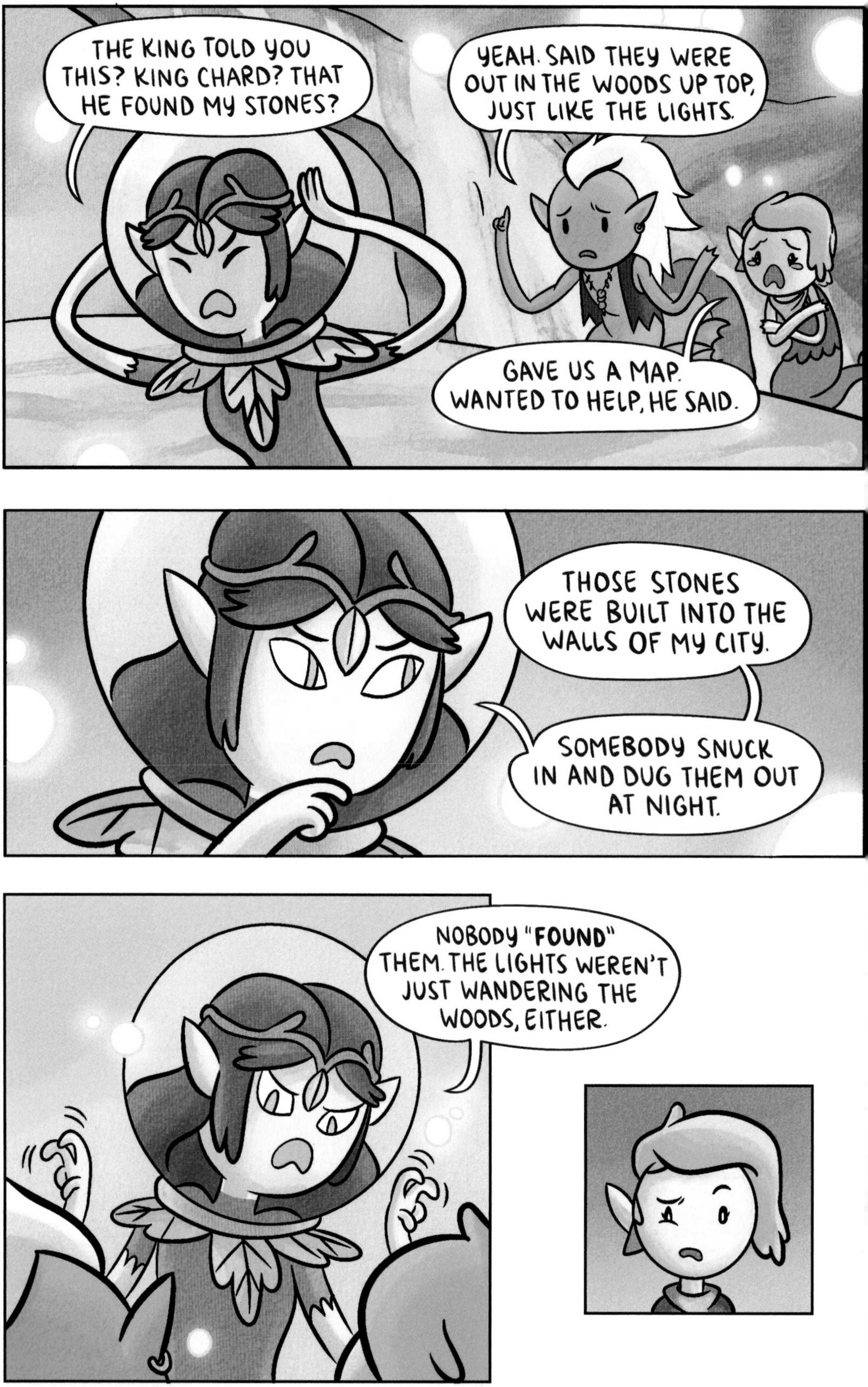
THE KING TOLD YOU THIS? KING CHARD? THAT HE FOUND MY STONES?
YEAH. SAID THEY WERE OUT IN THE WOODS UP TOP, JUST LIKE THE LIGHTS.
GAVE US A MAP. WANTED TO HELP, HE SAID.
THOSE STONES WERE BUILT INTO THE WALLS OF MY CITY.
SOMEBODY SNUCK IN AND DUG THEM OUT AT NIGHT.
NOBODY "**FOUND**" THEM. THE LIGHTS WEREN'T JUST WANDERING THE WOODS, EITHER.

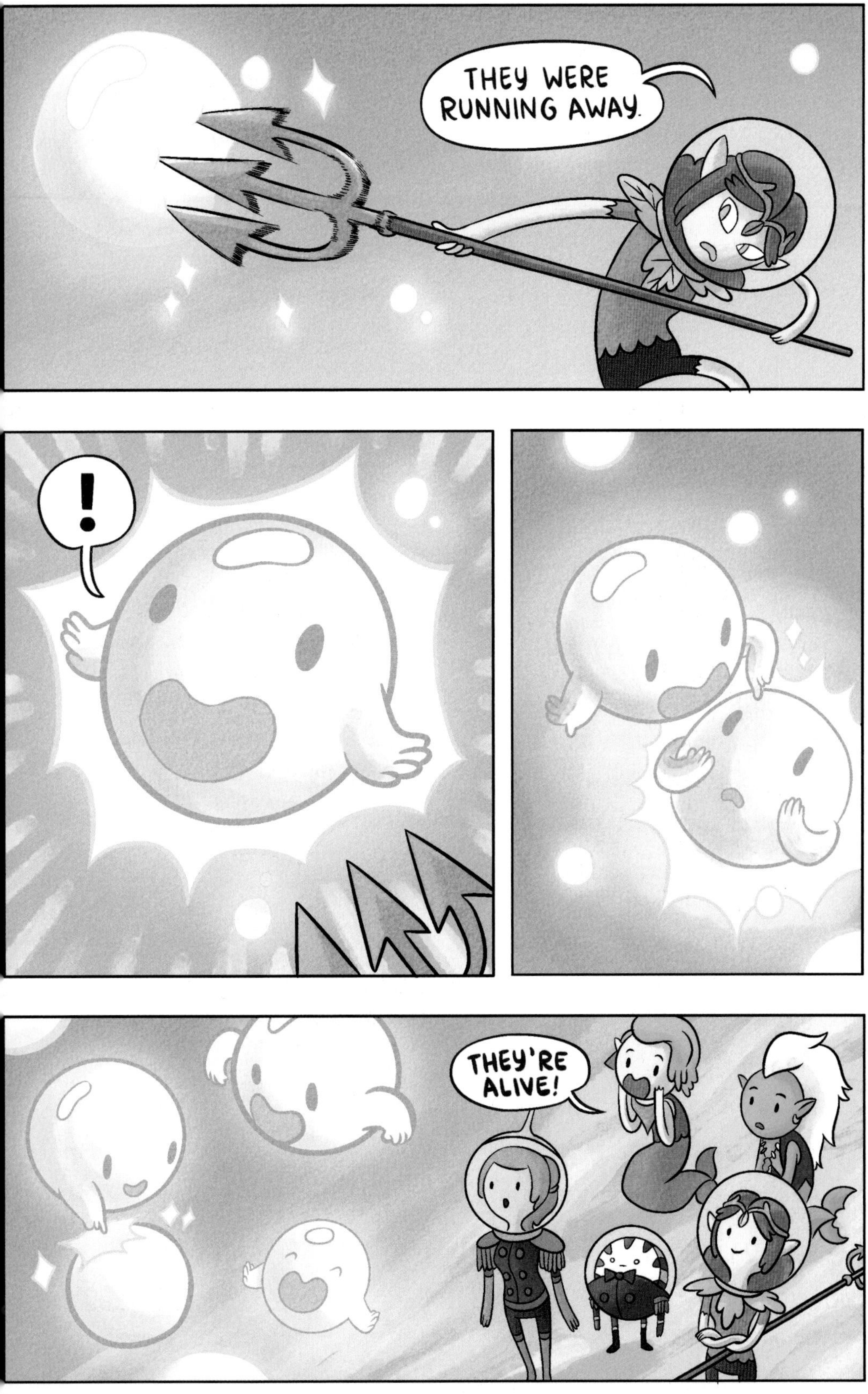
THEY WERE RUNNING AWAY.
!
THEY'RE ALIVE!

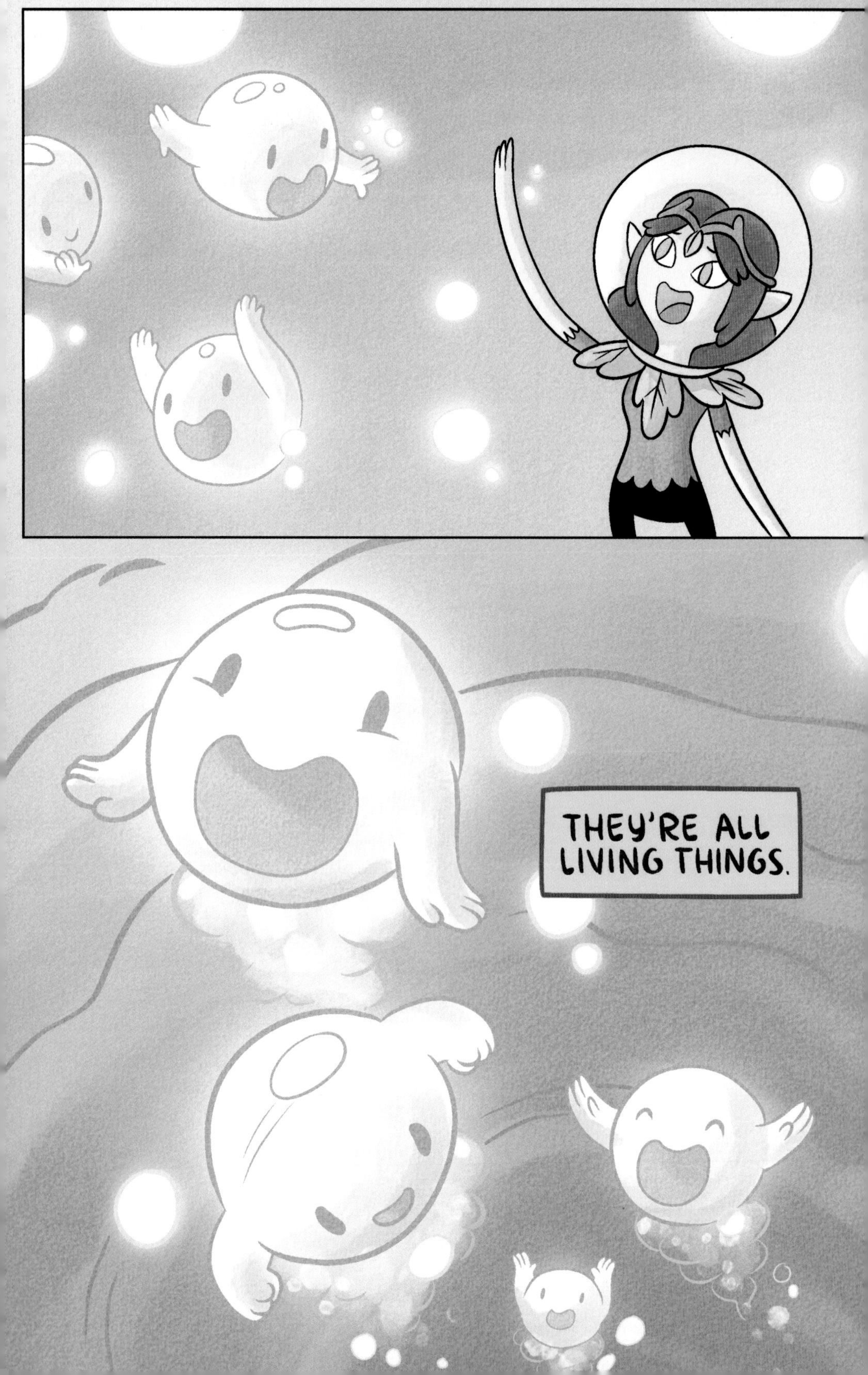
THEY'RE ALL LIVING THINGS.

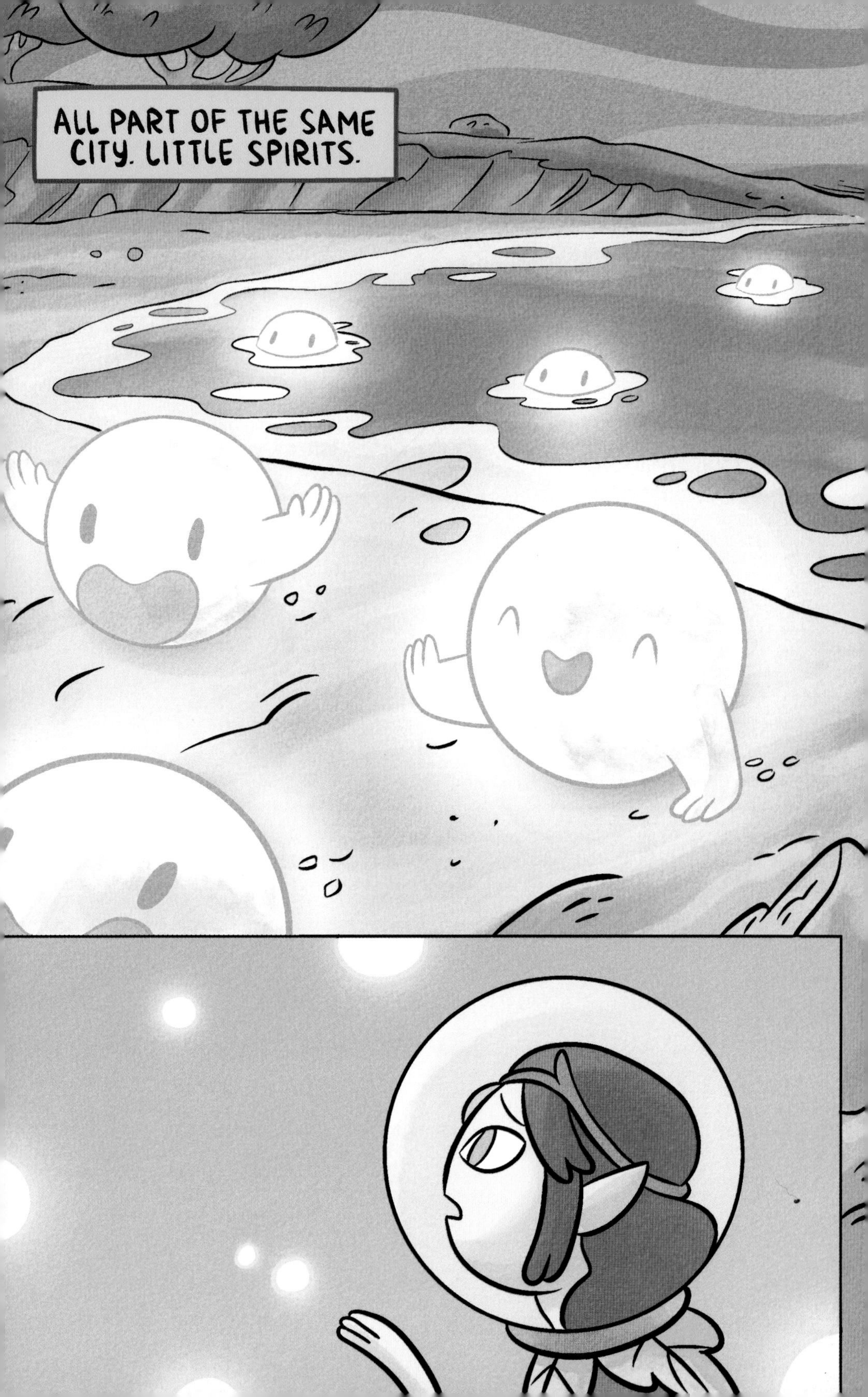
ALL PART OF THE SAME CITY. LITTLE SPIRITS.

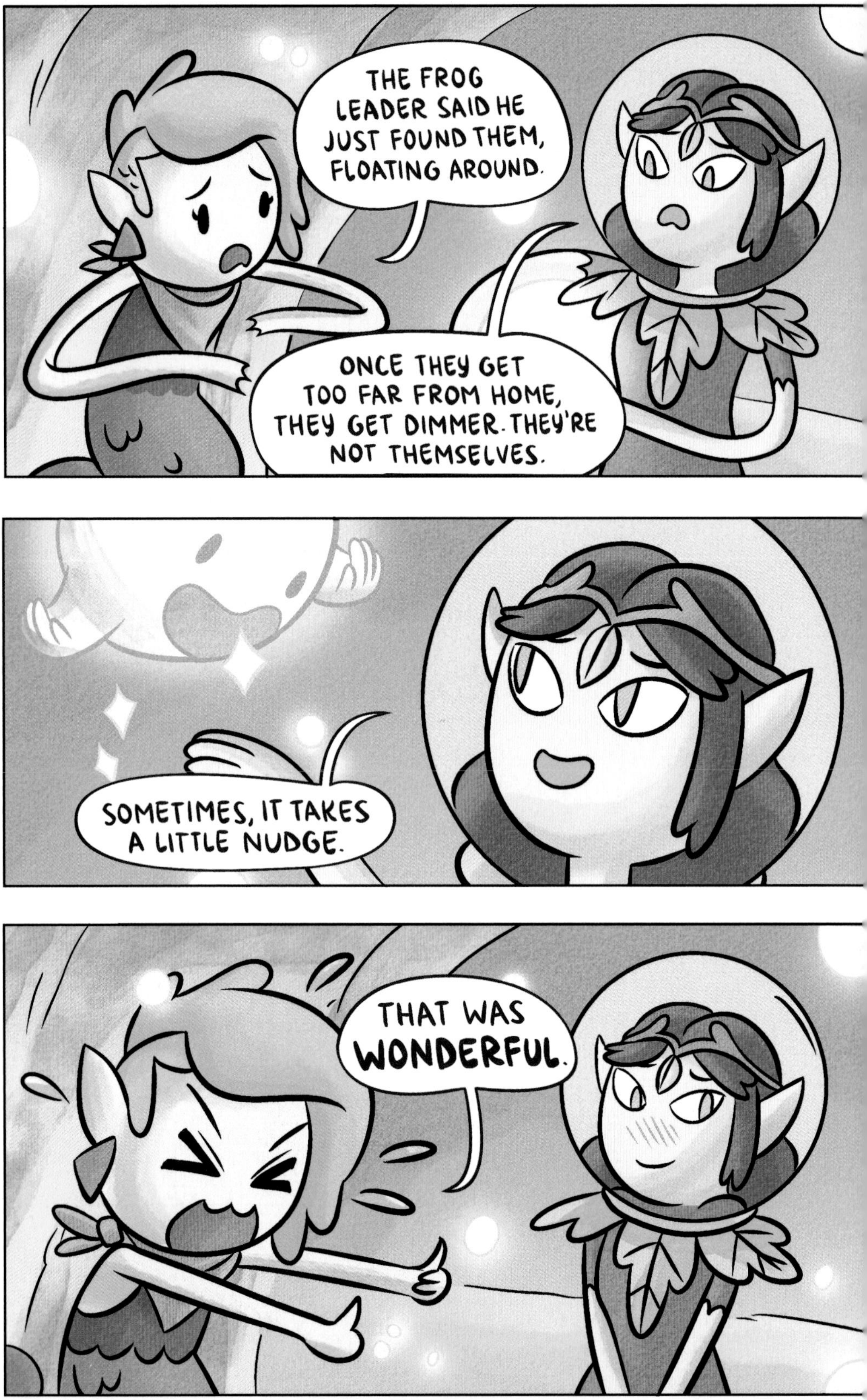
THE FROG LEADER SAID HE JUST FOUND THEM, FLOATING AROUND.
ONCE THEY GET TOO FAR FROM HOME, THEY GET DIMMER. THEY'RE NOT THEMSELVES.
SOMETIMES, IT TAKES A LITTLE NUDGE.
THAT WAS WONDERFUL.

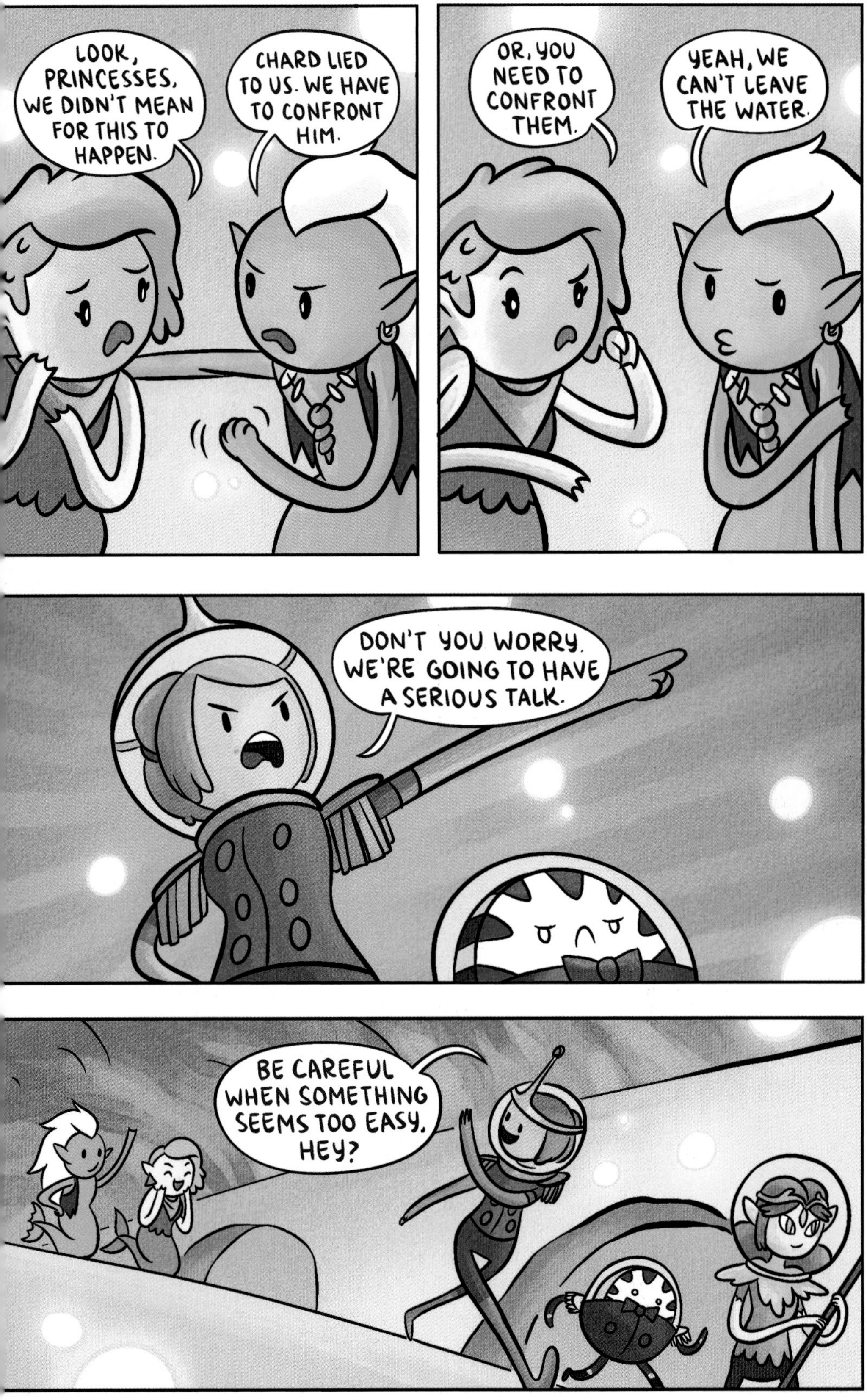
LOOK, PRINCESSES, WE DIDN'T MEAN FOR THIS TO HAPPEN.
CHARD LIED TO US. WE HAVE TO CONFRONT HIM.
OR, YOU NEED TO CONFRONT THEM.
YEAH, WE CAN'T LEAVE THE WATER.
DON'T YOU WORRY. WE'RE GOING TO HAVE A SERIOUS TALK.
BE CAREFUL WHEN SOMETHING SEEMS TOO EASY, HEY?

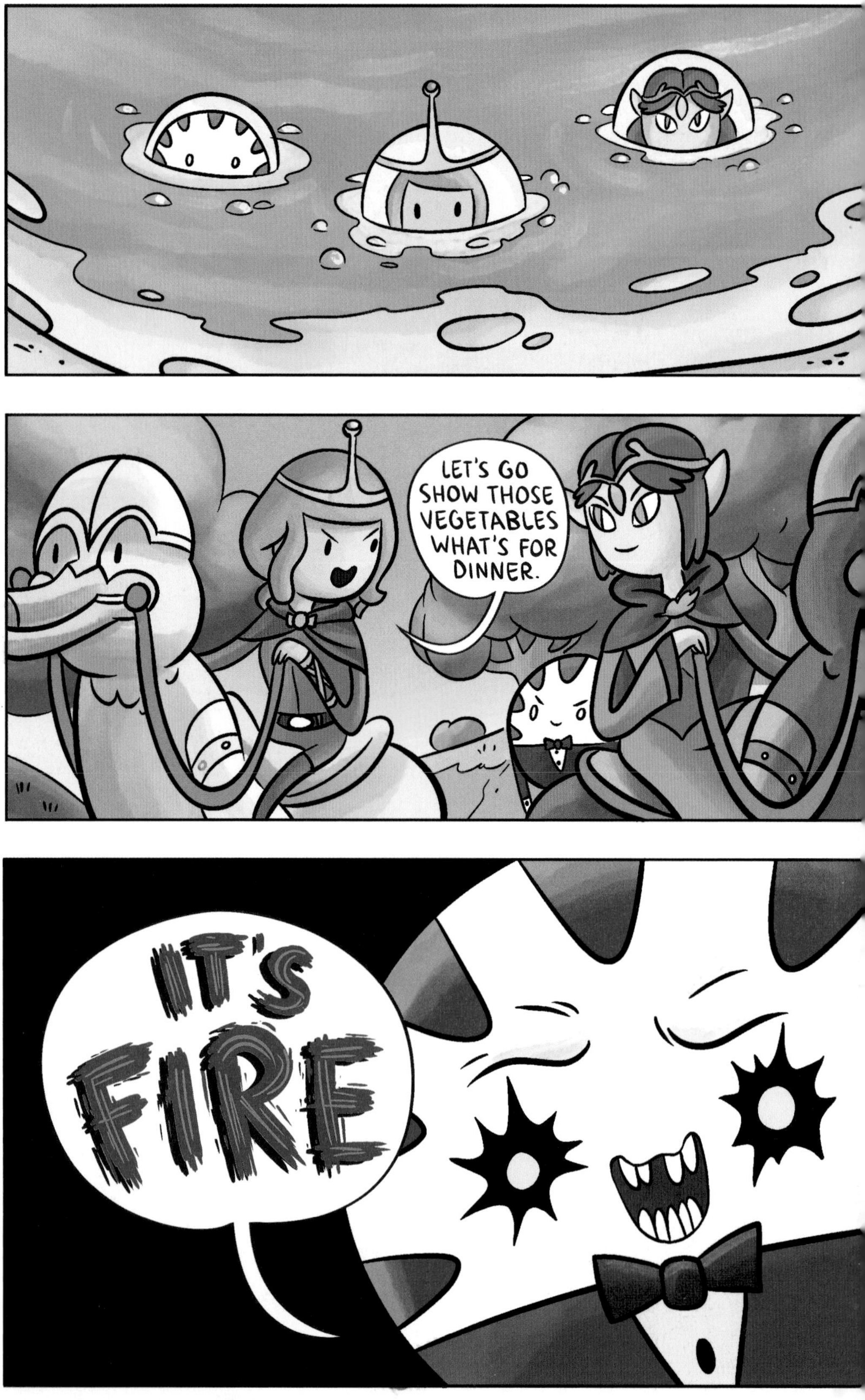
LET'S GO SHOW THOSE VEGETABLES WHAT'S FOR DINNER.
IT'S FIRE

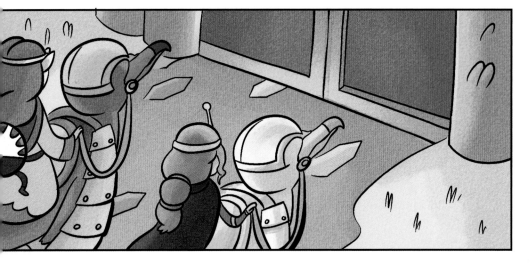

SALLY, GILLIAN-- HEAD BACK TO THE CITY. MAKE SURE THE LIGHTS FIND THEIR WAY, ALRIGHT?

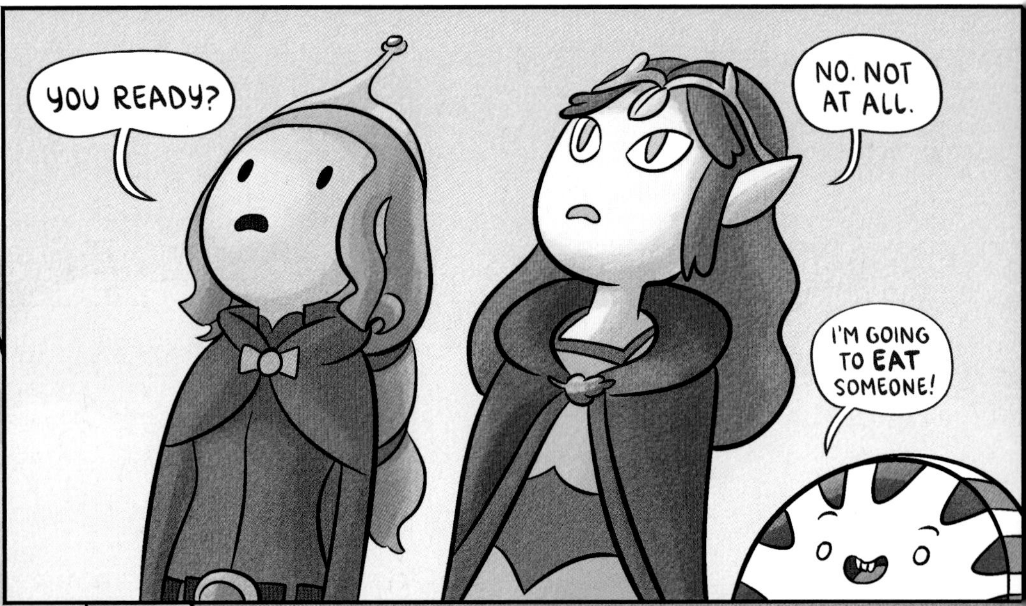
YOU READY?
NO. NOT AT ALL.
I'M GOING TO EAT SOMEONE!
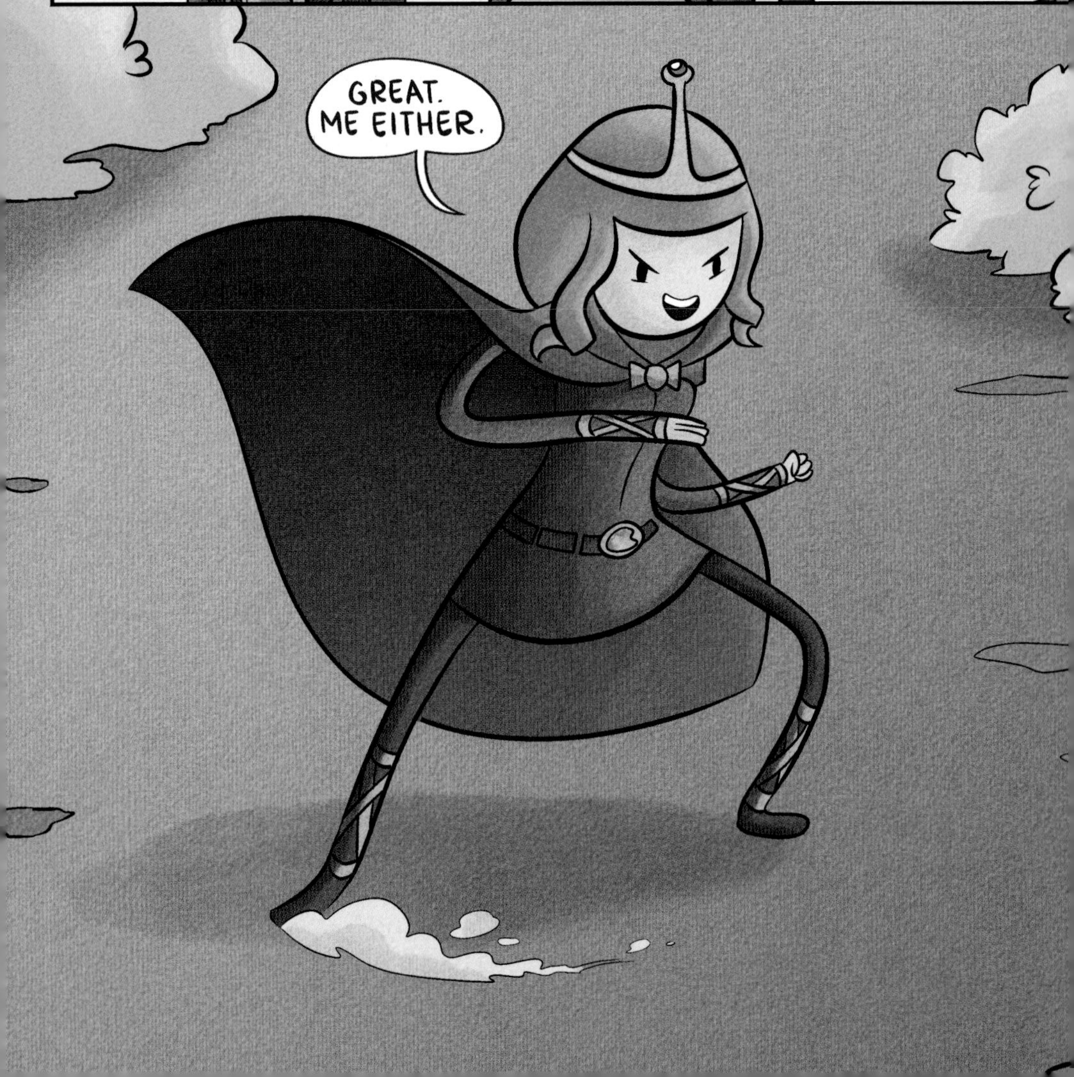
GREAT. ME EITHER.

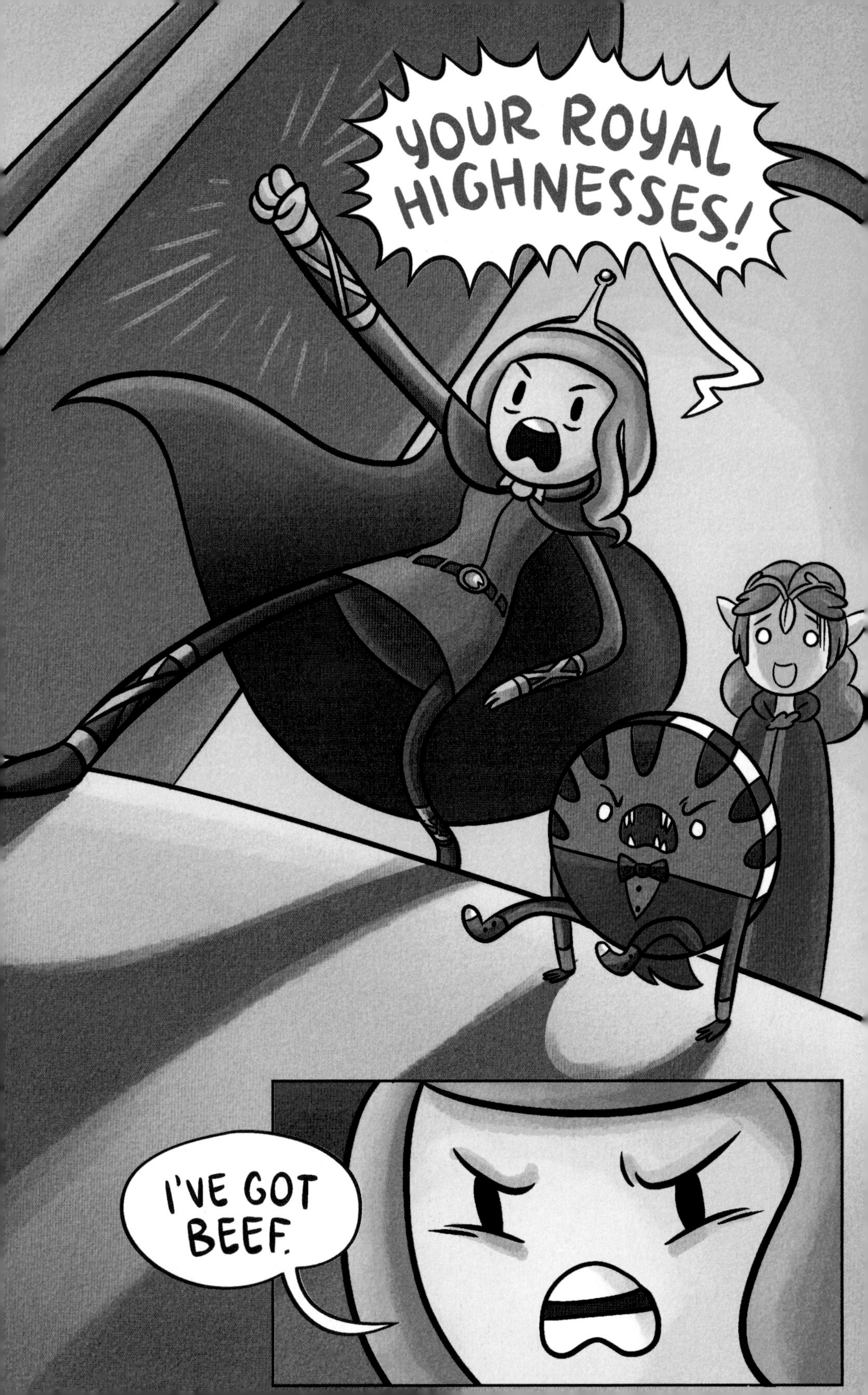
YOUR ROYAL HIGHNESSES!
I'VE GOT BEEF.

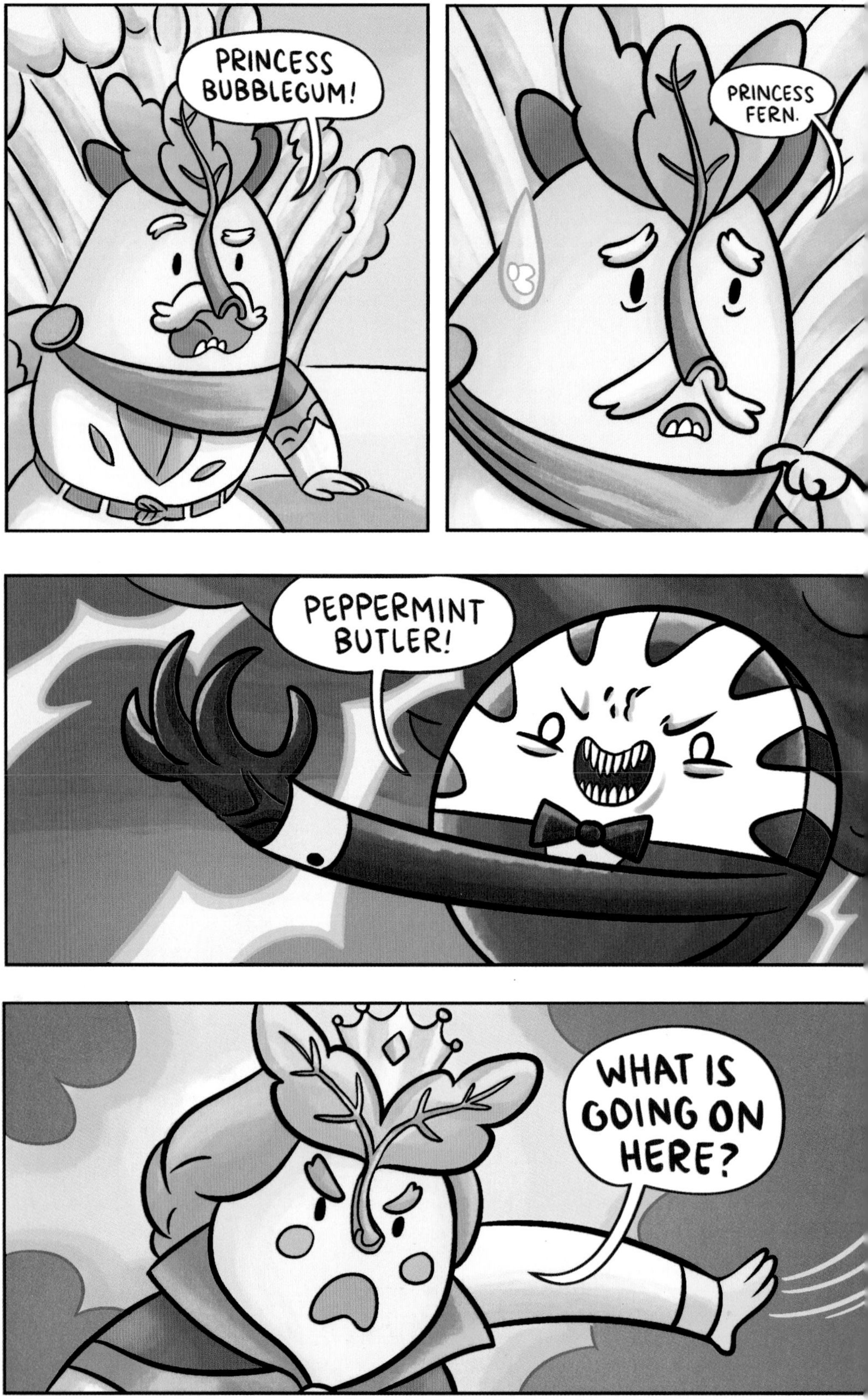
PRINCESS BUBBLEGUM!
PRINCESS FERN.
PEPPERMINT BUTLER!
WHAT IS GOING ON HERE?

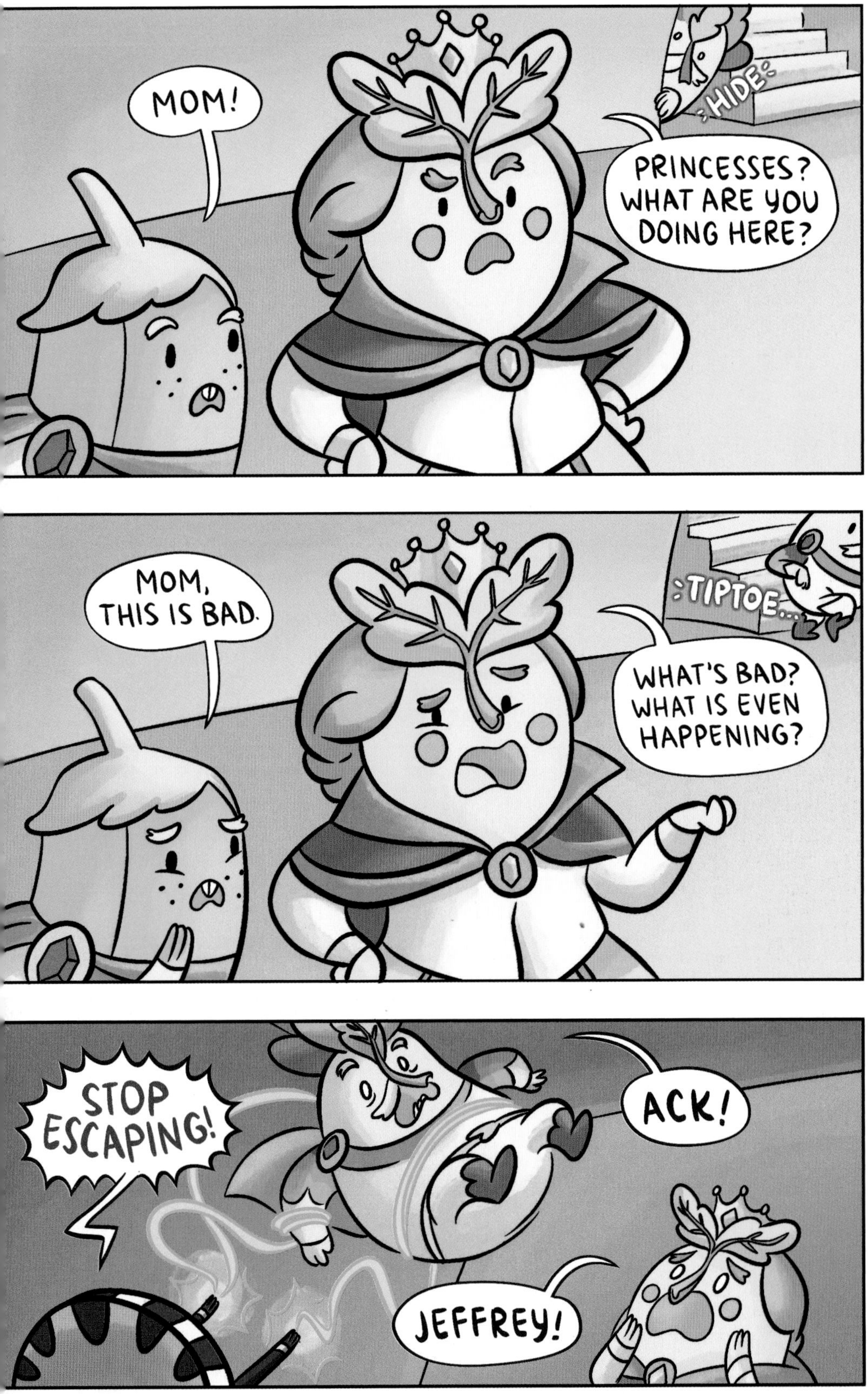
MOM!
HIDE
PRINCESSES? WHAT ARE YOU DOING HERE?
MOM, THIS IS BAD.
TIPTOE...
WHAT'S BAD? WHAT IS EVEN HAPPENING?
STOP ESCAPING!
ACK!
JEFFREY!

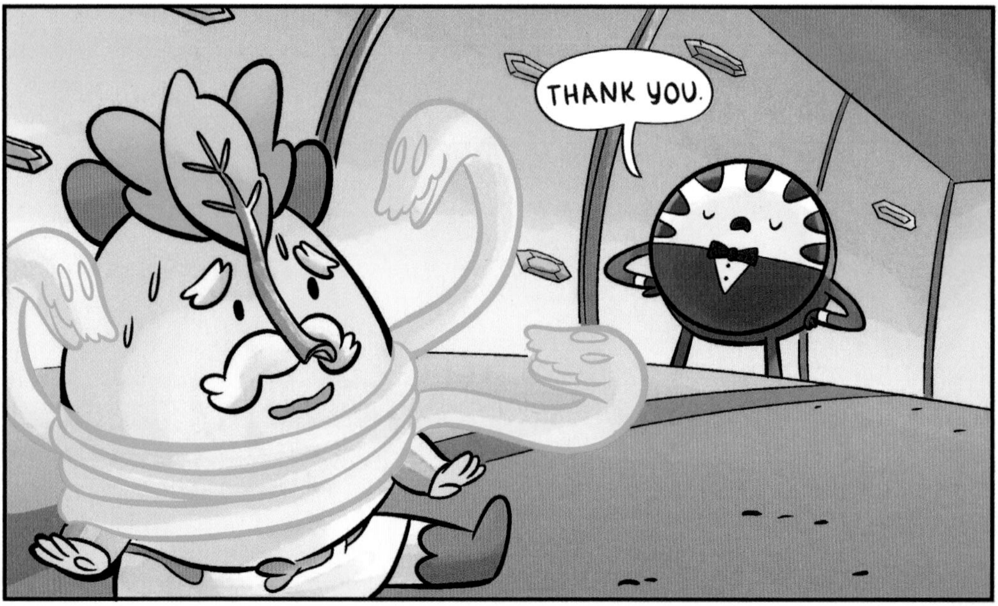
THANK YOU.

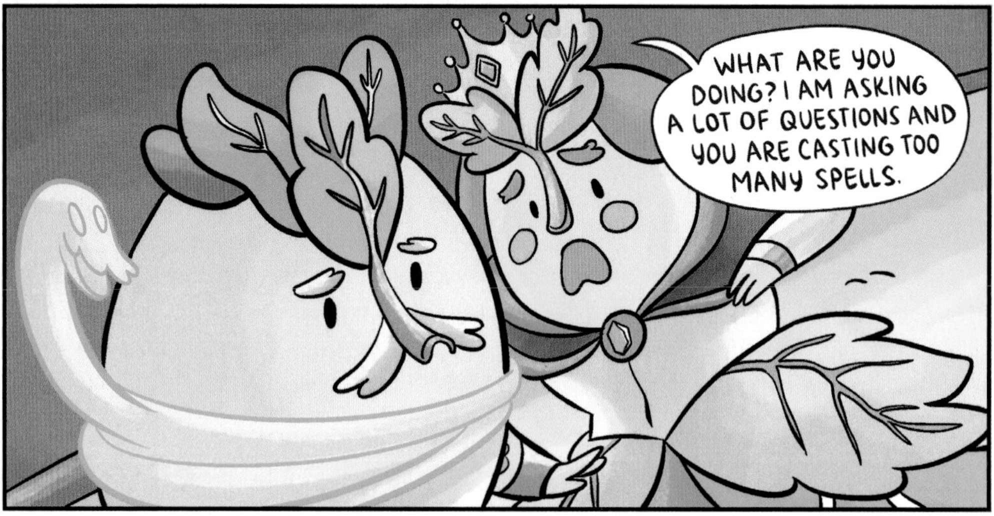
WHAT ARE YOU DOING? I AM ASKING A LOT OF QUESTIONS AND YOU ARE CASTING TOO MANY SPELLS.

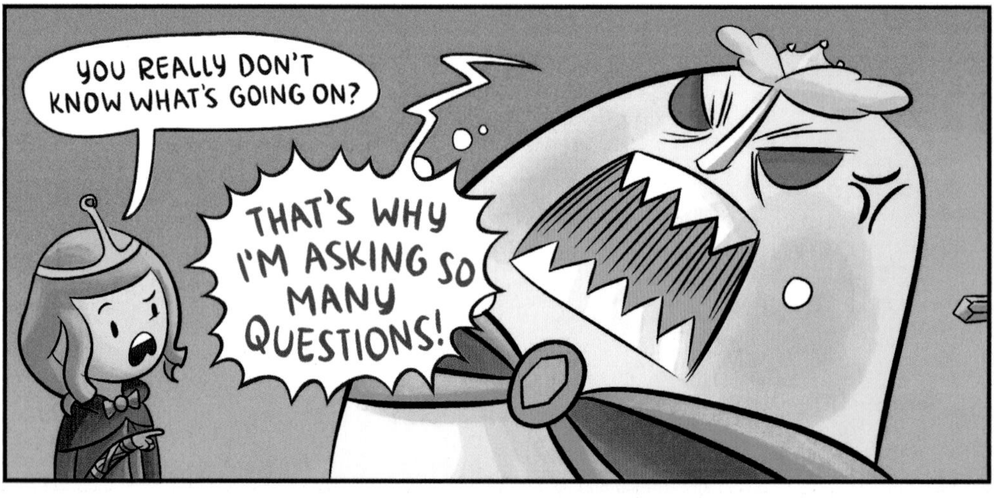
YOU REALLY DON'T KNOW WHAT'S GOING ON?
THAT'S WHY I'M ASKING SO MANY QUESTIONS!

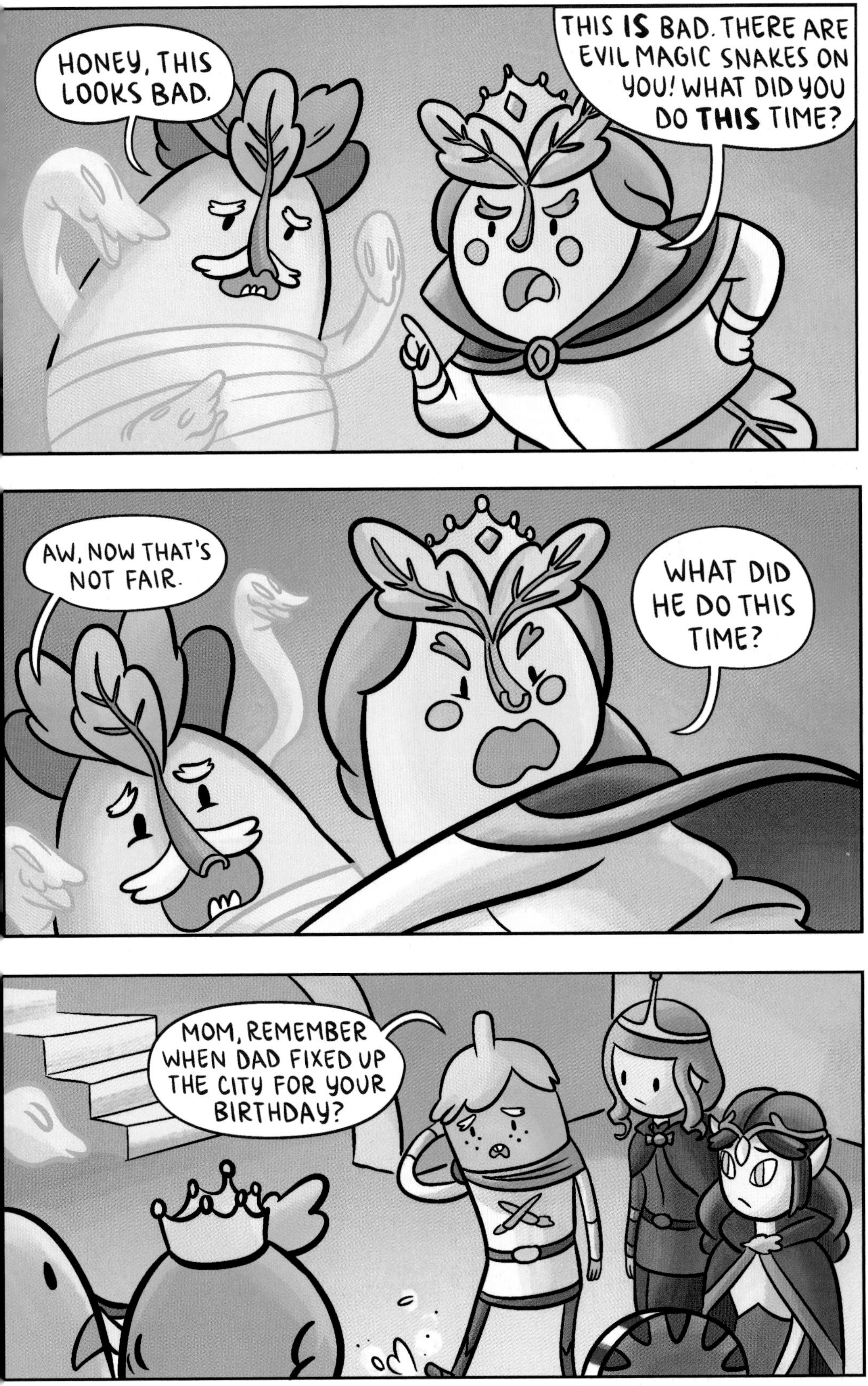
HONEY, THIS LOOKS BAD.
THIS **IS** BAD. THERE ARE EVIL MAGIC SNAKES ON YOU! WHAT DID YOU DO **THIS** TIME?
AW, NOW THAT'S NOT FAIR.
WHAT DID HE DO THIS TIME?
MOM, REMEMBER WHEN DAD FIXED UP THE CITY FOR YOUR BIRTHDAY?

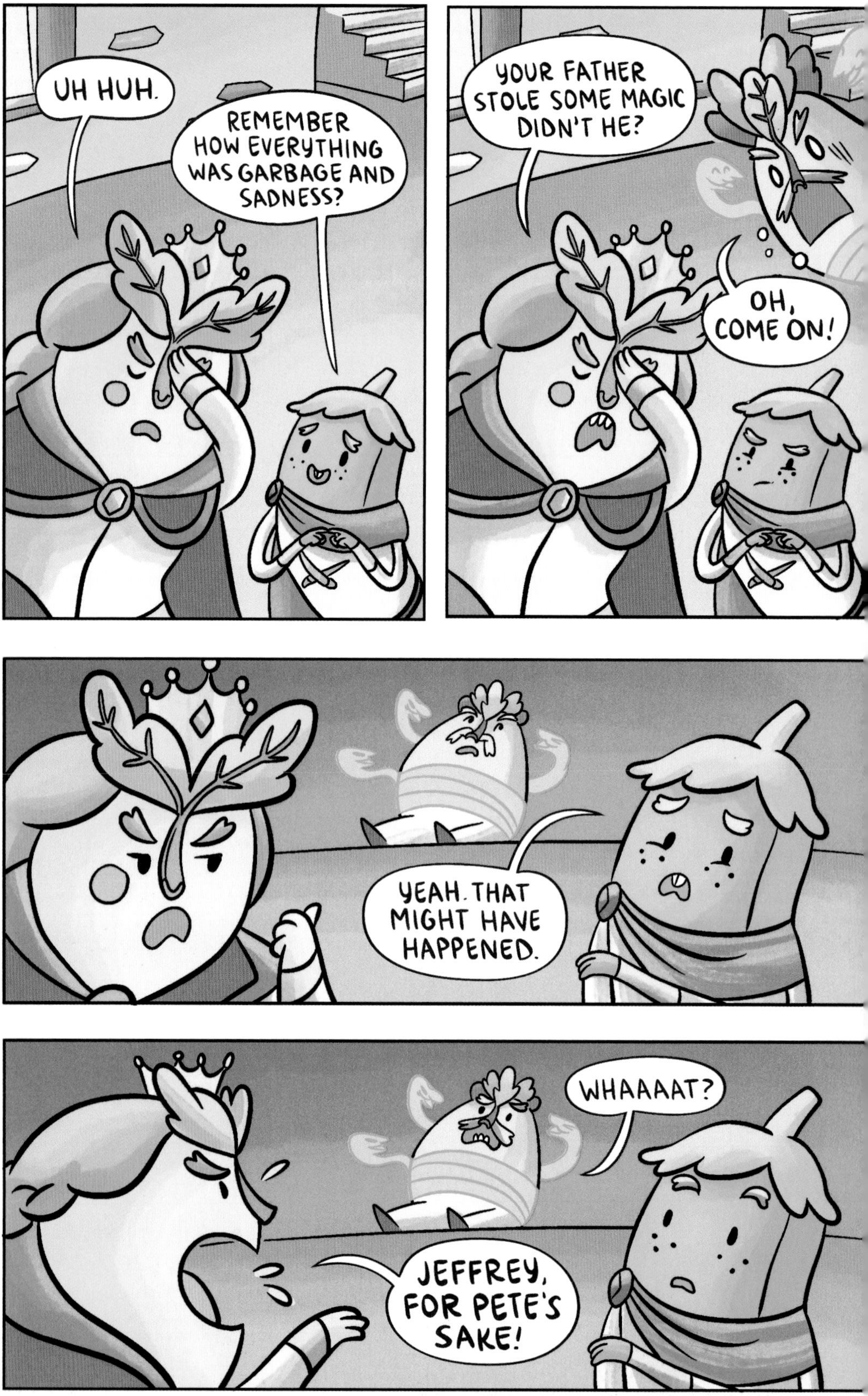
UH HUH.
REMEMBER HOW EVERYTHING WAS GARBAGE AND SADNESS?
YOUR FATHER STOLE SOME MAGIC DIDN'T HE?
OH, COME ON!
YEAH. THAT MIGHT HAVE HAPPENED.
WHAAAAT?
JEFFREY, FOR PETE'S SAKE!

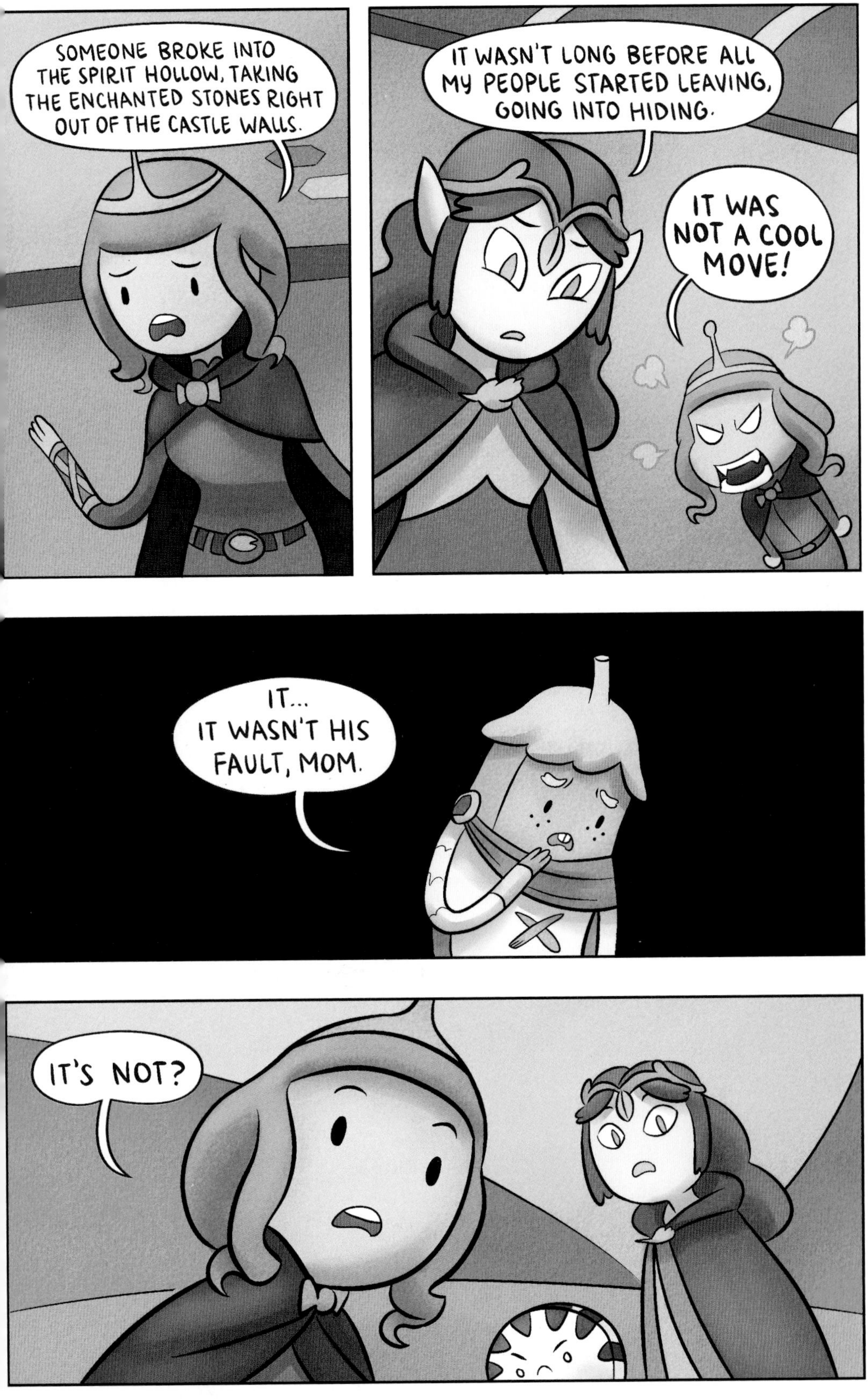
SOMEONE BROKE INTO THE SPIRIT HOLLOW, TAKING THE ENCHANTED STONES RIGHT OUT OF THE CASTLE WALLS.
IT WASN'T LONG BEFORE ALL MY PEOPLE STARTED LEAVING, GOING INTO HIDING.
IT WAS NOT A COOL MOVE!
IT... IT WASN'T HIS FAULT, MOM.
IT'S NOT?

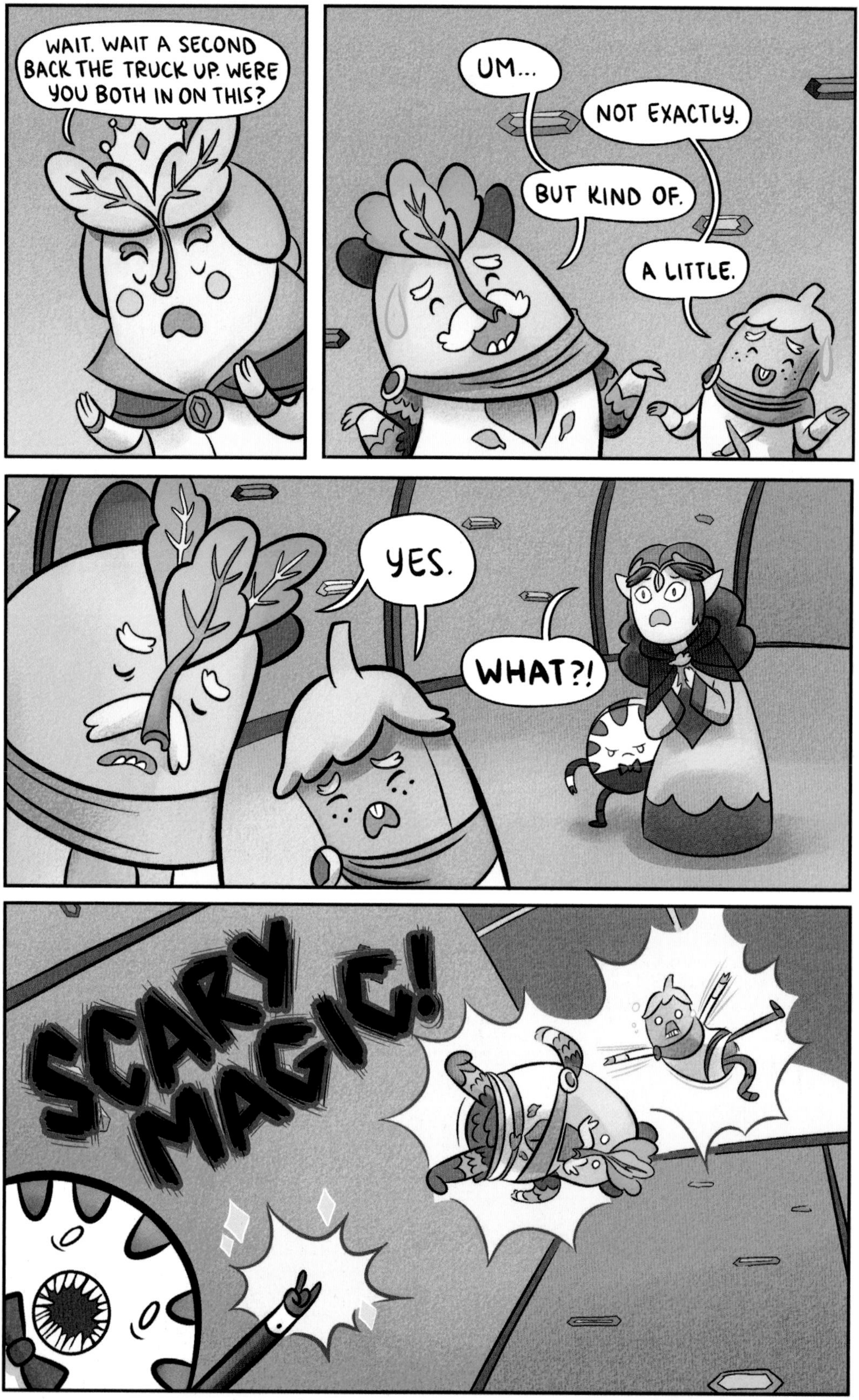
WAIT. WAIT A SECOND BACK THE TRUCK UP. WERE YOU BOTH IN ON THIS?
UM...
NOT EXACTLY.
BUT KIND OF.
A LITTLE.
YES.
WHAT?!
SCARY MAGIC!

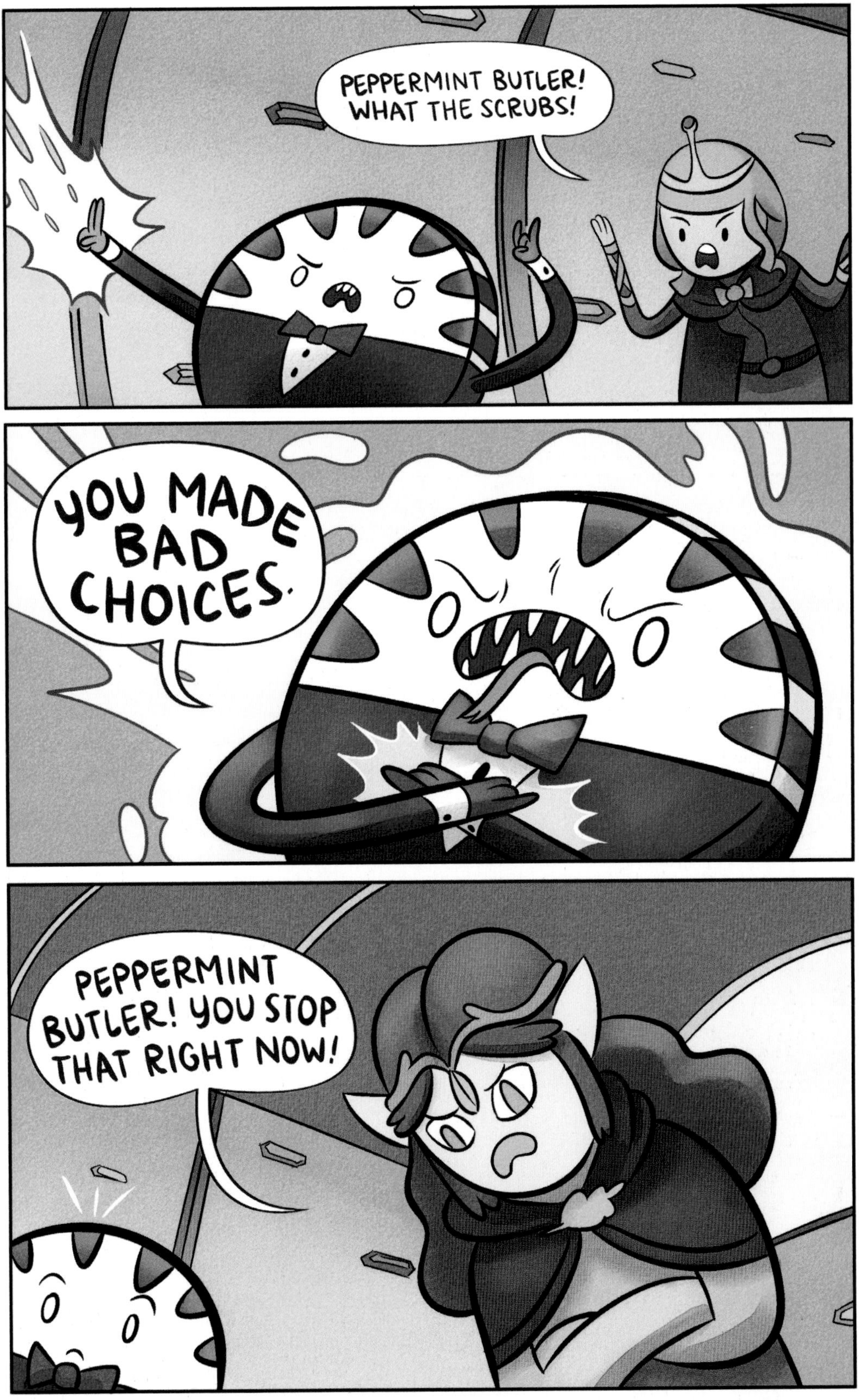
PEPPERMINT BUTLER! WHAT THE SCRUBS!
YOU MADE BAD CHOICES.
PEPPERMINT BUTLER! YOU STOP THAT RIGHT NOW!

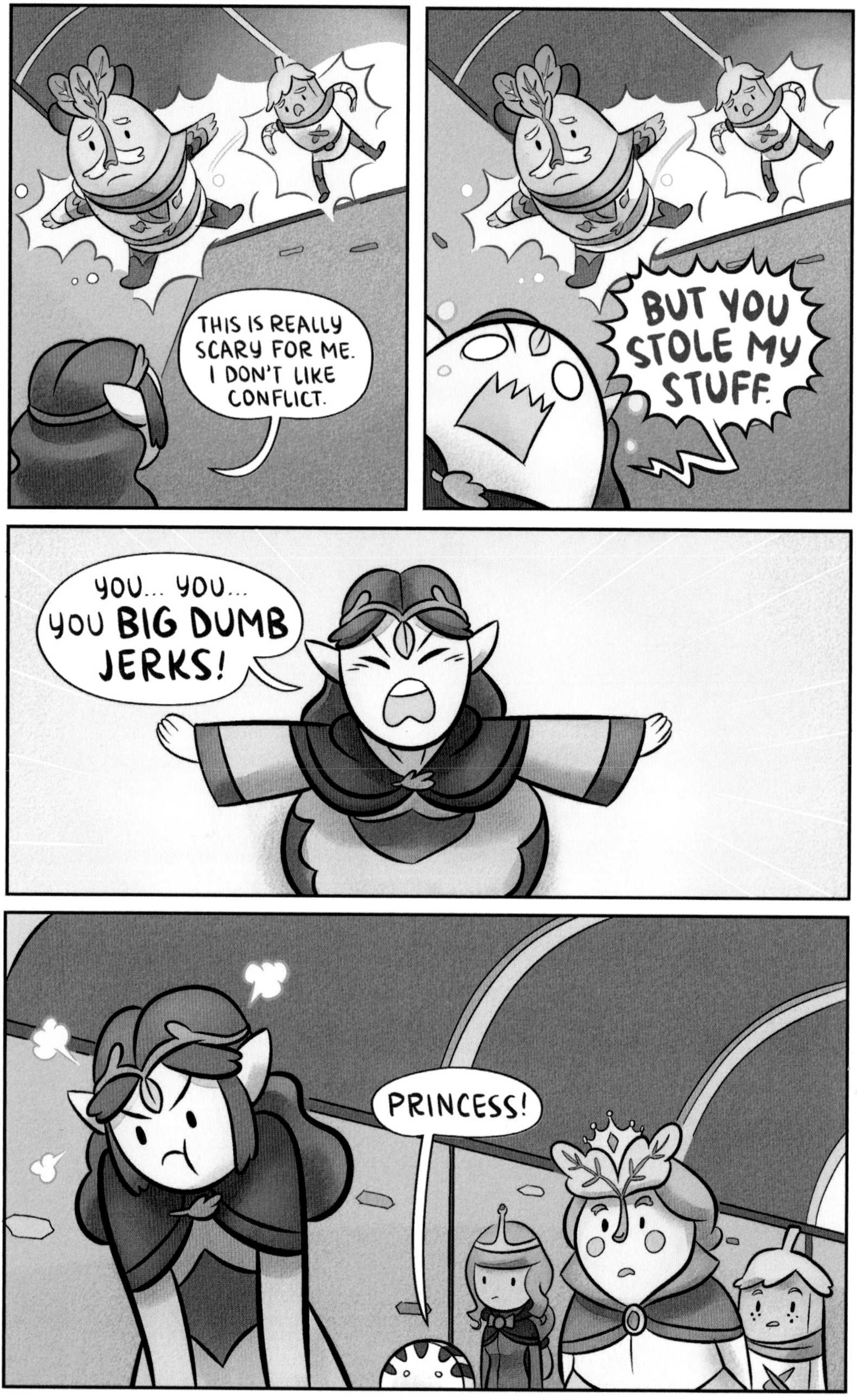
THIS IS REALLY SCARY FOR ME. I DON'T LIKE CONFLICT.
BUT YOU STOLE MY STUFF.
YOU... YOU... YOU BIG DUMB JERKS!
PRINCESS!

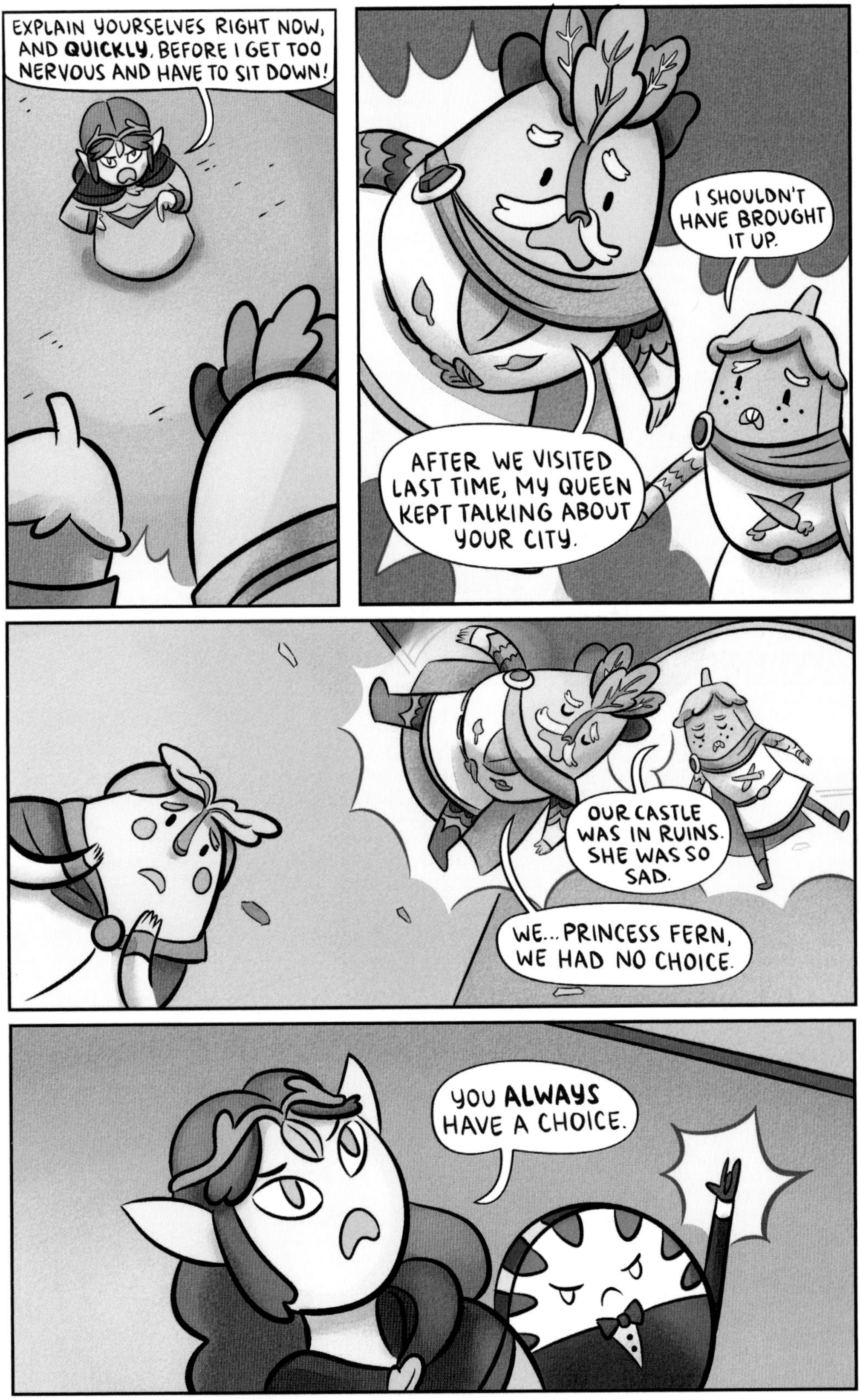
EXPLAIN YOURSELVES RIGHT NOW, AND **QUICKLY**, BEFORE I GET TOO NERVOUS AND HAVE TO SIT DOWN!
I SHOULDN'T HAVE BROUGHT IT UP.
AFTER WE VISITED LAST TIME, MY QUEEN KEPT TALKING ABOUT YOUR CITY.
OUR CASTLE WAS IN RUINS. SHE WAS SO SAD.
WE... PRINCESS FERN, WE HAD NO CHOICE.
YOU **ALWAYS** HAVE A CHOICE.

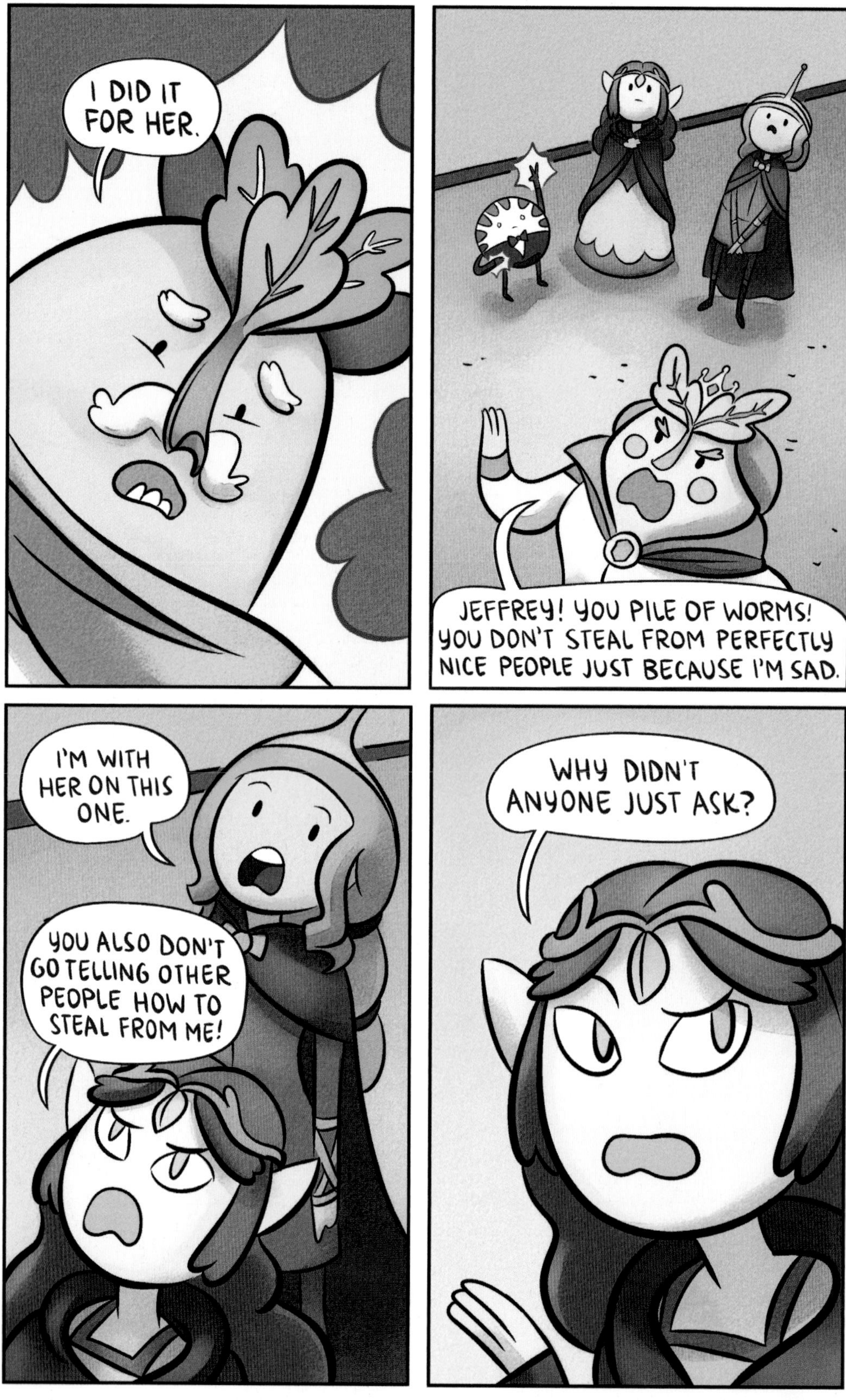
I DID IT FOR HER.
JEFFREY! YOU PILE OF WORMS! YOU DON'T STEAL FROM PERFECTLY NICE PEOPLE JUST BECAUSE I'M SAD.
I'M WITH HER ON THIS ONE.
YOU ALSO DON'T GO TELLING OTHER PEOPLE HOW TO STEAL FROM ME!
WHY DIDN'T ANYONE JUST ASK?

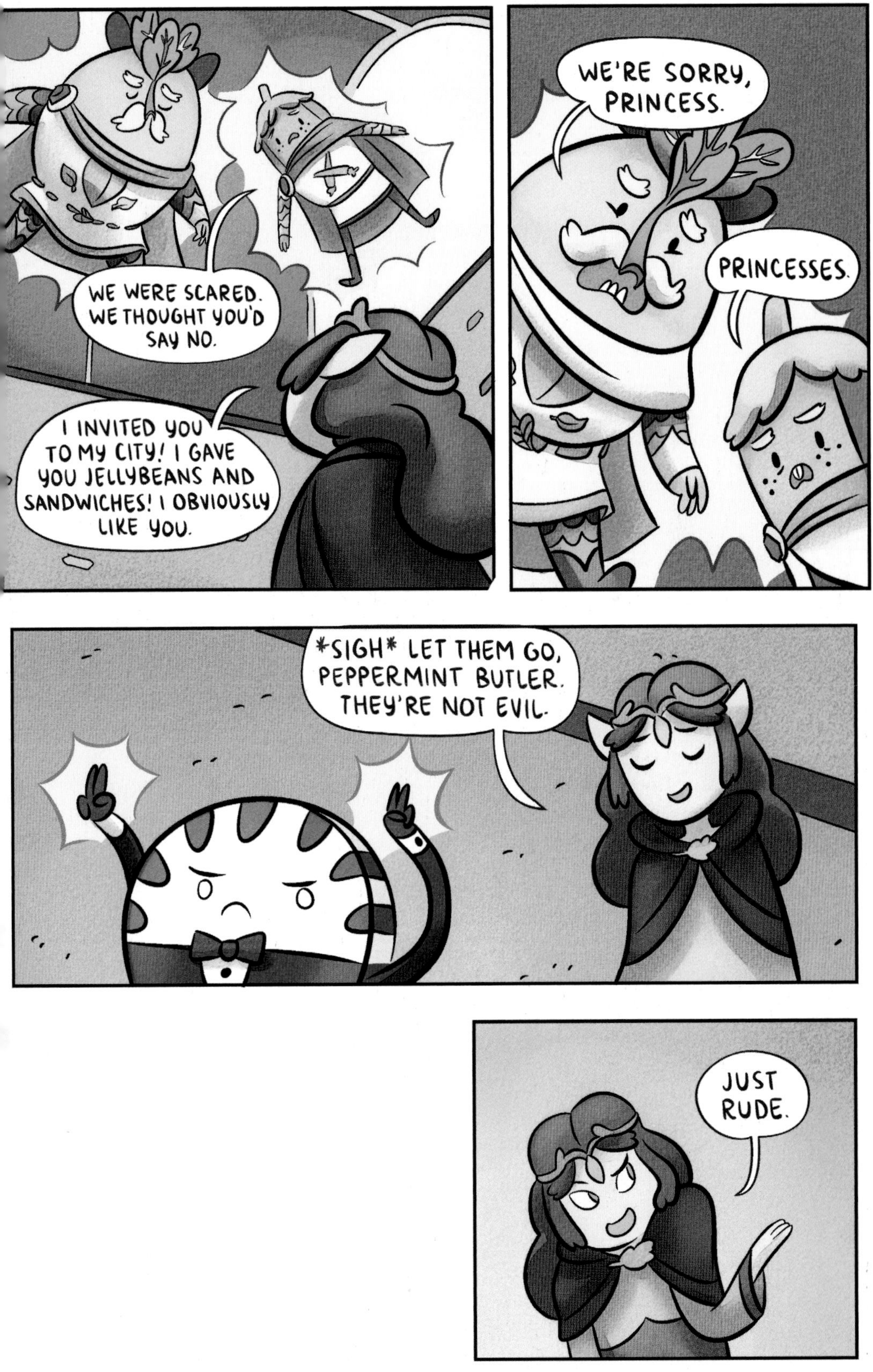

WE WERE SCARED. WE THOUGHT YOU'D SAY NO.
I INVITED YOU TO MY CITY! I GAVE YOU JELLYBEANS AND SANDWICHES! I OBVIOUSLY LIKE YOU.
WE'RE SORRY, PRINCESS.
PRINCESSES.
SIGH LET THEM GO, PEPPERMINT BUTLER. THEY'RE NOT EVIL.
JUST RUDE.

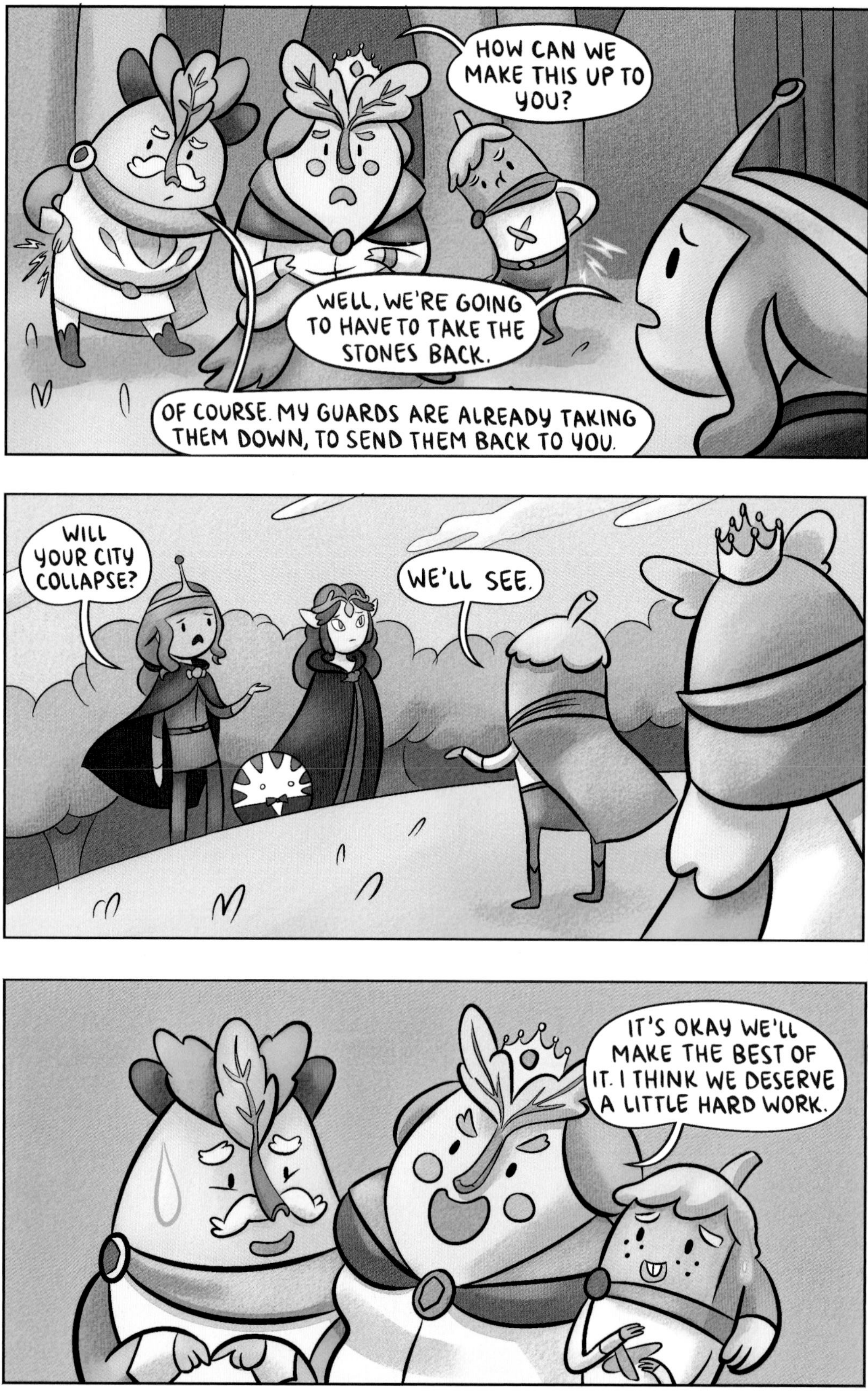
HOW CAN WE MAKE THIS UP TO YOU?
WELL, WE'RE GOING TO HAVE TO TAKE THE STONES BACK.
OF COURSE. MY GUARDS ARE ALREADY TAKING THEM DOWN, TO SEND THEM BACK TO YOU.
WILL YOUR CITY COLLAPSE?
WE'LL SEE.
IT'S OKAY WE'LL MAKE THE BEST OF IT. I THINK WE DESERVE A LITTLE HARD WORK.

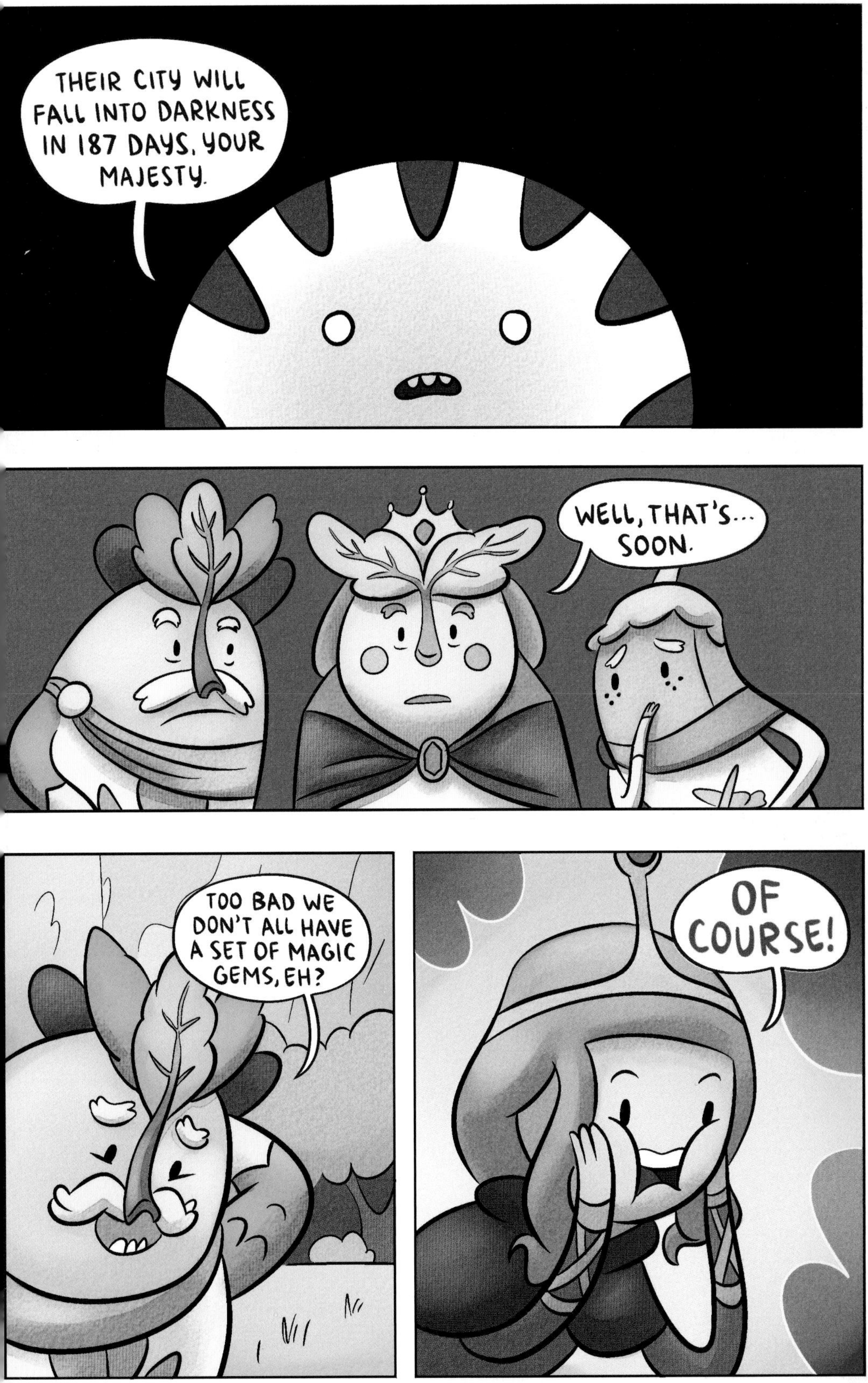
THEIR CITY WILL FALL INTO DARKNESS IN 187 DAYS, YOUR MAJESTY.
WELL, THAT'S... SOON.
TOO BAD WE DON'T ALL HAVE A SET OF MAGIC GEMS, EH?
OF COURSE!

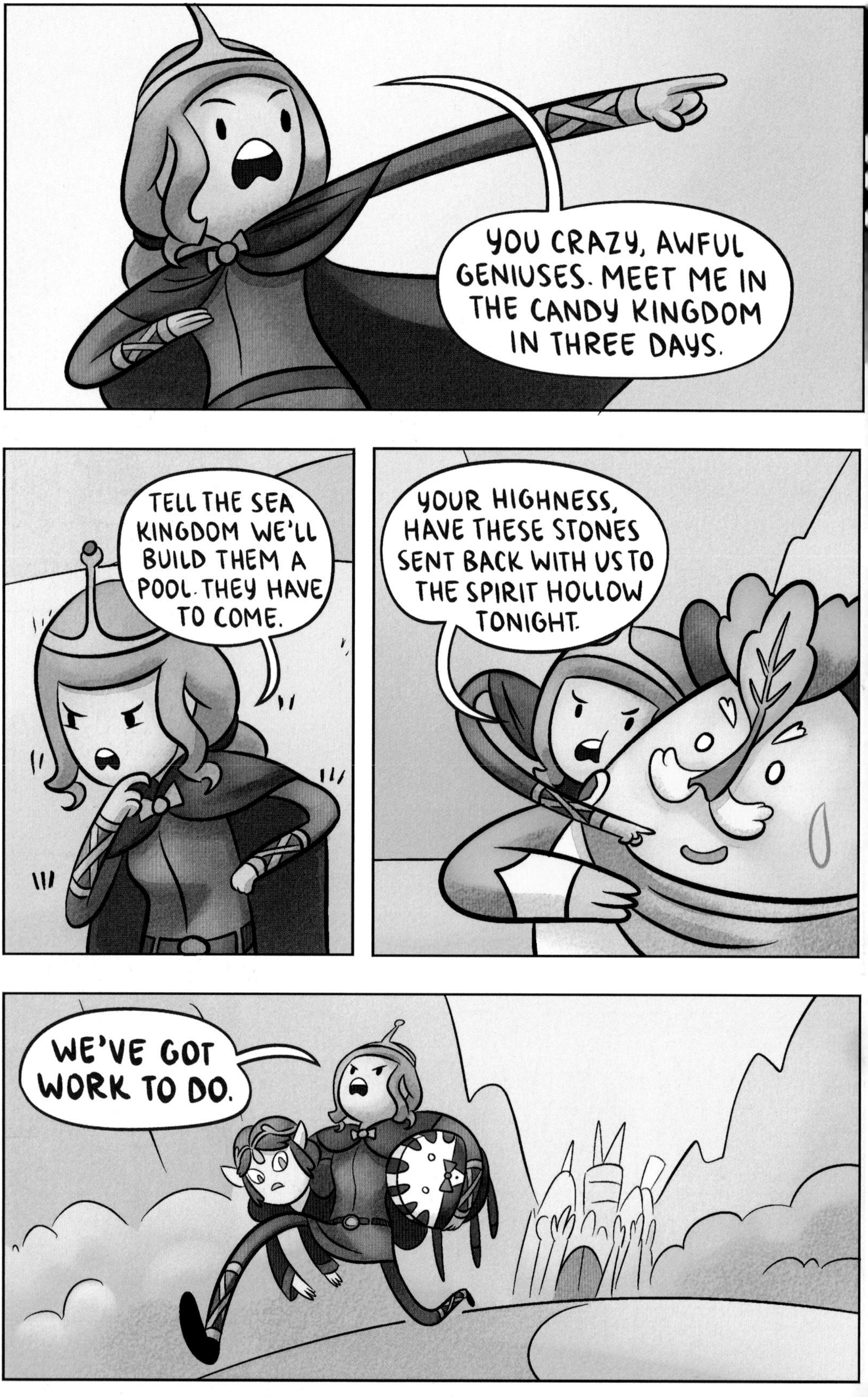
YOU CRAZY, AWFUL GENIUSES. MEET ME IN THE CANDY KINGDOM IN THREE DAYS.
TELL THE SEA KINGDOM WE'LL BUILD THEM A POOL. THEY HAVE TO COME.
YOUR HIGHNESS, HAVE THESE STONES SENT BACK WITH US TO THE SPIRIT HOLLOW TONIGHT.
WE'VE GOT WORK TO DO.

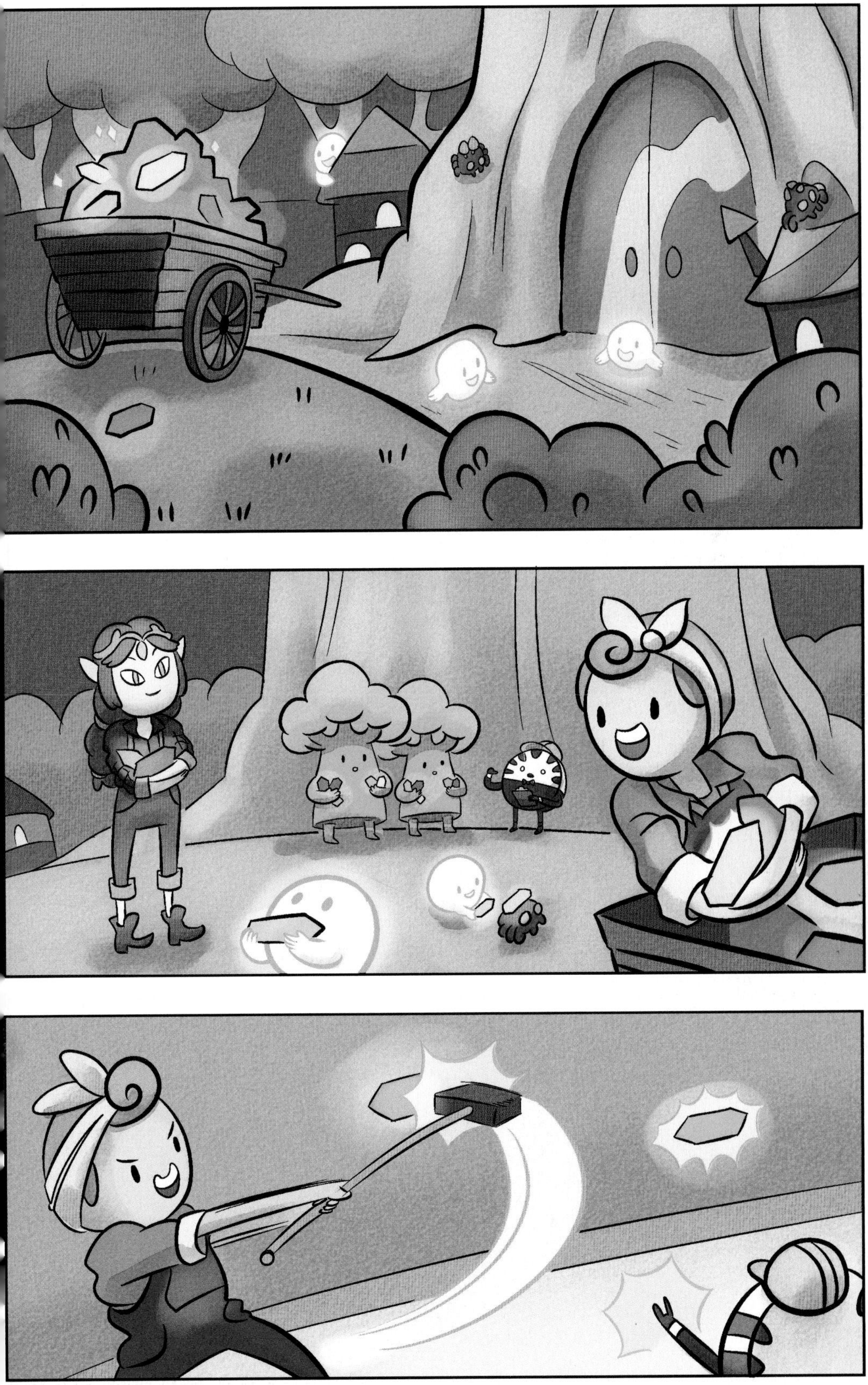

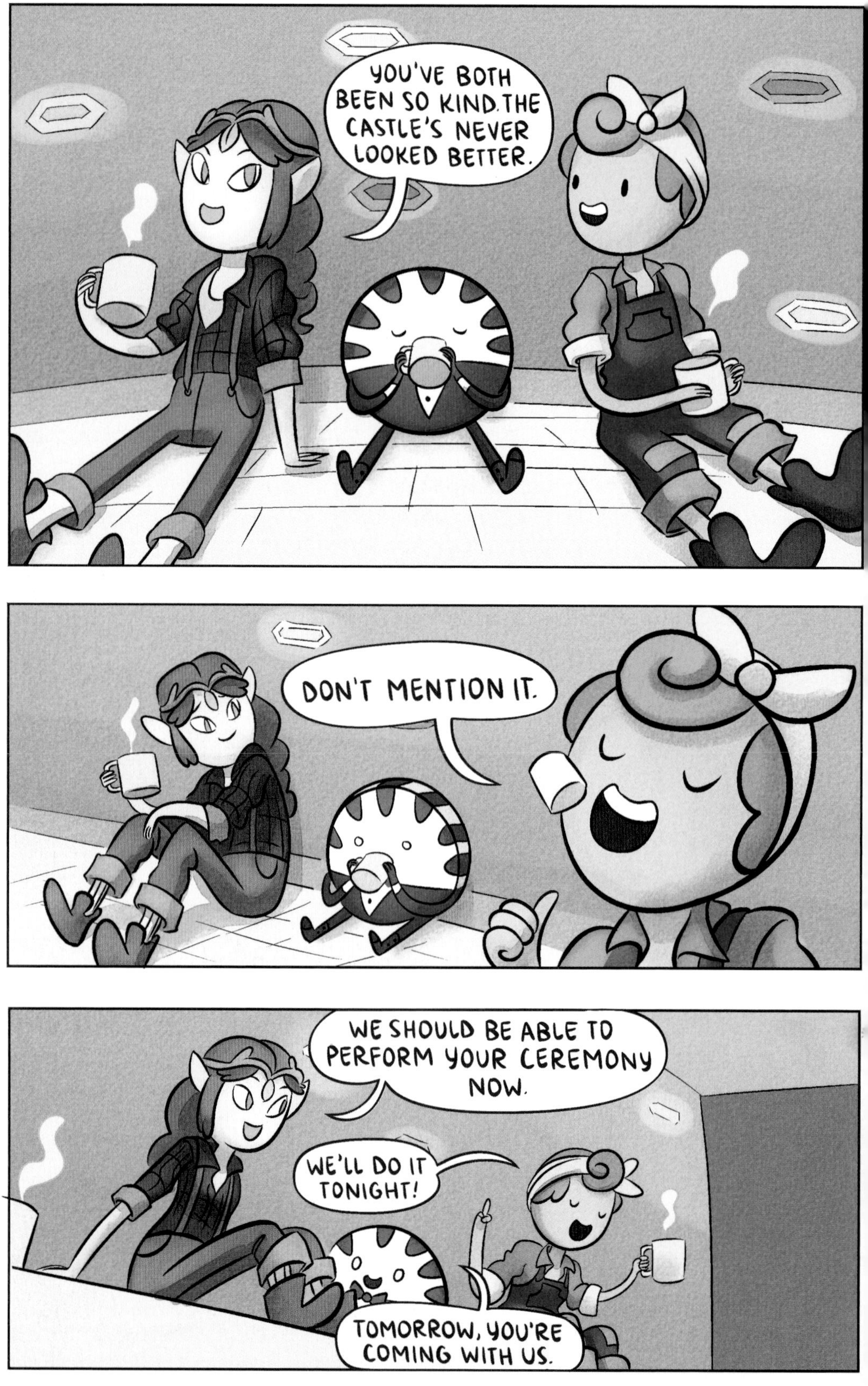
YOU'VE BOTH BEEN SO KIND. THE CASTLE'S NEVER LOOKED BETTER.
DON'T MENTION IT.
WE SHOULD BE ABLE TO PERFORM YOUR CEREMONY NOW.
WE'LL DO IT TONIGHT!
TOMORROW, YOU'RE COMING WITH US.

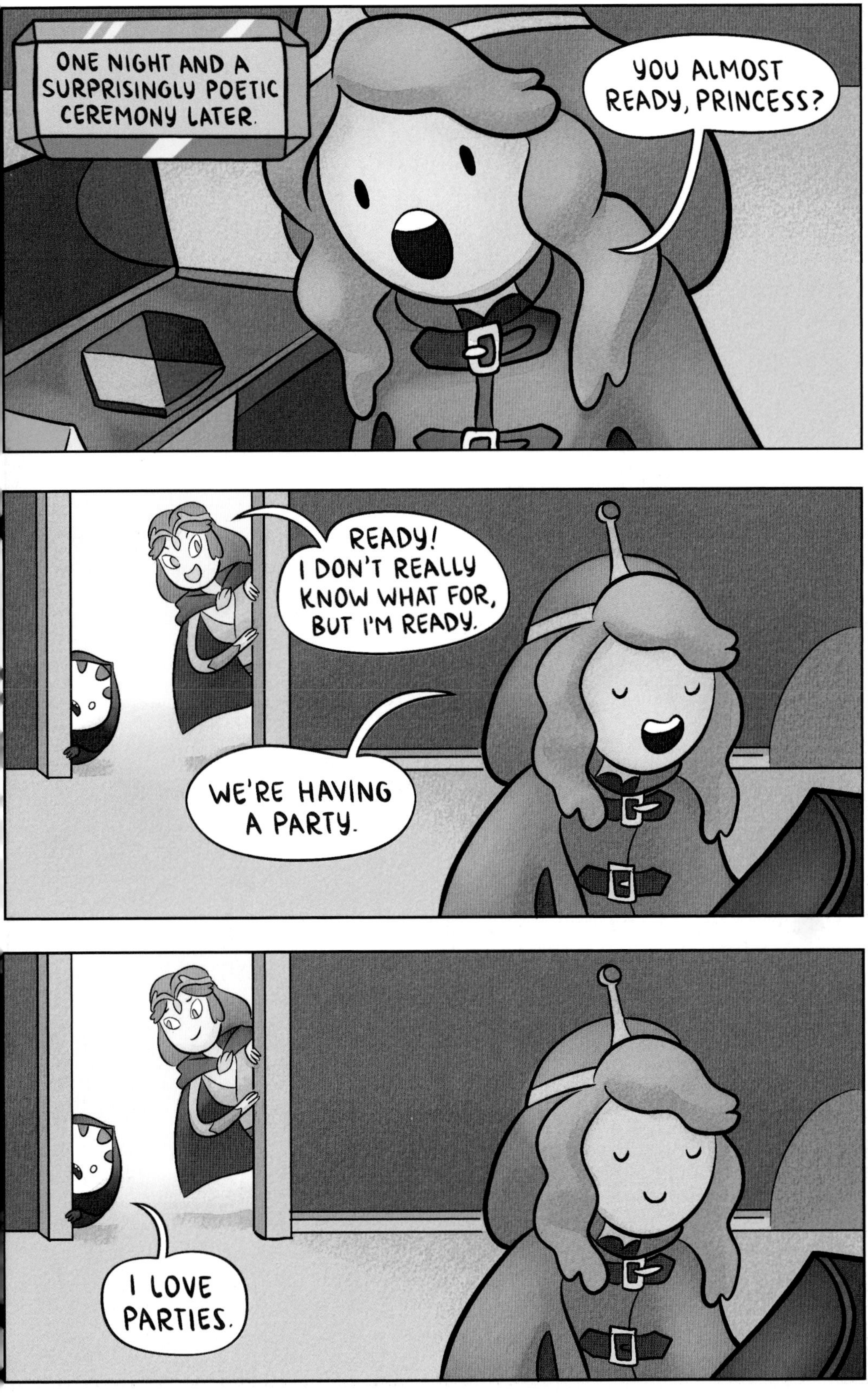
ONE NIGHT AND A SURPRISINGLY POETIC CEREMONY LATER.
YOU ALMOST READY, PRINCESS?
READY! I DON'T REALLY KNOW WHAT FOR, BUT I'M READY.
WE'RE HAVING A PARTY.
I LOVE PARTIES.

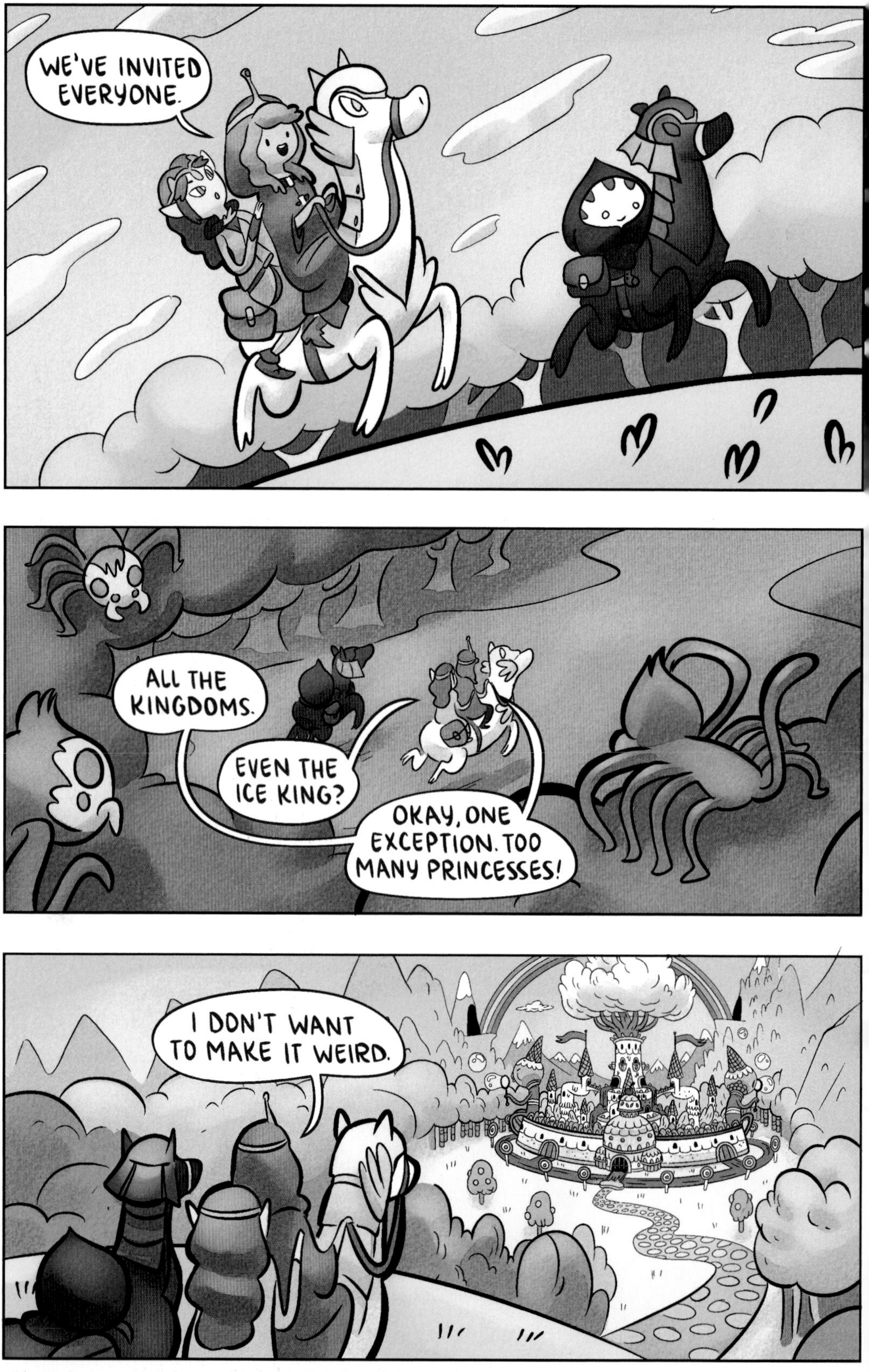
WE'VE INVITED EVERYONE.
ALL THE KINGDOMS.
EVEN THE ICE KING?
OKAY, ONE EXCEPTION. TOO MANY PRINCESSES!
I DON'T WANT TO MAKE IT WEIRD.

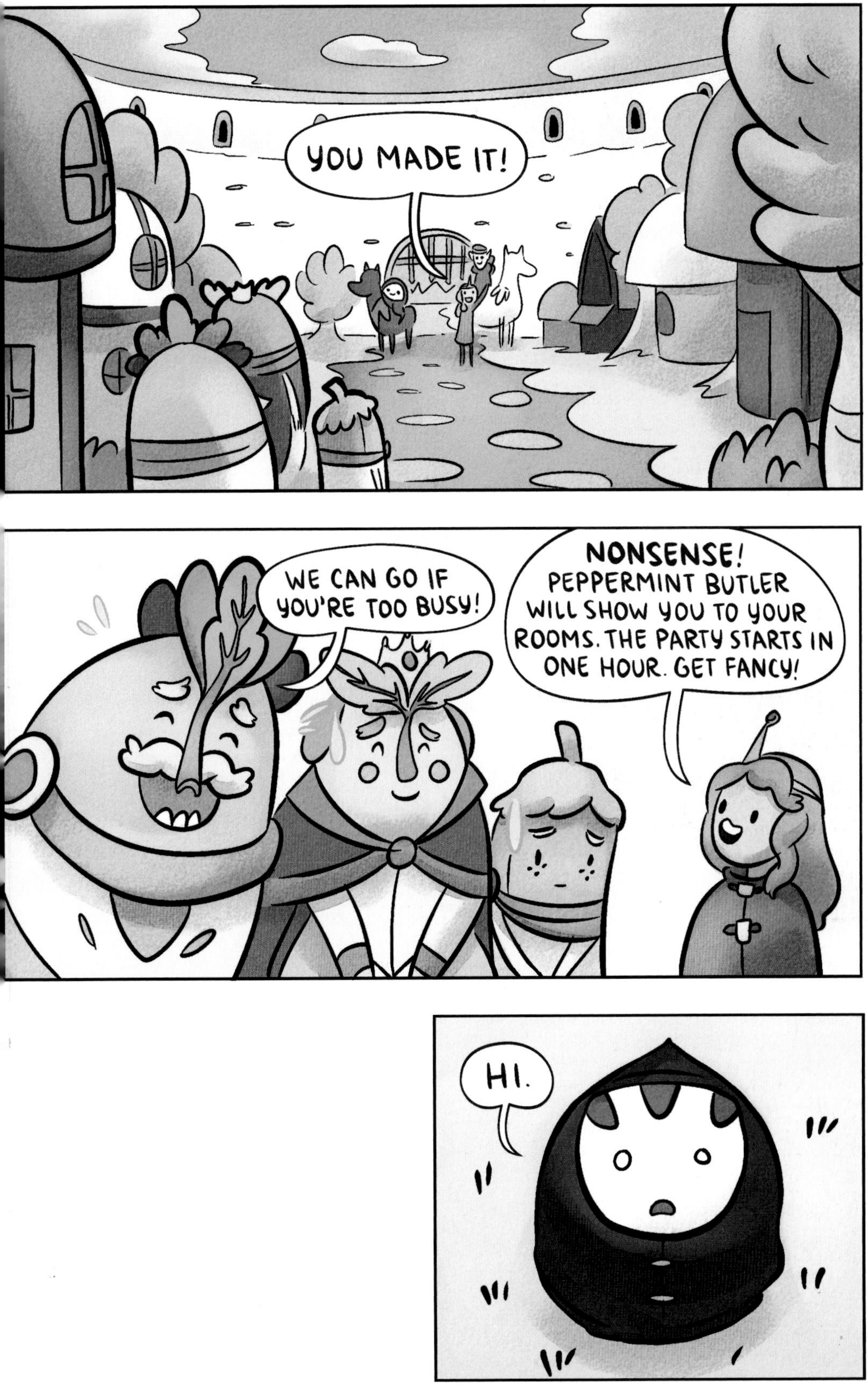
YOU MADE IT!
WE CAN GO IF YOU'RE TOO BUSY!
NONSENSE! PEPPERMINT BUTLER WILL SHOW YOU TO YOUR ROOMS. THE PARTY STARTS IN ONE HOUR. GET FANCY!
HI.

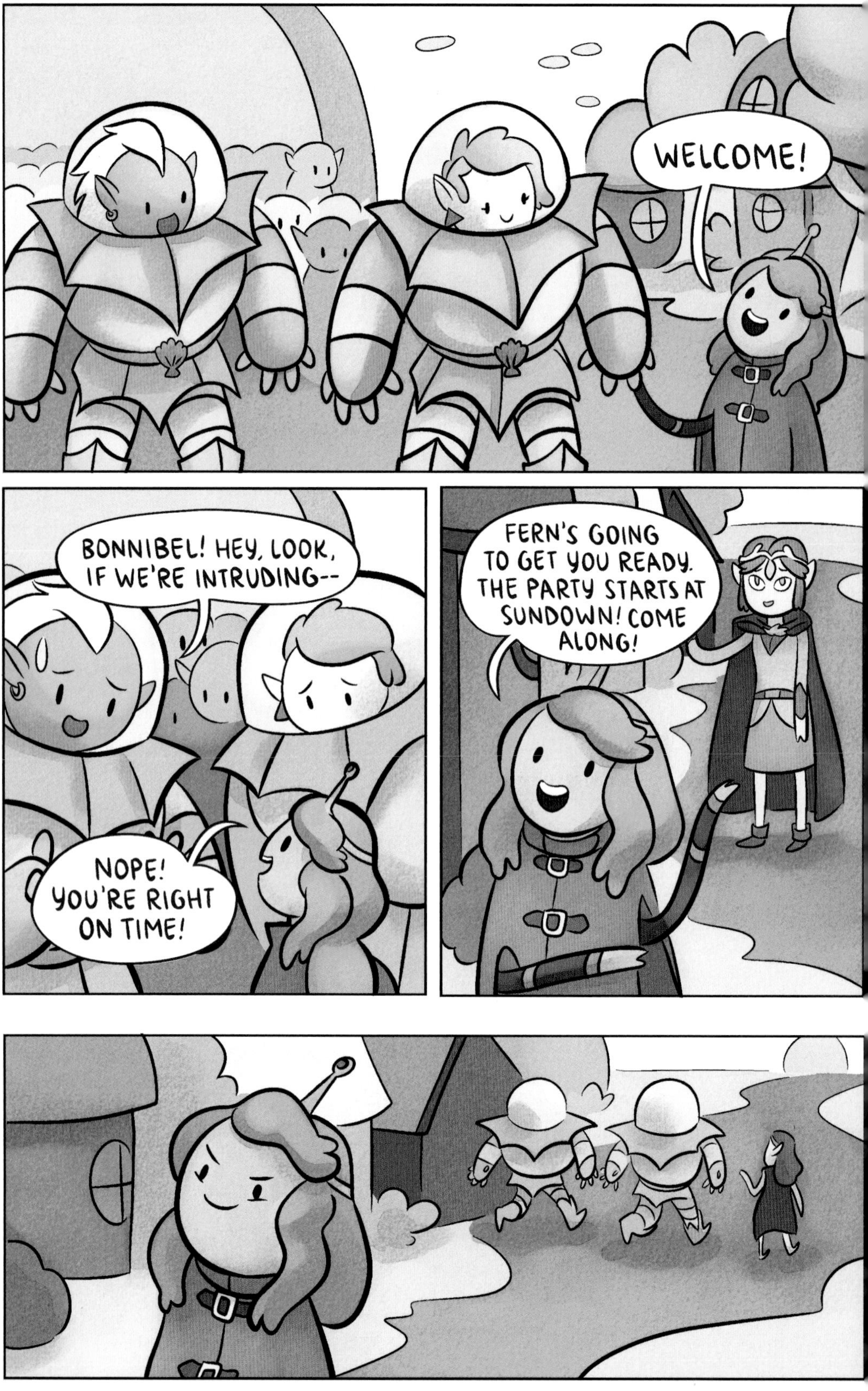
WELCOME!
BONNIBEL! HEY, LOOK, IF WE'RE INTRUDING--
NOPE! YOU'RE RIGHT ON TIME!
FERN'S GOING TO GET YOU READY. THE PARTY STARTS AT SUNDOWN! COME ALONG!

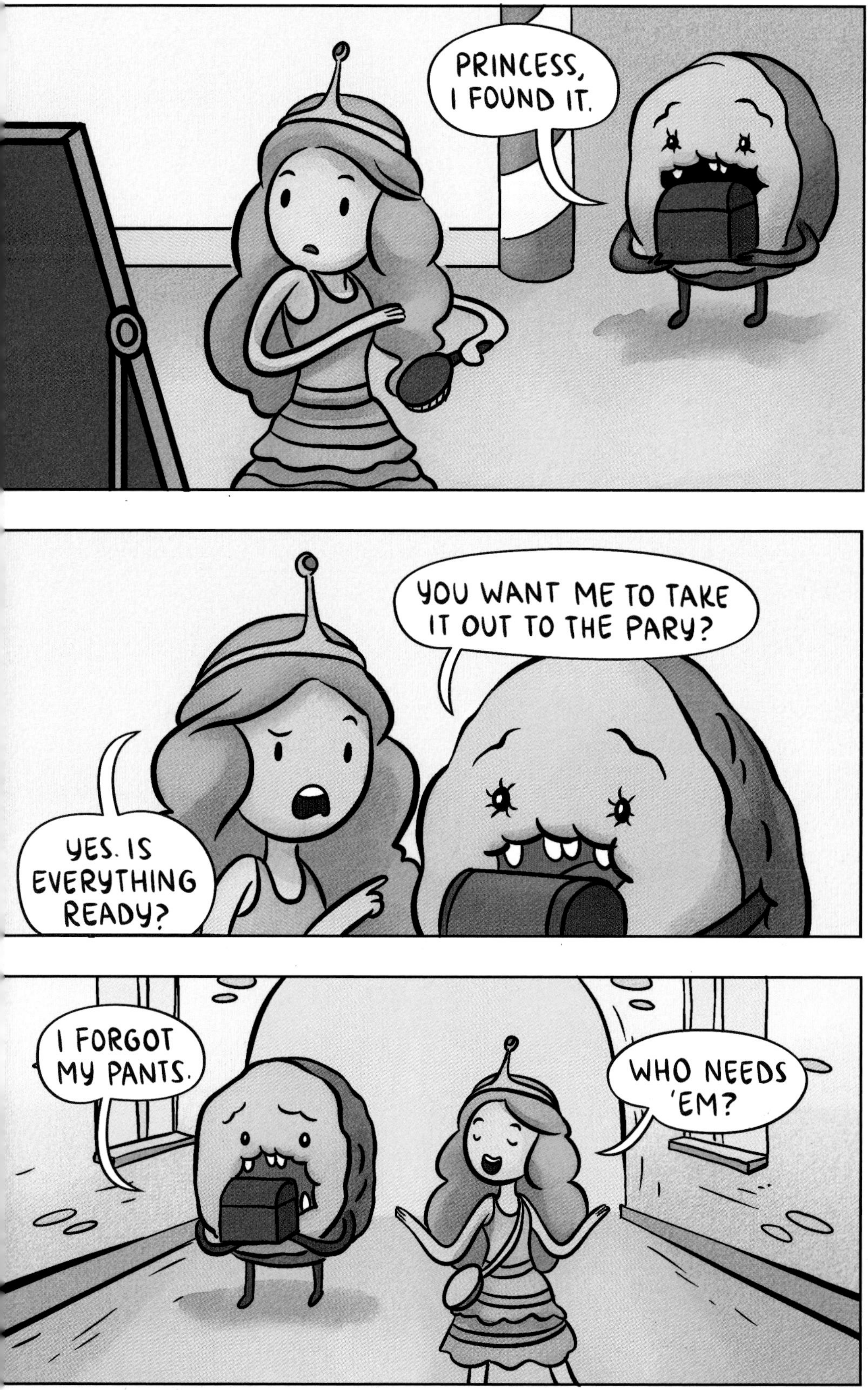
PRINCESS, I FOUND IT.
YOU WANT ME TO TAKE IT OUT TO THE PARY?
YES. IS EVERYTHING READY?
I FORGOT MY PANTS.
WHO NEEDS 'EM?

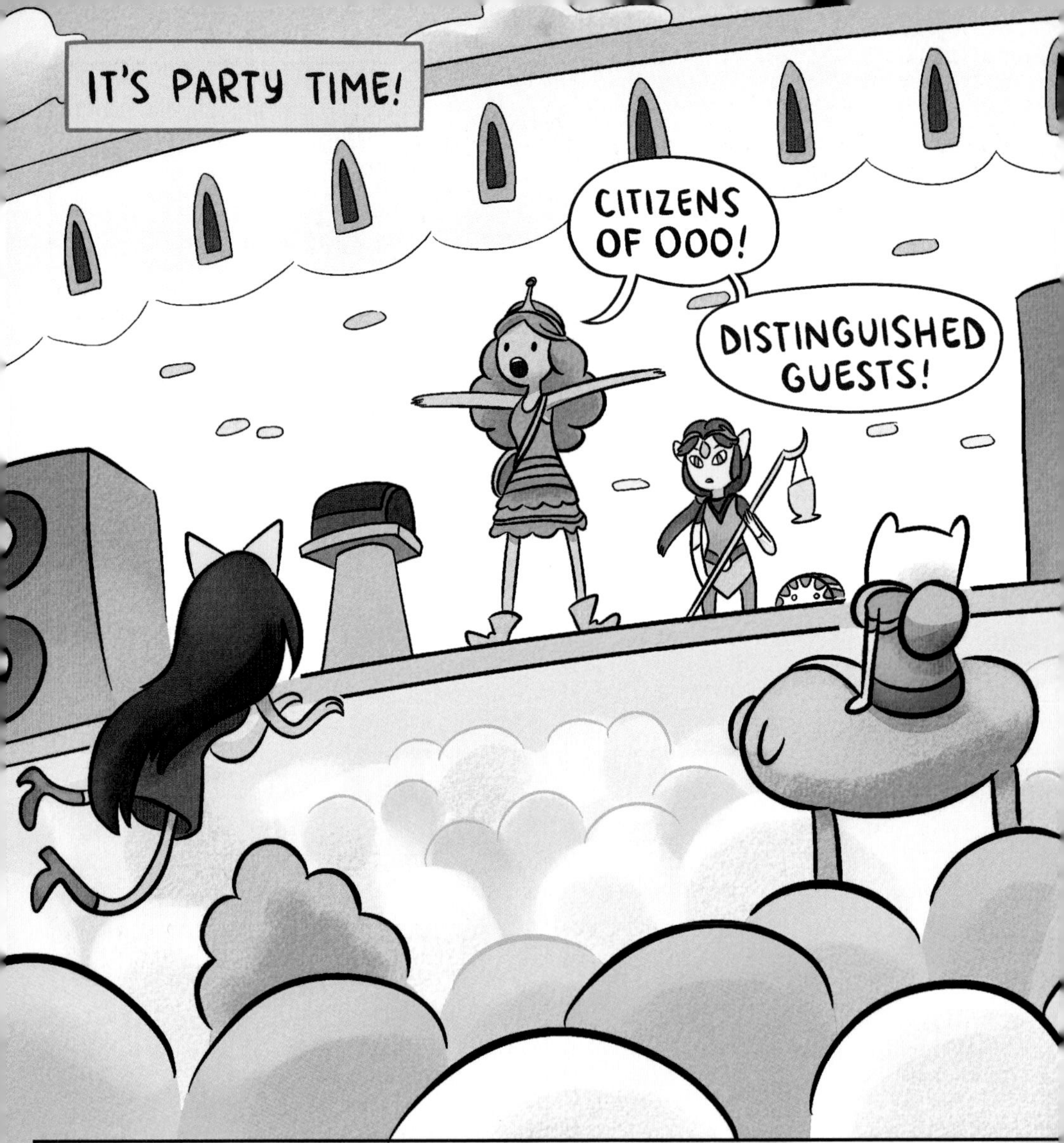
IT'S PARTY TIME!
CITIZENS OF OOO!
DISTINGUISHED GUESTS!

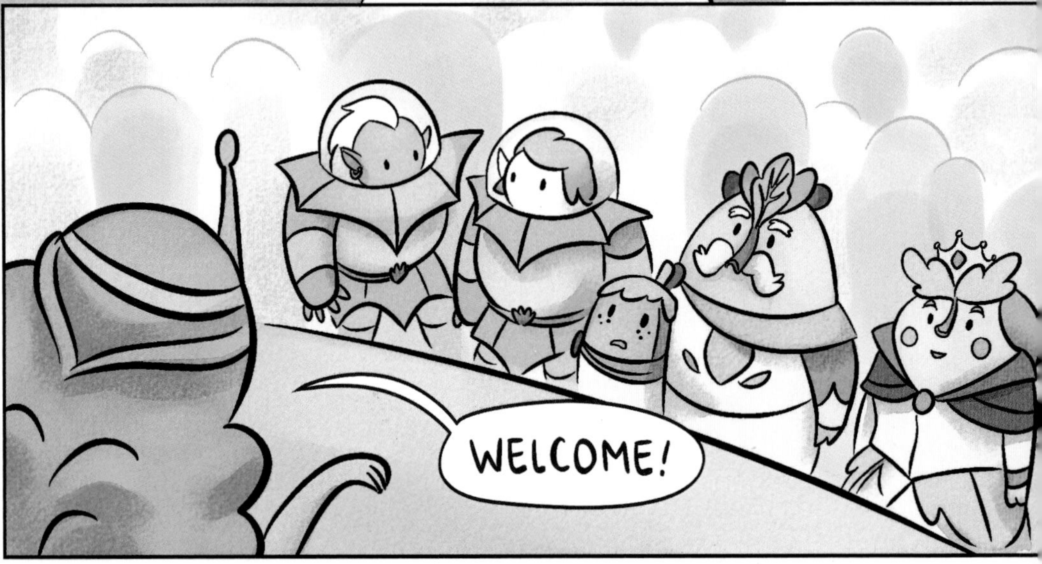
WELCOME!

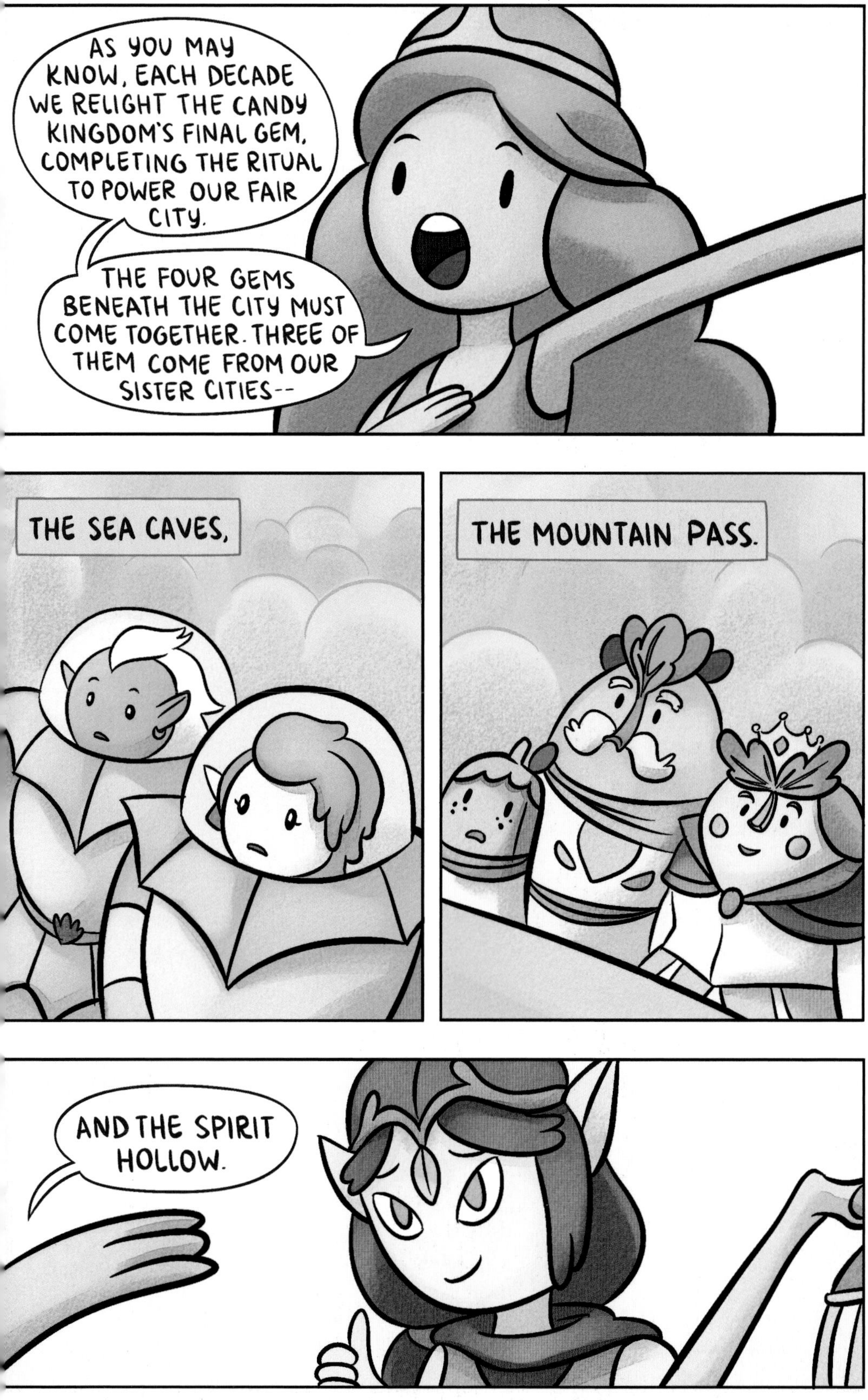
AS YOU MAY KNOW, EACH DECADE WE RELIGHT THE CANDY KINGDOM'S FINAL GEM, COMPLETING THE RITUAL TO POWER OUR FAIR CITY.
THE FOUR GEMS BENEATH THE CITY MUST COME TOGETHER. THREE OF THEM COME FROM OUR SISTER CITIES--
THE SEA CAVES,
THE MOUNTAIN PASS.
AND THE SPIRIT HOLLOW.

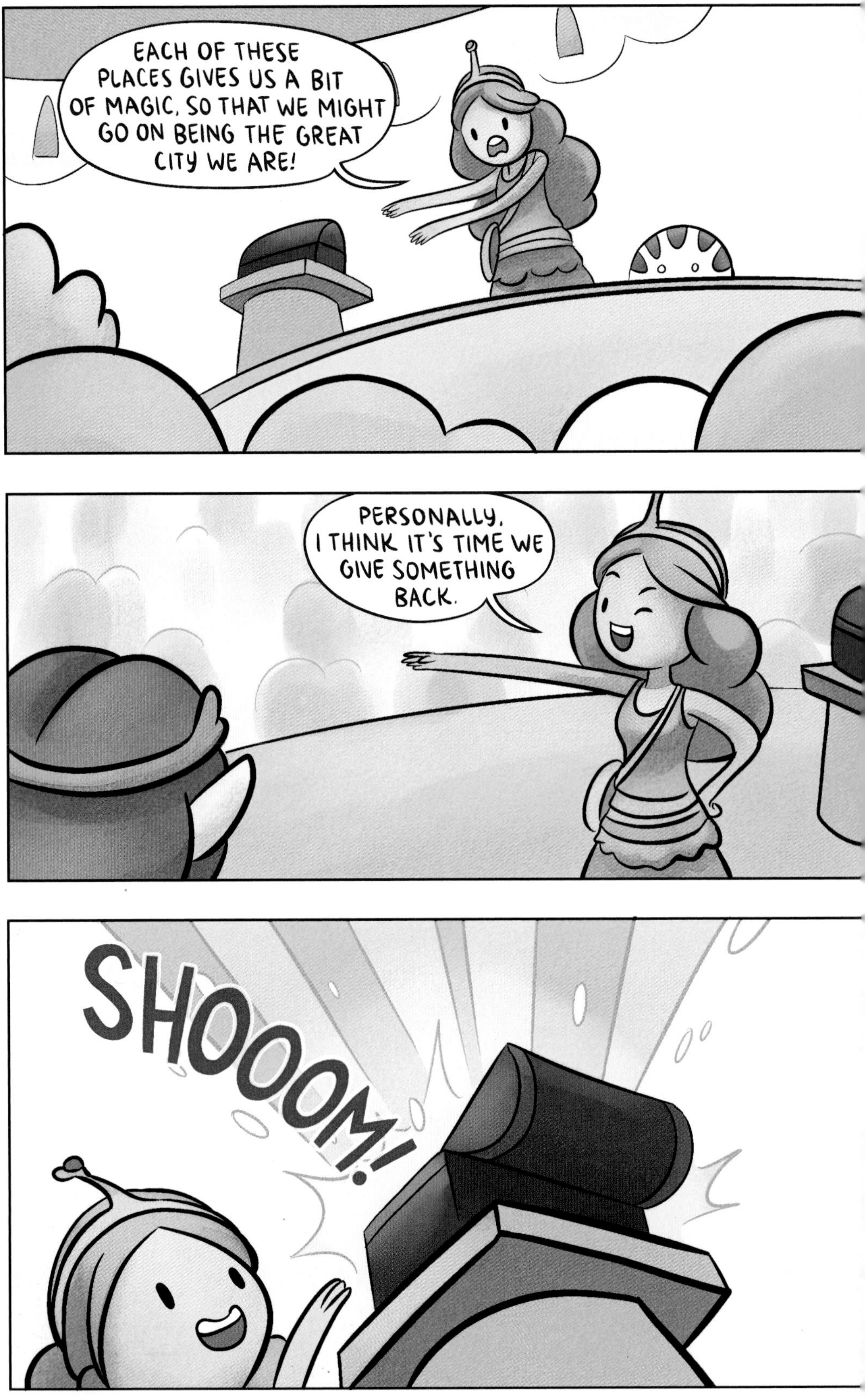
EACH OF THESE PLACES GIVES US A BIT OF MAGIC, SO THAT WE MIGHT GO ON BEING THE GREAT CITY WE ARE!
PERSONALLY, I THINK IT'S TIME WE GIVE SOMETHING BACK.
SHOOOM!

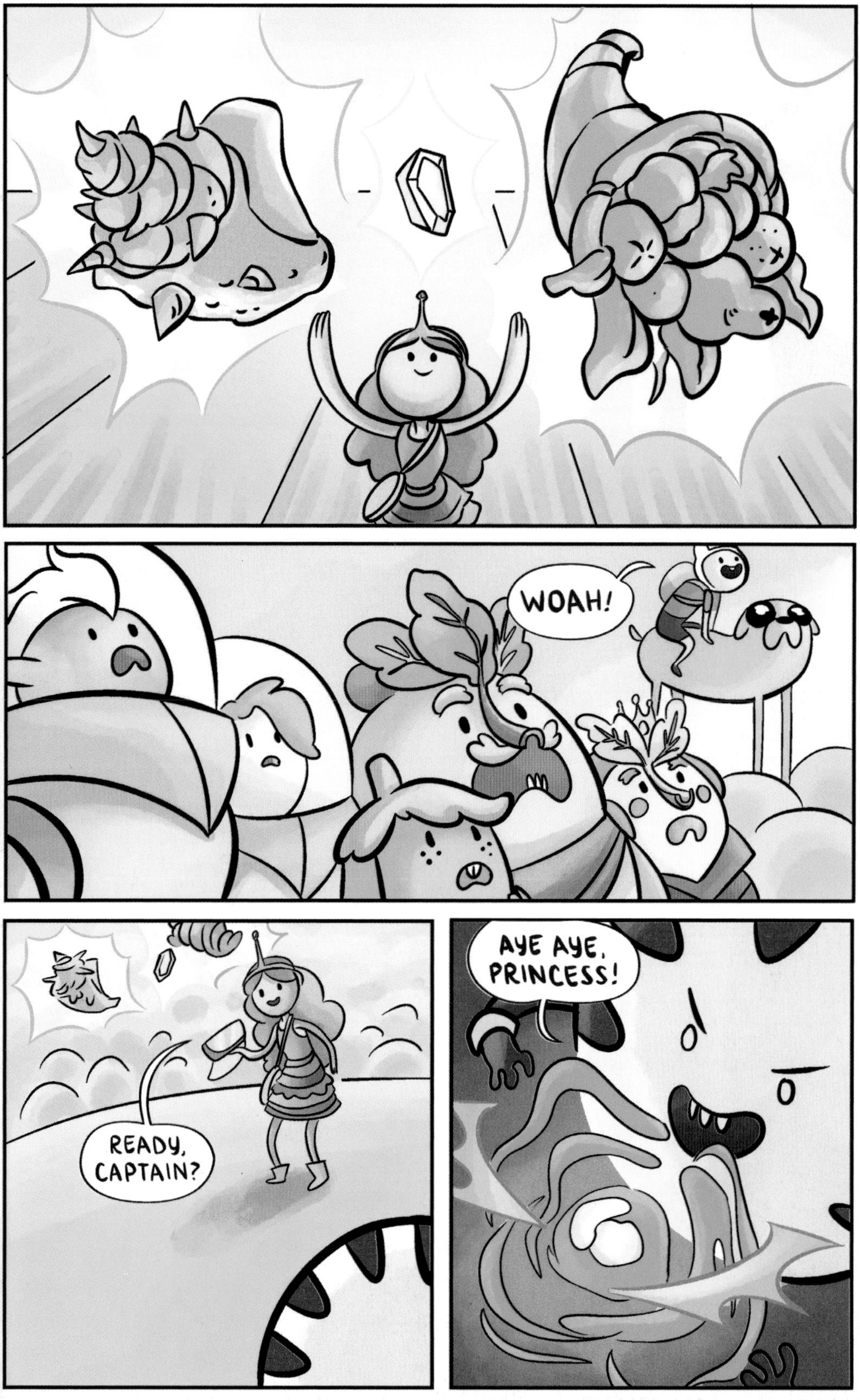
WOAH!
READY, CAPTAIN?
AYE AYE, PRINCESS!

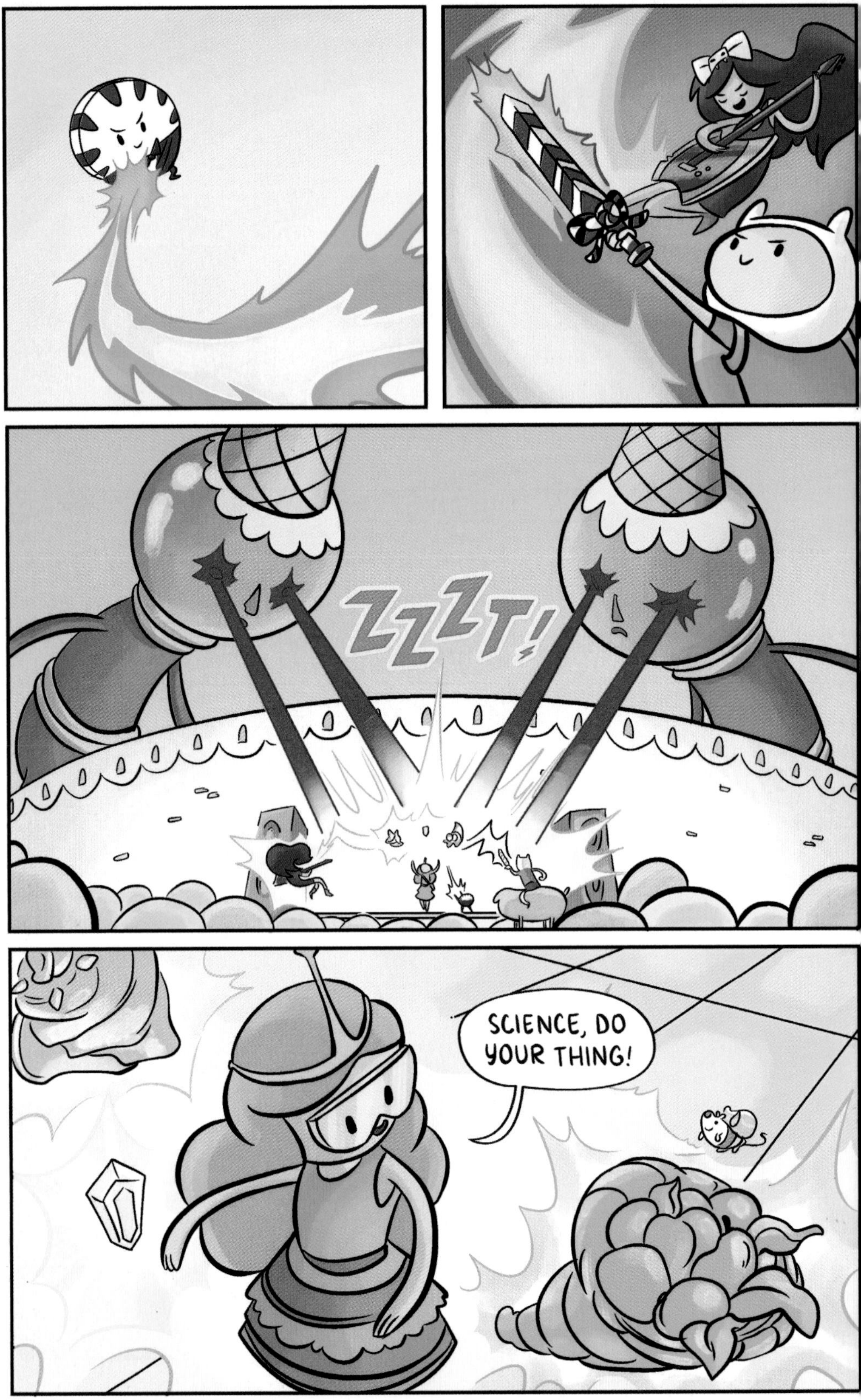
ZZZT!
SCIENCE, DO YOUR THING!

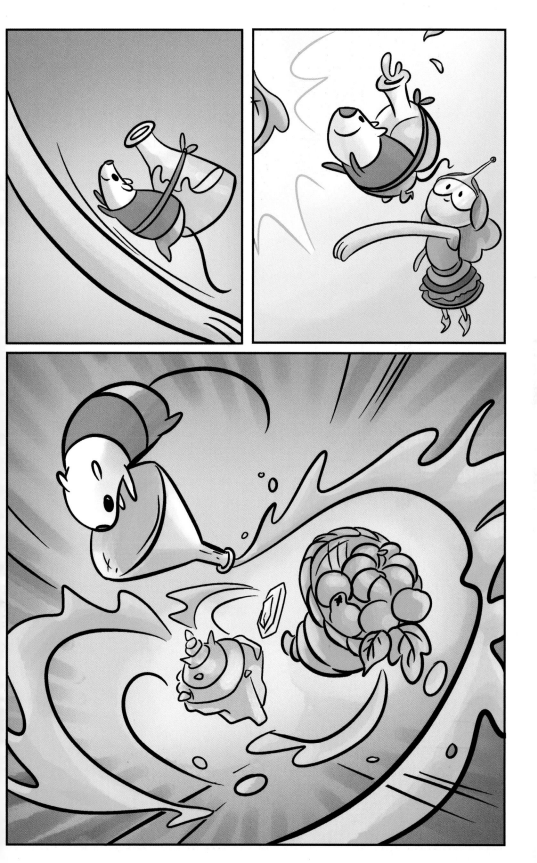

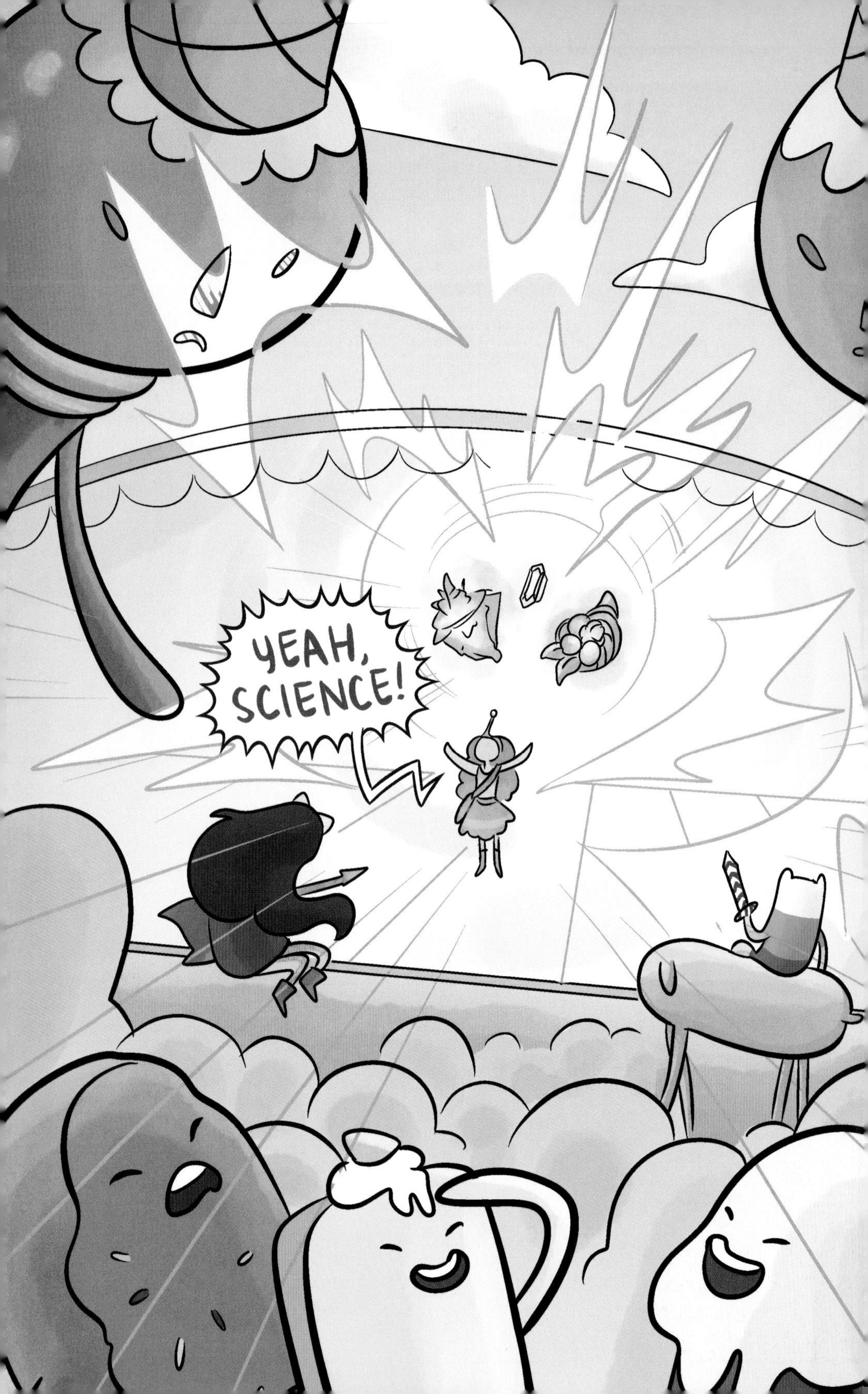
YEAH, SCIENCE!

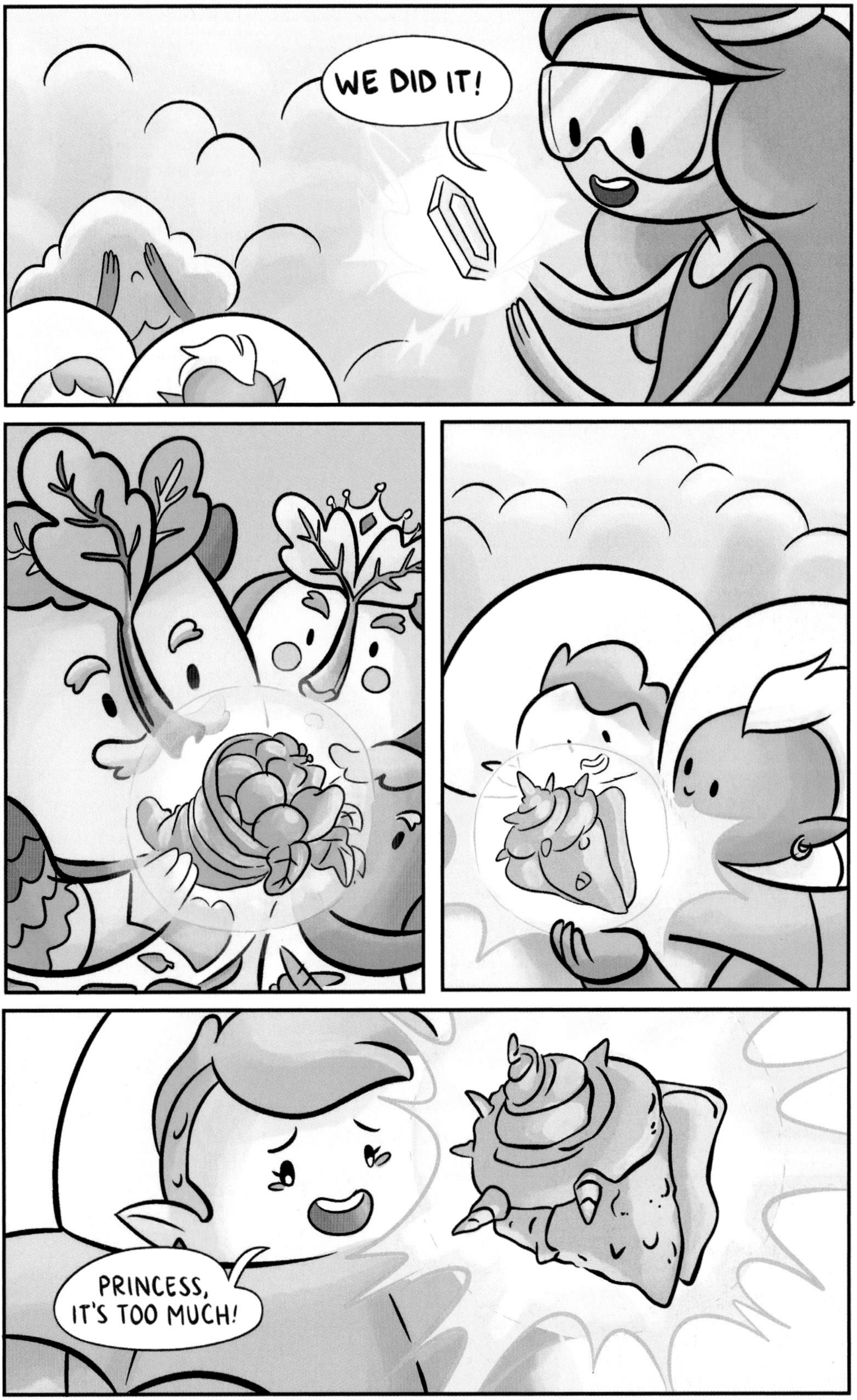
WE DID IT!
PRINCESS, IT'S TOO MUCH!

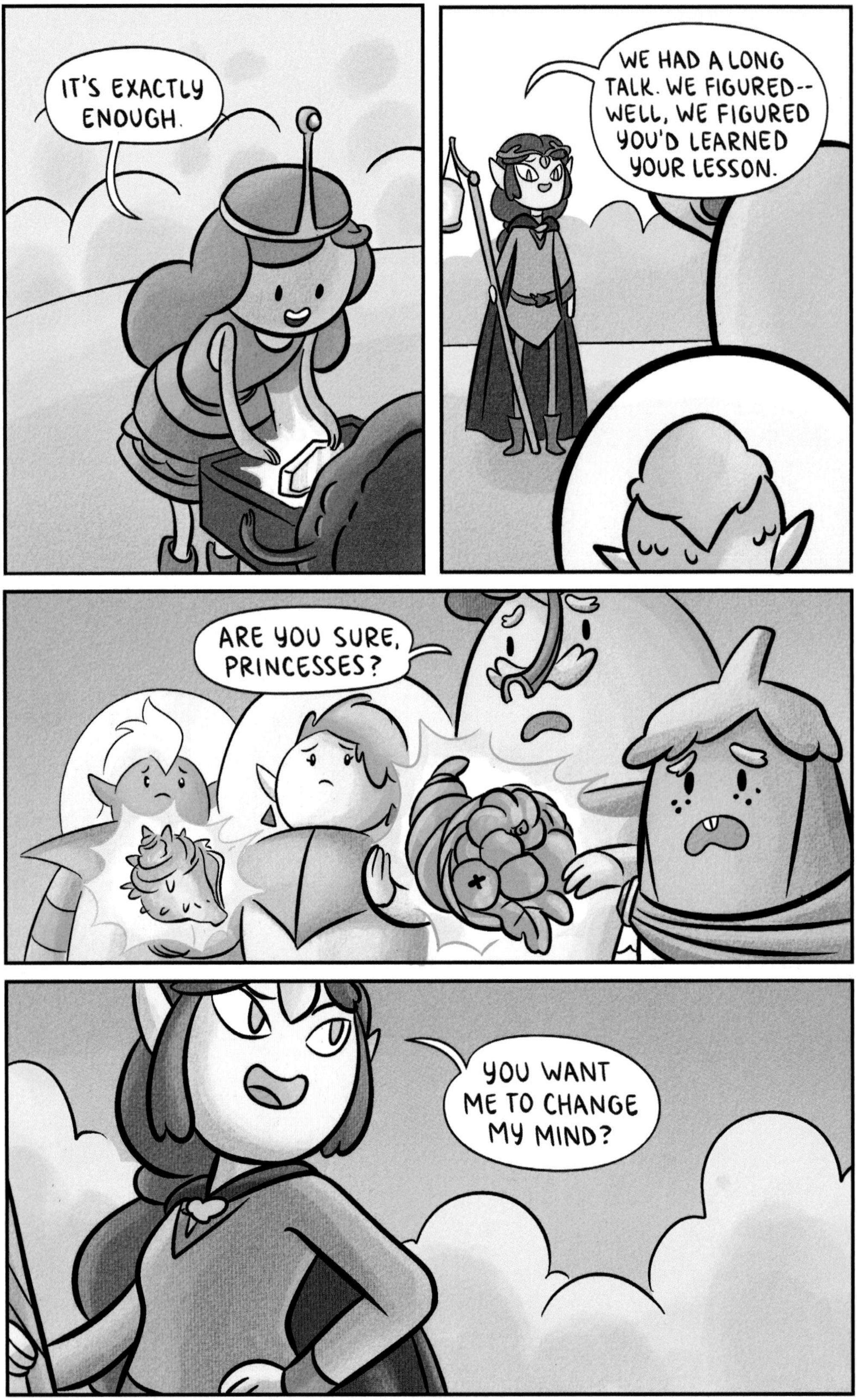
IT'S EXACTLY ENOUGH.
WE HAD A LONG TALK. WE FIGURED-- WELL, WE FIGURED YOU'D LEARNED YOUR LESSON.
ARE YOU SURE, PRINCESSES?
YOU WANT ME TO CHANGE MY MIND?

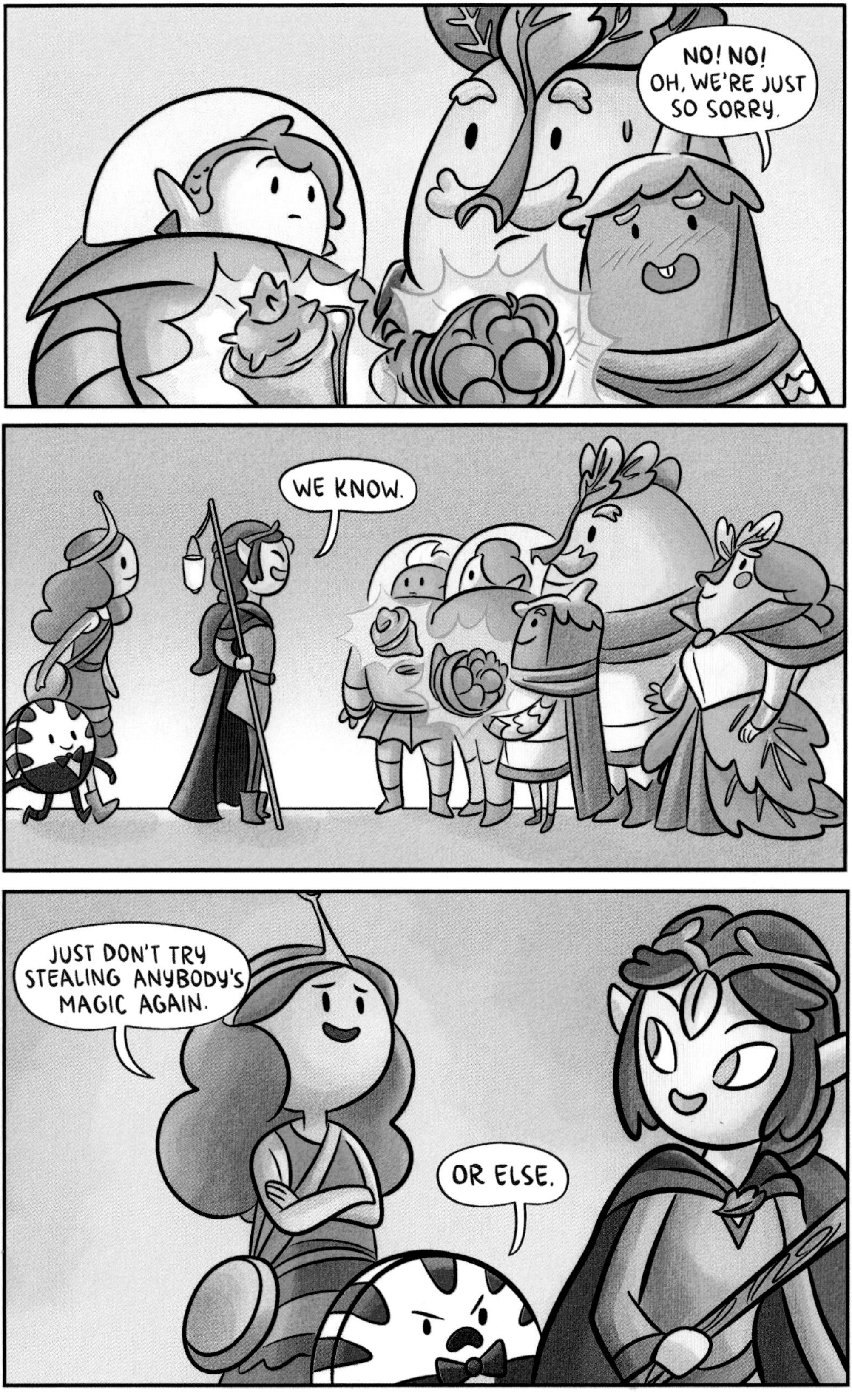

NO! NO! OH, WE'RE JUST SO SORRY.
WE KNOW.
JUST DON'T TRY STEALING ANYBODY'S MAGIC AGAIN.
OR ELSE.

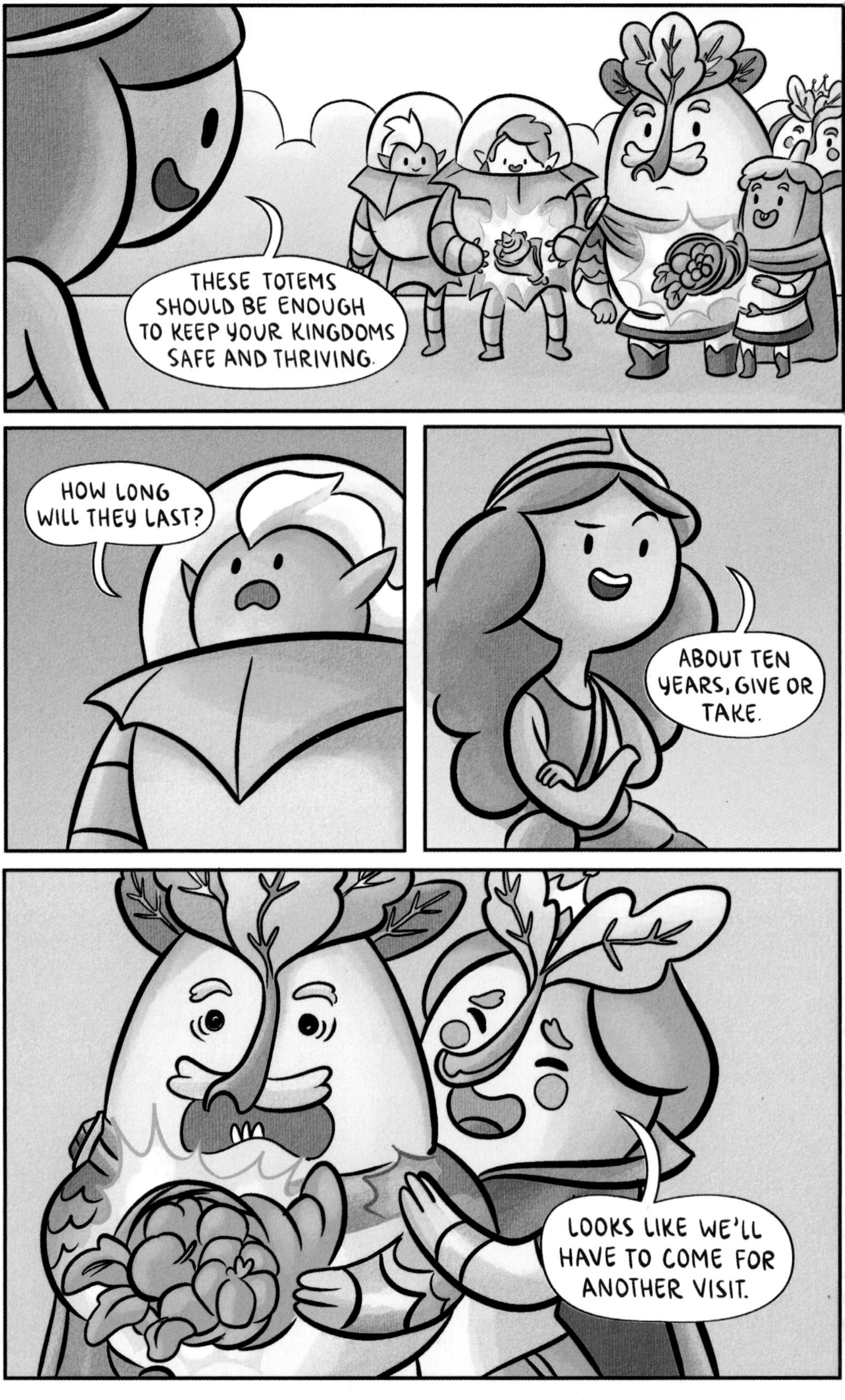
THESE TOTEMS SHOULD BE ENOUGH TO KEEP YOUR KINGDOMS SAFE AND THRIVING.
HOW LONG WILL THEY LAST?
ABOUT TEN YEARS, GIVE OR TAKE.
LOOKS LIKE WE'LL HAVE TO COME FOR ANOTHER VISIT.

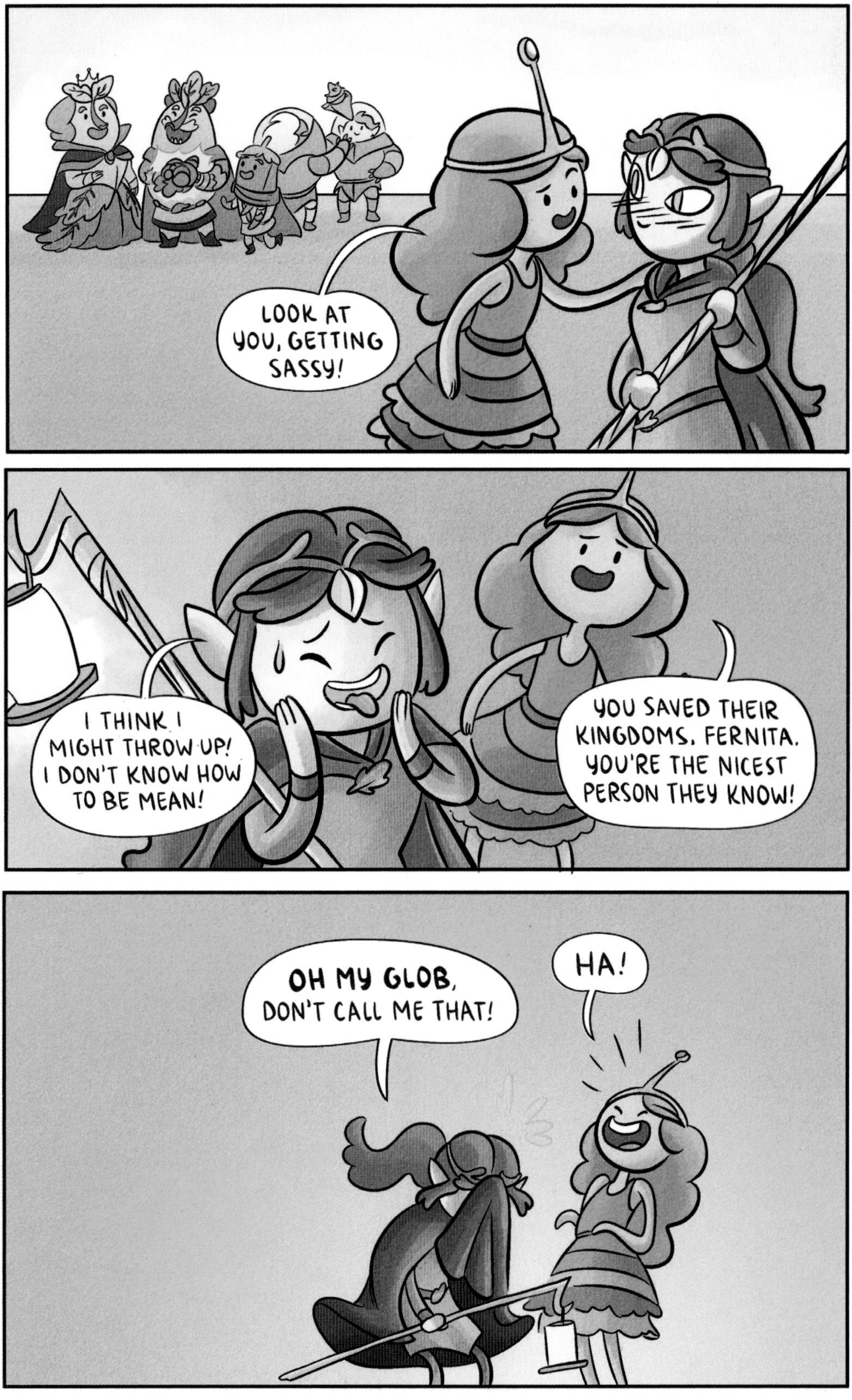
LOOK AT YOU, GETTING SASSY!
I THINK I MIGHT THROW UP! I DON'T KNOW HOW TO BE MEAN!
YOU SAVED THEIR KINGDOMS, FERNITA. YOU'RE THE NICEST PERSON THEY KNOW!
OH MY GLOB, DON'T CALL ME THAT!
HA!

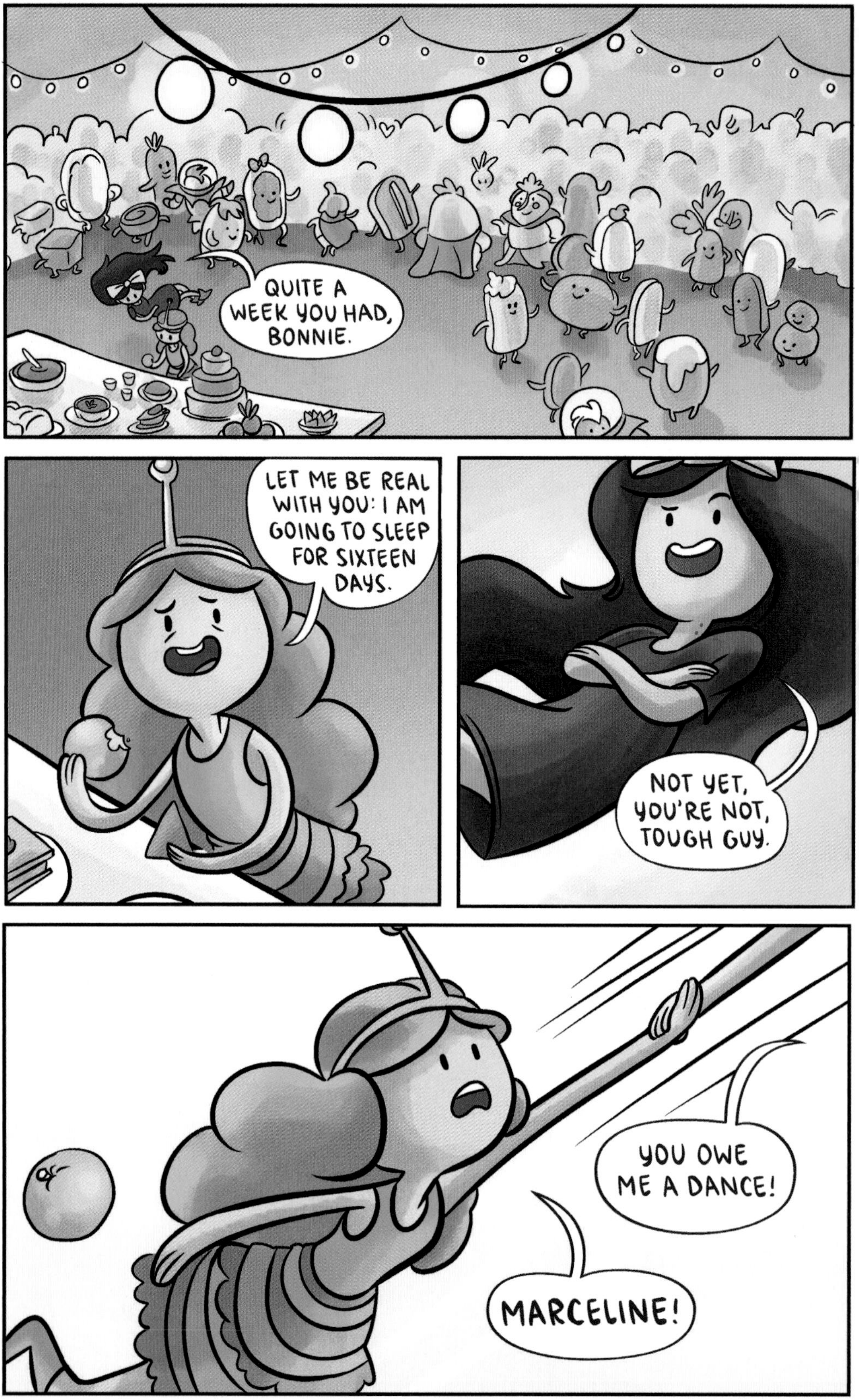
QUITE A WEEK YOU HAD, BONNIE.
LET ME BE REAL WITH YOU: I AM GOING TO SLEEP FOR SIXTEEN DAYS.
NOT YET, YOU'RE NOT, TOUGH GUY.
YOU OWE ME A DANCE!
MARCELINE!

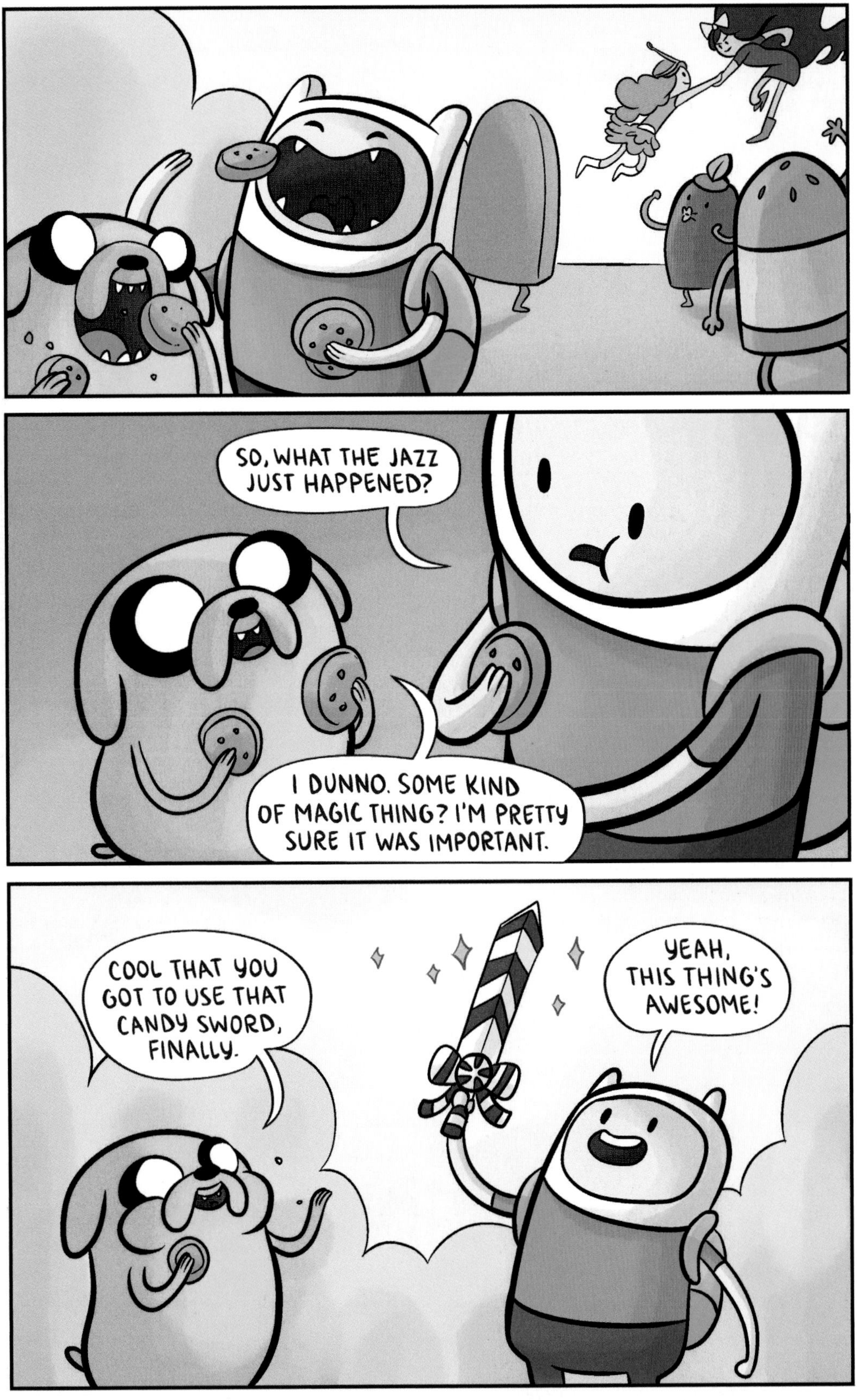
SO, WHAT THE JAZZ JUST HAPPENED?
I DUNNO. SOME KIND OF MAGIC THING? I'M PRETTY SURE IT WAS IMPORTANT.
COOL THAT YOU GOT TO USE THAT CANDY SWORD, FINALLY.
YEAH, THIS THING'S AWESOME!

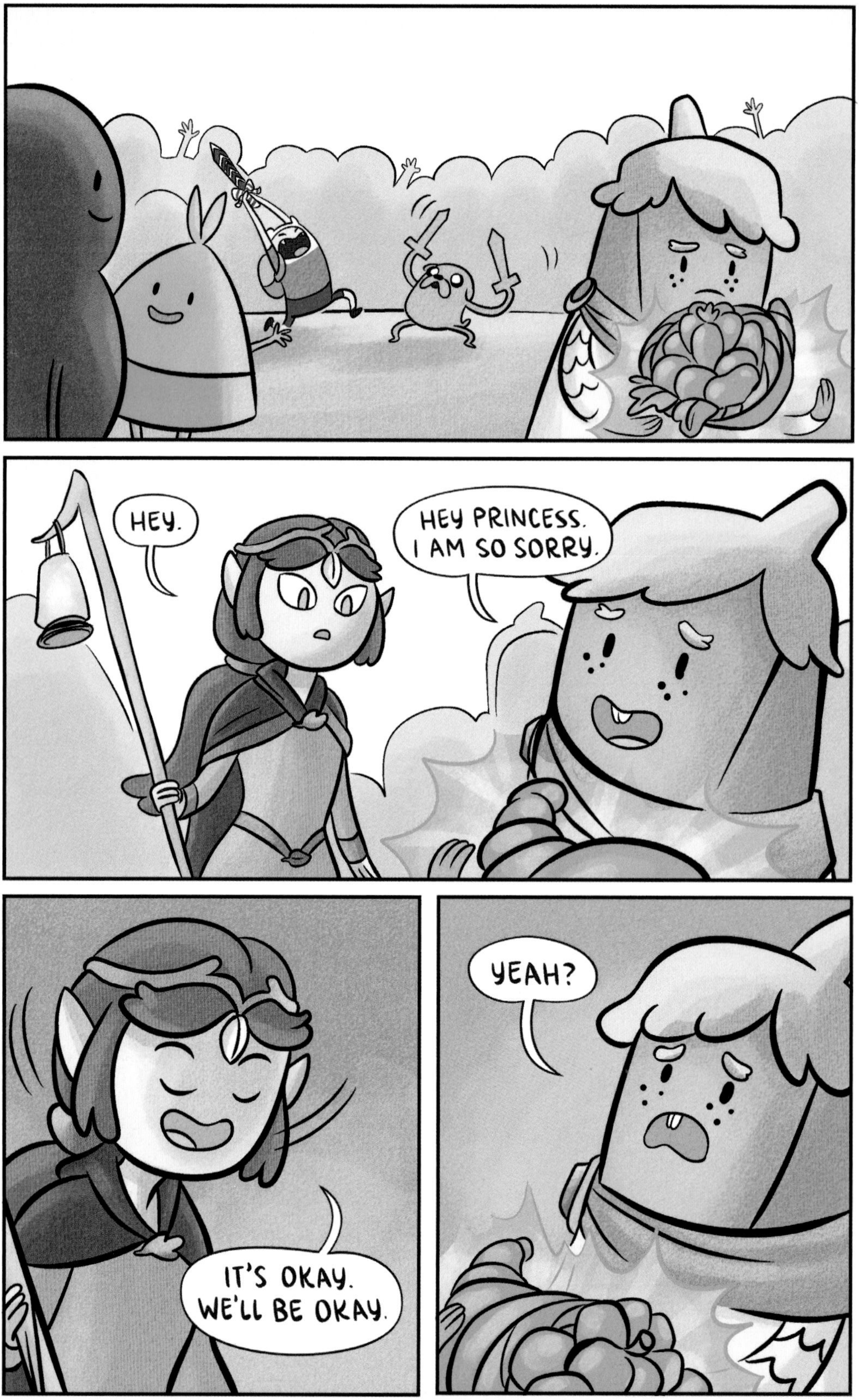
HEY.
HEY PRINCESS. I AM SO SORRY.
YEAH?
IT'S OKAY. WE'LL BE OKAY.

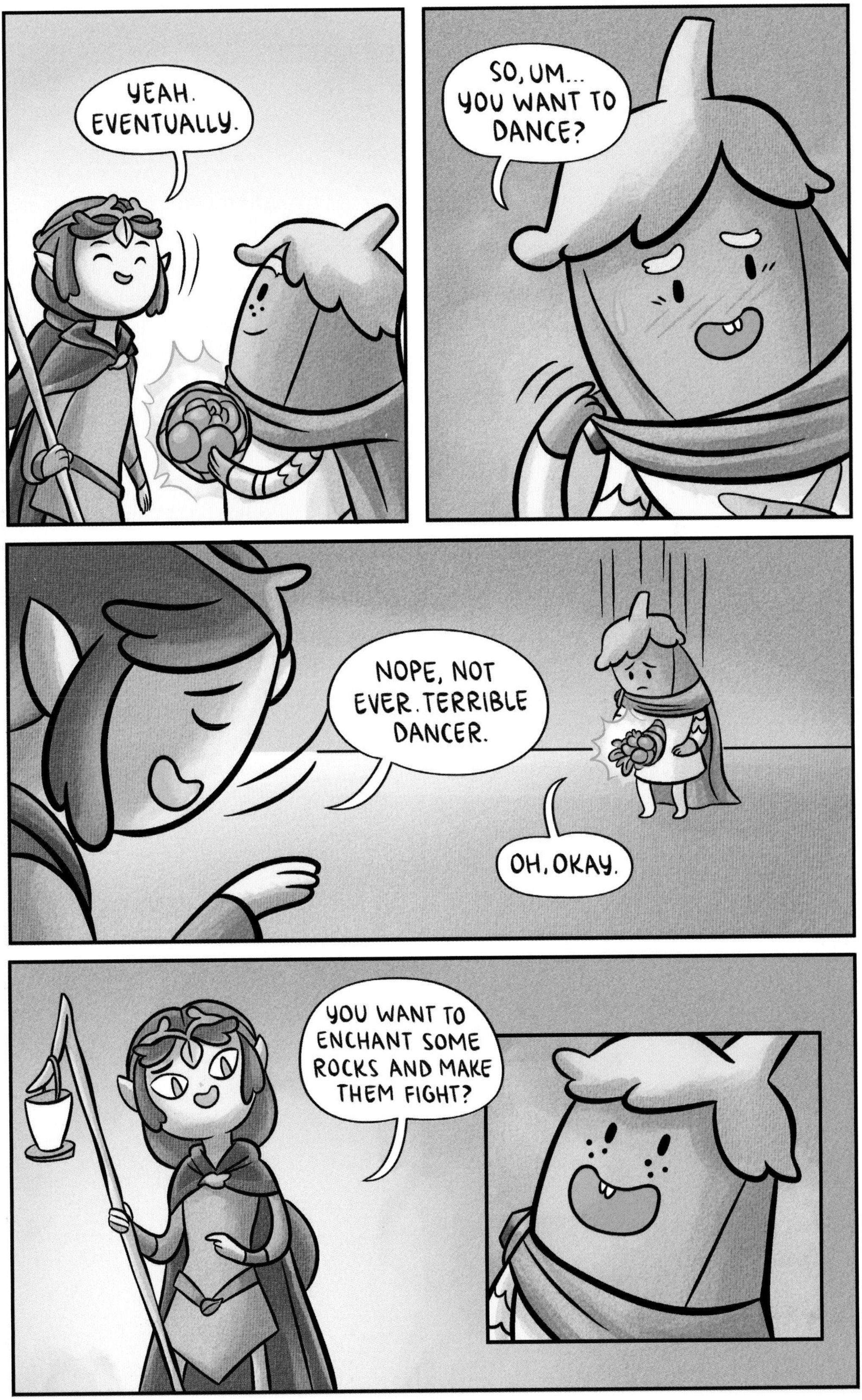
YEAH. EVENTUALLY.
SO, UM... YOU WANT TO DANCE?
NOPE, NOT EVER. TERRIBLE DANCER.
OH, OKAY.
YOU WANT TO ENCHANT SOME ROCKS AND MAKE THEM FIGHT?

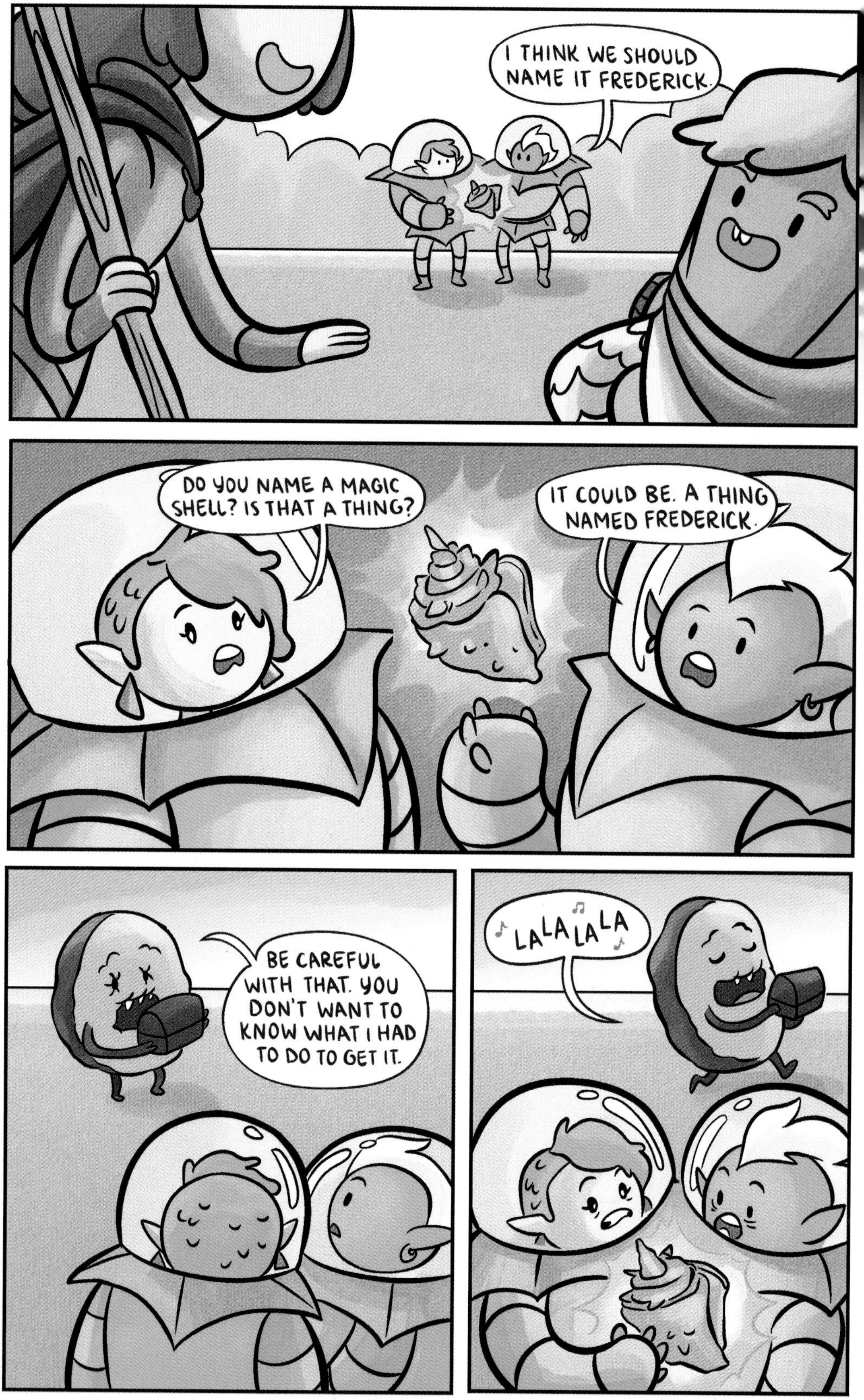

I THINK WE SHOULD NAME IT FREDERICK.
DO YOU NAME A MAGIC SHELL? IS THAT A THING?
IT COULD BE. A THING NAMED FREDERICK.
BE CAREFUL WITH THAT. YOU DON'T WANT TO KNOW WHAT I HAD TO DO TO GET IT.
LALALALA

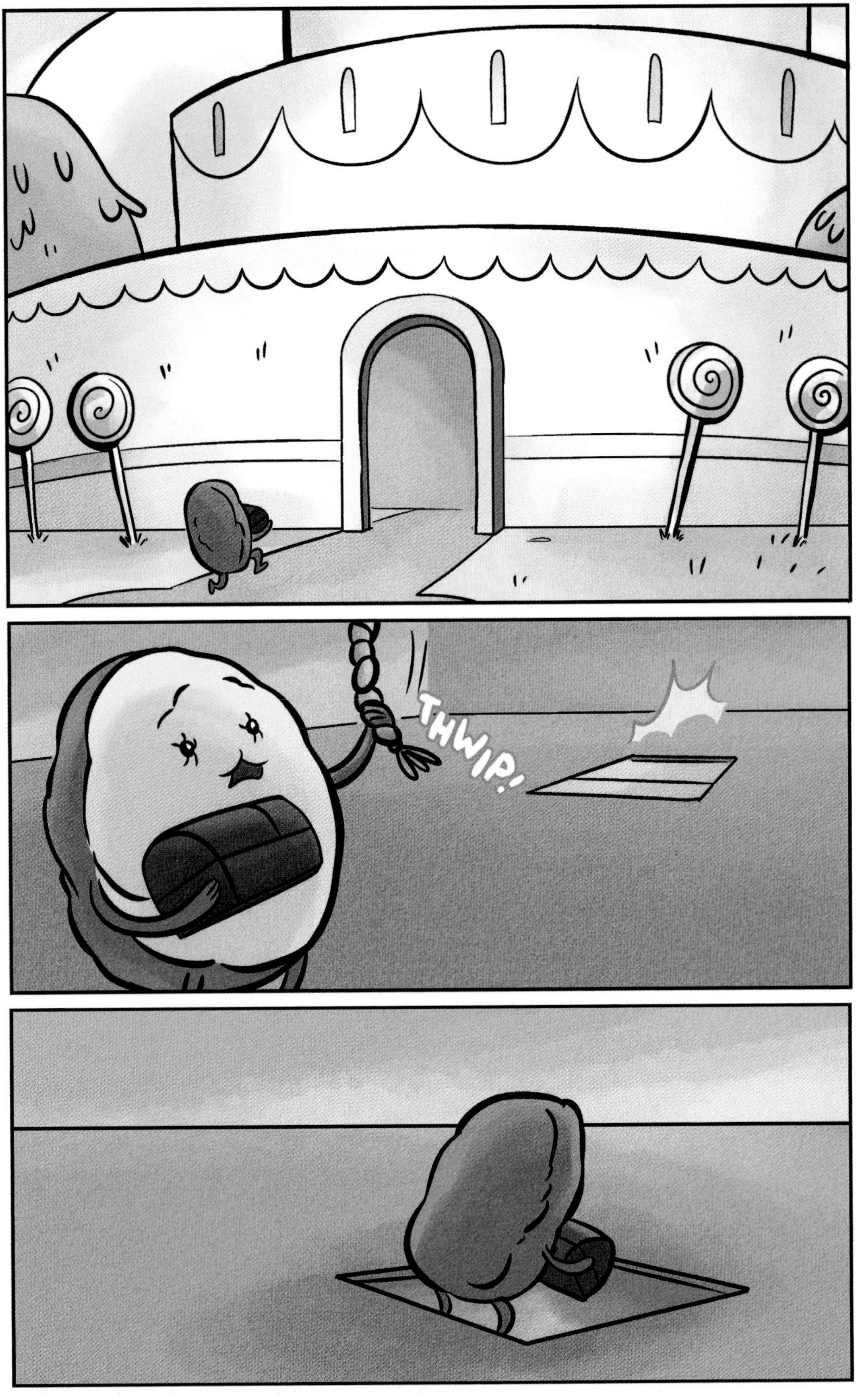
THWIP!

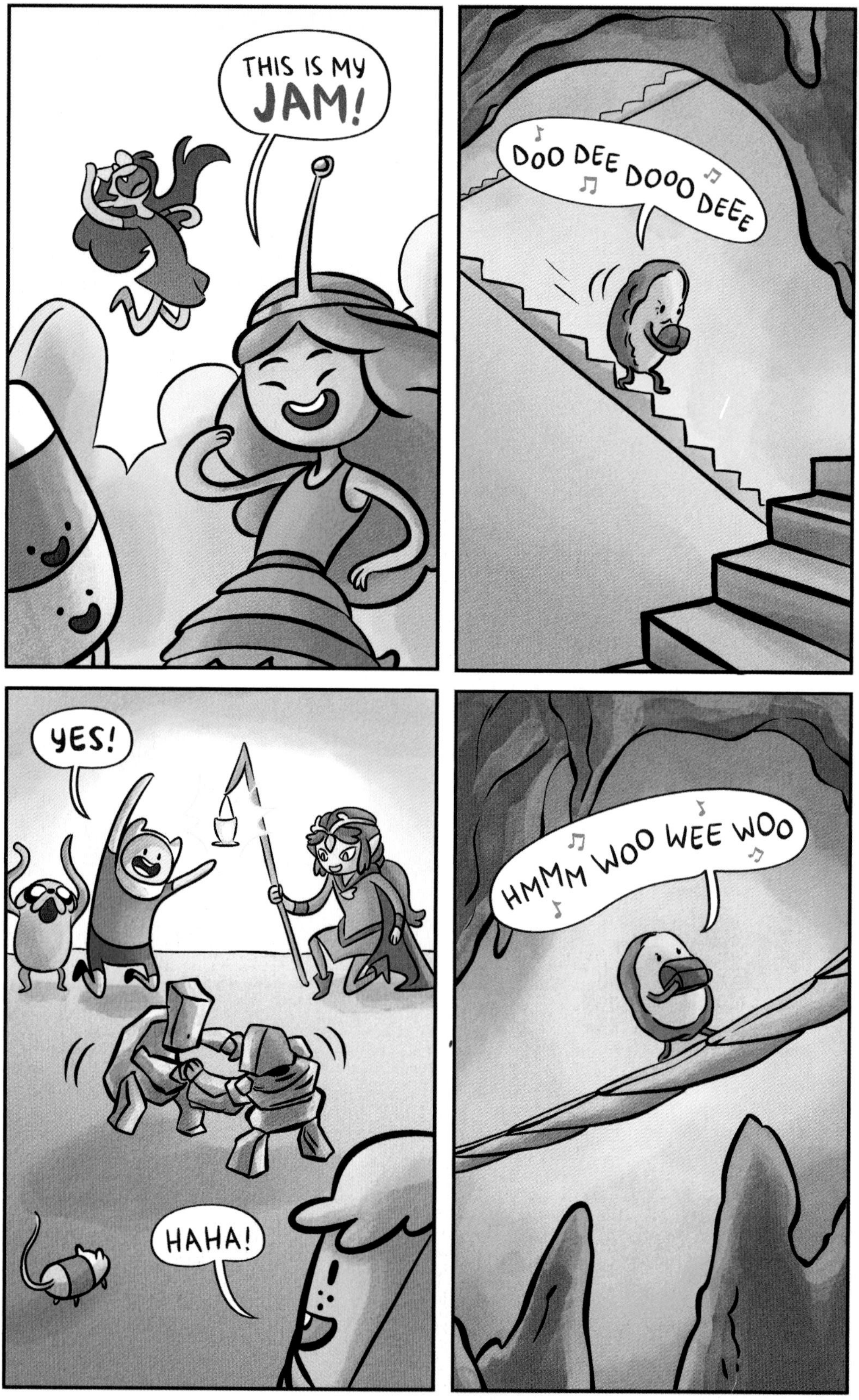
THIS IS MY JAM!
DOO DEE DOOO DEEE
YES!
HAHA!
HMMM WOO WEE WOO

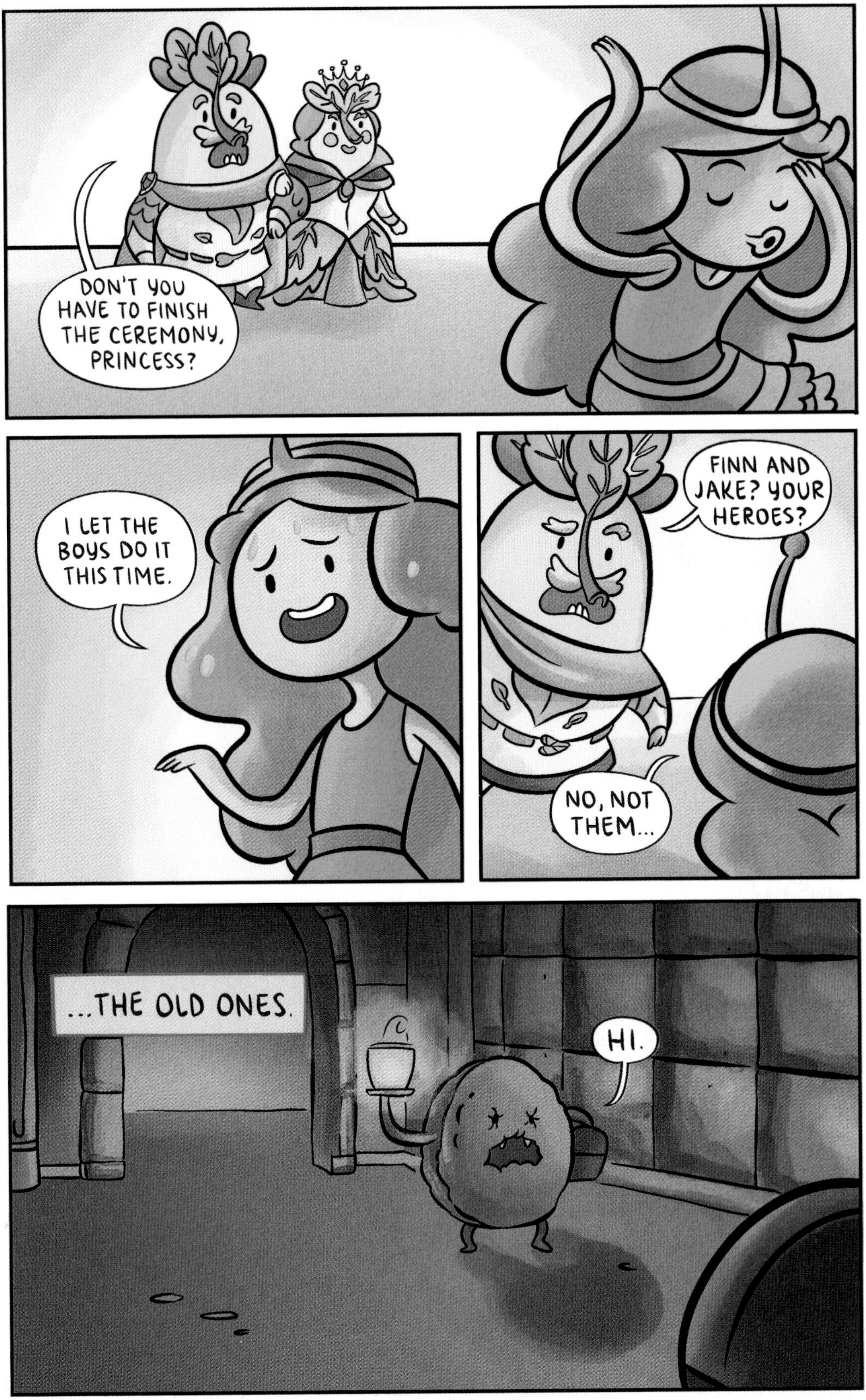
DON'T YOU HAVE TO FINISH THE CEREMONY, PRINCESS?
I LET THE BOYS DO IT THIS TIME.
FINN AND JAKE? YOUR HEROES?
NO, NOT THEM...
...THE OLD ONES.
HI.

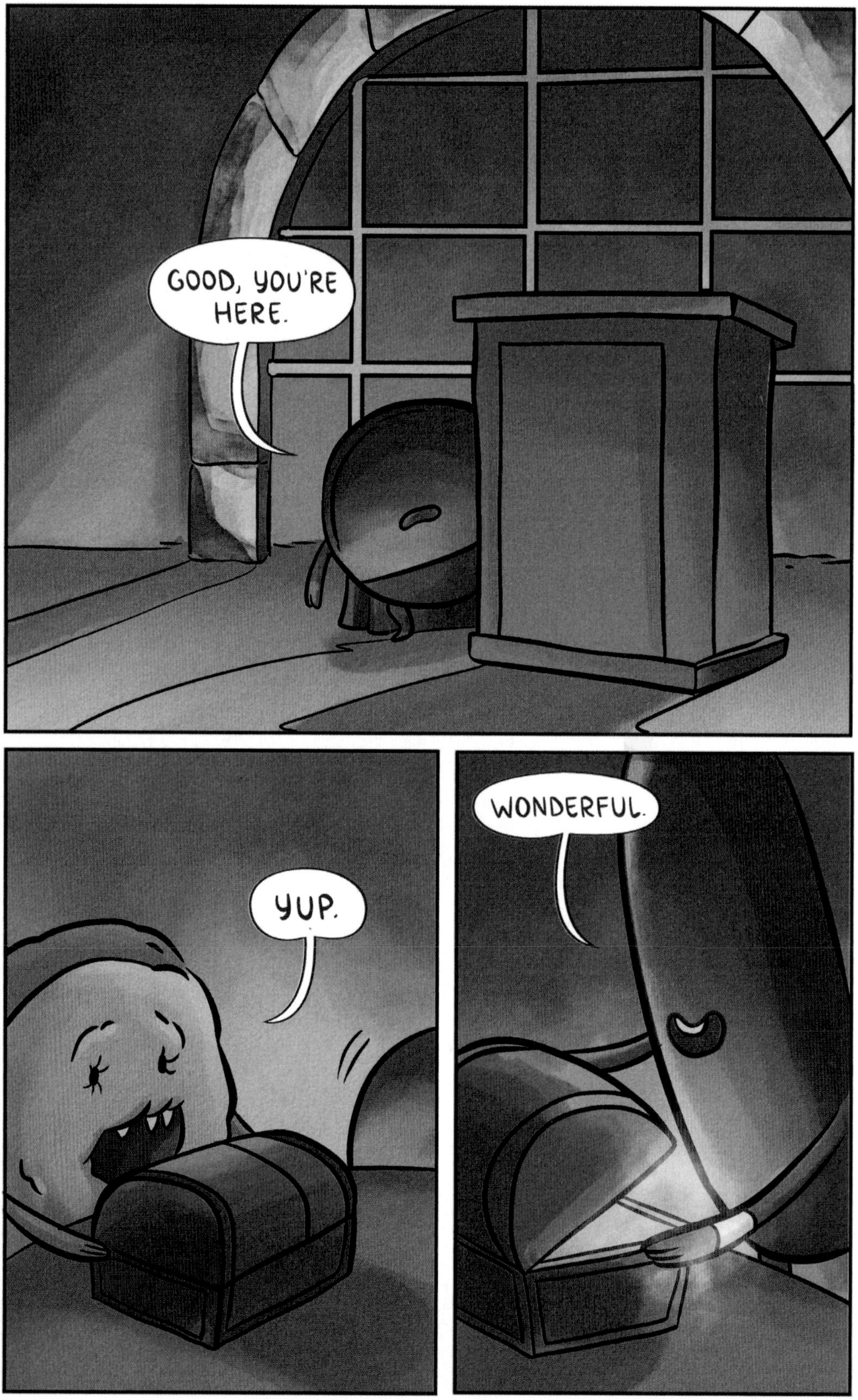
GOOD, YOU'RE HERE.
YUP.
WONDERFUL.

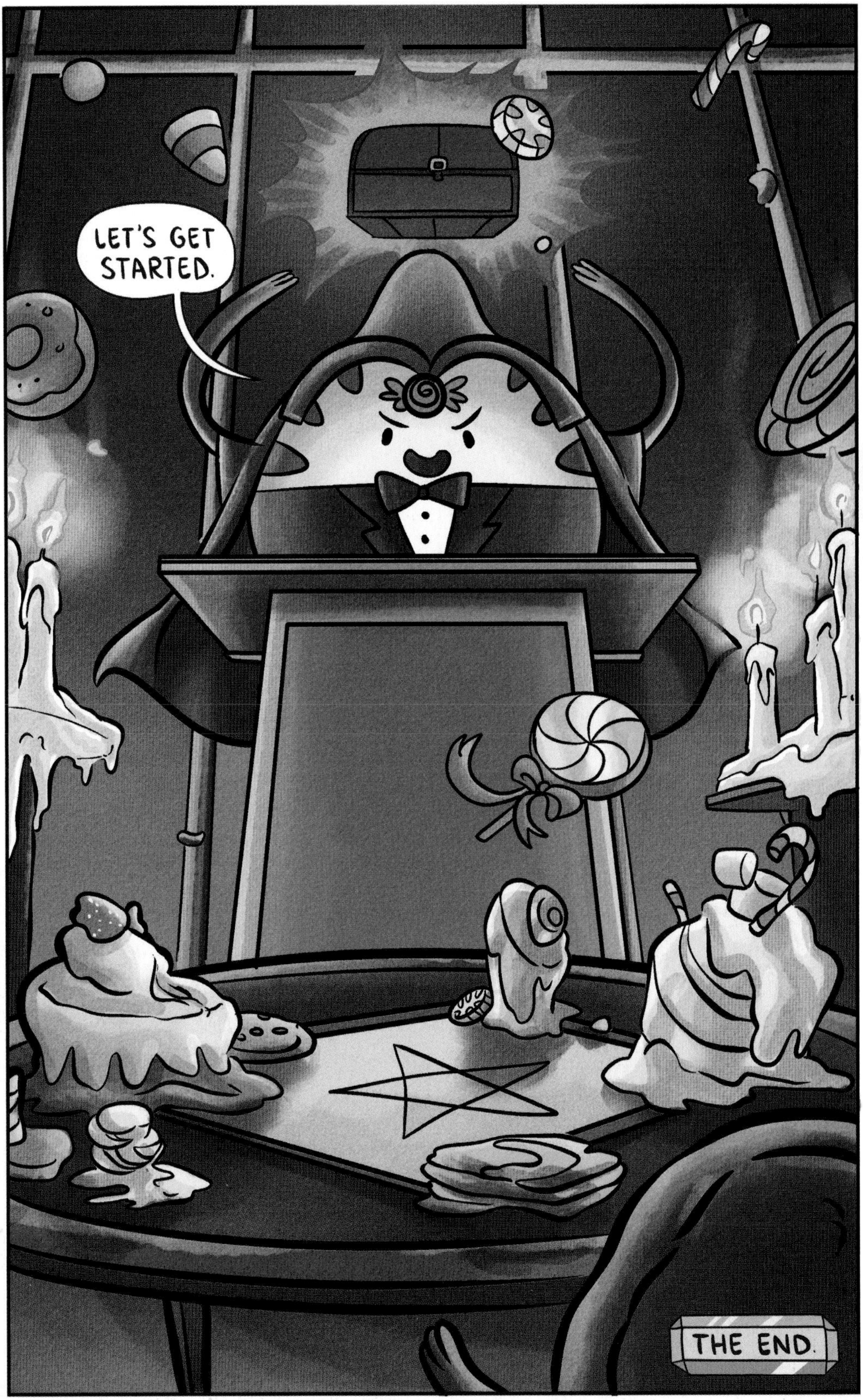
LET'S GET STARTED.
THE END.

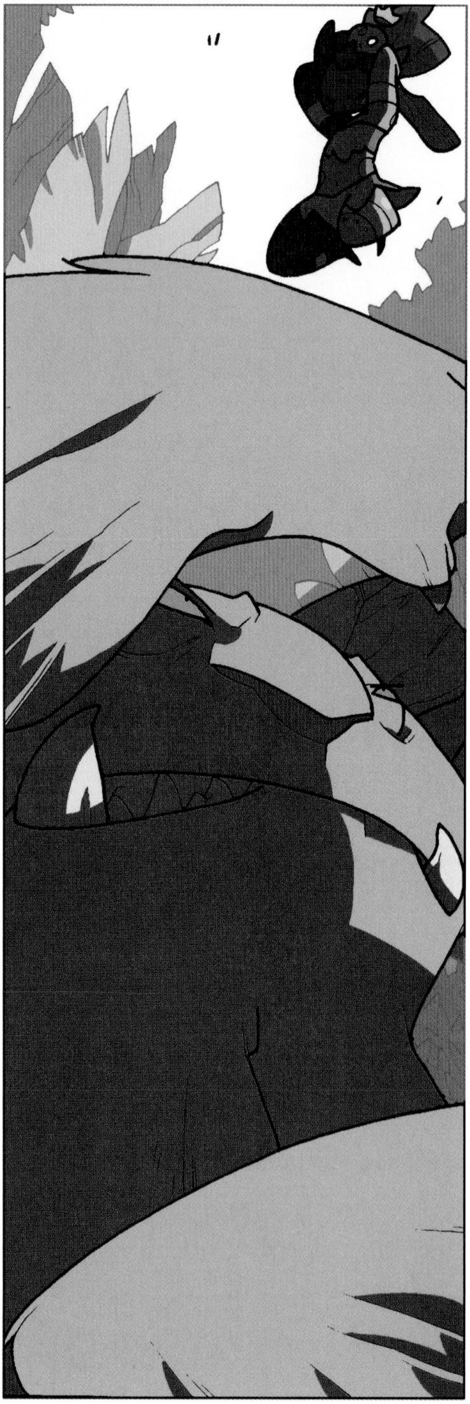

FOREST PRINCESS GETS A PET

written and illustrated by Meredith McClaren

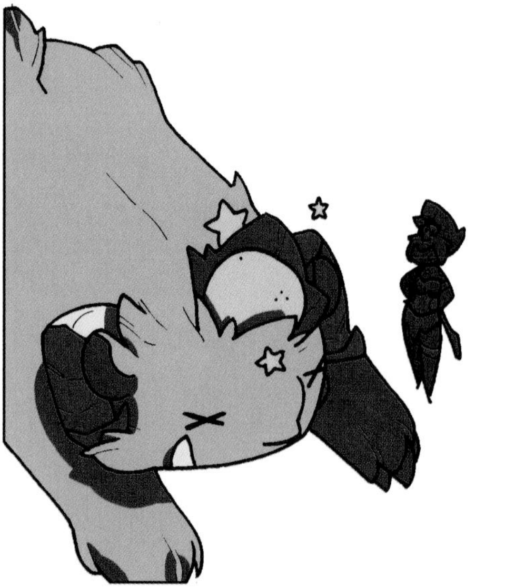

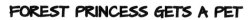

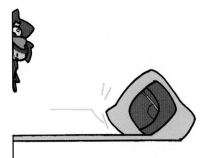

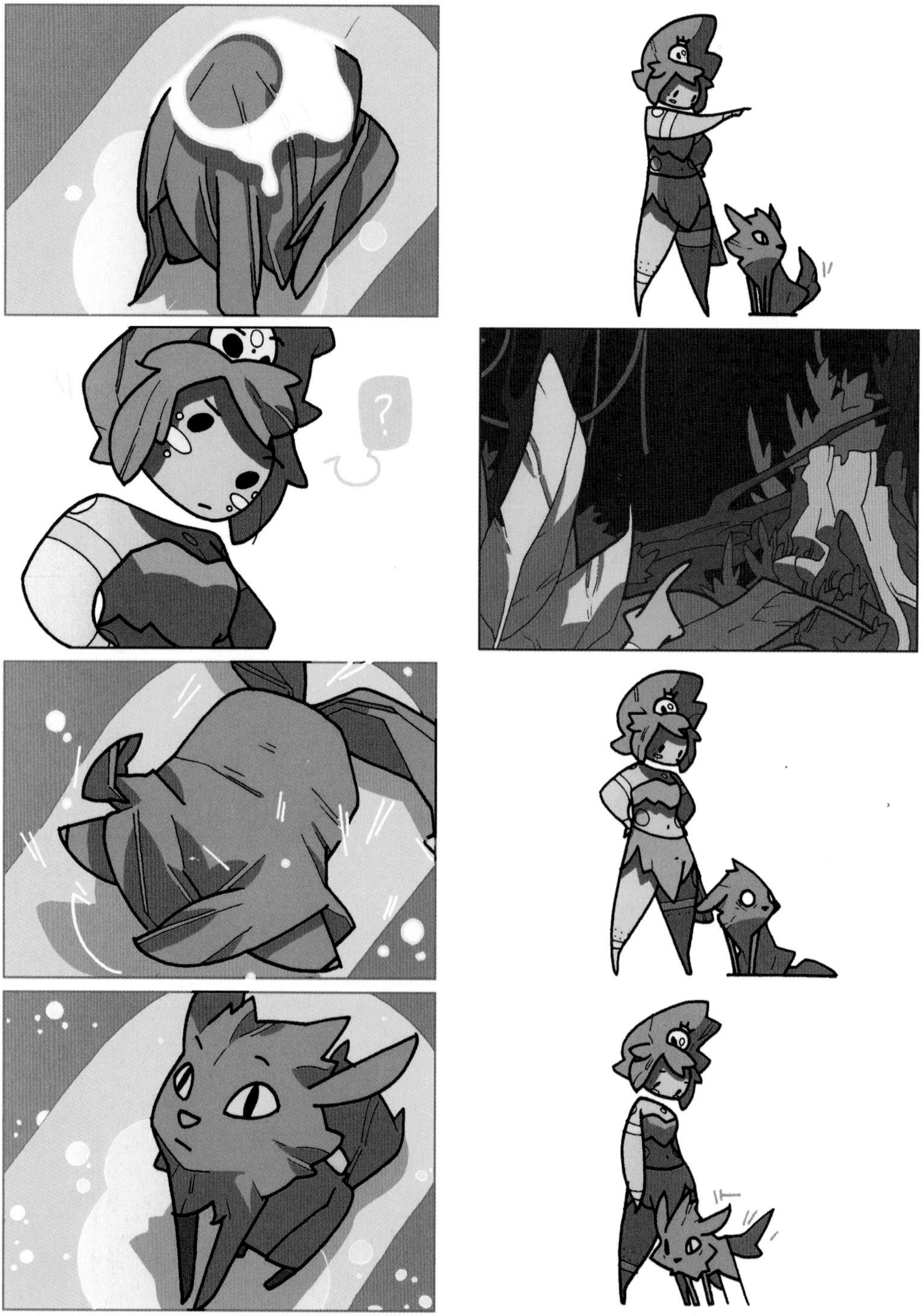
?

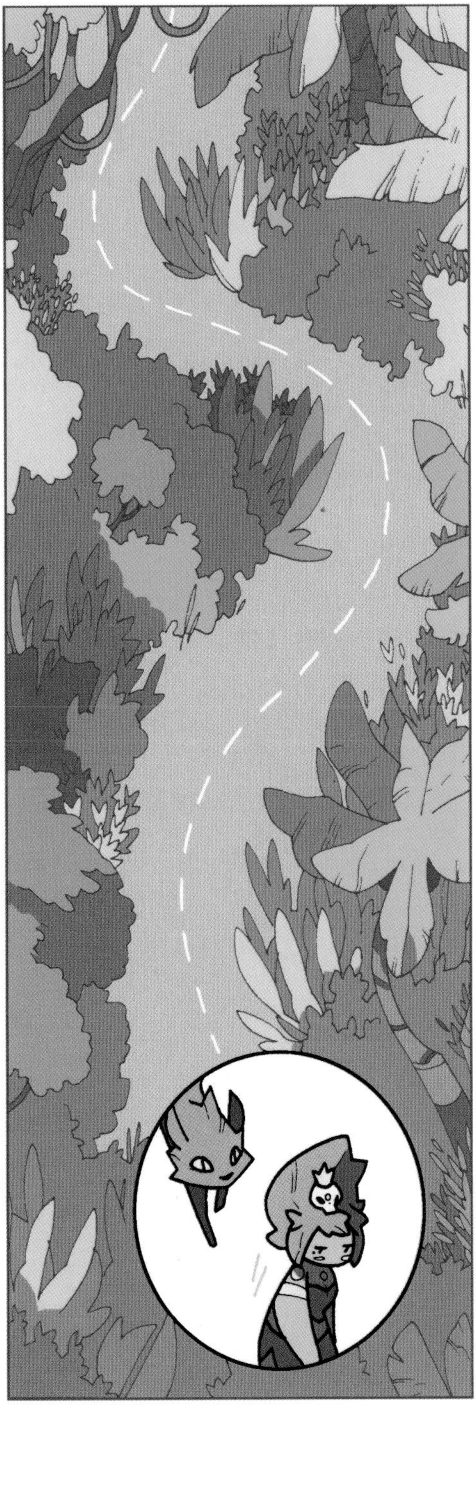

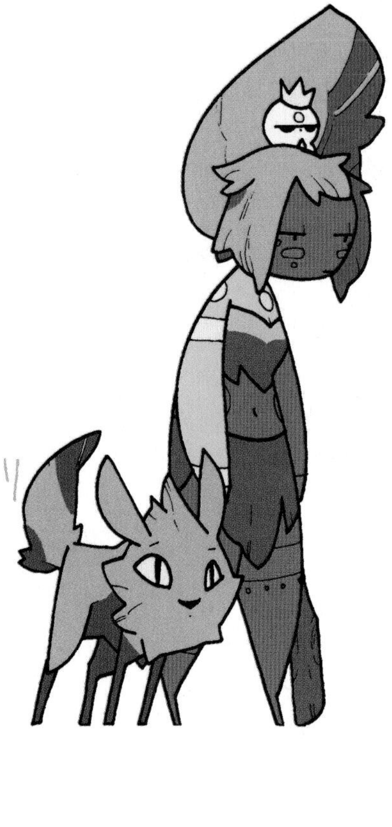

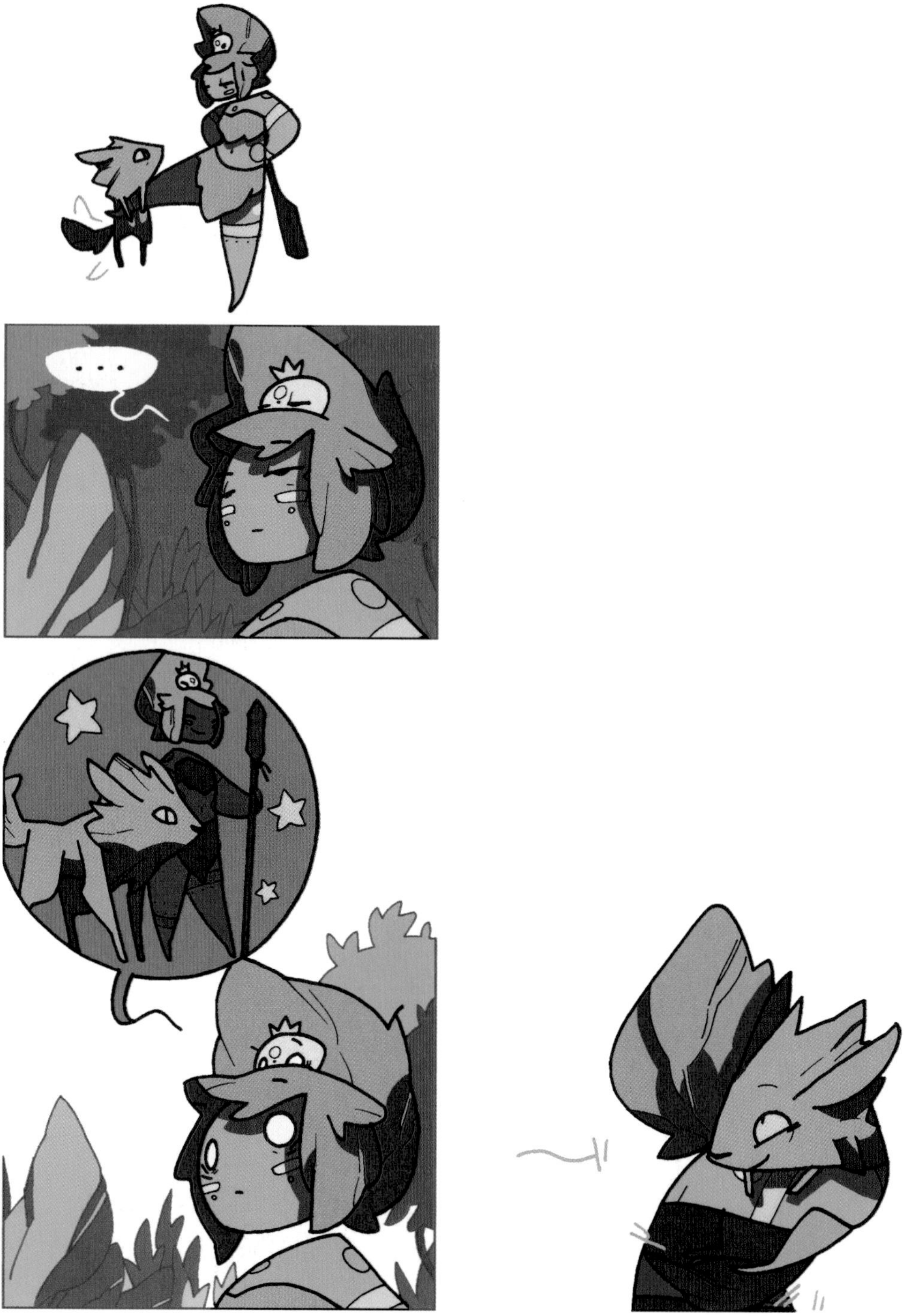
...

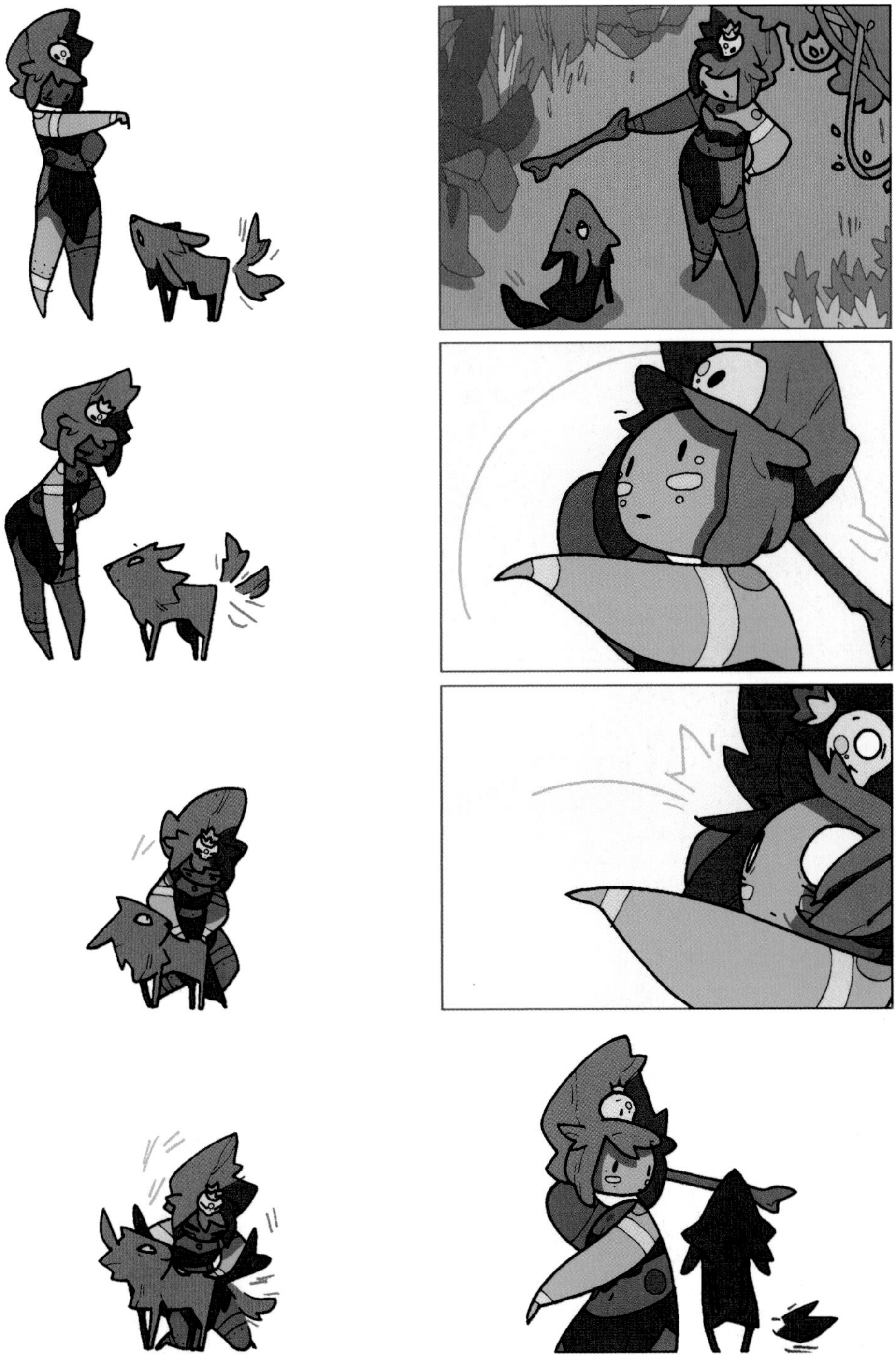

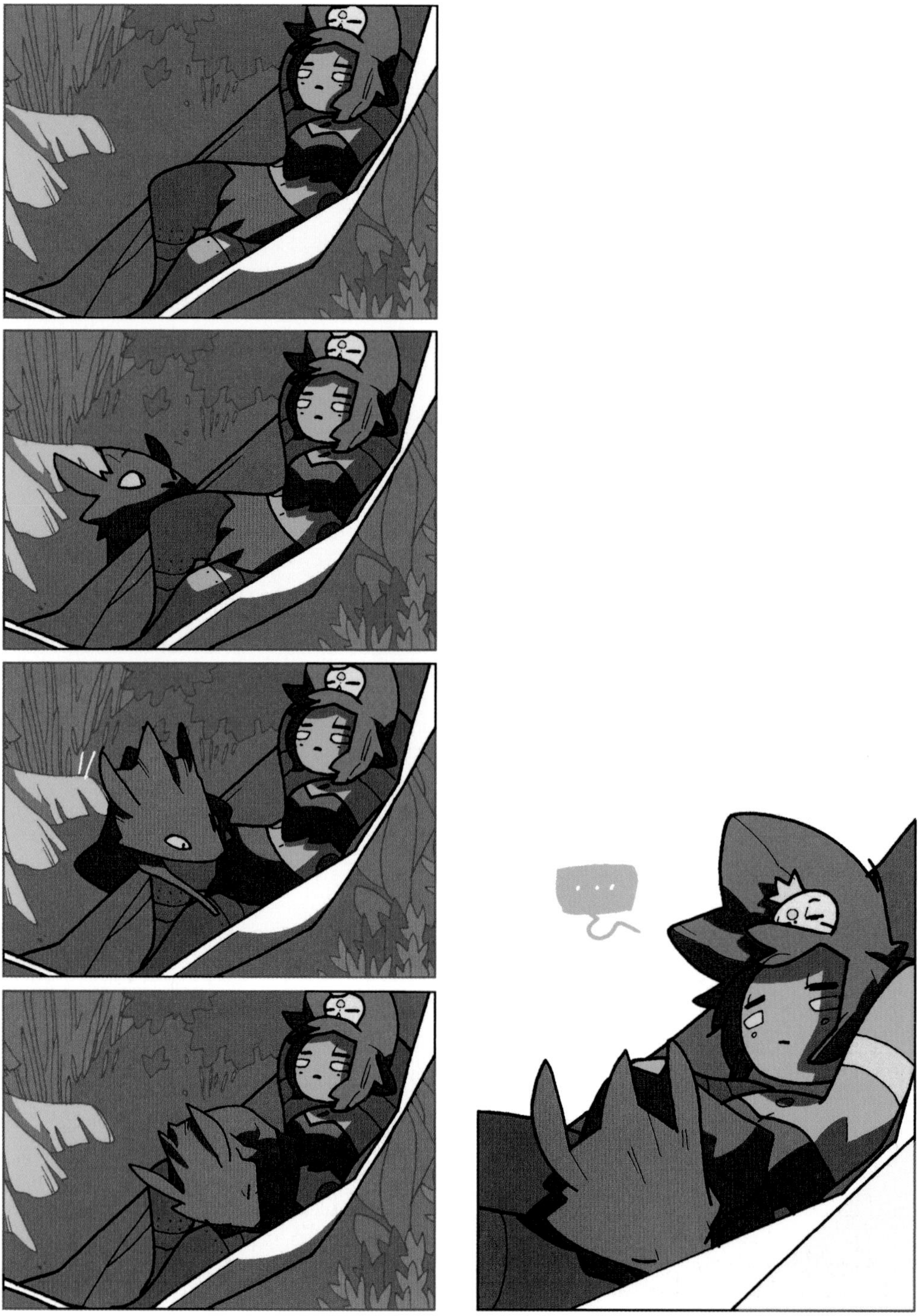
...

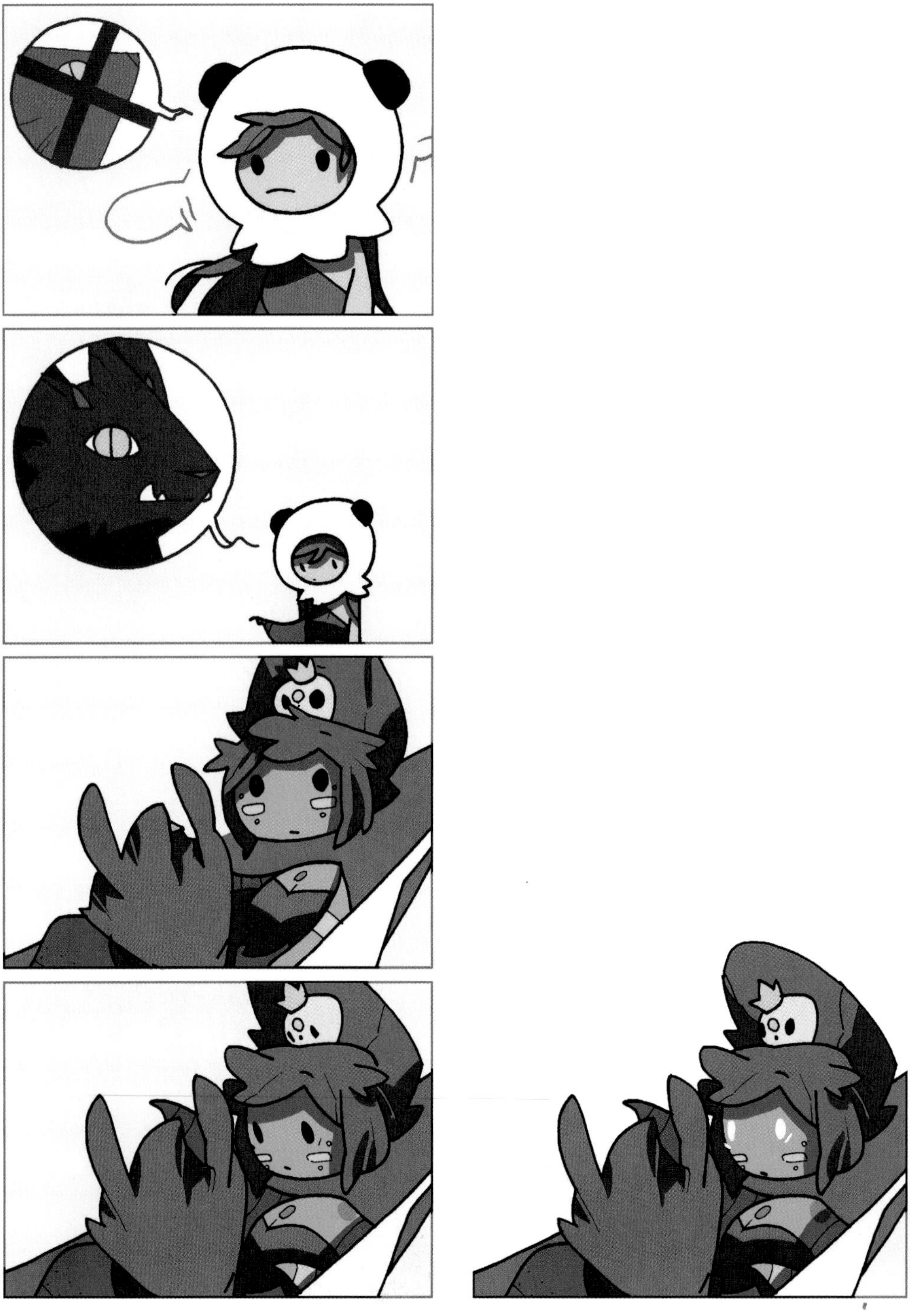

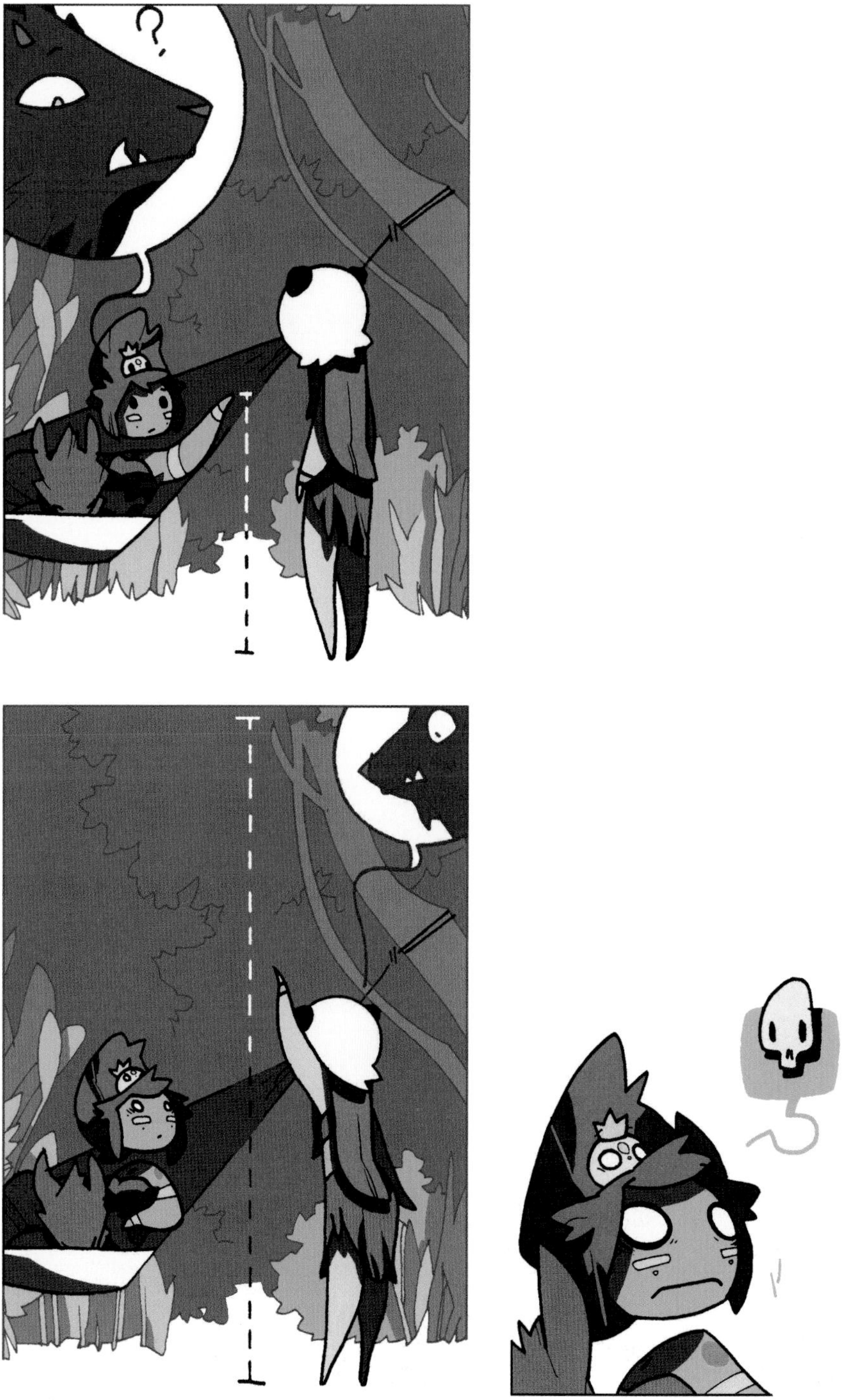
?

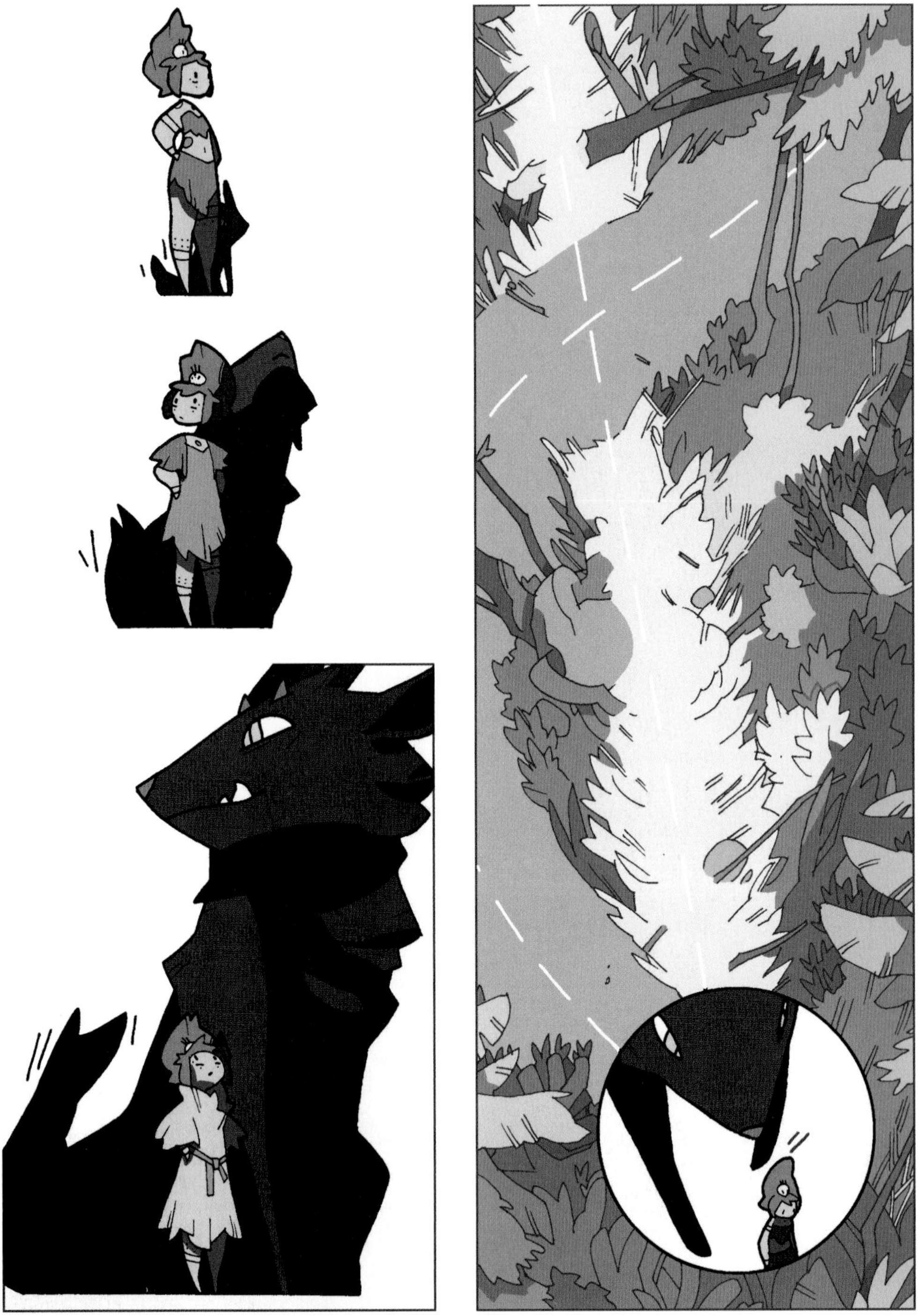

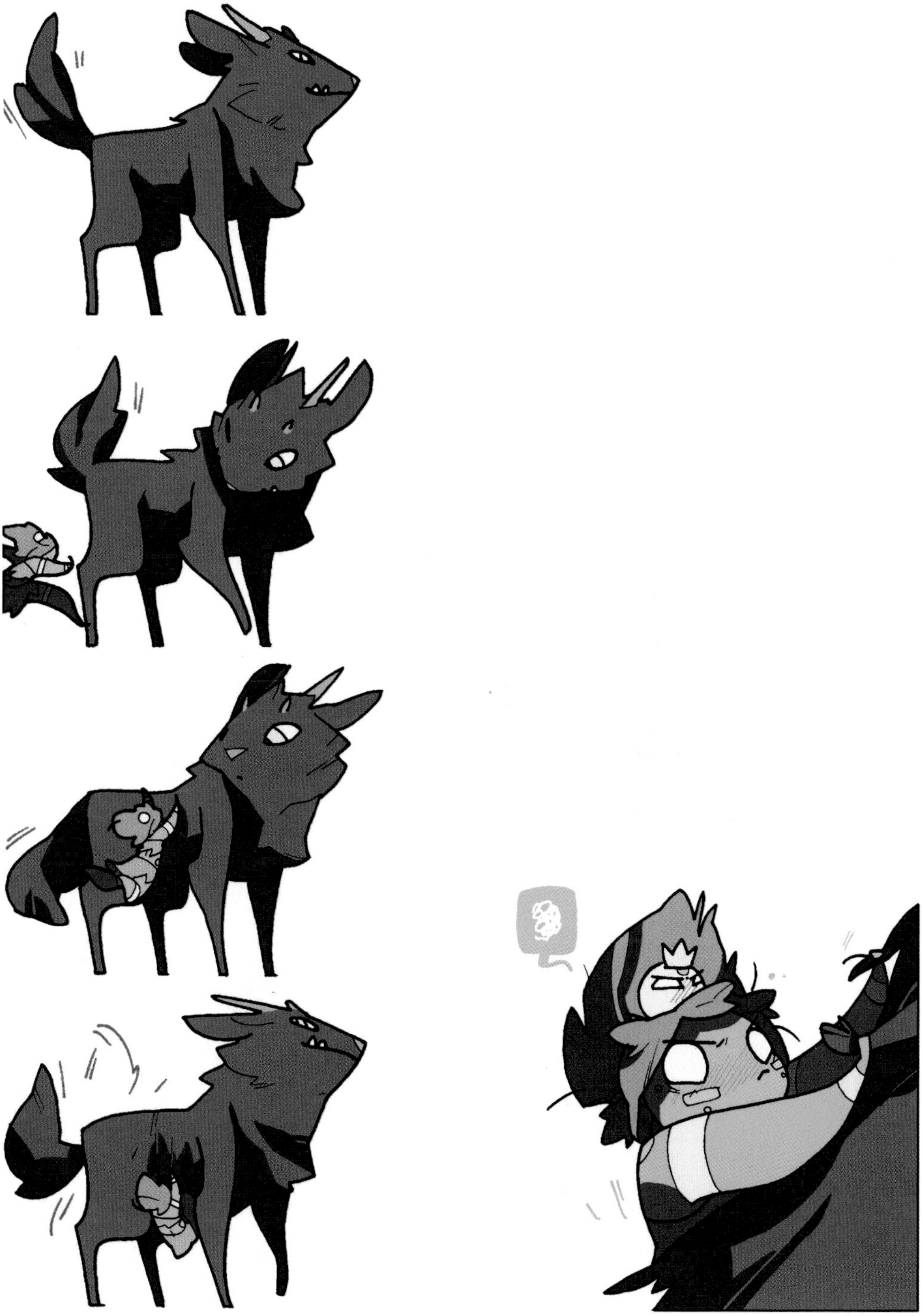

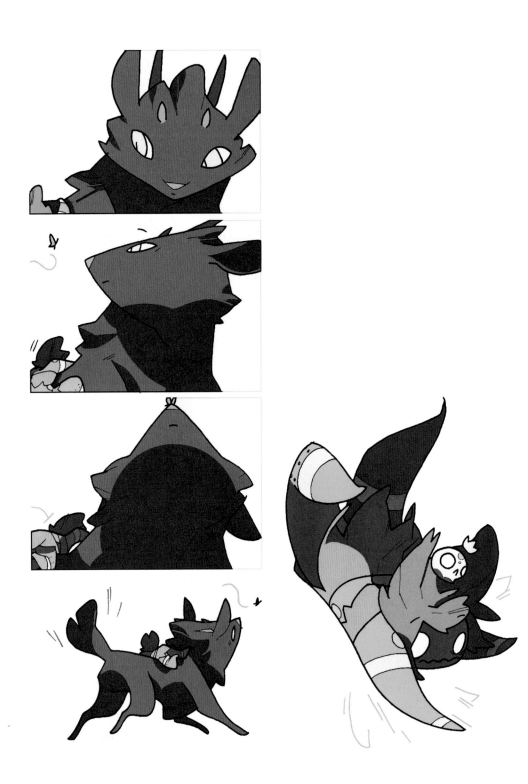

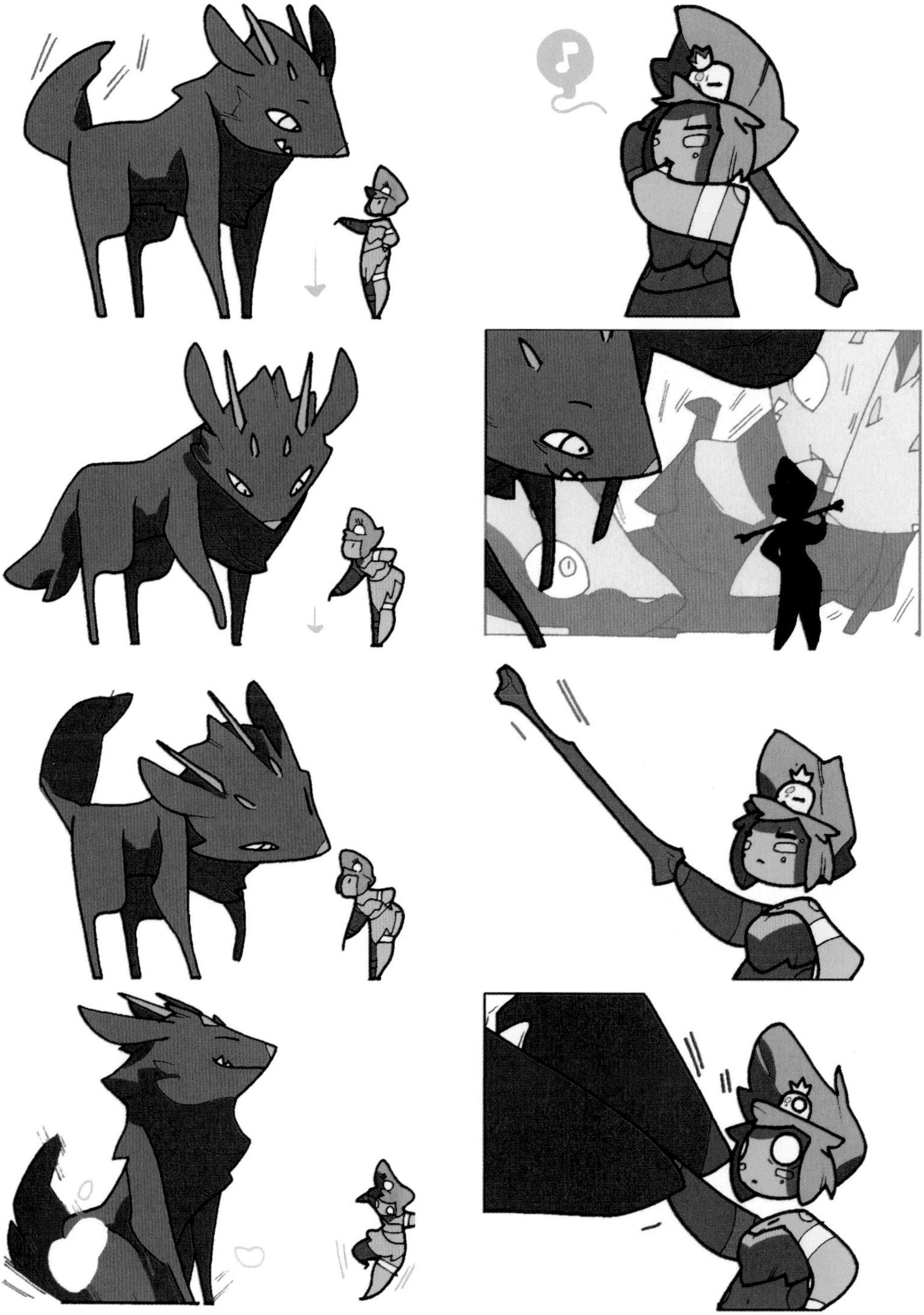

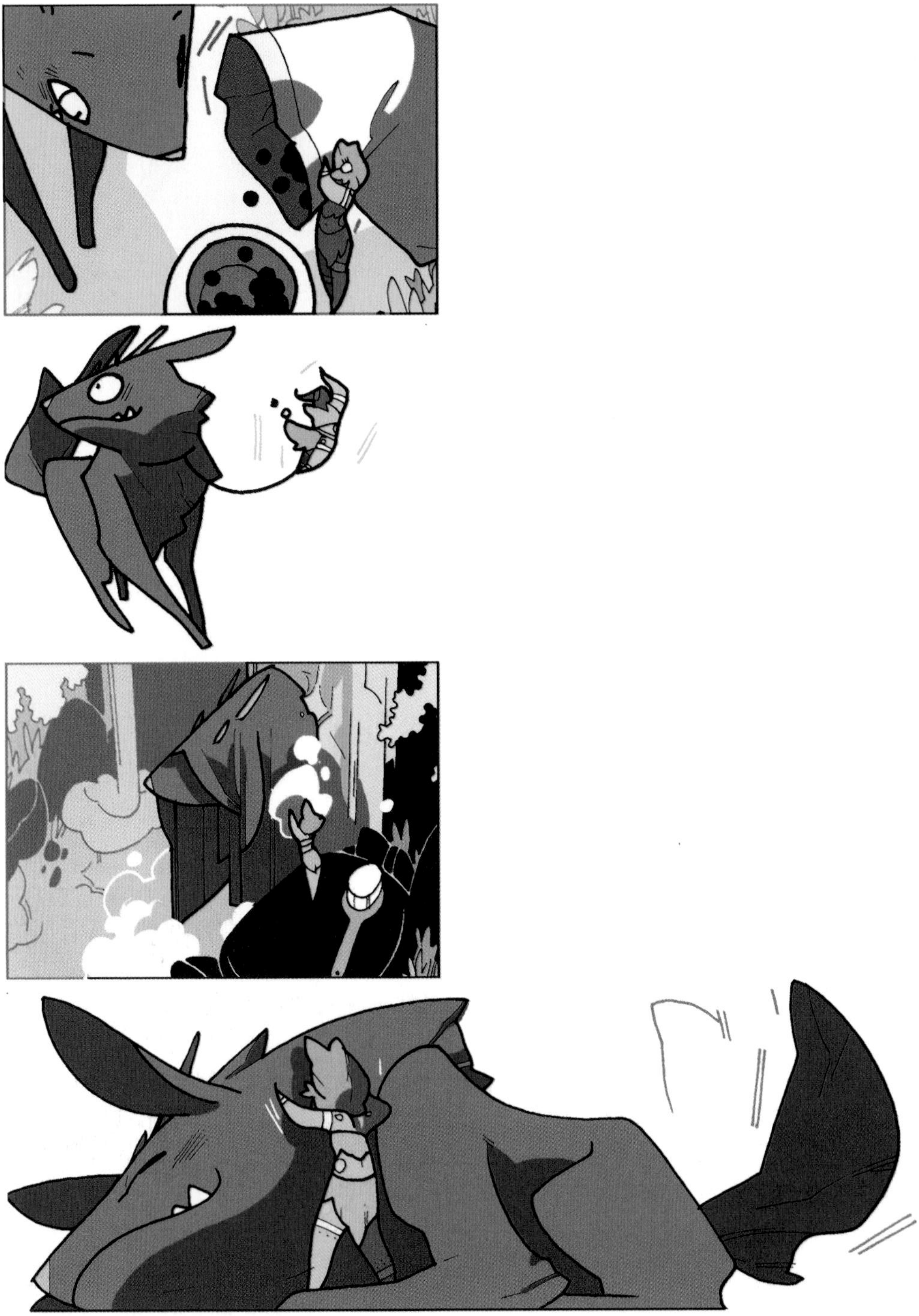

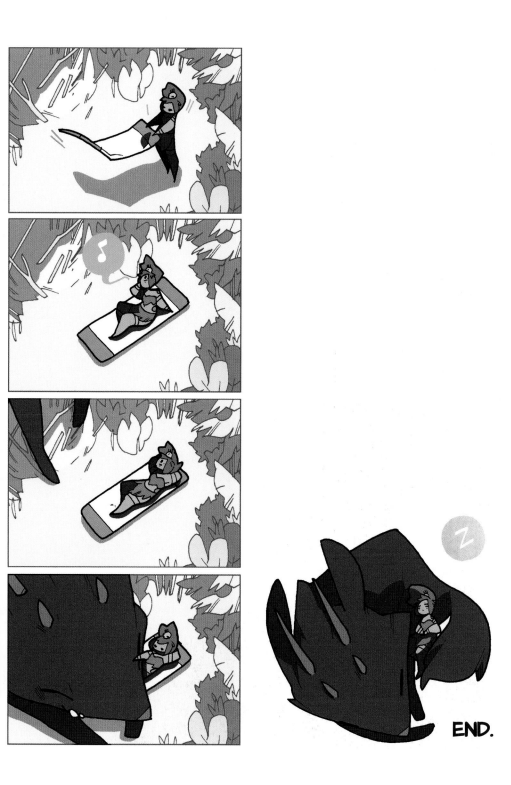

END.

ADVENTURE TIME™

VOLUME 5

SUMMER 2015

Written by **Danielle Corsetto**
Art by **Bridget Underwood**